RED NECKS IN LOVE

The Novel

By Charles Napier And Buck Flower

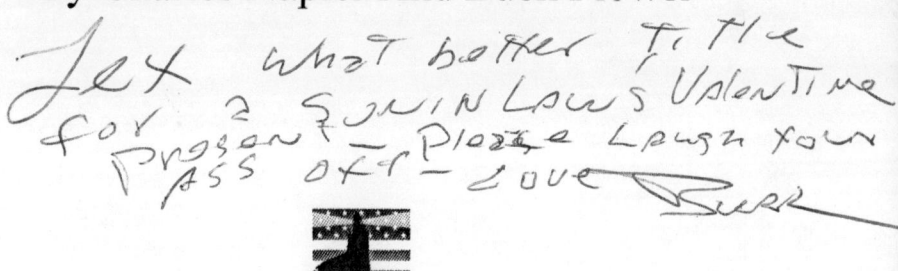

Jex what better title for a sonin laws valentine present — please laugh your ass off — Love Buck

AmErica House
Baltimore

ISBN: 1-59129-254-9
PUBLISHED BY AMERICA HOUSE BOOK PUBLISHERS
www.publishamerica.com
Baltimore

Printed in the United States of America

~ This book is dedicated to the innocent children, Whit, Hunter, Meghan, Kina, David and Roo, along with the suffering wives of two old Red Necks, Delores and Sybil ~

CHAPTER ONE
ANOTHER TOMORROW

Old Henderson let an ear-shattering fart.

It was loud. Possibly the loudest explosion of gas that had ever erupted from his body in the seventy-five years he'd been alive.

So loud, in fact, the audible rumble knifing its way through the antiquated, warped lumber that served as the walls of the old outhouse he presently occupied, undoubtedly traveled much farther.

It was probably, at this very second, journeying its way beyond the saloon. In all likelihood it would then continue past the defunct silver mine that sat slowly sinking into the barren combination of sand, eroded slate and limestone. These were the outlying boundary markings of what was left of the practically deserted, ramshackle town of Darwin.

If the audio mechanical energy transmitted by longitudinal pressure waves had indeed traveled that far, the gnarled old mining engineer reasoned, it had no doubt been also carried by the desert wind all the way beyond Telescope Peak.

That meant it could be heard across the endless array of sand dunes, barrel cactus and yellow boulders clear into the next county.

Ears could well have also perceived it, human and otherwise, in several directions.

The indecent sound some perceive as humorous, might have brought smiles to the personnel at the Naval station at China Lake near Ridgecrest. If, by chance, there was more than one person present at the place on highway three ninety five called Little Lake, they might also be sharing a giggle.

It may even have been heard as far away as Lone Pine. It was possible that the involuntary rumblings of the old rock hounds' gastronomic equipment had disturbed even the rattlesnakes on Maynard's Mountain.

It wasn't that the old man cared if he'd repulsed the reptiles on Maynard's Mountain. The same held true regarding any other living creature on earth or beyond.

He never worried about offending anyone or anything. However, he did feel his bowels had betrayed him. The old mans' solitude that he cherished so dearly was over. At least on this particular morning.

Old Henderson liked the equally old outhouse. Inside these walls he could shut out the fact that Darwin was no longer a hustling, bustling productive mining community.

He could forget that the village was on its way to rapid oblivion, occupied now by those who be otherwise homeless and a handful of idiots. All of them lacked the good sense to acknowledge the obvious fact that the silver supply in this particular part of the American desert had been permanently exhausted. These moronic hardheads were unwilling to admit that it would remain so forever.

Yes, the old man knew his privacy would soon be invaded and he hated it. He would spend his remaining living hours here if he could.

He found great solace in the comforting hum of the yellow jackets that lived in their little mud huts located in the rafters above his head.

He liked watching the busy, long tailed fluttering insects as they made entrances and exits through the numerous wide cracks in the old boards on all sides while he sat there. These same openings were also utilized by the desert sun to send in its long, dust laden fingers of illumination that crisscrossed the interior of the rickety old structure.

These shafts of light created an effect that reminded Henderson of the spotlights that he'd seen illuminating the bodies of those nearly nude dancers he'd watched with delight in the strip clubs in Reno at least a decade hence.

Sometimes he'd experiment with these lights by holding up pictures of the scantily clad ladies in the woman's underwear section of the catalogue placed in the outhouse for toilet paper. By twisting the retail publication this way and that he could often create the illusion that the shapely female bodies in the photographs were actually dancing for him just as the feminine flesh and blood bodies had long ago.

However there was no time for that particular ritual this morning. Due to an indiscretion on the part of his innermost organs, his time of privacy had come to an end.

The old man sighed as he tore a page from the catalogue. He ripped it from the farm equipment section of course. Old Henderson would never dream of defiling the woman's underwear pages.

He carefully laid the remainder of the retail publication aside and wadded up the paper in his hand.

Lifting his bare right hip, the senior citizen prepared to do what had to be done before the departure from his sacred sanctuary with its two holes.

"Dad? Dad, I know you're in there. God damnit! Answer me!"

The middle aged, windswept, rawboned owner of the flat, brittle voice that served to dissolve old Henderson's state of Nirvana might have been an attractive woman at one time. Any clues of this however, had been long ago erased by time and disaffiliation with the modern world and its feminine products.

Her eyes were as hard and brittle as the colorless rocks surrounding the saloon behind her.

Her thin bloodless lips seemed ready to crack at any second as she addressed the door to the upright wooden facility again.

"Dad? It's Darleen! Get your ass out here right now, or I'll break down the damned door!"

The rusty hinges securing the antique portal to the rest of the outdoor toilet groaned in protest as the gnarled old man stepped out from the dark interior of the small building.

He stood there for a moment adjusting his experienced eyes to the harsh desert sunlight and the glaring blue sky that seemed to wash over every thing in sight.

"Needs oil." He said looking at the hinges.

"Needs tearing down! That's what it needs! And I will too! If you don't start using the bathroom in the saloon where somebody can help you if you get in trouble! Can't you get it through your head you're old?"

The white haired, wrinkled man cast a caustic stare at this hard-bitten creature that had once been his sweet little girl. He shook his shaggy head sadly.

"Grepp-a-pax," he said.

"Dad! Now you stop that shit right now! You hear me?"

Old Henderson bit his leathery lower lip to keep from grinning. He was missing one of his yellowing front upper teeth. Darleen hated it when he talked Zorkanian.

He didn't care if he made her angry. She'd never tear down his beloved out house. The plumbing inside the saloon was far too unreliable for such a bold move.

She would never cause him bodily harm either. She was capable to be sure, and the aging mining engineer harbored no false illusions that his Daughter held any real affection toward him.

The reason she represented no physical danger to the old man was because she thought she needed him. Darleen, like the rest of the few foolish inhabitants of this forgotten area, was certain he would somehow find another vein of silver nearby and breath some life back into the collapsed lungs of this old town.

"I mean it Dad! No more of that shit about that space ship takin' you off to another planet up in the sky! No more gibberish!"

The woman's face almost softened as she continued, as if talking to a small child.

"Please Dad," she said. "Try to think straight. You were one of the top mining engineers in this country. You could be again if you'd just stop this foolishness about that spaceship that never existed."

The old rock hound burped as he hobbled over the rocks toward the ancient saloon.

Darleen never believed the story about the spacemen who'd grabbed him and taken him to live on the planet of Zorka for a whole month. He'd forgotten just how many years ago the adventure had taken place.

Henderson thought it was probably all for the best. They'd never let his Daughter on Zorka anyway. Her tits were too small.

"Dobo-brax-a-pu." He muttered.

"God damn you!" Snarled Darleen who was only a few steps behind him. "I told you to stop that! What did it mean anyhow?"

Henderson knew he shouldn't translate the phrase. No sense making his daughter anymore angry than she already was.

Besides, the construction of the human body being what it was, the Zorkanian suggestion was physically impossible anyway. He let another fart.

This one was nowhere nearly as loud as the old man's previous passing of gas. His daughter definitely could hear it, however. She stopped in her tracks and let the old man walk in through the rear entrance of the old saloon by himself.

Darleen waited for the early morning desert breeze to waft away her father's smell before she followed him into the ancient establishment. The falling down saloon was only still in business because Darleen had figured out a way to cash Welfare checks.

*** *** *** *** *** ***

It had been at least a week or more since Barney had even been near the old saloon over in Darwin, but he still woke up with a raging hangover. And even though he wasn't directly in its path, the morning sun that already blistered down on the Owens Valley a few miles south of Lone Pine, wasn't helping.

He tried shutting his eyes tighter. This only seemed to make what felt like lighting bolts shoot up through the inside of his already throbbing head.

He attempted to take his mind off his eyes and the pain by concentrating on the foul taste in his mouth that seemed to be increasing steadily by degrees.

He always awakened with a hangover. Barney couldn't remember when he had not. However, on this particular morning, he came to full understanding of the meaning of Uncle Trux's words, "Feels like the whole Damned Russian army marched across my tongue and every one of those slimy muthafuckers stopped for piss call!"

There was nothing really unique about Barney's present state of being. Most people in the Owens Valley awakened hung over, feeling the aftermath of too much alcohol consumption from the night before.

It was considered a rather natural condition, ranging all the way from Little Lake, as Far East to the almost ghost town of Darwin and continuing north to way beyond Lone Pine.

No, there was nothing unique about a hungover person in this particular part of the country, morning, noon or night. But Barney wasn't a person. Barney was a pig.

There were no papers in existence to testify to this fact, but fact it was. Anyone could see Barney was a pig through and through from his round pink snout that sloped its way back on either side of his scarred face, giving way to his long pointed black and white ears.

The curly tail sprouting from his wide round hair covered rump and the four cloven hooves at the end of his legs beneath his fat belly were also dead giveaways.

For a moment Barney wasn't exactly sure where he was.

In addition to the headache and the rotten tastes in his mouth, he was becoming aware of a foul smell that seemed to be invading the little round nostrils of the porkers' pink snout.

With some difficulty, Barney opened his right eye. Once this chore was accomplished, he worked on the left organ of vision

After what seemed to him like an eternity, Barney could finally see. He found himself to be beneath an old battered motor home. The same big utility rig that, for as long as Barney could remember, had served as home some of the time, and transportation, all of the time, for him, Daddy Farley and Uncle Trux.

He also found himself staring out beyond the underside of the over sized vehicle. Directly in front of his eyes were the bottoms of both of Daddy Farley's bare feet. They were only inches away.

The source of the smell was no longer a mystery.

Barney began wiggling his way out from beneath the stationary vehicle on his fat, round belly.

Suddenly a series of short explosive sounds began violating the morning air. This served to increase the pain in the pig's brain.

Barney knew that noise and who was making it.

Arty Dubs, the sheriff, or 'That Asshole' as Daddy Farley and Uncle Trux called him, was down at the Lone Pine dump shooting tires again.

Thus began another yesterdays' tomorrow in a pigs' paradise.

*** *** *** *** *** ***

In another region of California, considered paradise by many cultures,

Rodney Van Aukin hadn't suffered from a hangover in quite some time. That was because he hadn't consumed any beverage containing alcohol since shortly after arriving in the Golden State.

Nonetheless, he still had a headache. He was fully convinced the source of the pain to be the décor of his immediate surroundings.

The naked young man knew the discomfort behind his temples wasn't caused by the recently acquired padded toilet seat. The newest addition to the other facilities was welcomed in the posh, albeit tastelessly furnished, Beverly Hills bathroom he presently occupied. Even Rodney had to admit that particular purchase held merit.

Lack of cleanliness could not be blamed either. No one could fault the maid for dereliction of duty. The enclosure was spotless.

The heavy rose and lavender scent that permeated the room did make him a little nauseous. Rodney was certain that wasn't good for his skin condition, but the real cause of his headache was the frogs.

They weren't real frogs, but replicas of the webbed-footed amphibious creatures seemed to be everywhere. Pink frogs, yellow frogs, and even blue frogs. There were some in colors he couldn't even name.

Even the faucet handle he now turned to the left to shut off the combination of hot and cold water spraying down over his naked young body was fashioned to resemble a frog.

As the cascading flow of chlorinated liquid ceased, Rodney pushed back the soaking wet frog covered plastic curtain. He then stepped carefully over the edge of the frog shaped tub onto a bath mat sporting cartoon frog inlays.

To his right, as he stepped out of the shower tub combination, was a towel dispenser shaped like the wide mouth of yet another frog. From this, he pulled out a big fluffy towel covered with pictures of more frogs. He then closed his eyes and began drying his thin youthful body.

The headache began to subside somewhat as he rubbed the terry cloth material over his sensitive skin. He wondered, involuntarily, for just a second, if his fiancée's fixation with frogs might be due to the fact that she slightly resembled one herself.

Immediately he chastised himself for such an unkind comparison.

Louise was very attractive. The fact that she could stand to lose a few pounds only made her more desirable. He was fortunate to have found her. He told himself those very words many times every day.

However, he reasoned, after he and the young lady stepped beyond the upcoming vows of wedlock, and moved from her apartment into a place for both of them, a wise precaution might be separate bathrooms.

That way Louise could have her beloved frogs all to herself.

The naked young barrister finally opened his eyes. He wrapped the towel

10

firmly around his waist and tied the top ends into a knot.

He eased his thin lanky partially exposed frame across about one and a half squares of blue and pink tiled frogs and positioned himself in front of the frog shaped mirror.

He studied his strong but perennially puzzled face for any sign of his recurring skin condition, and prepared to shave.

As he picked up an aerosol shaving cream dispenser and his razor, Rodney tried to mentally push the remainder of his headache aside.

He began to reflect on his near state of matrimony. The upcoming event seemed to be the inevitable next avenue of progression in his mandatory stroll through life.

It hadn't been that long ago since Rodney Van Aukin was just another freshly graduated Bostonian law student. His marks hadn't placed him anywhere near the top of his class, but nonetheless, a graduate he was.

Then, almost as if it had dropped from the sky the previous February, a letter with a California postmark had arrived for him in his parents' mailbox.

The missive was from a prestigious Century City law firm. This was just one of the many West Coast legal organizations to whom the young man had mass mailed after graduation.

His father was in local politics and Rodney wanted to face the world on his own.

The only way to do so, he reasoned, was to get as far away from Boston as possible. This response, unlike the others, was not the usual form letter rejection.

He had actually been offered a clerical position in the legal organization of Herkimer, Herkimer, Herkimer, Herkimer. Attorneys at Law. His presence in California was requested immediately.

Rodney's speedy reply of acceptance had altered the young New Englander's life forever.

Rodney's memory was blurred from the moment the airplane had touched down in this sprawling jungle of neon, gold chains, swimming pools, and tanned bodies. He could recall only bits and pieces.

He remembered the lavish Beverly Hills garden party shortly after he was picked up and carried away in a limousine from the Los Angeles airport, or LAX, as it was called.

He definitely recalled the Vodka Gimlets on top of the numerous Bloody Mary concoctions it had taken to calm his fear of flying all the way from Massachusetts to the California coast.

Perhaps that memory alone was really the key to the next thing he clearly remembered. The following morning he awakened with, and in the bed of, the only daughter of one of the partners of the firm of Herkimer, Herkimer,

Herkimer Herkimer.

The frightened and fully remorseful young lawyer decided right then and there, that alcohol and Van Auken didn't mix. He vowed that his drinking days were over as he sorrowfully booked the next flight back to Boston.

Then he discovered that the father of the defiled young lady in question was not in the slightest bit angry. In fact Horace Herkimer seemed to be delighted.

Rodney was encouraged quite forcefully, to take the California Bar exam. By sheer coincidence, February was when the state test had to be taken without waiting for the next time frame opening.

He was not registered for the exam, but Louise's Father, Horace Herkimer obviously had some clout. Some very complicated strings were evidently pulled and the young man from New England had been let in under the wire.

The entire process didn't exactly seem legal, but the young Bostonian was rapidly discovering the term 'Legal' to be open for interpretation in the wonderful world of law.

Rodney was put to work as promised, after he had officially moved into Louise's apartment, taking care of the clerical duties in her Father's law firm.

Then, when the Bar exam results were posted at the end of April, to his own amazement, Rodney discovered he had passed. Not exactly with flying colors to be sure, but nonetheless, he hadn't failed.

Almost like magic, Rodney Van Aukin, late of Boston, now a citizen of California, was a real honest to God, lawyer.

As soon as it was official and the young man from Boston had taken the necessary following M. P. R. E. exam to make all official, he was granted permission by the powers that be, to actually practice his new profession in the Golden State. He was also made a partner in the firm.

A junior partner, granted, and the law clerk duties were still Rodney's to fulfill. Nonetheless, a partner he was. His name was even printed on the outer office door.

Almost immediately after this amazing turn of events, the freshly qualified California barrister was invited to a lavish luncheon at the Beverly Hills famous Rodeo Hotel Café.

Once there, he found himself and the pudgy Louise Herkimer to be not only the center of attention, but also the sole reason for the party.

Horace Herkimer had beamed as he announced the pending engagement of his daughter to the newest partner of his firm. Even though everything seemed to have miraculously been for the best, Rodney decided to hold to his previous vow to stay away from booze.

These phenomena had begun at least six months ago, and Rodney had started to work in the lavish offices in Century City, almost immediately.

Still, the newly appointed attorney had only met one of the senior partners other than his future father in law.

Horace's slightly younger brother, Harold Herkimer seemed to be the only other Herkimer working the firm's home office.

The president of the organization, Christopher Herkimer was never there. It seemed he was always traveling around America involving himself in civil rights movements, defending the downtrodden.

The remaining partner, W. P. Herkimer, Horace and Harold were reluctant to even discuss. However, it was common knowledge that all of the Herkimers involved in the firm were blood relatives.

W. P. evidently traveled at all times with Christopher, leaving the corporate law portion of the firm's business to Horace and Harold.

Civil rights law sounded much more exciting to Rodney than the business of preparing briefs for various businesses mainly involved in buying and selling. However, he went about the task of doing the clerical work assigned to him by his fiancée's father and her uncle without complaining. It seemed doubtful that he'd ever meet the other partners anyway.

"Rodney poo? You've locked the bathroom door again!"

The strident, slightly nasal, youngish female voice coming from the other side of the closed portal was accompanied by the sound of loud pounding.

Either would have pulled Rodney back to the present from his reverie. The combination of both caused his headache to return.

Behind him, the voice and the pounding continued and the display of ceramic frogs attached to the now vibrating door seemed destined to fall to the floor.

"I still don't understand why you always lock it. Geeze! Talk about women being uptight!" Louise called from the other side of the portal.

The daughter of Horace Herkimer wasn't really that fond of sexual activity, but she loved the exhibitionism of what she felt to be intimacy.

Rodney instinctively looked down to see if the towel still tied around his waist covered what it was supposed to be covering.

He picked up a washrag, trying very hard to ignore its embroidered frogs.

He rapidly began wiping shaving cream from his face as he called back.

"I.... That is....Sorry. Old habit. I'm still not totally used to sharing the bathroom....I mean with a pretty girl..... I mean with any girl.... I mean.... Sorry. Be right there."

Rodney had a tendency to stammer when he was faced with an unexpected situation or if he wasn't sure what he was supposed to say. He stammered a lot. He always had.

Unlike Louise, he hated it when somebody, male or female, preformed any of the natural bodily elimination functions in his presence. He also had

13

a terrible phobia against anyone watching him in the same situation.

The newly appointed member of the California Bar Association would rather pretend human beings didn't really do such disgusting things.

The shrill voice coming from beyond the now settling ceramic frogs, shifted gears and raised to an even higher peak.

The newest pitch would have made the sound of chalk being scraped on a black board resemble the plaintive "Mew" of a newborn kitten. Experience had taught Rodney this cackle was Louise's way of laughing.

He placed the washrag on the edge of the frog shaped sink. The young lawyer then took a deep breath of the rose and lavender scented air as he turned.

He began coughing as he moved to unlock and open the door.

*** *** *** *** *** ***

The air in the Lone Pine Dump didn't smell of lavender or roses, but it definitely boasted its own combination of strong odors.

Added to this quotidian stockpile of stench, which was growing stronger by the second as the blistering overhead sun climbed upward, was the unmistakable aroma of freshly detonated gunpowder.

This supplementary smell was immediately enhanced as a thick flame burst forth from the barrel of the .357 Magnum pistol. The weapon was held in the hairy left fist of Sheriff Arty Dubs.

Almost at the same second, a bullet from the gun tore into a lone tire rolling across the yard about fifty yards in front of the uniformed law enforcement officer. The glabrous, large, round black object flew backward into another ruined tire displaying signs of similar recent assault.

"That'll do her for this mornin,' Jiggs," said the sheriff, when the echoing sound of gunfire finally diminished.

It took some time for the audible reverberation to finish bouncing off the wrecked automobiles. Even more passed as the echoes continued making their way through the hollows of defunct and dismantled farm equipment, discarded appliances and other rubbish strewn about or piled within the confines of the tall fence surrounding the area of refuse.

The badge on the tall, left handed lawman's uniformed covered barrel chest gleamed as it reflected the rising sun shining down from above.

He shoved his broad brimmed hat back on his head revealing dark brown curly hair spilling down over a wide Neanderthal forehead. Then, he dramatically began to reload the Magnum.

Flashing a bucked toothed grin, the sheriff called across the junkyard again.

"Time to hit the highway and keep my eye open for the real thing now I know my peepers still got what it takes. You square away here and then hustle your hocks back to the Station. Gimme a shout on the radio when you git there."

At the far end of the dump, another uniformed man, this one hatless, peeked out from around the corner of the remains of a vintage John Deere tractor.

Deputy Sheriff Jiggs Mahoney reached up and ran a hand through his bright red hair as he breathed a sigh of obvious relief.

He finished emerging from behind the shelter of the old vehicle as he watched the sheriff walk through the gateway leading out of the dump. His surveillance continued as his superior climbed in behind the steering wheel of the marked patrol car before driving away toward the highway leading into Lone Pine.

Jiggs hated the sheriff's ritualistic morning target practice sessions. Especially since Arty insisted on the targets being exclusively tires. Jiggs had the job of rollin' out the rubber.

Arty loved to blow apart almost anything with that Magnum of his, but tires were the lawman's true passion.

Years ago, way back in the twentieth century, sometime in the early seventies, an actor named Clint Eastwood had starred in a movie called *Dirty Harry*.

Jiggs had never seen the motion picture. He wasn't even sure who Clint Eastwood was, but evidently in the movie, old Clint had shot out a lot of tires.

Ever since Arty had seen that show, shooting tires, whether attached to a vehicle or not, had become almost an obsession.

It was also Jiggs's duty to clean up the mess when these tire-shooting sessions came to an end each day. The early morning shooting schedule was never broken unless the jail held prisoners.

Even though Lone Pine boasted a fairly sizable enclosure of incarceration for a small town, except for Saturday nights and Sunday mornings, it was seldom occupied. Therefore, even though he didn't exactly relish what he was doing at the moment, Jiggs was definitely used to it.

Heaving a resigned sigh, the redheaded deputy moved forward and began picking up pieces of rubber, throwing them onto a huge pile of junk.

Then he had to get down to the real business of removing the remainder of the ruined, round doughnut shaped rubber, scattered about objects, from the center of the yard.

They had to be rolled back and placed on the huge pile of other discarded tires resting next to the south side of the junkyard fence.

The deputy paused in his labor to look through the tall, chain link barricade beyond the pile of tires.

About two miles away, or maybe even farther, he could see the old beat up Maynard motor home pulling away from where it had probably been parked for the night on the old Arroyo road turn off.

Jiggs was glad Arty hadn't noticed the rig during target practice. Just the mention of either one of the two middle-aged brothers could put the Sheriff in a foul mood for days.

Jiggs wasn't exactly why Arty hated Trux and Farley Maynard so much. Granted, they were a couple of hell raisers who stayed drunk most of the time.

They were also famous throughout the entire Owens Valley for their sexual encounters with women, most of them married and older. Some folks said they didn't always stick to the latter.

There were also many rumors regarding times they may well have ripped some people off, but that was just hearsay.

Farley Maynard did have a pet pig that followed the brothers around every place they went. But as far as Jiggs was concerned, none of these things necessarily made them bad people.

Everyone did something that might be frowned on by folks. Even Jiggs, who was considered by all, even those who only knew him by sight, to be an exemplary young man, had at least one skeleton in his closet.

There had been an occurrence in Tahoe, Nevada when he was working for the Forest Service that he was just as glad nobody knew about. That was right after he had finished high school and before he became a deputy.

It was in the past, but nonetheless a story he would just as soon not be circulated. What happened that time in Tahoe would definitely do nothing to enhance his standing with the young ladies in the Owens Valley were it to be made public.

There was one such pretty lass who lived right here in Lone Pine that Jiggs would certainly like to get to know better. Her last name was also Maynard and she was one of the main reasons Jiggs was hesitant to pass judgement on either Trux or Farley.

Arthell Maynard was possibly the sweetest young lady in the entire three counties that made up the vast Owens Valley, and by far the prettiest. Arthell was also the daughter of one of the two brothers. Which was actually the father, Jiggs wasn't sure.

This was also a matter none of the rest of the usually extremely well informed good citizens of the Owens Valley seemed to really be certain of. What everybody did know, was that the pretty girl bore the name Maynard with pride.

No matter how people felt about Trux or Farley, absolutely no one had any thing bad to say about Arthell.

As the deputy resumed his task, he glanced up to see the old motor home drive on to the highway and turn left, heading away from town. That was good. Maybe the Maynards' drinking would be done at the bar in Little Lake, across the county line tonight.

Or possibly they'd travel over to Darwin. Some folks said they sometimes lived in one of the Chinamen caves just outside the ghost town there.

Even if they ended up passed out on that mountain northeast of Little Lake they supposedly owned, it would be better for him, Jiggs reasoned.

He just didn't want them to get thrown in the Lone Pine jail. Courting possible disfavor with the lovely Arthell aside, Jiggs really hated the thought of having to clean up after that pig when it got drunk.

Farley Maynard claimed his pet Barney was as smart as any man alive. Jiggs wasn't an expert on intelligence, but the deputy knew all too well that the drunken pig had never learned to sit on the crapper.

He stood still for a minute as he squinted through the desert sunlight, watching the motor home disappear.

Jiggs suddenly realized there wasn't time at the moment to worry about the Maynards, their pig, or anybody else. He had to get the dump tidied up and get back to the sheriff's station. He must prepare to process traffic tickets.

Arty was bound to issue as many citations today as he could to those tourists passing through town on their way to Reno or Mammoth.

Those bound for Los Angeles, San Bernardino, or any number of other places Highway 395 with its dark multicolored pavement led in the opposite direction, were in just as much jeopardy.

No out of town motorist committing even the slightest moving violation could escape the eagle eye of Sheriff Arty Dubs. And God help their tires if they didn't immediately pull over when Arty flashed his over head lights and turned on his siren.

"Best hustle my hocks," Jiggs muttered aloud to himself.

Already the traffic was getting heavy. At least eight cars could be seen approaching town from the south. There had to be at least as many coming from the east.

CHAPTER TWO
SIMPLE ASSIGNMENT

Traffic was always thick as it crawled forward in either direction on Santa Monica Boulevard toward the pretentious smog shrouded skyline of Century City. This morning was no exception.

The culmination of tall, tasteless pinnacles of concrete, steel and glass were barely visible through the many layers of yellow, murky polluted air.

Beneath and between these obscenely caressed rows of towering edifices, a cacophony of blowing automobile horns, revving engines, jack hammers and blended radio announcer and D. J. voices, maintained its dutiful, deafening, daily roar.

In the middle of this melee of bumper to bumper motorized vehicles, a small, lime green vintage Karmann Ghia convertible, its make and model long ago discontinued by the people at Volkswagen, wove its way miraculously in and around the other automobiles without hitting any of them.

Cutting in front of an enormous Lincoln Continental, and narrowly avoiding the rear of a yellow utility truck, the little ragtop negotiated a left turn onto the thoroughfare ostentatiously claiming to be the Avenue of the Stars.

The screeching of additional brakes joined the audible melee of utter confusion as the German manufactured machine also ran a red light in the process.

Inside this small careening convertible, Rodney was strapped in the passenger seat gripping the dashboard in front of him with white knuckled fingers. His fiancée sat behind the vehicle's steering wheel.

The pudgy overdressed young woman wore thick makeup and false eyelashes beneath her outrageous hairdo. She operated the little car's controls as if there were no driver on the L. A. streets at the moment except herself.

She chortled happily away at Rodney who was obviously too frightened to hear her words.

Rodney had always wanted a convertible, and what with this new windfall that seemed to ensure the young lawyer a wealthy future, he had made the plunge. However, since his wealth was still forth coming, he'd found the Ghia to be the only convertible he could afford.

Louise loved it. She called it the Slum Mobile. At first her acceptance of his 'pre-purchased' automobile had pleased Rodney. He had learned quickly that there was no such thing as a used car in Beverly Hills.

18

However, his pleasure deflated rapidly when he discovered she even preferred the quaint little ragtop to her own nearly new Mercedes.

Rodney almost never got to drive the first convertible he ever owned.

"Married as soon as possible…," Louise was saying in her strident voice as Rodney saw the trunk of a Lexus looming toward him through the windshield.

He watched the side of the luxury automobile whiz past dangerously close to the window on his right as Louise somehow managed to maneuver around it at the very last minute.

Although Rodney was far too preoccupied to hear more than a smattering of her words, Louise continued as if the near brush with disaster had never happened.

"Of course, as to the actual date…."

The Beverly Hills Princess leaned forward and ground the gears of the little car's transmission as she missed a large battered laundry truck by centimeters.

She continued to talk while at the same time spinning the steering wheel sharply to the left. Somehow she successfully negotiated a u-turn in the middle of the heavy traffic.

"Obviously Mother will have to be consulted. I just hope she and Daddy are speaking again by then… It's an absolute bitch to have divorced parents when they aren't talking…Out of My way! You Geek! Watch it Lady!!! The sooner the better as far as Daddy's concerned… Filthy low class delivery truck driver… That's where I'm parking you piece of…"

The piercing horn blast belched out by the little ragtop Karmann Ghia succeeded in drowning out Louise's description of the poor operator attempting to park his van at the curb in front of her.

The sound also nearly caused Rodney to urinate in the crotch of his top of the line three pieced wash and wear, J. C. Penney's suit.

Just beyond the forward bumper of the Ghia, the delivery van driver somehow managed to swerve away from the stretch of red curb Louise was determined to occupy in front of the building that housed the firm of Herkimer, Herkimer, Herkimer, Herkimer.

Shaking slightly, Rodney quickly unfastened his seat belt and scrambled out onto the sidewalk. He really did have to pee now. His bladder felt so full, he was certain his heart was doing the backstroke to continue beating.

In spite of his discomfort, he still had to look around and marvel at the fact that his car had, once again, made this penetration into purgatory and remained unscathed.

Rodney danced about in front of the huge edifice. Shifting his weight from one foot to the other, he leaned forward to call across the car's interior to

19

Louise, attempting to tell her goodbye.

Louise was too quick for him.

"Goodbye, Rodney Poo!" she called as the little car moved forward away from the curb, causing a Cadillac driver behind her to stomp on his brakes.

"Tell Daddy I'm the reason you're late. He'll understand. Gotta jam lamb! Reservations at La Scalla and all that you know! Later on I've got a beauty parlor appointment. Call me. Use you're cell phone so you won't tie up Daddy's business lines. Kiss, kiss."

Rodney patted the upper right portion of his suit jacket where the cellular instrument he never used, nestled in an inside pocket. He was certain the controversial popular electronic leash would give him a brain tumor. He started to respond, but in a flash, both woman and car were gone.

He turned and began frantically to fight his way through the crowd, attempting to enter the building.

The young lawyer with his name on the outside of a door somewhere on the sixteenth level of this tall structure was trying to remember if there was a public rest room on the ground floor.

*** *** *** *** *** *** ***

High above, on that fifteenth level of the same building, neither Horace Herkimer or his brother Harold had any idea about the young man's present, urgent need to relieve himself of physical discomfort.

However, Rodney Van Aukin was still their center of conversation. Harold Herkimer sat behind an enormous, ornately carved and highly polished desk in the spacious, elaborately decorated office.

Harold was a thin man who appeared to be in his mid forties. He brushed lint from of the sleeve of his obviously expensive suit coat as he asked the other Mr. Herkimer a question.

"You're sure your future son in law is the right man for this project, Mr. Herkimer?"

Horace Herkimer stood facing a very well stocked bar situated against the wall on the far side of the room, mixing a pitcher of martinis. The velour jogging suit that covered his stocky frame was in direct contrast to his brother and partner's impeccable apparel.

Slowly stirring the ingredients of the silver container in his hand, he flashed a set of snow-white perfectly capped teeth in the middle of a well artificially tanned, closely shaven face. He reached behind the bar and selected two long stemmed crystal glasses.

After filling them both, the larger of the two men finally turned to answer the other occupant of the office across the top of a bulky mechanical rowing device that sat in the middle of the room between the bar and the desk.

"The little wimp is perfect, Mr. Herkimer. Those hicks will never suspect there's any real money involved if they're approached by someone so unimpressive. Why do you think I picked him? He was the cream of the crop out of a whole harvest of losers. I received an awful lot of applications at the end of last year after we discovered this project, Harold."

Horace Herkimer skirted the rowing machine as he crossed the room to give Harold one of the freshly mixed martinis. After taking a sip from the glass he retained for him self, he perched his broad, velour covered rear end sideways on the edge of the desk and reached across it's top to press a button on the intercom machine.

"Miss Wayling?"

"Yes Mr. Herkimer?" queried a fairly deep, definitely mature female voice as it came over the intercom speaker.

"Has Rodney come in yet?"

In the lavish outer reception office of Herkimer, Herkimer, Herkimer, Herkimer, Miss Agnus Wayling tossed her platinum blond curls, which showed signs of far too many bleach sessions throughout the years.

Why was she even being bothered with such a question when the person asking already knew the answer?

The overhead lighting of the outer office cast a sheen on masculine features made only slightly more feminine due to the assistance of several layers of make up. She looked up at a large gold-framed clock on the wall across from the desk she sat behind before answering.

The boredom in her voice matched the expression on her face as she finally spoke again into the interoffice communication devise.

"Of course not Mr. Herkimer. He's never been on time since he joined the firm. Why should this morning be any different?"

"Try reaching him on his cell phone."

"Wouldn't do any good. He never turns the thing on. He's afraid of it...."

A chuckle could be heard over the speaker before Horace Herkimer answered.

"Send him into my office when he does show up, Miss Wayling. Mr. Herkimer and I both would like to speak with him."

"Is that an order or a request, Mr. Herkimer?"

"A request, Miss Wayling. If you wouldn't mind?"

"I'd consider it a pleasure, Mr. Herkimer"

Miss Wayling allowed herself a smug smile of satisfaction. One had to keep those with superior positions in line. Otherwise they would take advantage of you. Always maintain the upper hand. This was something she had learned a long time ago.

When she entered high school, her unfortunate resemblance to her father dashed away all hopes of becoming one of the more popular young ladies in the secondary education atmosphere in any conventional way. Becoming a bouncy, bubbly cheerleader was not to be in her future.

However, neither was Agnus Wayling destined to become the school withering wallflower who ate lunch and went to the movies with other unattractive girls. She was also not about to be the lonely little thing who cried into her pillow alone at night. Agnus just wasn't made that way.

At first the girl cursed God for blessing her with masculine features. On further reflection, she realized she wasn't even certain there was such an entity. If indeed there really was a Supreme Being, the girl decided to tell Him to go take an aerial sexual assault at a rolling pastry with a hole in its middle. She would tackle this problem from another direction all by herself.

The unattractive teenager turned her energies to academics and one particular art. The art of oral copulation.

This was before a recent United States President had declared this particular activity not to be an act of sex. It is doubtful if this would have had any effect on Agnus anyway. Government politics were never of any interest to the young woman.

This may have possibly been an unknown American blessing. Conversely, it might have well constituted an unfortunate mischance for this society.

Her first strike of revenge against the popular goody two shoes girls cliques of her school, was to wrap her artistic lips around the male sexual member of the homecoming queen's boyfriend.

This historic event occurred in the back seat of a 1958 Chevrolet while the homecoming dance was in progress and the queen was desperately searching for her king. It never occurred to her highness to go hunting in the parking lot.

Of course, the boyfriend told everyone. Agnus wasn't about to become the trollop the whole football team hoped for as the news began to spread. She'd put far too much thought into her action prior to performance to let that happen.

Miss Wayling was meticulous in her picking and choosing. Only select leaders of the boys in the senior class were allowed the privilege of experiencing what this young lady with the manly features, the extremely magic feminine tongue and succulent lips of velvet had to offer.

Soon, her name was being whispered in the educational institution's hallowed halls among its male elite in terms of reverence.

Much to the chagrin of her popular female peers, she became a force to be secretly feared and respected. When on rare occasions, she was confronted by young women who suspected her of unzipping the fly of their betrothed,

Agnus neither confirmed or denied the accusation. She had also mastered discretion.

Miss Wayling had conquered the secret not necessarily to power, but control over those of the opposite sex who held it. She was a master of manipulation at the tender age of seventeen. Agnus was off and running when she graduated from high school and hit the big town of LA.

She discovered herself to be a unique woman. She was blessed with no illusions concerning her status in the world of big corporations, sex, drugs or rock and roll. She would never be in love, never suffer binding relationships, and more importantly, never be bound to some balding piece of funny putty the rest of her life.

Her looks were deceiving. When fully clothed, she was, by no means a head turner. However, undressed and stripped down to her panties, Agnus was white heat incarnate.

The lady who was decreed never to be cheerleader material had the ability to make both the least and most experienced Lothario scream out in ecstasy and beg for mercy.

Underneath that rather ordinary exterior beat the libido of a sizzling, merciless mama mink. She had the indisputable talent to send any man home to his wife, dog, cat or houseplant, utterly sated.

Her goals were not money or power, but rather domination of those in possession of both. Of course they had to be of the male gender or the Waling method wouldn't work. Since men seemed to be in charge most of the time in this big city, as long as the woman who was destined never to lead a high school cheer in front of the grandstand set her sights carefully, everything came up roses.

As Agnus entered the work force, she made her self indispensable to each employer. Slowly and methodically, she maneuvered her way into the positions she wished to be at the time, by her own unique method of sexual conquest. She knew full well that efficiency and loyalty alone were not sufficient.

As the years rolled by, when a job no longer suited her immediate purposes she moved on.

She had walked off her post previously held before joining the Herkimer team, shortly after lunch time one afternoon with no explanation. It was mandatory she leave but none at her place of business would have understood. She had received a call from another woman who had become a close friend throughout Agnus's adult tenure of manipulation in LA. The caller had been a grand lady named Harrington Fox who happened to be a middle aged heiress.

Harrington's philosophy toward life in general was far different from that of Miss Wayling. Harrington got married frequently, something Agnus would never even consider.

However, between the Harrington's marriages, the two ladies had discovered they did share one thing in common. Each loved turning whole groups of men into sniveling babies, leaving their victims sobbing for more even when past the point of functioning. It was a recreational delight for both.

Agnus really liked Harrington but she hated her name. She had tried in vain to get her partner in perversion to change it, saying that it sounded like that of some Civil War General. Harrington always laughed when the subject came up, but refused.

However, friends they were. On this particular day the heiress had called her from Acapulco and told her that her presence was required in what Harrington described as a forest of young stiff penises.

Miss Wayling was on the first thing smoking out of the city of Los Angeles on her way to Mexico.

Agnus had a wonderful time helping to level the forest down south, but when she returned she found herself once again unemployed. Her former boss's wife had moved in and taken over the business.

Agnus decided then and there she needed a job where such a move would be tolerated the next time.

One never knew when Harrington would be on the phone shouting 'Timber' again, and she was tired of changing companies. The lady knew she would find what she needed. She always did.

After her first interview with Horace Herkimer, Agnus nearly yelled, "Eureka." The firm, at that time was named only Herkimer, Herkimer and Herkimer and consisted of just Horace, his younger brother Harold and their older brother Christopher. It was the perfect spot for her to make her nest.

Horace was in charge of the home office. He had at one time taken the vows of marital bliss. However, this actually worked as a plus for Agnus' plan.

Due to the enormous amount of alimony he paid each month, there was not a chance that there would ever be a new wife to move in and take over while Agnus wasn't looking.

The corporation was controlled by the older brother. Since Christopher was always out of state working on civil rights cases, the chances of any such event occurring in his case were also extremely remote.

Younger brother Harold's wedded past was even more complicated than that of Horace. The youngest Herkimer of the brothers barrister, had so many ex wives, they would never be able to move in and take over. They wouldn't fit in one suite of offices.

All Agnus needed now was to make sure she gained enough control over each one and she would never have to look for employment ever again.

The minute Miss Wayling moved in, she went right to work on what mattered most. Corporate business would have to wait.

She had broken the two men down individually like shotguns. It was a complicated process. The Herkimer brothers proved to be almost dysfunctional.

It had taken nearly every weapon in her sexual arsenal. However, progressing carefully, taking each man forward in order, one step at a time, her accomplishments exceeded all expectations.

As in her high school days, discretion had been the key. Each sibling thought himself to be the only one. Although the memorable sessions of both that turned the tide ended in near disaster, prior to the actual state of cataclysm, each man was also convinced he had performed admirably.

Harold was first. The poor man's head was almost blown through the headboard of a Santa Monica hotel bed, when the amil nitrate he was sniffing exploded.

From that time on, he kept his distance from her, but would never dream of doing anything that would threaten Miss Wayling's security within the firm.

Horace's affirmation of total loyalty had taken more time. He was definitely the more adventurous of the two home based brothers, once Miss Wayling awakened certain sleeping dragons within his soul.

However, perseverance had prevailed. Agnus would never have to entertain even the slightest reservation regarding her permanent standing with Horace.

The older of the two home based attorneys, after his third night out on the town with the new secretary/ receptionist, experienced a mishap in his elegant Bel Air apartment that would endear the lady to him forever.

That was the night when Horace had the misfortune of a fairly large vibrator seeming to take on a life of its own. The battery operated toy deigned for stimulation had somehow slipped from the attorney's fingers and climbed not only up, but literally inside his anal orifice.

It was an accident, but in Agnus's mind, the ultimate in all strokes of good fortune. She could not have orchestrated anything better.

She had taken him to the hospital and discretely explained to the young intern in charge what happened. The young doctor had not really believed her and was attempting to keep a straight face when he bent over to examine the suffering lawyer.

The buzzing sound emitting from within, beyond Horace's hefty haunches had convinced him that the woman's words were true.

Agnus had faithfully stood by and held her new employer's hand while an unusually large team of doctors and nurses gathered to watch the removal of the vile instrument.

After the reeking devise was finally pulled free, Agnus wiped it off on the young doctor's coat and slipped it in her purse. She then ordered the other personnel out and sent the intern who had performed the operation for the hospital administrator.

For some reason the young man did as he was told. Not five minutes had passed when the administrator appeared. Agnus was never to forget the look on the man's face when he stopped dead in his tracks as he slid inside the circular curtain surrounding Horace's station.

Miss Wayling promptly dismissed the intern after warning him about privacy laws. She then ordered Horace to the private toilet.

Horace also did as he was told as he desperately grabbed at the slits in the humiliating gown he wore. The big time attorney was terrified that his insides would fall out at any minute.

Horace undoubtedly heard the muffled cries of delight coming from the administrator behind those curtains all the way through the toilet walls. However, the humiliated barrister said nothing when at long last, Agnus, who was finally alone, opened the door.

She had helped him get dressed and told him not to worry. Nobody would ever relate his embarrassing experience. The lady with the magic lips within the masculine face had done it again.

Her sexual tentacles had obviously reached into the very bowels of west Hollywood or at least this part of the miracle mile. Horace limped out of the medical facility that night with a new respect for his new secretary. An esteem that would last forever.

Unlike Harold, Horace still availed himself of the special lady's favors from time to time, but mechanical devises were now prohibited and never referred to. An unspoken rule between them except in the unlikely event Agnus should somehow find her job in jeopardy.

Agnus had finally met Christopher, the oldest of the three brothers and actual head of the firm, during one of his rare visits to LA and the Century City office.

Immediately she had set out to attach a similar hold on him. It was one of the few times in her life that she had failed.

The older man either was too distracted with his plans to leave and serve some minority cause elsewhere in the US, or he just didn't notice her advances. Due to a certain specific aspect of this particular Herkimer's physiology, she always felt it to be the latter.

Therefore, because of the particular circumstances, combined with the leader of the firm's personality, her ego endured no suffering.

Had she needed self assurance, which she did not, Miss Wayling could well have consoled her self with the additional verity that he never stayed around long enough for her to really work up a good game plan.

It didn't matter. Christopher Herkimer left all the firms real money making business up to Horace anyway. Christopher just held the reins guiding the direction in which these monetary gains were to be distributed.

Agnus learned soon enough that these reins were held in a very tight, controlling fist. A subject on which Horace was oft times heard to comment.

"I make the money. Mr. Herkimer controls it. I bust my hump catering to the rich, convincing them the need for high priced legal services. He spends it on people who can't afford lawyers. How's that for fair?"

Miss Wayling knew there was bitter blood on Horace's part toward his older brother but she also was well aware of how the firm was structured. As long as he was alive, Christopher Herkimer would hold his position as head of the law corporation. Even in the event of demise on the part of the former, there was no guarantee Horace would take over.

None of this concerned Agnus. All Agnus really cared about was Agnus. She concentrated on keeping both feet planted on solid turf and her antenna of sexual defense always on the alert.

Since she had come to work for the firm, one more Herkimer had been added to the list of partners.

Miss Wayling had managed to maneuver this one into her clutches a couple of times, but still didn't have the real hold on him she had hoped for. To say he was different was an understatement.

However, aside from being another small blow to Ms. Wayling's ego, he obviously approved of her presence in the firm and represented no threat.

The newest Herkimer stayed on the road with Christopher all the time and seemed to have no real influence in the firm at all. This latest addition to the firm before Rodney Van Aukin came along was a cousin, she was told.

While the 'cousin' was absolutely adored by the older Herkimer, he was openly disliked by both Horace and Harold. Agnus thought him to be a nice, if not unusual young man and not at all what she expected. However it was obvious to her once she met him, why her two immediate superiors were reluctant even to let their paying clients meet him.

She decided not to concern herself. Agnus had total control over those who mattered to her. Of that she was certain. At least she was until Van Aukin had entered the picture.

The bumbling little idiot was nothing more than a glorified law clerk. When he first arrived, had he not been so insecure and down right incompetent, Miss Wayling would have hardly noticed his presence.

Then, because the wimp was about to marry Horace's thunder-thighed daughter, he was made a partner and would soon be a member of the family. His name was even already on the door.

Had it not been for his complexion, the kid wasn't that bad looking. Still, she really didn't care for the squirrely little psychotic son of a New England politician.

The fact that he stuttered on occasion and didn't seem too bright didn't bother her. She thrived on any and all imperfections of her prey. But this one had a certain honesty about him. Agnus had learned way back in school that a combination of honesty and imperfection could be deadly.

Nonetheless, the lady knew the time would come when she'd have to lure the unsuspecting stammerer into some sort of sexual encounter. This business of job security just never seemed to end.

A light began blinking on a long electronic panel resting on the desk next to Miss Wayling's computer keyboard. She'd have to worry about the distasteful task of debauching young Rodney later.

Her husky voice was extremely pleasant as she spoke into the tiny microphone attached to the headset entangled in her almost colorless hair.

"Law offices of Herkimer, Herkimer, Herkimer, Herkimer. How may I help you?"

*** *** *** *** *** ***

The lobby beneath the prestigious law firm was filled with beautiful, provocatively dressed young women. Rodney was too busy at the moment being irritated with the owners of the building to notice.

The recently accepted member of the California Bar Association had no idea the amounts of money they collected each year in leases. Whatever the figure, he was sure the landlords could at least afford more than one urinal in their ground floor public rest room.

He was also attempting to look at his watch while he zipped up his fly. This further averted his vision.

Somehow he made it through the crowd of women and managed to push the up button on the elevator direction panel next to the sliding doors.

He glanced at his watch again. Louise always managed to make him tardy for work, but he'd never showed up this late. He just hoped nobody noticed.

Miss Wayling would know of course, but if she didn't tell anybody else, maybe Horace and Harold Herkimer wouldn't. It would be nice if they just assumed he was already in that little closet they called his office, attending to his usual clerical duties.

Finally, the elevator doors in front of him opened.

Before Rodney could step inside, a throng of well-endowed career girls swarmed forward in front of him. The young fellow only managed to barely wedge his own body inside before the doors slid closed.

Immediately, the conveyance invention zoomed toward the top of the multimillion-dollar edifice through the very center of its extravagant bowels.

As the elevator streaked upward, Rodney, close to the door, pushed button number fifteen with his forefinger. His whole arm was immediately shoved aside by a stunning redhead reeking of what was probably Channel Number Five. She giggled as she ran her manicured long fingernails down the entire panel. Immediately all the lights began to glimmer.

As the car came to a sudden halt, Rodney nearly lost his footing. He murmured an apology to the two young women he had fallen against as the doors opened.

Four more career females of various size and color pushed their way inside. This addition of feminine flesh and corresponding products forced the lone male occupant of the car back against the wall farthest from the door.

After what seemed to Rodney an eternity, the elevator finally arrived at the fifteenth floor. He tried to worm his way toward freedom through and around the maze of beautiful breasts and buttocks. His valiant attempt was doomed.

Once more he was driven back to his suffocating prison of cashmere and cleavage. The doors closed, and, as before, the elevator car continued upward.

Finally on the twenty-second floor, Rodney managed to escape.

The doors slid closed and the tired young man stood in the foyer, attempting not only to catch his breath, but also to decide if he should push the down button.

He had two options. The young attorney with his name on a door somewhere inside this building could try the elevator all over again or take the stairs back down to the fifteenth floor.

After a moments thought, in spite of the extra required physical effort, Rodney chose the latter. He headed for a door marked, "Stairway."

*** *** *** *** *** ***

When the portal leading to the elevator's alternative into the fifteenth floor corridor finally opened, Rodney stumbled out of the stairwell into the hall. He was grateful for at least three things.

He was not only delighted that, at long last, he was only a few doors away from his destination, the junior barrister was thankful for the fact that his trek had been downward instead of the opposite direction. He was also pleased that he'd only fallen down once.

Attempting to make his forth-coming entrance look normal, Rodney stood up straight and walked down the hallway to the third doorway on his left. He paused before opening the portal to look at his own name in gold letters.

Right there on there on the door, now directly in front of him was printed, "Herkimer, Herkimer, Herkimer, Herkimer." In much smaller letters, but none the less, also in gold leaf, it said, "and Van Aukin." Rodney began to feel much better as he pushed open the portal and entered the outer reception office.

The mood of the young lawyer with his name on the door was immediately dashed to realistic perspective. Miss Wayling greeted him before he had both feet over the threshold.

"Mr. Herkimer wants to see you!"

Rodney attempted to buy some time. "Which Mr. Herkimer?" he asked. He suddenly had a strange feeling this older woman was staring at his crotch. He let his right hand stray downward. Perhaps his fly was unzipped. It wasn't.

At his engagement party he had overheard some vile whispered gossip regarding Miss Wayling and Horace Herkimer. The spreader of inner office corporate scuttlebutt was some lady who had evidently been a nurse before she married a diabetic wealthy businessman. She and her husband had been seated near the young couple of honor at the time of the glorious event. Before she realized Louise was listening and shut completely up, the guest had begun painting an obscene verbal picture about the two that Rodney had never believed.

Of course he still didn't. However, the focus of the masculine faced secretary's eyes at this moment did make him think about the story and cause him wonder.

He had to be mistaken. Maybe she was looking at his shoes, or quite possibly something behind him. He turned back to make sure he had closed the door correctly.

"Both Mr. Herkimers. They're waiting in the big office. Mr. Herkimer said for you to come immediately. The minute you showed up."

There was nothing amiss with the door. It was closed. He turned back. This time there was no mistake. She was indeed staring at his crotch, no where else. It made him very uncomfortable.

He started to walk away toward the corridor leading to the executive offices, then, attempting to keep the front of his trousers twisted away from her line of vision, he paused. He really should find out which Herkimer had actually issued the order and if he was supposed to show up with any particular paperwork.

Rodney was just about to ask these questions, when another light in the panel on top of Miss Wayling's desk lit up.

"Law offices of Herkimer, Herkimer, Herkimer, Herkimer. How may I help you? To which Mr. Herkimer do you wish to speak, please?"

Agnus continued to stare in the direction of Rodney's crotch even though she no longer had a direct line of vision as she waited for an answer. Her question had obviously stumped the party on the other end of the wire, and she'd been momentarily put on hold.

Her thoughts strayed idly to Harrington, whom she knew was at this moment celebrating the divorce of her seventh husband at a plush restaurant in Beverly Hills. What would she would think of this jerk?

When the time came, maybe Harrington would help. Forget it, Agnus. She thought to herself. Harrington would puke. Miss Wayling would have to bite the bullet, or whatever, and go this one alone.

Rodney considered taking advantage of this pause that followed to remind this strange woman whose eyes were still attempting to focus his crotch, to not only voice his queries, but to remind her that his name was also on the door.

He changed his mind regarding both and turned away to investigate for stains as she began speaking again. Perhaps that was the reason the woman would not avert her eyes.

"I'm sorry. That Mr. Herkimer is still out of the state with Mr. Herkimer. Would you care to speak to Mr. Herkimer or Mr. Herkimer? Which Mr. Herkimer? Oh, that Mr. Herkimer is the Mr. Herkimer the Mr. Herkimer you just asked for is out of state with. Very well. I'll tell him as soon as he checks in. Would you…?"

Miss Wayling continued to rattle on as Rodney, forgotten for the moment by the mistress of manipulation with the masculine features, fearfully disappeared around a corridor corner.

He moved slowly down the second hallway toward what Miss Wayling had referred to as the big office and the two Mr. Herkimers who were not out of the state. He checked carefully. There didn't seem to be any spots on the front of his pants.

He hoped he wasn't showing up without documents his superiors expected him to be bringing with him. He also hoped neither of them would comment on his tardy arrival to the office.

*** *** *** *** *** ***

"You're at least an hour and a half late Rodney! Please don't take another hour and a half coming through the door."

Horace Herkimer's oversized posterior, at one time boasting an implanted vibrator, was now firmly settled on the seat of the rowing machine. One of his hands gripped an oar while the thumb and forefinger of his other, delicately held the stem of his half-full martini glass.

His words were addressed to Rodney who stood hesitantly in the open doorway leading out into the hall from whence the young man just came. Harold Herkimer still occupied the chair behind the desk beyond the rowing machine.

"I'm' really sorry Mr. Herkimer. I mean my apologies to you too, Mr. Herkimer... I... That is..." Rodney stammered as he moved into the room with trepidation slowly pulling the portal closed behind him.

"Hey! You're talking to two guys who used to be married, here. Just because we've both been divorced an innumerably collective amount of times, doesn't mean we still can't remember what it's like to be in love. And my daughter's a beautiful young woman. They're all beautiful before you marry them. That's the reason we have to get you to the church as quickly as possible. Nothing like being married to make you want to get out of bed in the morning and go to work. Right Mr. Herkimer?" said the stocky man in the expensive jogging suit as he drained his glass.

Quickly rising from the rowing machine, he brushed past Rodney on his way back to the bar where he began pouring himself another drink.

"Right Mr. Herkimer," said the other senior partner. He leaned forward and picked up a folder filled with papers. "We really should get right down to business," he continued.

"Absolutely!" replied Horace Herkimer before raising the martini glass to his lips. After pouring a good portion of the clear liquid past his extremely white teeth, he moved forward toward Rodney who was now trapped between the two men.

The youngest man in the room moved his head rapidly from right to left, then left to right, as he looked from one to the other. The Bostonian law school graduate looked as if he might be watching a tennis match.

"B... Business?" Rodney knew he was still stammering, but he couldn't seem to stop.

Horace Herkimer nodded as he carried the remainder of his drink to a large, oblong, digital blood pressure machine hanging from the wall next to the bar.

The heavy attorney in the expensive jogging suit held the glass aloft with his left hand while inserting the forefinger of his right into a little hole in the medical contrivance.

"Rodney, we've decided to relieve you of your wretched clerical duties... At least temporarily."

Rodney, looking slightly shocked, yet pleased said nothing as Horace Herkimer read the unhappy results on the blood pressure machine gauge screen. Without even changing expression, the older attorney returned to the bar and proceeded to top off his drink

"We're entrusting you with a very important assignment, Rodney."

"That's wonderful news Mr. Herkimer." Said Rodney, finally able to speak without stammering.

"If you can pull this off, son, you'll be well on the way with the firm. That's important to me, considering how soon you'll be officially part of the family. Don't let me down Rodney."

"I won't sir," said Rodney, attempting make his voice sound deeper. "You know I received my best grades at law school in courtroom procedure."

At the bar, Horace Herkimer rolled his eyes as he looked past Rodney to the other Herkimer. "This isn't exactly a court room assignment, Rodney," he said. "Mr. Herkimer here will fill you in."

Rodney turned toward the other Herkimer who was spreading the papers from the folder out on the desktop in front of him.

"Rodney, you're going to represent our firm on a very crucial project which will involve your going out of town for a few days," said Harold Herkimer.

"A business trip? Dynamite sir!" The younger man responded. Rodney was obviously pleased.

"Where? Chicago? New York? Not back to Boston?" he asked hopefully.

"Not exactly," said Horace Herkimer who still stood behind Rodney. "You're taking a trip to the country."

The look of pleasure immediately vanished from the young man's face. Rodney hated the country. He suddenly found himself fighting back an urge to vomit as he turned back to look at Louise's father.

"C...country?" He was stammering again. There was very little in this world that Rodney Van Aukin could say he really disliked. The country was at the top of that short list.

"That's correct. The country," said Harold Herkimer, as he began spreading out a map on top of the other papers in front of him.

Rodney's neck was beginning to hurt as he twisted it back around toward the seated Herkimer who was now pointing to a particular spot on the map with a manicured nail.

"Lone Pine, California to be exact," the executive continued. "Right here, Rodney. Let's see... Beyond Mojave.... And before Bishop...."

Harold Herkimer, evidently tired of looking at the squiggly little lines, turned his attention to the business of folding the map. Once this was accomplished, he rose to his feet and handed the bulky object across the desk to Rodney.

"Don't worry. Just follow the map. Your assignment is to locate two certain parties known as the Maynard brothers and get their signatures on these documents," he said, as he stuffed the rest of the papers back into the folder, which he also gave to Rodney.

"Our firm has been retained by a contracting company to purchase the Maynards' property. We've tried corresponding with them to no avail. So, we're sending you to find them and close the deal. It's very important. Any questions?"

"Only one, sir," replied Rodney. "Why Me?"

"Because you're the most qualified, Rodney," responded Horace Herkimer, as he moved up behind the young man and gave him a pat on the back. "Give him the envelope, Mr. Herkimer."

Harold Herkimer leaned forward and opened one of the desk drawers from which he withdrew a thick envelope. This he also handed to Rodney.

"Be careful with this," he admonished with a serious look on his face. "There's twenty two hundred dollars in there, cash. Two thousand for the purchase after the Maynards have signed over the property, and two hundred for your own expenses. You'll be traveling in your own car. You'll bring back receipts of course."

Rodney stood there with both hands now full. He appeared to be not only quite lost, but also thoroughly confused.

He looked around at Louise's father as the other man spoke. Horace was climbing back onto the rowing machine. The portly attorney in the jogging suit was being very careful not to spill the remainder of his martini in the process, as he now took his turn talking to the young man with a mission.

"Why don't you take the rest of the day off? I'd get an early start tomorrow morning if I were you."

Rodney was sure he'd misunderstood. "T...tomorrow? Tomorrow's S...Saturday, sir."

"That's right. Good day to travel, Saturday. Less traffic. I think you should be on the road before daylight. Think that's a good idea?"

Even though Louise's father had phrased his last sentence as a question, Rodney knew he was being given an order. He said nothing.

"Yes," continued Horace. "An early start to where you're heading's the only way. I've been told that desert can grow ghastly hot as the day wears on."

Rodney was fighting back tears. "Country? Desert? I've got this skin condition...."

"Nonsense!" Harold Herkimer moved swiftly from behind the desk.

He took Rodney by the arm and began ushering the unhappy fellow out the door before he could say anymore.

"Just get an early start. It's extremely important we see you back here in no less than three days with those documents signed."

Rodney disappeared into the hallway.

Harold Herkimer firmly closed the door behind him. He listened for a minute to the young man's departing footsteps before turning back to his brother.

Horace was still seated on the rowing machine and was obviously pleased with the way the meeting had been handled.

"Well, that does it. You and I buy the property for two thousand and sell it for two million. Not a bad return I'd say," he stated proudly as he stepped off the rowing machine and headed back to the bar.

Harold Herkimer remained by the door.

"The firm's money to be accurate. It's been a year since that area was surveyed before we were approached to handle this transaction. Then, they said next spring. Now it's the end of this summer. It's already almost the end of this summer! Every thing's been moved ahead. We don't have much time."

"So? You know how bureaucracies work, Harold. Unusual to have a date set sooner instead of later, but in reality it works in our favor. We can't buy that property and hang onto it when we're using the firm's funds. We have to unload it immediately. Even though you and I are supposedly the only ones besides the select few in the contracting company we represent that knows why that mountain's valuable, I've always been a little nervous. Now there's no danger of anyone else sneaking in ahead of us. The sooner we move, the sooner we're independent and off the Herkimer hook. We don't need that much time. Fortunately we were afforded an ample amount to put our pigeon in place. The little bird is primed and ready to fly."

Harold made a distasteful face. He started back around his brother and partner still seated on the rowing machine, heading back to his behind the desk.

"I shudder to think off the consequences should our partners ever catch wind of this," the younger of the two middle aged executives said. "I know you have it set up for young Van Aukin to take the fall if they do, but...."

Harold paused as he reached his destination and a new thought interrupted his old one. " Of course if it works, when it's all over, you'll have to find a way to get rid of Rodney before he ... If he were ever to mention this to the other Mr. Herkimers...."

"Mr. Herkimer," said Mr. Herkimer, interrupting the other Mr. Herkimer, as he raised his glass to the same Mr. Herkimer, "it's going to work! And fuck Herkimer and Herkimer. What they'll never know can't hurt them. Fuck Van Aukin too! Either way he'll be history. The idea of having that stupid little bastard in the Herkimer family's laughable. W.P.'s embarrassment enough. It took some fancy maneuvering to talk my daughter into bed with that little New England nerd, but believe me, I'll have no problem at all

35

talking her out."

*** *** *** *** *** ***

Rodney wasn't allowed in Louise's bed at all that night.

He was only permitted inside her bedroom long enough to pack the belongings he needed for the trip he had to take the following morning.

She made it clear she wasn't permanently kicking him out, she was just mad. She wasn't only angry with him, but her father had incensed her as well.

The reason for the spoiled young woman's irritation wasn't because Rodney would be absent for an uncertain amount of time. The wrath of Louise was brought about due to the fact that The 'Slum Mobile' was being taken from her.

She'd even called Horace Herkimer and offered her own Mercedes for Rodney to drive during his out of town excursion. The telephone in his Bel Air residence was answered by Miss Wayling.

At first she thought this to be a good sign. Her father almost always gave her whatever she desired when Horace and the secretary with the rather coarse features were at his place working late. When that happened, for some reason his cooperation could almost always be guaranteed.

This became an evening of exception. Her father was adamant. Rodney was to drive the Karmann Ghia and he didn't care to discuss the subject any further.

Louise made Rodney sleep on the couch alone because she was furious with both of the men in her life.

"Daddy's a rectal eliminator and you have no testicular fortitude!" She screamed in her strident voice as she slammed the door to the slumber chamber.

"There's no such word as 'eliminator' and 'fortitude' in that context is ambiguous," he called to the now locked door, attempting to draw on his training from law school.

"Go to Hell Rodney!" Louise countered from the other side of the door.

"I am. At least I'm on my way there tomorrow…." he responded in a tiny voice. The frustrated young man looked ready to burst into tears.

A light of hope glimmered momentarily in his eyes as the bedroom door opened.

Perhaps Louise had discovered the error of her ways and had decided to forgive him.

He instantly knew better when his cellular telephone come flying out through the bedroom doorway. It struck him in the temple before bouncing onto the sofa.

Immediately the door closed again and Rodney could hear it being locked from the other side. Rodney decided this last act might well have been a sign of at least partial reconciliation as he looked down at the dreaded portable communication invention.

At least Louise wanted him to call. Surely this place called Lone Pine wasn't so primitive that it didn't have pay phones. He really didn't wish to risk developing a brain tumor.

As he began to undress and prepare for his last night in Beverly Hills on the uncomfortable sofa before his mandatory venture into the depths of Hell, Rodney searched his mind for something positive. Norman Vincent Peale had been required reading back in law school.

The unhappy junior member of the firm of Herkimer, Herkimer, Herkimer, Herkimer and Van Aukin could only come up with one detail that wasn't totally negative about his present situation and the impending doom that lay ahead.

As he finally drifted off into fitful slumber alone on the Beverly Hills sofa, he consoled himself with one comforting thought.

At least, after his shower the following morning prior to his departure, he wouldn't have to look to look at the frogs in Louise's bathroom anymore. Not for at a couple of days anyway.

CHAPTER THREE
UNKNOWN HORIZONS

The Beverly Hills bathroom was at least two hundred miles behind him but here was another frog staring up at Rodney. This one was real.

At first Rodney thought his mind was playing tricks on him. After all, he hadn't gotten much sleep the night before and the fact that Louise still wasn't speaking to him when he left was in itself unnerving.

This, followed by the tremendous psychological struggle of maneuvering the little green German manufactured automobile through the early morning traffic out of Los Angeles before daylight, could cause even the strongest of mental faculties to waver.

When he'd finally stopped in that dreadful town known as Mojave for gas, he knew he should have used the rest room. But at six a.m. the sun was just coming up over the eastern desert skyline.

It looked to Rodney like the fires of Hell were creeping toward this place that had the appearance of the Dominion of Death. He paid for the fuel and drove on as fast as he could.

Before he had traveled even fifty miles, his bladder began to remind him of his failure to be mindful of proper duties at proper times. This was a basic rule that should have over ridden his feelings of fear toward the small city.

Unfortunately, now there wasn't even a building in sight, let alone a toilet facility.

The young traveler had spotted a grove of trees a short distance from the highway on the right. There seemed to be a drastic decrease in vegetation in the distance ahead.

Since there appeared to be no other promise of privacy in sight, he had parked the Ghia on the shoulder of a slight bend in the road and exited the vehicle.

After putting the top up on the small convertible and making sure it was locked, he had then hurried toward the trees.

Now, here he was, urinating in the middle of a bunch of trees and a frog was looking at him.

He dismissed the thought that the creature might be delusional when the slimy gray, green, wart covered little monster started croaking.

Figments of the imagination didn't croak. Of that, Rodney was fairly certain. The fact that it was real didn't make him feel much better. It was still watching. He hated that.

Whether the web-footed creature was protesting the invasion of its privacy by this two-legged humanoid in the three-pieced suit, or making a comment on the size of his penis, Rodney had no idea. The thing was still looking at him as he went to the bathroom. He wished it would just go away.

Suddenly his wish was granted. The young lawyer instantly regretted having made it. A strong wind, seeming to come from nowhere, forced him to begin twisting his body about in different directions to keep from urinating all over himself.

By the time he was finished, the frog was indeed gone. The wind, however, had become so strong he was sure he was going to be killed by one of the whipping overhead tree branches coming dangerously close to his head.

Clearly out of his element, arms and legs flailing madly, the terrified young traveler ran out of the mayhem of madness that had only a short time ago been a peaceful, sleepy looking grove of trees.

Fighting an act of what some ascribe to God, he finally made his way back to his little green car parked on the shoulder of the highway in the middle of a curve.

After experiencing a great deal of difficulty, Rodney at last was able to climb into the vehicle and pull the driver's door closed behind him.

Once inside the little automobile, the attorney took a deep breath. He tried to stop himself from shaking as he managed to finally get his fly closed.

Suddenly, his eyes grew wide as he looked in the rear view mirror. A very large eighteen wheeler truck complete with a very long trailer, was coming around the bend. The enormous machine was bearing down on his small parked convertible at a very high rate of speed.

The gigantic vehicle thundered past the Karmann Ghia. The dangerous looking truck barley missed the little car as the mechanical monster and its long trailer finally completed rounding the turn.

Unfortunately, the eighteen wheeler's natural slipstream, combined with nature's high wind, tugged at the convertible top of the little automobile with so much force, the material was ripped totally free from the rest of the car.

Behind the steering wheel of the freshly mutilated Karmann Ghia, all expression was gone from his face as Rodney looked through his windshield. Beyond the glass in front of him, he witnessed the remains of what Louise used to call 'The Slum Mobile's cute little ragtop' careening down the highway like a tumbleweed, following the truck.

He crouched low in the seat as the wind continued to whip around both him and the defiled little German vehicle. The frustrated traveler picked up his brief case from the passenger side of the floorboard.

Being very careful not to give the wind access to the contents of the flat leather container, such as the envelope containing the cash and the other items, including the map given to him by Harold Herkimer, he pulled out the dreaded cellular telephone.

After looking at the instrument for along while, he returned it to the briefcase. He made certain the latch on the case was securely closed, then placed it back on the floorboard.

The wind whipped at his hair and clothing, as he then leaned forward and inserted the key into the Ghia's ignition.

*** *** *** *** *** ***

The wind was still blowing but compared to what he had experienced earlier that morning, fifty miles out of Mojave, it felt to Rodney like a gentle breeze.

His nemesis now was the overhead blistering sun. Without a top, the Karmann Ghia's air conditioning unit was useless. There was no overhead protection at all for his sensitive skin.

He'd removed his jacket and his vest. He was afraid he might ruin his image if he took off the tie.

For a while, he'd tried tying the jacket around his head to protect himself from the sun that grew hotter as it crept toward the center of the sky.

The youthful barrister learned very quickly that he'd come up with a foolish plan when the garment slipped over his eyes and he nearly ran off the road. It also made him even hotter.

He had tried a another variation of the same technique by wrapping one of his extra shirts he'd taken from the suitcase behind the seats of the Ghia, around his head. This didn't work either.

Not only did the shirt also keep slipping down over his eyes, the garment's particular placement may have been the cause of further problems. When he'd stopped to ask how far it was to Lone Pine at a place called Little Lake, a withered old lady in front of a trailer house, had set her dogs on him. Rodney had barely avoided those snapping teeth.

Rodney wasn't quite sure why the old lady wanted the canines to eat him. He wasn't familiar with the term 'Foreign Raghead.'

However, he had decide to play it safe and brave the elements bareheaded from that moment forth.

The sun was nearly to the point of being exactly overhead now. Rodney felt like a freshly baked potato. Still he drove on toward what had been dictated by his superiors as his destination.

In addition to every thing else, added to his confusion was the highway itself. Rodney could swear it kept changing colors.

Instead of a normal, sensible gray as everyone knew pavement was supposed to be it, for a long time now, it had been a variety of different hews. Some times it was dark blue, other times almost chocolate brown, but mostly a dark, brick red.

He was beginning to feel like he might be the victim of a very cruel joke. Maybe this place called Lone Pine didn't even exist.

Perspiration seemed to ooze from every pore of his entire body as he peered through the windshield in front of him around the carcasses of deceased, squashed insects pasted to its other side.

Finally he saw a sign announcing it was only two more miles to Lone Pine.

Unless the State Highway sign painters were in on the gag, there really was a city out here in the middle of absolutely nowhere with that name.

Elated that he was finally about to reach his destination, he pressed his right foot down on the accelerator as he peered closer through the bug-encrusted glass for any sign of the city itself.

Fortunately, he saw the sheep in the middle of the road just in time to slam on the brakes.

A substantial amount of rubber was disengaged from the Ghia's tires and left embedded in the strange colored asphalt beneath and behind it, as the little car screeched to a halt.

Miraculously, the topless green vehicle managed to somehow avoid colliding with any of the wooly, bleating creatures filling up both lanes of the thoroughfare leading from and toward Lone Pine.

The road was overflowing with sheep. Rodney was sure there were at least a hundred, and they smelled terrible.

In actuality, there were only fifty-five, and they weren't all on the highway.

Some had already gained access to the other side. Others were just stepping onto it, adhering to the edict handed down to the chicken ever since evolution had developed that particular creature, or the road, whichever came first.

There was, however, no denying the smell. Rodney dug frantically into the pocket of his trousers for a handkerchief with which to cover his nose.

One of the foul smelling wool covered creatures had evidently heard somewhere that the shortest distance between two points was indeed a straight line. Therefore, the animal decided to proceed over the automobile in its path rather than around it.

The sheep leapt into the rear space behind Rodney. It paused just long enough to leave a rectal deposit on his suitcase, then jumped out, joining its companions on the other side of the Ghia.

Another of the flock, an old ewe, decided to take a break before continuing onward. She stopped to nibble at the remains of the small car's ragtop.

Rodney held the handkerchief over his nose as he tried to convince the odorous old female to continue onward

"Shoo!" he managed to blurt out between gagging sounds. "Get away!"

The old ewe paid no attention to the driver of the car and continued to munch away at her newly discovered delicacy.

Rodney finally spotted a young freckled-faced girl who looked to be about twelve years old following the remainder of the sheep across the highway. She seemed to be fighting a battle with her budding breasts that were attempting to work their way free over the top of tight, faded gingham dress.

The girl also wore a shapeless old straw hat over her tangled straw colored hair. She walked toward Rodney and the nibbling ewe.

Once again, the young man attempted to keep his stomach from turning over as the smell of the sheep invaded his sensitive nostrils.

"Excuse me," he managed to ask. "Would you happen to know the Maynard brothers?"

The girl evidently decided to give up the battle of the breasts for the moment and reached into the front of the car the past the empty passengers seat.

In spite of her awkward position, she managed to slap Rodney squarely in the face. The handkerchief he was holding to his nose flew out of the Ghia onto the other side of the road.

"I ain't that kinda girl Mister!" she said savagely as she withdrew her hand to push an escaped nipple back behind the gingham.

Using the same extremity, she reached out and cuffed the ewe on its ear. "Come on Flossie. Git!!"

The old ewe reluctantly gave up the ragtop remains and moved around the front of the vehicle to join the other sheep. Almost all of the wooly animals were now on the other side of the road heading across the desert toward a large barn.

Rodney attempted to regain his physical composure as he remained in the car. He watched the girl. She was still pushing her growing womanhood back into the top of her tight fitting dress as she urged the bleating creatures onward.

He then looked in his rear view mirror to survey any apparent injury his face might have received from the blow she had inflicted. He was also certain that his sensitive skin would be showing considerable damage from all this vile exposure to the elements.

Amazingly there seemed to be no new bumps or blemishes. Even those he'd seen in Louise's frog shaped mirror earlier the same morning, which now seemed like at least a year ago, were no longer visible.

He could see no telltale marks from the recent slap either. This could well be due to the fact that his entire face was now turning a very bright pink.

Rodney was sure that before long, both epidermis and the dermis itself would peel away, exposing his skull. Louise would sever all ties with him forever if he returned to Beverly Hills looking like the top part of a warning symbol for poisonous substances.

The suffering young lawyer turned away from the mirror to look once more at the freckled faced girl still herding the sheep toward the barn.

He was fairly certain, due to her recent, violent reaction, that she did, somehow know the Maynard brothers, or at least who they were.

Rodney, himself, was honestly sorry he had ever heard of either of them.

*** *** *** *** *** ***

"Trux Maynard was here yesterday and picked up his mail. The lady said she had no idea where his brother was and didn't care. Except she didn't say it quite that nicely," Rodney said into the mouthpiece of a pay telephone receiver.

He was standing just inside the open doorway of an old fashioned phone booth, located beneath a waving American flag that flew from a long, upright pole in front of the Lone Pine Post Office.

His Karmann Ghia, windshield still smeared with the splattered remains of a variety of insects, stood a few feet away, parked at an earthen curb just off the main drag of the small city. It seemed so strange to be in such desolate blistering surroundings with the majestic snow covered peaks of the Sierra monitions in the background. The poor little totally topless vehicle looked sad and neglected.

"And when I asked the lady where they lived, she slammed the window shut on me," Rodney continued. "This really is a strange place, Louise."

Louise was wearing a string bikini which made her look like the 'Before' part of a television weight loss work out infomercial. She was lounging at the moment on a Gucci foam pad beside the pool of her Beverly Hills apartment building.

She cuddled a green stuffed replica of Kermit the frog beneath one pudgy arm while she talked into a frog shaped cellular telephone, which she held in her other hand.

"Rodney," she said, "I'm not interested in the details of your work. You know that. I just want to know how the 'Slum Mobile's doing."

In front of the Lone Pine Post Office, Rodney looked at the pathetic, dirty little molested machine in question and crossed his fingers before answering.

He hoped he didn't turn immediately into a pillar of salt.

"All things considered, she's holding up fine just fine," he said, growing braver by the second. "The air's real clear here so I've got the top down."

Louise shifted her position and rolled closer to the pool. Her strident voice remained pleasant, but held just a hint of warning as she spoke once more into the cell phone.

"I just hope you're putting it up when the sun's out. I wouldn't want her sweet little seat covers ruined."

He wanted to tell her that the sun hardly ever shined in this area he'd arrived in. He couldn't. The round fiery ball up above had absolutely no interference as it glared down with no mercy from the clear blue sky. Rodney decided it was time to bring this long distance conversation to an end.

"Don't worry. Gotta go now. More boring business. I'll call you."

Back in Beverly Hills, Louise was rising to her feet. She carefully lay the stuffed frog aside. She then stuck her wide round bikini clad behind way up in the air as she bent over to roll up her Gucci foam rubber mat.

She cradled the cell phone between her chubby shoulder and the side of her right lower jaw as she continued to talk into it.

"Make sure you do. I need to know when you're coming home. There's a new play opening at the Mark Taper I'm just dying to see. I'm not sure why you let Daddy send you away in the first place. Rodney! Stop saying 'But.. But.' You're starting to sound like a motor boat. Just do whatever Daddy sent you there to do and get back here with the 'Slum Mobile.' I've got another call anyway. Bye. Kiss Kiss. Hello? Oh, hi Mirna. No, nothing important...."

Rodney hung up the pay phone and turned to see what looked like two shabbily dressed Native Americans draped over the side of the Ghia.

The bronzed faces of both individuals peeked out from beneath the broad brims of shapeless western style hats with large feathers protruding from the bands as they shared a bottle of wine.

He took a deep breath of the Lone Pine air before approaching them. It went against his better judgement to admit it, but the act of inhaling actually felt good. The attorney wasn't used to breathing something he couldn't see.

"Hi there," said Rodney, to the two men leaning on his car. "Nice weather we're having."

The recipients of his greeting gave him a bored look as the one on the right took a drink from the bottle before passing it back to the one on the left.

"You fellows Native Americans?"

For a minute it looked like there would still be no forth-coming response. Then finally, after the man on the left took a long drink that nearly drained the bottle, he spoke.

"I'm a native alright. Borned right outside of town on the Reservation.

44

Druther be called a Human Bein though."

"Druther not be called at all if there's no money involved," said the other man.

"Show a little class. Dude wasn't talkin' to you," the first individual countered before turning his attention back to the sweaty young stranger wearing the tie.

"Don't much like that word ' American.' Way I see it, this lands been all fucked up ever since some white eyes invented it."

"He's a God damned Indian," said his companion taking possession of the bottle. "Just like me. He's Standing Up, and he's a God damned Indian!"

Rodney wasn't quite sure why the fellow was telling him about the man in question's physical position at the moment. The young attorney could see he was standing.

"I ain't from no India," said the other. "And Italy where you're from ain't in India neither. Italy's some other place."

"Screw your self. I ain't from Italy. I was born right here in Lone Pine same as you."

"Your stupid Grandpa come from Italy, Sitting Down!"

"You're Italian?" queried Rodney, Who was becoming very confused with the conversation. Both men were standing. On the other hand, he guessed it was possible the fellow's ancestor might have made the trip across the ocean sitting down, although it sounded extremely uncomfortable.

"Hell no. I'm Awopaho. From the great hills of Sicily."

Both of the drinking companions seemed to find the last remark very funny. Laughing, they began to stagger away.

Rodney called after them.

"I saw 'Drums Along The Mohawk' three times."

The two staggering men paused and mumbled to each other. Then they turned back, giving the stranger a very curious stare.

Rodney immediately decided to get down to business and eliminate any further small talk while he still had their attention.

"I was hoping you gentlemen might be able to help me," he said. "I'm trying to locate the Maynard brothers. A Mr. Trux Maynard and a Mr. Farley Maynard?"

The pair looked at Rodney a little while longer without speaking. Then they looked at each other.

"You're right, Standing Up," said the one who claimed to be 'Awopaho' to the one who claimed to be a Human Being. "Sum bitch does smell like sheep."

Without further comment, the two turned away and headed for the main part of town.

45

Rodney assumed they were off to replenish their wine supply. He had seen several liquor stores among a multitude of bars along with eating establishments on Main Street, when he first entered Lone Pine.

He stared after them trying to make at least a semblance of sense out of what the two had been talking about.

The young lawyer would have been even further stymied were he to have been made privy to the conversation of the pair as they continued their trek unhurriedly onward toward the main part of the small town.

They were now speaking to each other in languages that were not remotely connected to English. To complicate matters even further, the languages each spoke was totally different from the one in which the other was speaking. It was obvious neither understood what his companion was saying to him.

It was also apparent that what each was saying to the other was not very nice. Several people on the street saw the arguing pair, but appeared not to even notice.

These two Native Americans, both in their middle thirties, wearing the same big hats they had worn since anyone could remember, were fixtures in Lone Pine.

At least a small portion of the confusion encountered by Rodney during his attempted conversation with the two would have been clarified had he but known their names. The young barrister was probably the only one within the city limits of Lone Pine except those in their automobiles on main street just passing through, that did not.

Sitting Down Twogood and Standing Up Blackstone had no actual family ties. Sitting down's grandfather, as Standing Up had only recently stated in a derisive tone, was reportedly a white man from Italy. That may have been the reason Standing Up even refused to admit he and the other man even belonged to the same tribe.

Sitting Down confirmed this. Possibly because it was fact. Then again, perhaps he just didn't want anyone to think him too analogous to Standing Up. Even a Native American reported to have Italian blood flowing in his veins is entitled to a certain amount of pride.

The Reservation outside of Lone Pine where both were born was called the Paiute Shoshone. Therefore, the two may have been telling the truth. No Caucasian citizen in the Owens Valley knew for sure.

If those citizens of the reservation had actual factual documentation on this piece of trivia, they weren't talking. Native Americans receive tremendous satisfaction when keeping the heads of those with invader ancestry off balance.

The origin of the rather unusual names bestowed up on the two in question, was unknown. Some say their parents were simply honoring an age old Native American tradition. Others, mostly Native Americans, are more inclined to speculate in another direction.

This theory follows a much less esoteric trail. Maybe the fathers of both boys, while their mothers were still pregnant, were out in the desert somewhere sharing a pipe filled with something other than tobacco. Perchance at that time they decided it might prove amusing to watch the struggle of kids growing up with screwy names.

Whether the unusual appellations had any bearing on their early lives is a matter of personal opinion. However, it is fact that both chose to leave the reservation and the Owens Valley when barely in their teens.

They left to explore the world around the same time, but not together. Each went his own separate way.

Standing Up didn't really journey that far. He ended up living somewhere near the Kern river in northern California with another tribe of Native Americans known as the Kioawasua.

Very few Kioawasua are left on this earth. Maybe that is why they were willing to take in somebody with such a ridiculous name. Perhaps Standing Up used an alias during his stay with the Kiowasua.

Young Sitting Down's travels took him much further. For a period of time, he ended up living with a white trash family in Alabama. Then, the teen age native of California's Owens Valley took up with a tribe of Gypsies and ended up in a trailer park in Tuckaho New Jersey.

Never good at begging, the youth who somebody had named Sitting Down when he was far too young to object, was eventually kicked out of both tribe and the trailer park. He took away two attributes.

From the Gypsies, he had learned the art of making beautiful creations from silver and was excellent at it. He also was now fluent at speaking Rom, their language.

Sitting Down was in his early twenties when he finally came back to Lone Pine and the reservation. He found that Standing up had returned the previous year.

No one was quite sure how it happened, but during his absence with the Kiowasua, Standing up had become extremely proficient at creating marvelous paintings with watercolors, oils and all most anything else. The man was a masterful artist.

When the two young men met after so long a time, They greeted each other. Standing Up spoke the tongue of the Kiowasua. Sitting Down answered him in Rom. Neither understood the other. Both found this to be hilarious.

As the years went by and the two men became almost inseparable. They had much in common.

They both had strange names. Both were really talented artists. Together they managed to eke out a living selling their creations to occasional tourists passing through town on their way north to the ski resorts or Reno.

More importantly, they shared a fondness for the same cheap wine and the occasional use of certain organic hallucinatory drugs.

From the moment of their reunion after returning to Lone Pine, they continued the periodic practice of talking to and berating one other in the two respective tongues the other did not understand.

It was a ritual they fell into whenever the fancy seemed to strike. Each received extreme personal special satisfaction this practice brought to the faces of others. The world around them had become their own personal collective source of humor.

Back in front of the post office, the young lawyer from Century City continued to watch them in wonder. Rodney had never seen anybody like those two in his life.

He only wished he might have understood what they were talking about. He may have missed out on being the recipient of valuable pearls of wisdom. Rodney had read somewhere that the American Indian holds the secret to the future of all mankind.

Finally, as they came closer to main street and their destination, Sitting Down reverted to English. He had a very important question for the other man who was still cussing him out in Kiowasua. One that did involve the immediate future of at least two members of mankind.

"You got money for wine?"

"Does a bear shit in the woods?" said Standing Up, answering in English with a question of his own.

"How the Hell would I know? Suddenly I'm an expert on bears?"

"You been all over. Surely when you was travlin' with them Gypsies, you run across some bears."

"Not with the Gypsies," replied Sitting Down. "Back in Alabama, I did seen one take a crap in a garbage dump once. Got no idea if they shit in the woods."

"They don't, you're gonna' end up awful thirsty."

"Did that white eyes with the pink face back at the post office stink or what?"

"Bear shit smells better," admitted Standing Up.

"Wonder what he wants with Trux and Farley?" Sitting Down pondered aloud.

"Maybe one of em' knocked up his grandma."

"Somebody's grandma wouldn't get that close enough to get knocked by anybody smells that bad. Bet he's a bill collector. Really did smell like sheep, but he's dressed too fancy to be a sheep herder."

"Maybe his grandma's an old ewe. Never know about you white dudes. Specially them with pink faces. Ever body knows them Maynard brothers'll hump anything," responded Standing Up as the two men rounded the corner onto main street and disappeared from Rodney's sight.

The young man from Boston had no idea his odor or any member of his family were being discussed. He did suddenly remembered why he was here.

This was not a holiday he had been sent on by his superiors. There was business to be taken care of. The Maynard brothers must be located so he could return with their signatures on those papers in his briefcase. Rodney had no time to stand around watching Indians.

As the attorney started to open his car door. He looked down to see an old dirty mongrel dog sniffing at the Ghia's tires.

"I don't suppose you know the Maynard brothers?" Rodney asked the canine as it started to lift its shaggy old leg.

The aging mutt looked up at him and sniffed. Immediately the animal turned and fled with its tail tucked firmly between its legs.

CHAPTER FOUR
TWILIGHT ZONE IN THE AFTERNOON

"Hell yes, I know them assholes!"

This emphatic statement came from the mouth of short, round attendant wearing greasy coveralls. The fellow was, at the moment, filling the Karmann Ghia with gasoline as it sat in front of the pumps of a service station located at the extreme south end of Lone Pine's main drag.

Rodney stood near by. He seemed oblivious to the traffic and pedestrians moving back and forth on the street and sidewalks behind him.

The young man's pink face now had a slight whitish tinge to it, and he was far too busy to notice anything. He had immediately set out in search of a drug store when he left the post office.

When he finally found one, he had entered and purchased a tube of skin block and a very large bottle of strong smelling cologne.

He had already smeared the cream on his face. The remainder of the tube was nestled in the Ghia's glove compartment with the pair of binoculars Louise always used when she journeyed to Malibu with the Beverly Hills Bird Watchers Club.

He was now dousing himself and his clothing all over with the cologne.

"And I know where I wisht they was too!" the attendant continued as he replaced the Ghia's fuel tank cap after securing the hose to the gas pump.

The short round man in the greasy one pieced garment maintained his complaining tone as he picked up a pail of dirty water and a long handled squeegee before moving toward the wind shield of the dirty little green car.

A barely legible tag over the coverall's left breast pocket announced the fellow's name to be Larry.

"Six foot under by God!! You know what them low life bastards done?"

Three little boys, dressed in torn T-shirts and jeans, were now dancing around Rodney as they giggled and pointed at him.

Beyond the small trio of dancing hecklers, a group of very informally dressed townspeople of both sexes were also enjoying the show.

The lawyer gave the small impudent harassment committee a dirty look as he moved away from them to deposit the now empty cologne bottle in a trash container next to the gas pumps.

In front of the Ghia's windshield, Larry kept right on talking as he scraped the dead bugs away from the glass.

"They come in here about a month ago with that old piece of shit motor home of theirs! Them and their god damned pig! Took on a whole tank full of my best high test. Then you know what that slimy buttwipe, Trux done?"

Rodney was certain the greasy man was going to tell him whether he asked or not. The young man's assumption was absolutely correct.

"Flipped a quarter in the air, said I lost. Just like that. Then they hauled ass outta here, burnin' me for a whole tank of high test! Hell yes!! I know them assholes!!!"

"Surely you reported them to the police?" asked Rodney sounding genuinely concerned.

Larry kept on scrubbing away at the dead bugs.

"I did. But by the time I'd got hold of Arty Dubs, he's the sheriff, they was long gone. Probably off to Darwin to them caves they live in sometimes. Darwin's cross the county line. Sides, nobody in their right mind goes there. Like goin' to one of them furrin countries like that there Israylee or Eyerack 'thout a gun. This ud' be a good lookin little car it uz' ever cleaned up. Damned shame it ain't got no top."

The windshield was finally free of the carcasses of squashed insects. The short round man stepped back to admire his handiwork for a second. Then he reached down to open the front of the little car.

"Sounded like it was runnin' a little ragged when you drove her in though, I'd better check under the hood. Got a feelin' you need a new water pump. You're lucky. Just got in a whole shipment of new ones for this very model. Sell you one real reasonable."

Rodney was a little embarrassed. He really didn't wish to insult a professional, but he felt he had to point out the man's honest error.

"That's the trunk. The engine's in back. And it's air-cooled. It's really a Volkswagen."

Larry was only at a loss for words for just a moment. "I knew that," he said as he quickly withdrew his hand from what he now knew to be the handle of the trunk and immediately returned to his former subject.

"What you want with the Maynard's anyhow? Hope you got bad news for em."

"You said they live across the county line? Could you give me directions?" Rodney asked as he paid the man.

"That is after I've used your restroom," he added. Rodney wasn't about to make the same mistake twice in one day. Who knew how far it was to this place called Darwin?

*** *** *** *** *** ***

Rodney was sure he must have somehow accidentally traveled through some sort of dimensional space warp and ended up on the moon.

He was terrified that the fast food hamburger he'd picked up on the way out of Lone Pine, and devoured on the way, may have well been his last meal on earth.

All around him as he drove forward, there was absolutely no sign of even a hint of life, human or otherwise.

Heat waves and dust devils shimmered and danced about on the barren landscape as far as the eye could see.

The road he traveled appeared endless as the little green topless automobile wound its way in and out of red rock canyons. He seemed to heading into oblivion.

Rodney was about to give up and turn around when suddenly he saw something in the distance in front of him. A ghostly settlement seemed to be rising slowly from the very bowels of the earth.

As the nervous young man drove closer, he could see many houses collapsed due to the passing of time and total neglect.

As he entered what at some time must have been a town, he looked to the left of the opened-topped Ghia.

Embedded in the foothills of a mountain was a gigantic old metal and wooden structure that might possibly see two winters before totally succumbing to time and the desert.

There was almost no clue even for the keenest observer that these pathetic ruins had, at one time been a silver mine. An enterprise not only productive, but lucrative as well. Today it looked more like a cemetery.

Rodney slowed the car to crawl as he continued onward into the spooky community. A weathered hand printed sign sticking crookedly up out of the sand just beyond the right side of the now very narrow road said, "CITY OF DARWIN. KEEP THE FUCK OUT!"

Rodney swallowed hard and considered taking the crude missive's advice. Mysteriously, some force inside of him that he wasn't really acquainted with urged him onward.

As the Karmann Ghia continued to creep forward, a shadowy figure appeared in a doorway of one of few upright shacks several yards to the left of the road.

After a minute the same figure scurried through the shadows, evidently heading for another structure.

Somehow Rodney and the little German car found themselves on the deserted main street of the town they had both been warned to keep the fuck out of.

The wind whipped the tin roofs of the buildings on both sides of the spooky thoroughfare, giving off eerie sounds of danger as Rodney passed the remains of an old hotel.

As the car moved slowly onward, another shadowy figure peered out through a broken window of the dilapidated old building's second story.

Finally the Ghia came to a stop at the end of the street in front of a crumbling false fronted saloon. Two battered empty pickups stood outside the establishment.

Rodney, grateful to at last see some sign of life, pulled up and parked next to one of the trucks.

He cautiously climbed out of his vehicle, then reached back into it for his coat. After shrugging into the garment, he straightened his tie. This accomplished; the young barrister pulled his briefcase from the rear of the Ghia.

He took a deep breath, then cautiously approached the saloon. He could see there were at least two people inside because the front door was missing.

Darleen's windswept features appeared somewhat softer inside the old drinking establishment, than they had in the early morning sunlight the day before when she was ordering her father out of the old two holer toilet out back.

Even some the brittleness seemed missing from her eyes as she looked through the semi darkness of the saloon's interior past a rough looking man wearing a dirty sleeveless under shirt and even filthier jeans. A metal hard hat covered the majority of the dirty man's head.

The focus of Darleen's attention was a strange looking young fellow wearing a suit and tie and carrying a briefcase. He stood in the front entrance looking in over the threshold from outside.

She quickly glanced at Old Henderson, the only other person present. The white haired vintage gentleman was seated at a corner table. If her father noticed the stranger, he gave no indication.

The old man seemed to see nothing except a pile of small stones piled on the table top in front of him, which he peered at through a jeweler's glass he held up to his right eye.

In the pathetic excuse for a doorway, Rodney surveyed the building's interior. He wasn't sure if he possessed the nerve to make an entrance.

The inside of the building resembled the town behind him. The dark interior seemed to epitomize gloom and desolation. The floor was cracked concrete. Much of the furniture was falling apart or already broken. The cracked and shattered windows were either boarded up or covered with worn burlap bags.

Timidly, Rodney forced himself forward and walked slowly to the bar.

The Old man at the table continued to look at his rocks. The burly man still seated across from Darleen turned immediately toward the newcomer. He pulled the hard hat from his head which was revealed to be not only greasy

53

and grimy but totally without hair.

The metal headgear made a loud ringing noise that made Rodney jump as its owner slammed it down forcefully on the bar.

"Names Jake, Mister. You wanna fuck or fight? Don't make no difference to me!"

Behind the bar, Darleen reached down and pulled a baseball bat into sight. She shook the piece of scarred sporting equipment menacingly at the rough looking man.

"Don't you go startin no more shit in here Jake! You still owe me for the door you tore off last night! Now you back off right now or I'll cut you off till your next welfare check comes in! I mean it Jake!"

The man called Jake looked from Rodney to the woman. He then took a long hard look at the baseball bat.

The sullen expression remained on his face and he left the hard hat on the bar, but the belligerent man with the dirty bald head seemed to have no more to say for the moment.

He gave Rodney one more threatening glare and picked up a tall glass in front of him that appeared to about half full of straight whiskey. Apparently no ice was available on this particular day in the Darwin saloon.

Darleen lowered the bat as she turned her attention on the pink faced stranger with the briefcase in his hand. The poor young man looked totally out of place in these surroundings wearing his rumpled suit and tie.

She gave the young man what was supposed to be a flirtatious smile.

"Anyway, he's kinda cute. Smells good too. Whatcha got on honey?"

Evidently the cologne Rodney had doused himself back in Lone Pine was working.

Old Henderson finally spoke up from his corner table.

"He's got a hard on. But he didn't know you could smell it!"

The old man obviously found his own remark extremely funny. He doubled over with loud laughter.

It was evident that Darleen failed to share her father's sense of humor. She yelled across the bar past Rodney and Jake at him.

"Shut your fucking filthy mouth Dad!"

The old man continued to laugh as she turned back to Rodney.

"Don't mind him. Mind's gone south. Usta be one of the country's top mining engineers till he disappeared for a few days one time. Long time ago. We found him wanderin in the mountains and he ain't been right since."

Rodney continued to listen as the rawboned woman leaned forward and lowered her voice.

"Claimed a space ship picked him up and took him to another planet."

If Darleen had hoped for her father not to hear her last words, she had failed miserably.

The old man laid down the jeweler's glass and called toward the bar again. His tone seemed to be serious this time.

"The planet Zorka!" he said. "Terrible place. Fulla women with big tits and no pussies."

Darleen shot the old man a look filled with a combination of disdain and despair. Her tone had lost much of its friendliness as she spoke to Rodney again.

"Ignore him. Outsiders ain't allowed to talk to him nohow."

Without warning, a cloud of suspicion crossed her hard features.

"You ain't here to talk to my dad are you?"

The combination of the smell of stale whiskey and the totally outré atmosphere was giving Rodney a bad case of the jitters.

He attempted to give her a reassuring smile along with an honest answer. He knew he was stammering again as the words tumbled awkwardly past his parched lips.

"N.. No. I..I'm I..looking for th…the M…M…Maynard b.. brothers."

The baseball bat was held in Rodney's direction now and Jake evidently felt it was safe to enter into the conversation. He posed a question that was dripping with suspicion and sarcasm.

"You know them Maynards?"

"W..Well, no I…I…"

"Didn't think so. You wanna know what I do think?"

Rodney really didn't. But he felt an honest response wasn't in order.

"I think you're a stutterin' lyin little piece of sissy smellin' candy assed shit!"

Darleen failed to come to his defense this time.

Rodney started backing away as the much larger man drained his glass. The mean looking individual with the glabrous dome pulled a pocketknife from the pocket of his grungy jeans. He began to open the portable cutting tool as he rose to his feet.

Its blade looked extremely long and lethal to the young lawyer from the Century City law firm who had only come to town looking for the Maynard brothers.

"I think you're here to talk to Old Henderson! And if you don't get your sorry ass outa Darwin right now, I'm gonna slit your bag and stick your skinny leg through it!"

Without saying so much as another word, Rodney immediately turned back toward the establishment's main doorless entrance and began to run.

Zigzagging his way around the mangled and maimed furniture, the young man from Boston with the promising future, held his brief case aloft as he scrambled out of the saloon as fast as he could.

Rodney came racing out into the mid afternoon sunlight and the foreboding shadows of Darwin's main street.

He nearly tripped as he ran around the two pickups still parked in front of the saloon. Somehow he managed to retain his footing and his grip on the handle of the briefcase as he surged onward to his own automobile. Finally, when he reached the driver's door of the Ghia, he stopped and looked back.

The young man licked his cracked lips in relief. Evidently neither the ruffian with the knife or the mean looking lady with the baseball bat had decided to follow him.

Without taking his eyes off the front of the building from which he had just fled for even a second, Rodney tossed the briefcase in back and leaped into the Ghia without even bothering to open the door. After he started the engine, he put the little car's transmission into reverse.

Finally pulling his gaze from the gaping entrance of the saloon, he looked over his right shoulder as he prepared to back up.

His pink face immediately took on a catatonic expression.

Old Henderson, seeming to have appeared from nowhere, was now sitting in the passenger seat beside him.

The old man winked as he pulled a big Navy Colt revolver from beneath his worn khaki shirt.

"Keep on truckin' boy. We'll see maybe can we pick up the Maynards' scent for ya'. Git your ass outa here quick fore them inside knows I'm with ya. That daughter of mine's an ice cold bitch and ole Jake's meaner'n a red assed ape, but I'd hate to have to shoot either one of em."

Rodney decided to do as he was told. He turned the Ghia around and headed back down the decaying street.

"See where them buzzards is circlin' around over that dead cat cross from the old hotel?" asked Old Henderson. "Hang a left there and head on out east. Keep goin' till I tell ya not to no more."

Rodney looked out at the carcass of the deceased feline as the Ghia reached the indicated corner and he turned the steering wheel to the left, obeying orders. He was certain the poor creature's body hadn't been there when he'd passed this way before.

"Probably dropped dead from starvation," said the old man, as if reading the young stranger's mind. "Don't worry. Won't be there for long. Someone'll come by and take it home for dinner 'fore them buzzards git it. Times is hard in Darwin."

Rodney gave out with a visible shudder as he drove east on this newest old street following the directions he had been given.

Beside him, his white haired companion shoved the gun back beneath his shirt and leaned closer to the driver. The old gentleman pulled his lips back into what became a grotesque grin.

"See this missing tooth? A pretty senorita knocked it out with the golden heel of her high heeled slipper."

The old mining engineer leaned back in his seat and howled with laughter as they continued eastward between the rows of vacant, falling down structures.

Henderson's guffaws began to diminish as he looked around at the ruins and beyond them. His leathery features turned serious as they had inside the saloon when the subject of the space ship had come up.

"Me and my old Cajun daddy discovered this place," he said, when he finally spoke again.

"Knew we was onto somthin' good when we seen that mountain over yonder was shaped just like a tit. It's 'tother side of the county line, but it looks a lot closer. Belongs to them Maynards yer lookin' for. No silver on the son of a bitch, but I love lookin' at it just the same. Both Me'n Pap loved tits. I still do. Ain't much good when no pussies come with em' though. Turn right here."

Somehow Rodney was able to successfully negotiate the sudden turn without running over a pile of old boards. Beside him the old man continued talking.

"Yeah, Pap was a hard rock miner if they ever was one. Me too! Sept' there ain't much use for the likes of me or my old dead Pap round here no more. Silvers all gone. There's them don't wanna believe it, but it's true."

Rodney didn't know quite how to respond. He discovered no response was expected as the old man continued.

"Some do," he admitted, amending his prior statement.

"Ole Hefferoid Hogg's got a Borax mine up above Dirty Socks. Don't pay goat squat, but he grubs outa livin. Better'n the stupid shits hangin round here. All of em' hopin some how silver's gonna grow up outa the ground like some sorta weed. Little over a year ago some surveyor come through. Everbody was sure he was gonna find silver. Hell! Turns out he was some sort of geologist. Wouldn't know silver if somebody shoved it up his butt. He was lookin' for prehistoric shit. Don't know if he found what he was lookin' for or not. Sure as Hell didn't find no silver though. Good thing he left the country. Ole Jake back there and some others, they wanted to hang im' then slice the poor son of a bitch up into tiny little pieces with Jake's chainsaw for getting their hopes up. Dumber'n a pile of five year old horse turds is what they are. I shoulda stayed on Zorka. Pussies or no pussies, they do have silver on Zorka!"

He pointed ahead with a gnarled forefinger as he squinted through the glass of the car's windshield.

"Okay. When you come to the last of what's left of them buildins' up ahead, kinda geegaw sideways a little to yer left and head on up that canyon. I better tell ya, soon's I put you on their scent, I'm gone. Gotta be yer own dog."

Rodney had no idea what the strange old man was babbling about, but he did as he was told.

As the little topless dirty green car and its occupants entered the designated canyon area, Rodney couldn't help but observe that the hills on either side of himself and the old man were honeycombed with crude man made caves. Old Henderson followed the younger man's gaze.

"Call em' the Chinaman caves. Chinese dug em' out a long time ago to live in when they come over here to mine silver. Stop here!"

The Ghia came to a halt and both men got out. Rodney followed the old miner who made a bee line to two of the caves nearest the road.

Old Henderson pointed as he paused just short of two of the caves.

"There's where the Maynard's keep their stuff. They don't much live nowhere. Most of the time, they just run around the country in that old motor home they call the HOWDY HOSS," explained the old man.

Rodney stared at the caves in disbelief. He finally mustered up enough courage to move forward and inspect them. As he came closer to the first one, he could see a crude door blocking its entrance. The second also sported a similar rotting portal. Small pieces of fluttering paper were attached to both barriers.

Rodney turned to speak to the old man but his tour guide was no longer anywhere to be seen. The lawyer looked back at the parked Karmann Ghia. Old Henderson had not returned to the automobile.

He scanned the hills on both sides of the canyon to no avail. The hard rock miner with the missing tooth had totally vanished.

Rodney was more frightened than ever. None the less, he seemed to be driven on by the futility of it all. He moved forward to get a closer look at the still fluttering paper on the door of the nearest cave.

There were words scrawled crudely on the paper, which read: PLEASE DON'T TAKE MY SHIT. The missive was signed: FARLY MAYNARD.

Rodney moved to the other cave door. This message was not only more legible, it was written in much bolder print: ANYBODY WHO COMES IN HERE WITHOUT MY PERMISSION GITS HIS DICK RIPPED OUT. GONE TO DIRTY SOCKS LAKE TO TAKE A BATH. It was signed: TRUX MAYNARD.

A following postscript furnished more information: P.S. THE CHICKEN SHIT NEXT DOOR AND HIS RINKY DINK PIG WENT WITH ME.

Rodney looked around once more to see if the old man who'd brought him to this place had come out of hiding. The senior citizen of Darwin was still nowhere in sight.

The young messenger was disappointed. Not only was he terrified to find himself totally alone in these bizarre surroundings, he'd decided he liked the strange, senescent character, even though the old man's state of mind was obviously delusional.

He also wished he had somebody to share the moment with him. In spite of his fear, the young man was suddenly experiencing a strange feeling of elation.

He reached out and touched the note that was supposedly written by the Maynard brother named Farley.

He was afraid to even go near the one from the other brother because of the awful threat to a certain portion of the anatomy to anyone who did. But Rodney had made progress. He was closer to his reason for being in this land. A place he sure God had forgotten. Then again, he wasn't even sure The Almighty knew of its existence.

It stood to reason that since the notes hadn't been blown away by the wind, they had to have been recently written.

Following this same path of logic, he felt he might well be on his way back to the civilized world much sooner than originally anticipated.

It only stood to reason that two poor souls that were so poverty stricken they were forced to live in caves, would be only too happy to sign away a worthless piece of property for two thousand dollars in cash. Rodney just hoped there that was a place named 'Dirty Socks Lake' on the map in his briefcase.

He'd heard Old Henderson mention it in passing when the old miner had been lamenting the loss of silver, but the young lawyer hadn't been paying very close attention. Even if he had, it was very doubtful he'd know where to find it from just the conversation.

He also sincerely hoped that the Maynard named Trux and Henderson hadn't been using some sort of local colloquial reference.

Since the old man had left him, and there was no one to ask, he had no choice but to return to his car and look at the map himself.

He looked at his wristwatch as he walked back to the waiting Karmann Ghia. In spite of the fact that it seemed like he'd been gone from Los Angeles forever, it was only three o'clock in the afternoon. He raised his hand to his brow and shaded his eyes as he looked up at the clear blue sky. Due to the vast horizon in this particular part of America, the sun seemed as if it might be hanging around for still some time prior to totally retiring for the day.

Maybe, Rodney reasoned he could still take care of his business and be on his way back before dark.

If he were allowed to do that, perhaps he could find someplace to spend the night on the outskirts of LA and find some place to have the Ghia's top replaced before returning home. He'd still have an extra day before his deadline at Herkimer, Herkimer, Herkimer, Herkimer.

If he could accomplish both, Louise would never know what a terrible thing he'd let happen to her precious 'Slum Mobile' and both the young lady and her Father would be happy with him.

He reached in behind the driver's seat of the little green car and pulled out his briefcase.

Lying the portfolio on the Ghia's hood, he opened it and pushed aside the envelope filled with cash, the papers the Maynard's were supposed to sign in return for same, and his never used cellular phone.

He then withdrew the map, and, after carefully closing the case, spread the bulky paper ontological unit filled with graphical representations of the region out on the hood beside it.

Beads of sweat from Rodney's forehead dropped onto the paper. He had the uneasy feeling that somebody was watching him as he traced his finger along the maize of lines on the map.

He made a distasteful face as he found the town of Darwin. However, his reddened features broke into a broad smile as his digital found the three words, Dirty Socks Lake.

According to the footnotes on the map, the place was some sort of desert mineral hot springs. Rodney didn't care what it was. He now knew where it was. Or at least he knew where to find it.

Without even bothering to fold the map, he threw both it and the brief case back into the Ghia. The young man was so taken by his discovery; he lost the feeling that he was a victim of surveillance. Rodney decided to urinate right then and there.

A giant desert tarantula crawling toward the sound of splashing water convinced the young lawyer to void his bladder rapidly and take care of the business of putting his equipment away and zipping up his fly after climbing back into the car. Nevertheless, he felt better than he had in a long time.

He finished doing what had to be done and started the Karmann Ghia.

Putting the little machine's transmission into drive, he took advantage of the vehicle's short wheel base and turned around in the middle of the narrow road heading back in the direction from whence he originally came.

"I'm not afraid anymore," Rodney said aloud to himself as he drove forward through the canyon.

Suddenly the intrepid traveler's face froze. He screamed in total terror.

Directly in front of the little topless automobile and its driver as they rounded a bend in the road was an ancient old buck board with iron wheels. The antiquated vehicle, apparently self propelled, was gaining speed as it rolled right at them.

The Karmann Ghia screeched to a halt. The antiquated wagon flew by missing the little car only by inches.

If not for the reddish color added to the pigment in Rodney's face by the overhead sun, it would have been ashen white. Every fiber in his entire body seemed to be trembling.

He sat there praying for some salvation from this madness as he watched the buckboard smash into one of the crudely excavated caves on the lower side of the road. Suddenly, the extremely loud roar of an engine with no muffler rendered the air.

Rodney looked in the direction of the obnoxious noise and nearly suffered a heart attack on the spot.

The source of the sound was immediately disclosed. Jake, the ruffian from the saloon, was now directly in front of him walking down the middle of the road. The hard hat was covering up his glabrous pate again and beneath it he wore a sadistic grin.

He held a lethal looking chattering chain saw in his hands as he moved forward toward the little green car. Two raggedy unshaven men with hollow looking eyes, brandished pick handles as they walked on either side of him.

All Rodney could think of at that terrifying moment was a horrible movie he had seen when he was around ten years old.

He couldn't remember the name of it. One particular mean little boy he was attending school with at the time, had managed to sneak the video tape out of his father's collection. They, along with some other small adventurous friends, had watched it on the friend's VCR when no adults were present. That video taped reproduction of an original film had been responsible for at least two years worth of unbearable nightmares.

It had been an old movie at the time. At least as old as Rodney was. He couldn't remember the name of it right now but never would he forget the horrible rough looking men in it.

Men who looked much like the three advancing figures kept coming right down the middle of the road.

The ruffians in that movie had done vile, unspeakable things to another man in the same movie. Rodney was certain these three meant to do even worse things to him. He frantically looked around for a way out. There was none.

The menacing men moved closer. The awful roar of the chainsaw was deafening.

In the front seat of the Ghia, Rodney gripped the steering wheel with both hands. He stiffened his whole body, preparing for the end of his stay upon this earth.

As he did so, his right foot pressed down hard on the Ghia's accelerator pedal. The little topless automobile shot forward.

In front of the suddenly rapidly moving green machine, the two men on either side of Jake leaped out of the way.

Jake himself however, was determined not to be diverted. He made a pass at the Ghia's windshield with the murderous moving teeth of the saw still in his grip.

Millions of gigantic sparks shot out in every direction. The blade of the machine of destruction made a horrendous sound that echoed off the surrounding canyon walls as it glanced off the apex of the little car's windshield frame. The saw lurched backwards, literally flying out of Jake's hands.

The large mechanical cutting tool, its murderous teeth still rotating, and its engine still screaming, careened through the air in one direction. Jake's filthy hairless head was suddenly exposed to the elements as his metal hat sailed away in another.

The mean looking bald man, recently in possession of both of these items, no longer looked quite so mean as he tumbled end over end off the road.

The German car zoomed forward through a thick cloud of dust, screaming it's way through the remainder of the canyon toward freedom.

CHAPTER FIVE
OUT OF THE FRYING PAN

After his unbelievable, terrifying experience in the canyons outside of Darwin, Rodney had decided to abort the whole mission and go home.

Not home to Beverly Hills. He knew if he returned there with the Ghia in its present condition with out fulfilling his assignment, his days were over with both Louise and her father's firm.

He had decided to drive straight to Boston. He was sure his parents still loved him. They would accept the fact that he had failed. His father would be terribly disappointed, but they wouldn't kick him out in the streets. At least not right away.

There were several reasons why this scenario was never to reach fruition. The frustrated young fellow had become hopelessly lost when he finally made his way out of the canyons beyond Darwin. Quite by accident, he found Dirty Socks Lake before he could locate the main highway.

By that time he had realized that he didn't have enough money to get him back to Boston unless he pilfered the funds meant for the Maynards.

Rodney wasn't a thief. He knew that the two words 'Honest Lawyer' constituted an oxymoron, but he was cursed. He was simply one of those people whom, if he found a penny lost by someone else, he would be forced by a little demon deep inside him to find the owner of that penny and return it.

The young man was also unable to lie. As son of a New England politician, this was considered far worse than a curse. His father called it a birth defect and blamed it on his mother.

Rodney's mother had pointed out that, according to history, George Washington had been afflicted with the same malady.

This did give the senior Van Aukin some hope. If, indeed the story of the cherry tree were true, the Father of America's prevarication inability had obviously, somehow, been conquered. Otherwise, he couldn't possibly have become President. Rodney was sent to the doctor.

The family physician had assured his parents that the child's propensity could be compared to masturbation or picking ones' nose. A phase he would eventually grow out of.

The young attorney hadn't picked his nose for years and he never masturbated. The latter activity was prohibited because he had not been able to shake loose from the parasite of honesty. He was afraid if he were to masturbate, the demon would someday, force him to tell someone what he had been doing. He walked away from conversations regarding the subject for fear he might even be compelled to confess the urges.

Shortly after he and Louise had gotten together, Louise had discovered his integrity abnormality. Like everybody else who became privy to his deep, dark shameful secret, his fiancée had become alarmed. She had recommended he see a psychiatrist.

The very word 'Honesty' seemed to make the Beverly Hills shrink nervous. The doctor of mental disorders had, in turn, recommended immediate electric shock therapy. Rodney had given up and decided to live with his defect.

Throughout the years he had discovered the 'Honesty monster' would leave him alone as long as the topic of integrity didn't come up. Today, he regretted not trying the shock treatments.

He'd have to somehow figure a way get those funds back to the firm without touching them. He certainly couldn't use that particular money to return to Boston.

Almost all the rest of the cash in his possession posed the same problem. The additional two hundred dollars given to him by Harold Herkimer was to be used as expenses for a specific purpose. If he spent it for anything else, that would also be stealing.

The only other alternative that he could come up with was to risk a brain tumor by using that cellular telephone to call home for monetary assistance.

When he'd finally discovered himself to be in the neighborhood of his original destination before experiencing a brush with death back at those caves, he'd at least finally stopped shaking. The poor young man had already lost several mental wrestling bouts with his unreasonable set of ethics. Since he really didn't really want to consider the only other option that seemed to be open, he made the decision to go back to the original plan.

According to the California Highway Department public relations people or whomever it was that wrote the informative footnotes on Rodney's map, Dirty Socks Lake was not only a mineral hot springs, it was also an oasis.

To Rodney it didn't look like any oasis he'd ever imagined. The lake itself was fairly big, but the surrounding scrub brush certainly didn't say 'Oasis.'

However, there was an old battered motor home parked near the lake, and when Rodney focused Louise's binoculars, he could read the name 'HOWDY HOSS' printed on the rear of the vehicle. He remembered Old Henderson telling him that was the name given to the Maynard's motor home, sometime before the strange aging miner had so mysteriously disappeared.

There were also people down there. He had actually caught a brief glimpse of what he was certain to be human movement behind that motor home next to the lake.

Satisfied that he had at last found the parties he was looking for, the young man who'd decided not to return to Boston lowered the field glasses.

He returned to his car that now looked even worse. The ugly gouge in the upper part of its windshield frame recently inflicted by the chain of the maniacal cutting machine back in those canyons, made its missing top seem almost incidental. The abused little automobile was parked about a half a mile away from the body of water on a dirt road leading down to the lake. The wind shifted and a foul smell invaded his nostrils.

Remembering the dead cat back in Darwin, the lawyer looked up in the sky to see if there might be buzzards circling over head.

None could be seen, but he forgot the smell when he realized how much time he'd spent wandering around lost. While daylight visibility seemed to be still unlimited, the sun was much closer to the western horizon than when he had last looked at it and his shadow on the ground was now extremely long.

He glanced at his watch. It was nearly five. Rodney decided circumstances being what they were; he was fortunate the Maynards seemed to like long baths.

Thus ended his plan of wrapping up negotiations and heading back to LA before nightfall.

Then again, he reminded himself, as he slid in behind the steering wheel of the Karmann Ghia, for awhile, he hadn't been exactly sure what his plan was. He noticed the smell again as he set the binoculars aside and started his car.

Putting the little vehicle in gear, he drove onward, down toward the lake.

*** *** *** *** *** ***

The Ghia fishtailed as it came up behind the motor home, nearly sideswiping the much larger vehicle.

Rodney finally gained control of the little green car that he had accidentally driven into a puddle of water, and safely braked it to a halt a few feet away.

He could hear more water splashing on the other side of the motor home.

The Maynards must still be busy with their bath. It wouldn't be polite to interrupt such a private endeavor. He would be ready for them, however, the minute they were presentable.

Following the protocol of his profession, Rodney struggled into his suit coat again. He looked in the rear view mirror to straighten his tie.

The face that stared back at him was still quite pink, but no blemishes had appeared since the last time he looked, and the skin still hadn't started to peel.

The young attorney took this as a positive sign. He sent out a mental message of gratitude to good old Norman Vincent, wherever he might be.

The odor here at lakeside was even stronger than it had been from his earlier observation point. The aroma wasn't nearly as vile as his memory of the sheep's stench he'd encountered before he arrived in Lone Pine, but it was still more than slightly repugnant.

He opened his coat and lowered his head to sniff the front of his shirt hoping that some residue of the cologne's scent might still be present to offset the offensive aroma. It was. He made a silent vow to never again complain about the lavender and rose perfumed air in Louise's bathroom back in Beverly Hills.

While Rodney inhaled the remaining fumes of his clothing, he realized the other smell was somehow familiar.

It was reminiscent of a bag of dirty laundry Louise had once overlooked in the bottom of his closet back at her apartment in Beverly Hills.

Suddenly it dawned on him that it was the water beyond the motor home that was responsible for the other smell.

The footnote on the map had said the lake was the result of several mineral springs and the young man had read that such bodies of water were high in sulfur content. He had also read that sulfur possessed an odor similar to that of unlaundered stockings. Obviously that was how the place had gotten its name.

Rodney chastised himself for his lack of immediate perception as he picked up the briefcase and exited the Ghia. He hadn't been able to think straight since this trip started. He wanted it over as soon as possible.

As he started toward the motor home, a loud, very high pitched nasal feminine scream came from the other side of the large vehicle.

"Damn you Farley Maynard!"

Keeping close to the side of the battered oversized combination of automobile and trailer house, Rodney crept forward. He reached the rear corner of the rig beneath the sign that declared it to be known as the 'HOWDY HOSS' and peeked around the corner.

Two, extremely large Rubenesque young women, appearing to be somewhere in their early twenties and very pretty in spite of their sizes, bobbed up and down in the dirty water. The enormous nippled mammary glands of both were quite visible.

Rodney watched from his hiding spot around the rear corner of the 'HOWDY HOSS' with wide eyes filled with wonder. He would never even in the deepest crevices of his mind, ever think of Louise as being overweight again.

If the remainder of their bodies, still immersed beneath the water, were at all proportionate to the rest of their anatomies, he reasoned, each had to rival the dimensions of the average hippopotamus. However, the skin covering the enormous visible bulk of both was firm and tan. Neither sizable female body displayed even the slightest hint of cellulite.

Rodney immediately discovered the nasal voice he had heard while still on the far side of the motor home, to belong to the smaller of the two oversized water nymphs. Unlike her nude companion, the girl now speaking appeared to weigh no more than two hundred pounds.

"I told you to leave that pig in the motor home, Farley! He's swimin underneath me and nibblin on my birthmark."

About ten feet up the shore line, no more than two feet inland from the surface of the lake, an extremely tanned shaggy haired man with a beard hiding the lower part of his face, stood in a mud hole. He appeared to be in his mid forties.

He was also totally naked and his practically non-existent bare rear end was sticking upward toward the sun. This undersized posterior contrasted greatly with his over sized stomach as he bent over washing the belly of a pig that seemed to be of medium proportions.

The man wasn't fat, especially when compared with the young women in the water. The abdominal area of his body simply created a lower profile within his overall physical structure, that would be considered unflattering in most fitness centers of America.

He called over his shoulder to the equally nude, complaining, rotund girl. His voice was deep and gravely and held an injured tone of indignation.

"Everbody's always blamin' everthing on Barney."

The pig looked up and offered his own grunt of vexation as he heard his name. The bearded man continued.

"He ain't nowhere near yer birthmark, dang it, Squeeze Chute. He's over here with me, gittin his belly warshed."

In the lake, the girl with the nasal twang let out a high squeal and leapt into to the air above the water's surface, proving the lower part of her anatomy to be even more spacious than the upper.

"Well, something keeps biting me!"

She turned to the even larger young woman who stood in the water only a few feet away.

"Ain't nothin been bitin your bottom, Catch Pen?"

Before the even larger girl could answer, a male body exploded up out of the water between the two big feminine creatures.

A full head of curly blond hair appeared first. The hair was, in turn, followed by a wide grinning mouth so full of big, natural teeth; they rivaled the quantity of ivory keys on a Steinway piano. A jaw resembling an anvil supported the broad grin.

The owner of these outstanding features rose up to a standing position, He was also tan all over. He appeared to be slightly younger than the other man still occupied with the pig in the mud hole, and also somewhat taller.

His naked body was obviously in better shape and he was far better endowed in the manly equipment department.

In defense of the bearded man in the mud hole, the blond broad shouldered male individual who had just emerged from the water, was much larger than almost all other members of his gender in that particular department.

Rodney, still peeking around the corner of the motor home, was sure the sun shining down on the water must be creating some sort of an optical magnifying allusion.

In addition to devilish smile, the broad shouldered man had an impish gleam in his clear, crystal blue eyes as he leered at the girl called Squeeze Chute.

She immediately started squealing as she began splashing water on the freshly emerged individual.

"Damn you, Trux Maynard! Was that you bitin my birth mark?"

The larger of the girls threw her head back in laughter. Almost immediately, her mirth turned to a shriek of anger as she spotted Rodney peering out from his observation hiding place around the corner of the old recreational vehicle.

"There's a strange man lookin' at us nekid!"

All other eyes in the vicinity, including those of the pig, turned and looked directly at the sheepish looking young lawyer.

In the water, the curly haired man with the big chin called out to him.

"You just gittin your jollies, or is they somethin' we can do for you?"

At the motor home, Rodney attempted to pull himself back out of sight as he timidly called back.

"I.. I'm sorry… I.. that is…."

"Show yourself God dammit! Come out here where we can see you."

"No Trux!" said the heftier of the two girls. "Don't let some strange man see me and my sister nekid!"

"He already seen you Catch Pen. Gotta admit in your case it is a big deal, but he ain't dropped dead yet," said the man called Trux before yelling at the hiding attorney once more.

"You're startin' to piss me off, pal! Get your sorry ass out here!"

Rodney had endured enough local wrath for one day. He knew he couldn't handle any more, especially from those with whom he was duty bound to conduct business.

Clutching the briefcase and attempting to keep his eyes averted from the multitude of nudity both in the water and on the shore, he walked into full sight from around the corner of the motor home. He tried very hard not to stammer.

"I'm l..looking at.. I.. that is.. I mean I'm looking for some gentlemen named Maynard. A Mr. Trux Maynard and a Mr. Farley Maynard?" The young lawyer managed to finish with out too much difficulty.

"You was right the first time. You are lookin at em. 'Sept we sure as hell ain't no gentlemen. Appreciate it if you didn't use that word again. 'Specially when they's women present."

"Trux!" squealed Squeeze Chute. "Make him go away. Me'n Catch Pen don't want no stranger seein' us nekid!"

"Oh, George W. Bush on a fuckin' crutch!" said Trux as he shot the heavy girls a disgusted glance. He looked on shore at the subject of the girl's concern. "You gotta name?" he asked.

"Rodney. Rodney Van..."

Trux interrupted him. " Rodney, this is Catch Pen and Squeeze Chute. The Hogg sisters."

The man with the curly blond hair and the oversized chin called over his shoulder as he waded out of the water.

He spoke directly to the girls behind him as he walked toward the mud hole where Rodney first spotted the bearded individual with the pig.

The other man was now standing at the edge of that mud hole and was busily pulling a pair of shapeless old boxer shorts up over his skinny legs and posterior beneath his flabby stomach.

"Catch Pen and Squeeze Chute, this here's Rodney. Now you ain't strangers no more. So quit complainin' or cover your tits! Farley, hand me that grass sack!"

Farley plucked a large, worn cloth bag from the branch of a piece of scrub brush and gave it to Trux as the latter walked up to him. In spite of their obvious physical differences, there was indeed, a strong resemblance between the two men.

Behind them, still in the mud hole, the pig was now standing. He eyed Rodney with more than just idle curiosity.

Trux wrapped the sack around his middle as he turned back to the young man holding the briefcase.

"I'm Trux Maynard," he said. "This fuzzy faced fart with the puss gut, wearin' the bombed out boxers over his scrawny butt's my brother Farley. Some bitch ain't got enough ass to make a sick man a bowl of soup, but he's still my brother. What can we do for you?"

Rodney felt like a hundred years had past since he'd departed Beverly

69

Hills early that same morning to seek out these two men now standing in front of him. They were very strange and so were the circumstances under which he'd finally found them.

However, nothing about this day could be considered normal. At least he could now complete his business and return to civilization. He hoped it still existed.

Had the two born and bred Owens Valley middle aged male siblings facing the young attorney the power to read minds, they would have been highly offended. Neither considered himself or the other the least bit strange.

In reality, the Maynard brothers were really no more than slightly exaggerated personifications of almost any male member of that group referred to as Red Necks. A breed that can be found in every single state within the boundaries of this land so proudly known as the USA.

They represent the results of an evolutionary chain depicting centuries of Anglo Saxon copulation, rape and mayhem, combined with a certain amount of scattered incest throughout the decades. Family trees fully branched out become considerably tangled due to lack of pruning.

Aeons ago, some of the ancestors of Trux and Farley Maynard undoubtedly had some social standing. However, fate and perhaps Karma had at this stage, had dropped them like cannonballs into pure raw reality.

They now occupied a very low rung on that same social ladder. They weren't aware of this, but had they been, neither would have had any desire whatsoever to climb any higher. The view was better from the bottom.

Neither could be considered heavy thinkers. Farley had a tendency to lean in that direction on rare occasions but had never really developed the mandatory mental muscle to accommodate the lifting.

Prior to entering puberty, the brothers had stolen a watermelon from the garden of an old, since passed on soul, called the Widow Armstrong.

The angry elderly lady had rallied the neighbors and a posse had tracked the fruit thieves and their loot to the park that still rests in the middle of Lone Pine.

They found the two young culprits involved in a disagreement over whether the melon which now sat on top of a picnic table, was ripe or not.

The heated argument proved to be so fascinating, the crowd, instead of moving in and grabbing the delinquents, was compelled to pause and watch.

For at least an hour, or so the event is related by those still living who were there and those hearing the story from someone who claimed to have been present, the Maynard boys had circled that melon. Each thumping away at it from every conceivable angle. Finally, they pulled out their pocketknives and began plugging holes in the stolen round green gourd.

By now the gathering of onlookers had grown. However, instead of a

70

group of citizens sitting in judgment, they had transcended into an amused audience watching this amazing display of youthful stupidity. Supposedly, even the angry widow was beginning to giggle.

When at long last, the brothers still had not come to a meeting of the minds regarding the melon's edibility, they put away the knives and began punching one another.

During the fist fight, Farley knocked the melon off the picnic table. It broke into hundreds of pieces as it splattered all over the ground. Since it was now apparent the fruit was indeed not fit to eat even if it were ripe and ready, the boys had stopped fighting and apologized to the widow. She could have the melon back.

After suggesting she might consult someone on proper gardening methods in the future, the preteen white trash brothers had then departed. They left the crowd to pick up the pieces and the seeds.

Trux and Farley were both in their forties now. Farley was slightly older but Trux, unless Farley disagreed with him, which seldom happened, was considered the leader.

As they passed through and beyond the various stages of puberty, their tastes had turned from stolen fruit to what they felt to be more fulfilling conquests. However, with only one exception, the manner of how the brothers handled life had altered little.

They were just two more Good ole red blooded American boys who, once they crossed the necessary threshold of becoming twenty-one so they could legally buy booze, saw no reason to seek further maturity.

While they had indeed developed individual personalities as they grew older, the Maynard brothers remained inseparable, marching essentially to the beat of the same drum. Except for a few homespun tenets handed down by their departed father and a handful developed on their own for convenience, that personal percussion throb was simple and straight forward.

People meet, people fight. All, again with one exception, should fornicate whenever possible. Laughter is important and on rare occasions, so is love. Nothing else really matters. In the end, no matter what has happened in between, all will die. Build as many happy memories as you can before the trap door beneath your toes trips open.

Our nation is filled with many who share this basic philosophy and may well be a better place because of their presence.

"Ain't my fault I got a puss gut," said Farley defending the last derogatory statement Trux had made regarding his physique. The pig, now standing beside the bearded brother, grunted in agreement.

"Because he drinks beer so damned much," Trux informed Rodney.

Once again the creature on the ground with the cloven hooves, voiced a

71

guttural affirmation. Trux now spoke to the pig.

"You ain't got no room to talk, Barney. Your guts damned near as big as his is."

Farley ignored Trux and gestured toward the talkative animal.

"And this is Barney," he stated proudly. "Don't think you'll make him feel bad lookin' at them scars on his face. Barney's proud of em'. Got them scars fightin rattlesnakes. Hell on rattle snakes ole Barney is."

Rodney smiled weakly down at the pig as it grunted up at him.

"Best say howdy to im'." Farley's deep voice held just the hint of an edge of warning. "Hurts Barneys' feelins', folks don't say howdy to im'."

The young lawyer felt extremely stupid talking to a pig. He wasn't really that concerned if he offended an animal. However, upsetting either of these two whose signatures he really needed would be a grave mistake. He decided nothing would be lost were he to give it a try. He even threw in a little wave.

"Hello Barney." He hadn't even stammered. This was a good sign.

Barney nodded and grunted again. At least it looked like he nodded. Rodney was certain the animal had grunted.

The sound of girlish giggling came from the lake. The nervous young man from Boston involuntarily turned toward its source.

Both large young women were now lying face up, floating in the water. They looked very much like two lazy whales with out a care in the world. Obviously they had taken Trux at his word that the newcomer was no longer a stranger.

Trux flashed his big teeth as he winked at his brother. His tone held a hint of friendly conspiracy as he spoke to the younger man again.

"That's a lotta woman for just one scrawny little dude like you, but if you really want some of it, Me'n Farley'll be glad to put in a good word for ya'."

The lantern jawed man's totally unthinkable suggestion brought Rodney immediately back to reality and the reason he was here. He shifted his eyes quickly from the bounteous beauties in the water and extended his hand toward both of the brothers.

"I'm Rodney Van Aukin. I represent the firm of Herkimer, Herkimer, Herkimer, Herkimer and…"

Farley turned to Trux before the young man was able to list his own name in the firm.

"Sounds like he's got a bad case of hiccups."

Rodney attempted to push onward. "I'm here to talk business," he began.

Again he was interrupted. This time it was by Trux.

"You really wanna do that?"

"It's why I'm here," replied Rodney. "I've been authorized to offer you both a proposition I'm sure you'll find extremely beneficial. It's my

73

understanding that you gentlemen own a certain piece of property."

Trux held up his hand. "There you go, usin that word again. Don't make me tell you no more. Only property me'n Farly owns is that old mountain our daddy left us when he fell through the trapdoor. You talkin about that?"

"Trapdoor?" asked Rodney.

"Means when he died," translated Farley.

On the ground, Barney nuzzled the bearded brother's bare leg with his snout in sympathy.

"You lookin' to buy that ole mountain?" queried Trux.

"Yes, I am," replied Rodney as he began to gain confidence. He lifted up the briefcase for them to see. "I have the papers and payment right in here. If we could just…"

Once again Trux held up his hand halting further verbal dissertation.

"If you're really serious about this, don't say no more till you take off your clothes."

Rodney had obviously misunderstood. He tried to smile as he indicated the fact.

"I beg your pardon?"

"Don't never beg if you're big enough to steal," was Trux's quick retort. "You heard me. Our ole daddy told both me and Farley never to talk business with a man less we got a good look at his pecker."

"That's what he told us," said Farley as he nodded. "Daddy was a great one for lettin' it all hang out. Always said it was the fella really out to fuck you that kept his pecker outa sight."

The young lawyer attempted a laugh.

"That's really very funny. Now if we could…"

It was Farley's turn to interrupt. "Daddy wasn't laughin' when he said it. He was real serious."

"Damned straight it ain't no joke!" Trux's tone was growing impatient. "Either strip down or ship out. You really got somethin' to say, Me'n Farley'll take time to look at your small pecker, but we ain't got time for your small talk if you're lookin to fuck us. Our breeze don't blow in that direction."

Rodney's mind raced during the long pause that followed. Flashbacks of that horrible movie that had come into his mind during that awful moment back on the road beyond the caves outside of Darwin came back to him.

The images in his memory were monstrously more vivid now. He even remembered the title. The film was called *Deliverance*.

Actually, in its time, the cinematic endeavor had been considered a box office success and by many, a marvelous work of realistic art.

It had been adapted from a best selling novel by the original author, James

73

Dickey who also portrayed the sheriff. Masterfully directed by John Boorman, the movie had helped to launch the careers of several noteworthy film personalities of the last century. Among these were Burt Reynolds, Ronny Cox, Ed O' Neal and that marvelous character actor William A. McKinney.

The piece had also starred an already well established actor, Jon Voight and started a really fine actor named Ned Beatty on his way to an extremely lucrative career.

Rodney was far too young to have anything other than a remote idea who any of these people were. Some of the names, were he to be quizzed, would not have been familiar to him at all.

He had heard of Burt Reynolds. He was some famous old man who used to be married to an equally famous old woman named Lonnie Anderson. Rodney thought she did some sort of soup commercial for a while.

While he had no knowledge of anything else about yesteryear's Ned Beatty, he vividly remembered the character the thespian played as he was being brutally raped by the uncouth, nefarious mountain men. It was a scene he would never forget and hoped never to see again. For months after viewing the pilfered video, the New England boy had slept with his back against the wall.

Rodney had been unbelievably frightened when the bald man in the tin hat back on the road beyond those caves earlier that day was coming at him with that chain saw. That fear paled in comparison to the trepidation he felt welling up in his throat now.

Was the fate of that poor man in the movie he saw so long ago what these two brothers had in mind for him? In front of the fat women? Afterward would he be fed to the pig? He tried desperately to clear his head. There really was a way he could avoid this if these two men really planned on doing to him what had been done to that fellow in the movie.

Unlike the earlier unpleasant situation, when those other brutes had tried to kill him with the chainsaw, he apparently was allowed to walk away from this one. The Volkswagen engine in the Karmann Ghia did get excellent gas mileage even if it was a long way to Boston.

He could surely find a pay phone along the way that could be used to call his parents for just a little money. His father would understand that just because he'd chosen the law for his profession, didn't mean he had to sink to the lowest of levels.

Then he remembered what the senior Van Aukin did for a living. His father was a New England politician. A politician did what ever was necessary to get the vote. He would understand nothing except his son's failure to bring those signatures back to his superiors.

74

There was also the chance that he could possibly be mistaken. He knew nothing of rural protocol. He had observed enough in the short time that he had been in the Owens Valley to come to the conclusion that the local people were not what could be considered normal human beings. Possibly the viewing of another's genitalia really was a custom prior to discussing business in this benighted society.

Even this proved to be true, such a blatant invasion of privacy still made his blood run cold. On the other hand, were he to later discover they had really wanted nothing else from him, and his refusal to comply with local ritual proved to be the reason for his failure…He didn't want to think anymore. The young law school graduate's scrambled brain seemed to be running low on power.

"Bout time you was leavin' Mister," said the man called Trux, looking Rodney straight in the eye. "Plan on walkin' outa' here on your own two feet or you need a little help?"

Hoping desperately that the broad shouldered man with the clear blue eyes and the lantern jaw's previous comment regarding the two Red Neck brother's 'Breezes not blowing in a certain direction', could be interpreted in a positive way, Rodney handed him the briefcase.

The younger man's fingers trembled as he reached up to remove his tie. Try as he might, he was unable to rid his mind of the continuous, swirling flooded images of Ned Beatty screaming like an animal being slaughtered alive.

Nevertheless the tie came off. Shadows of vehicles, sparse vegetation, people, and at least one animal were now extremely long. They visibly grew even longer as this stranger in an even stranger land continued disrobing.

He was barely breathing as he doffed his clothing at sundown; right there on the shore of a stinking lake in front of two nearly naked grown men, two totally nude obese young women and a pig.

For this attorney, it had indeed been a very difficult day at the office.

CHAPTER SIX
YOKEL TRADITIONS

"He's hung bettern' you are Farley," Catch Pen called from where she and her sister still bobbed about in the water as the sun finally disappeared completely from sight.

"A grasshopper's hung bettern' Farley!" Trux yelled back at her as he showed his overabundance of teeth.

"You girls be quiet! We're talkin' business here!" said Farley. It was obvious that the bearded Maynard did not wish the subject of manly endowment to be carried any farther.

Both he and his brother were fully dressed now. Technically the only ones present who could be considered totally nude now were the two girls in the lake and the pig.

Rodney still wore his shoes and socks as he sat on the lakeside sand. He was trying very hard to hide at least the crotch of his otherwise totally exposed body with the open briefcase on his lap. His underwear, shirt, tie, trousers and jacket lay in a neat little pile beside his bare buttocks.

The young man had been more than greatly relieved when his preferred interpretation of Trux's statement about blowing breezes proved mercifully to be correct.

The Maynards had honestly meant it when they said they only reason they wanted him to remove his garments was to discuss business. Both would have thought it funny but would have been mildly shocked in their own rough hewn way, had they been aware Rodney thought they had anything else in mind.

The late Mr. Maynard really had passed his own personal rendition of just one of the many philosophies attributed to Henry David Thoreau, down to his sons. Said offspring were but acting upon advise handed down from the dearly departed.

Trux, Farley and the pig sat in front of the young lawyer. Each of the two men now held a can of Blue Ribbon Beer in his hand. Farley was sharing with Barney by pouring a portion of his metal container's contents into the crown of an old floppy hat that lay upside down in front of the pig.

"Don't mind them, young fella. Keep talkin," urged Farley. "We're listenin."

"That's about all there is, really," said Rodney. "You sign the papers and I give you the money. Can I put my clothes back on now?"

"You really got two grand cash for us?" asked Trux, giving a nod of approval indicating the young man could now get dressed.

Rodney closed the briefcase. He kept it on his lap as he picked up his jockey shorts and began pulling them on underneath the portfolio, still trying to keep his genitalia from sight.

"Right here in this briefcase," he said as he realized his shorts were coming on backward. He began pulling them off again. "I still don't understand why you didn't receive all this information in the mail. I know Mr. Herkimer wrote you several letters about it."

"We didn't get no letters bout nobody wantin to buy our mountain." Farley said as he scratched the pig's back. Barney, however, was looking up at Trux, giving the broad shouldered blond man an accusing grunt. Farley followed the pig's gaze.

"Did we Trux?" he asked

Trux avoided his brother's eyes as Rodney finally succeeded in pulling on his shorts. The blond man with the big chin sneered down at the pig.

"When the hell you gonna start mindin your own business, Barney?"

"It is his business. Barney's family, too. Did we get any of them letters Trux?"

"Okay, damnit! I threw em' away," he said after a short pause. Immediately he continued in a defensive tone. "You know I swore I'd never open another God damned letter after I got my draft notice when I turned eighteen. Shit! I wasn't even old enough to buy booze and they wanted me to go kill people I didn't even know good enough to be mad at."

"You still shoulda tole' Me'n Barney bout' em', Trux."

A long moment of silence followed. The brothers looked at each other as Rodney put the brief case to one side and rose to his feet.

He was bending over to pick up the rest of his clothing when Barney's ears and the hair on his back suddenly stood straight up. The pig looked at the far side of the lake as he gave out with an excited squeal.

Without further warning, an extremely loud explosion shattered the stillness.

In the lake itself, Catch Pen and Squeeze Chute emitted squeals of their own. Water cascaded in every direction as both immediately struggled to their feet in total panic.

Squeeze Chute's nasal voice rose to a terrified wail as she and her sister created separate tidal waves running toward opposite sides of the murky body of smelly, sulfuric liquid.

"It's Heffaroid!" she screamed.

His clothing forgotten for the moment, Rodney straightened up and looked around for the source of the explosive noise.

Behind him Trux had already discovered it. His wide blue eyes above his even wider jaw registered genuine alarm as he threw aside his beer can and looked across the lake.

"Oh shit! It's their God damned fat brother, Heffaroid Hogg!"

On the far side of the odorous body of dirty water, an unkempt man, much larger than either Catch Pen Or Squeeze Chute, sweated and groaned profusely as he attempted to climb over a barbed wire fence.

One of the reasons the gigantic fellow seemed to be having so much difficulty, in addition to his tremendous bulk, was the hindrance of a huge, smoking double barreled held in the crook of his enormous right arm.

As he did gain access to the lakeside of the barrier, he reached into a pocket of his tight fitting ragged bib overalls and withdrew a fresh shell.

The huge fellow began reloading the weapon as he lumbered forward around the left side of the lake, heading toward the people beyond him. As he came closer, there was no missing the murderous look in his angry dark eyes.

"Quick! Into the HOWDY HOSS!" Trux yelled as he picked up Rodney's briefcase and slammed it into the startled young man's bare stomach. "Ole Heffaroid'll kill anybody seen his sisters nekid! Shit! He was supposed to be gone for the day!"

"Days over Trux!" said Farley who had already scooped Rodney's clothing up from the sand and was running toward the motor home. Barney danced about on his short legs, oinking with frenzy.

Rodney clutched the briefcase with both hands as Trux physically propelled him around the corner of the HOWDY HOSS and in through its side door. Farley stuck his head out through the same portal as his brother, now also inside, leapt behind the steering wheel and started the engine.

"Come on Barney!"

The pig, evidently satisfied that his troops were now all properly assembled, displayed amazing speed for a member of the swine family as he raced into Farley's arms.

At the left side of the lake, Heffaroid still charged forward past Squeeze Chute who was unsuccessfully attempting to hide her wide girth behind a scrubby bush.

Her Brobdingnagian brother slipped on a reminder that Barney had been a recent visitor to the premises. He fell forward. The ground shook as he landed face first in the mud.

The shotgun slipped from his grasp. The weapon too, landed in the mud, both barrels stuck downward, directly into the mire.

Rising to his knees, and pulling the old relic free, the enormous man hoisted it up to his shoulder.

He pointed the gun at the now departing motor home and squeezed back both triggers at the same time. The tremendous recoil of the firearm, as its two mud filled barrels exploded, sending the huge aggressor flying backward.

"You ain't hurt are ya Heffaroid?" asked Squeeze Chute as she peeked around a branch of the scrub brush.

Inside what was apparently the bedroom area in the back of the shabbily furnished, rapidly departing motor home, Rodney kneeled on a mattress covered with wadded up blankets that, in turn, rested on a raised platform about two feet high. The base of the bed was apparently part of the big recreational rig's initial construction.

He peered through the vehicle's rear window as he struggled into the rest of his clothes.

Beyond the streaked glass, he could see the little Karmann Ghia and the lake, both becoming smaller.

He turned toward the rest of the interior of the HOWDY HOSS. He looked between the frayed and worn curtains, which, evidently, when pulled together, separated the bedroom area from the remainder of the inside of the large recreational rig.

Trux still sat behind the steering wheel with his foot pressed down on the gas pedal operating the controls as he headed the big machine elsewhere.

Farley, balancing his body against the gravitational sway, was busy pulling more cans of Blue Ribbon from an old icebox. Barney, seemingly oblivious the everything except the beer, looked up at Farley with an expectant look on his scarred face.

"My car," said Rodney, almost ready to cry, "It's still back there. And I left the keys...."

Farley continued to manage balancing himself as he moved to the rear of the motor home where he opened, then handed the grief stricken young attorney, a fresh can of beer.

"Either your car or your ass, Mister," he said before turning away and lurching back toward Trux with another beer he still held in his hand.

From his position behind the steering wheel, which he seemed to be continually spinning, Trux called back over one of his broad shoulders.

"That's right hoss. Heffaroid ud' shoot you in a minute. You not only seen his sisters nekid, you was nekid your own self."

"Dumb move gettin caught nekid with the Hogg sisters," said Farley as he handed his brother a beer before heading back to the icebox for more.

Rodney held the full can he had just been handed bearing the Blue Ribbon logo, like it was some sort of foreign object.

"But I wasn't ... You made me..."

"Come to think on it, maybe you wasn't. Don't know how long he'd been lookin. Maybe you was just climbing into your drawers when he first seen you. That ud be even worse to ole Heffaroid's way of thinkin." Trux called back again as he manipulated the steering wheel with one hand and lifted the container of Blue Ribbon up to his lips with the other.

At the icebox, Farley now was pouring some beer into a bowl that seemed to be secured to the motor home bulkhead for just such occasions.

As soon as the bearded man stopped pouring, Barney shoved his snout in the bowl and began thirstily lapping away.

Rodney looked out the rear window again. Neither his car nor the lake was now in sight. Without even being aware of his actions, he took a drink of the beer Farley had handed him.

Even back in his college drinking days before he'd taken the pledge to stay away from alcoholic spirits, he'd never liked this particular beverage. For some reason, right now, it tasted wonderful.

"He wouldn't really have killed me would he?" The young man asked as he picked up his briefcase with his free hand and attempted to move forward up the aisle within the moving rig. He didn't do the balancing act nearly as well as Farley.

"Most likely worse," commented Farley, as Rodney lurched up beside the bearded brother and the busy beer drinking pig.

"Worse?" echoed Rodney as Farley finally raised a full beer can to his own lips and kept it there until the container was completely empty.

Trux had slowed down somewhat now, and was driving at a more reasonable speed. Through the windshield, darkness could be seen at long last descending on the desert outside. He leaned forward and turned on the headlights.

The big chinned Maynard brother crushed his empty beer can with the hand that wasn't occupied with the steering wheel at the moment.

As he casually tossed the ruins of the aluminum container on the floorboards beneath his feet, he called over his shoulder again.

"Whoever don't die'll end up havin' to marry one of them bank mules." He said in a very matter of fact voice as he turned the steering wheel sharply to his right without bothering to apply the brakes.

The headlights through the windshield played on an outside road sign announcing that the old recreational vehicle and its passengers would now be headed back toward Lone Pine.

This was, of course contingent on being able to gain total access to the road leading north without turning over.

Trux added one more verbal thought as he completed negotiating the change in direction, ignoring the squeal of tires rending the early evening desert air that filtered in through the motor home walls.

"Them Hogg girls is a lot of fun to skinny splash and screw around with, but I think dead ud be better than bein' married to one of em."

"Dead ud be better'n bein' married to anybody," said Farley displaying amazing agility as he rescued the beer that flew from Rodney's hand when the lawyer fell back into an old cracked leather covered seat as the motor home made the sharp turn.

A narrow door built into the interior structure of the rig opposite where Rodney had landed in the old leather seat, slammed open.

Beyond the portal entryway he could see a tiny toilet bowl inside extremely cramped quarters.

Still holding the rescued beer, Farley moved across the aisle and quickly closed the door.

"Don't use the crapper, by the way," the bearded man told the young lawyer. "Useless son of a bitch plugged up a while back. It was a mothafucker to get it clean and to stop smellin'. One of these days we gonna' dump the tank underneath."

He shifted the conversation to a more favorable subject, the can of beer in his hand.

"No harm done. Didn't spill a drop," Farley said again as he offered the still nearly full aluminum container to the now seated Rodney. "You headin' for Lone Pine?" he called to the front of the motor home's interior.

"What's it to ya?" Trux called back

"Nothin. Just figgered you was. Only time you drive like that's when your runnin' from pussy or runnin' to it."

Rodney shook his head at Farley, declining the offer of the remaining beer in the can that had slipped from his grasp. It tasted too good. All he needed right now was to become inebriated on top of all the other terrible things that were happening to him.

With daylight no longed coming in through the windows, it was becoming much harder to distinguish details, but Farley readily recognized the beer was being rejected.

The man with the protruding stomach and almost no rear end shrugged. He turned to the pig that was looking up at him with eager anticipation.

"Tell you what, Barney, Daddy Farley'll split it with ya. Okay?"

"We never did finish our business," Trux called back again, this time addressing Rodney. "Wanna bring up them papers n' and gimme a gander at em'?"

Rodney wasn't quite sure what the man in the drivers seat meant by the word 'Gander', but he rose to his feet again and began carrying the briefcase carefully up the aisle through the ever increasing darkness of the motor home's interior.

"Don't worry. We ain't gonna make you show yer pecker again. We already seen it. It ain't much, but like the fat lady said, it's bigger'n Farley's."

"We got a little bit of whisky left," called Farley, evidently eager to change the direction of the current conversation.

"Bring it on up." Replied Trux. "You oughta' look at this shit too." He continued as Rodney arrived at his side. The young man awkwardly attempted to balance the briefcase on the dashboard of the moving motor home as he opened it and removed the requested papers. Trux reached over his head and turned on the driver's dome light.

Farley moved up behind Trux. He had a clear glass pint bottle in his hand now, which displayed about an inch of amber liquid sloshing about inside near the bottom.

Trux kept one hand on the steering wheel as he held the papers beneath the overhead light with the other as he looked at them.

Rodney was terrified the man was going to run off the road, but somehow the old recreational vehicle seemed to keep going straight, almost as if it might have been on automatic pilot.

"Don't know if I want to sell that ole mountain. How about you Farley?" Trux asked his brother who was now peering over his shoulder at the deed in Trux's right hand.

"Don't hardly seem fair to take that much money for it," replied the bearded man as he traded the now open bottle for the papers and started to look at them. He glanced down to see the pig at his feet grunting up at him.

"Was you sayin' somethin' Barney?"

The pig grunted again. Farley handed the papers back to Rodney as he spoke to his brother who was in the process of draining the contents of the small whiskey bottle as he continued to drive.

"Pull over Trux. Barneys' gotta go."

Trux heaved an exasperated sigh. He tossed the empty pint bottle on the floorboard where it made a resounding clank as it struck the crumpled beer can. He then began to apply the brakes.

"You know better'n to feed that damned pig beer while we're drivin,"

The headlights of a lone automobile briefly shined on the motor home as it passed, but otherwise, except for the HOWDY HOSS, the highway to Lone Pine seemed to be deserted.

The old recreational vehicle lumbered off the road and stopped near a cluster of scraggly bushes that looked somewhat grotesque beneath the natural glow of the nearly full, rising moon.

The lights of the motor home went out and shortly thereafter, it's side door opened and the occupants of the big rig began to pile out into the night.

Farley and Barney, in the lead, immediately headed for the bushes. Trux leapt out behind them.

"Come on Barney. Daddy Farley knows when a feller's gotta go, a feller's gotta go." Farley's guttural voice trailed off as he and the pig disappeared into the brush.

Rodney, still in possession of the briefcase, stood on the bottom step of the open doorway deciding exactly which direction would afford him the most privacy if he were to take advantage of this respite, since the inside facility was out of order. In spite of the fact that the moon had only recently peeked its way up over the distant horizon, it was much easier to see out here than inside the motor home.

As he finally began to make his descent, he realized Trux had already unzipped his own fly and was nonchalantly relieving himself directly in the young barrister's path.

"Tell you what," said Trux, raising his voice slightly to be heard over the sound of his own splashing urine, "I do know where there's some property for sale's supposed to have a gold mine on it. Not guaranteed of course, but it still might be a helluva lot better buy than that old mountain of ours. Ain't nothin' up there sept' old rocks, rattle snakes and buzzard shit."

"But I have orders to buy this particular property," Rodney replied as he averted his eyes and quickly stepped backward to regain his prior footing on the motor home step for safety. "This mountain... Your mountain as you call it..."

Farley and the pig returned from the bushes.

"Barney's all done," The bearded man announced to anyone who might be interested.

"You check him for worms?" asked Trux.

"He only hadda do number one."

Trux turned his attention back to Rodney. "You really got two thou for us? No shit?"

The younger man sat down on the top step behind him that was, in reality, the beginning of the motor home floor. He began to open the briefcase again. Maybe he was at least about to accomplish something. He still had no idea how he was going to retrieve the Karmann Ghia.

He produced the envelope and pulled the top of it open, displaying the hundred dollar bills inside. The moonlight illumination gave the money an almost surrealistic appearance.

Trux looked at his brother and flashed his overabundance of teeth. Farley grinned back.

"Now if I can just find a pen." began Rodney, as he rummaged around in the bottom of his briefcase beneath the dreaded cellular telephone. His hand not occupied in the search still held the envelope.

Trux stopped him.

"Nah. We don't wanna make no decisions tonight. But since you got all them greenbacks, You might's well loan me some of it."

Before Rodney could think of a response, Trux leaned forward and gently extracted a hundred-dollar bill.

Farley moved in beside his brother and took another hundred from the stash of cash.

"Me'n Barney could use a little ourselves," he said.

Immediately the pig began to grunt. "Barney says we sure do thank you," the bearded Maynard added.

Rodney started to protest. Then a small piece of his legal training somehow wormed its way into his confused and cluttered brain.

The Maynard brothers had now accepted some money. That meant the deal had entered a period of commencement and was therefore now subject to litigation. If nothing else, They could no longer legally sell the property to someone else. It was at least a start.

In addition to these extremely official reasons, he was also afraid to ask them to give it back. He had a feeling that neither Trux nor Farley, or even Barney for that matter responded well to pressure.

The young man with the legal mind that really felt more like tangled spaghetti at the moment, carefully placed the envelope still containing the majority of the purchasing funds, this time, into the inside pocket of his suit jacket. He then closed the briefcase.

While the Maynards were stuffing their own recent acquisitions into the pockets of worn Levi's, Rodney rose to his feet.

"We'll call it a down payment," he said, trying very hard to sound confident and official.

"Call it goat barf if you want to," said Trux. "To me'n Farley it's still just a loan. Since you got so much of that green stuff inside your coat next to your tit there, you wont mind if we take a while to pay it back," The man with the big chin continued, obviously not privy to Rodney's legal information.

"Course if we do sign them papers, you can give us the rest of it and you'll have your self a mountain and we wont owe you nothin," added Farley.

Trux's statement gave Rodney an uneasy feeling. Farley's comment, however, at least made him feel better regarding the transaction. He had another subject that still weighed heavily on his mind at the moment.

"Do you think it's safe to go back to the lake? I really do need to get my car…"

Trux responded with absolutely no hesitation.

"I wouldn't chance it," he said, looking very serious.

Rodney's mouth opened in almost anguished protest. "But.. But…I can't just….You don't understand…." The ugly stutter monster had its talons in his tongue again.

Trux's wide contagious grin reappeared as the tall man with the big chin and the broad shoulders attempted to console the frustrated young fellow from the city.

"Come on. Ain't that bad," he said. " Sometime tomorrow ole Heffaroid's gonna have to git back to his borax mine. Ain't got no choice. Poor fat son of bitch can't afford no help! Me'n Farley'll scope it out and give you a hand when the times right."

"Anyway," Farley joined in, "couldn't do it right now nohow. We ain't done our socializin' yet."

"S...Socializing?"

"We wouldn't even think about signin' them papers 'thout first socializin' with ya," said Trux good naturedly, "Way me'n Farley do business. Ain't no other way with me and my brother."

" A..Another rule h..anded d..down by your late F..F...ather?" Rodney was still stammering, but the question was asked with genuine respect and interest.

It was taken the way it was delivered. Trux had to stop and think about the answer, though. "No I think this un's our own idea. Maybe Farley's. He's the deep thinker in the family."

"Who gives a shit?" Farley spoke up modestly. "Maybe Barney come up with it. Anyhow it's how we operate."

Rodney was afraid to ask, but he felt the question was mandatory.

"What did you have in mind?" He seemed to have regained control of his tongue. "Dinner? I am a little hungry."

"Hell no!" Trux spat out. "We don't eat more'n once ever two or three days if we can help it. 'Specially when we been drinkin'. Fucks up our buzz!"

Farley's eye's twinkled merrily in the moonlight. "Ever been trollin' Rod?"

"Fishing? No, but...."

The twinkle faded from the bearded brother's eyes. His tone became cranky.

"I'm talkin' bout pussy not fish, damnit! You do know what pussy is?"

Trux started to snicker. The twinkle in Farley's eyes returned as he looked at his brother and also began to laugh.

"By God, come to think on it, they is a connection," Farley managed to blurt out between convulsive snorts of merriment.

Total confusion had become Rodney's natural state of mind. He just stared as the brothers shared the joke that had obviously sailed way past his head.

It was just as obvious that the humor of whatever had just transpired had not escaped the pig. Barney was dancing up and down and omitting grunting noises that sounded uncannily like giggles.

The young man felt totally left out and terribly alone. Two more automobiles passed on the highway beside the stationary old rig and its passengers. Each was traveling in an opposite direction from the other.

Suddenly he felt himself being pushed back into the motor home as the Maynard brothers and their cloven hoofed companion stormed the darkened entrance of the old vehicle.

"Well shit howdy!" cried Trux as he elbowed the young attorney aside on his way to the steering wheel. "We goin' trollin' we got work to do! HOWDY HOSS gotta' be all cleaned up."

"Stocked up too!" chimed in Farley as he pulled the door closed. "Can't do no trollin ' thout bait. Soon as we get her spiffy, don't forget to stop at the liquor store, Trux!"

The pig grunted loudly in total agreement as Trux started the engine and eased the old recreational vehicle back onto the highway.

"Sooner forget my ass, Farley!" Trux called back through the darkness. "We'll get her spiffy while we're pickin up bait! Yes sir! We'll have her all together. Might even get in a little snooze time before the bars close in Lone Pine! Can't do no trollin' till the bars close in Lone Pine!"

"Been a spell since me'n ole Trux went trollin'. You're gonna love it," Farley assured Rodney.

The young attorney settled back in the old leather seat. He didn't even have a clue as to what now lie in store for him. All he'd really gleaned from the conversation was that they really couldn't start trolling, whatever that was, until the bars closed in Lone Pine. He probably wouldn't have acquired that much information, if Trux hadn't said it twice.

He wondered vaguely if skin had starting falling from his face now that the sun was gone. The poor young man was so exhausted he didn't even care. He lay his weary, confused head back and closed his eyes.

CHAPTER SEVEN
TROLLIN'

The old clock above the darkened entrance of the even more antiquated red, brick bank building read two am as the battered HOWDY HOSS, its head lights on dim, cruised slowly down the main street of Lone Pine.

Rodney was now seated in the driver's seat operating the controls of the vintage vehicle. Behind him, the Maynard brothers crouched in the semi darkness of the motor home's rear interior.

They murmured to one another, and occasionally the pig that lay next to the icebox, as they peered out through the side windows of the old utility rig.

The moon was now clearly over head. The only other lights on either side of the street that could be seen through the now surprisingly clean glass, were those of the small city's drinking establishments and the head and tail lights of an occasional car or pickup weaving away from one of these places of business.

Occasional yells of revelry from the drivers of the departing vehicles floated upward toward the moonlit mountains in the near distance.

The snow capped peaks seem to be smiling down on all the drunken human behavior attesting to nature's tolerance toward human stupidity.

Lone Pine's nighttime entertainment hot spots were obviously in the process of suspending operations until the following day.

Rodney wasn't sure how he came to inherit the designated driver's position. He felt it was probably all for the best considering the amount of alcohol the others, including Barney had, and were continuing to consume.

The young Bostonian didn't really believe any of the three had stopped drinking since the beer had first been brought forth back at Dirty Socks lakeside.

Later, he wasn't sure how much of their recently 'Borrowed Funds' they'd used to purchase more. He knew they had amply replenished their supply of the Blue Ribbon brand foamy beverage.

They had also acquired what seemed to Rodney to be an enormous amount of bottles containing various brands of a vast variety of much more potent libations.

These acquisitions were added to inventory almost immediately when they had stopped behind that country liquor store. This was shortly after they had decided Rodney must join them in their 'Socialization' project.

Perhaps they might have paused in their alcohol consumption while they cleaned up the motor home. It was also possible that later they may had abstained when they were throwing the trash that had littered its floors and elsewhere into the huge Dempsy Dumpster behind the roadside booze emporium.

They had been gracious enough to allow him to get some sleep during most of that activity so he really couldn't account for their actions during that period of time. He'd even managed to pick up a little something to eat and use the restroom in the liquor store, before he collapsed on the old messy bed in the rear of the HOWDY HOSS.

It had been fitful slumber at best, filled with nightmares. Monsters with chain saws with dirty bald heads, fat men and giant frogs kept chasing him.

The frogs had turned into Louise, her father, and Harold Herkimer, while the Khamann Ghia slowly sank beneath the surface of the water in Dirty Socks Lake.

Somewhere in one of the sporadic dreams, Old Henderson was back in Boston. The senescent miner had been stroking his mother's bare breasts while he examined her nipples through a jeweler's glass that seemed to be growing out of his eye.

He had awakened to find the interior of the rig not nearly so filthy as he remembered, and Barney, staggering slightly, grunting in his face.

He had been told by either Trux or Farley, he couldn't recall which, as both began rapidly making the bed they had allowed him to nap on, that it was now time to go trolling. He was also informed at that time that he, Rodney, had the privilege of being the chauffeur.

The brothers had changed into much cleaner clothing. However, the sleepy eyed barrister harbored a grave suspicion that neither they nor the pig had discontinued even an iota of their booze consumption during the transition period.

The young man from civilization was still terribly confused. Since this state of mind seemed to have become his modus operandi since he had first received this absurd assignment, he was becoming accustomed to the feeling.

He sat in the driver's seat now, accepting his new delegated duty, cruising slowly down the main street of Lone Pine in the middle of the night.

"Slow down, Rod," Trux called in a very loud conspiratorial whisper. The energetic man was speaking from what seemed to be his post at one of the windows of the moving vehicle in the semi darkness behind Rodney.

The old motor home was already moving at no more than a snail's pace. Nonetheless the young lawyer complied.

Through the now surprisingly clean windshield, he could see three unescorted middle aged ladies beneath the glow of the outside combination of moon and artificial light. They seemed to be attempting to balance themselves on extremely unsteady legs as they exited a bar on the right hand side of the street.

Behind him, Trux and Farley had also spotted the trio of drunken damsels. The brothers exchanged delighted looks. Trux's whispering voice was filled with boyish excitement as he called again to Rodney.

"That's us! Stop this sucker!"

Once again the befuddled driver complied with the man's request. Barney let out with an excited squeal and scampered up beside Rodney. To the young man's surprise and subsequent dismay, the pig then leapt up onto his lap.

Almost immediately the young appointed driver realized Barney's motivation was to have a better view of the street. Both driver and animal watched as Trux and Farley piled out of the HOWDY HOSS and approached the three women.

Man and pig continued their observation through the glass as Trux immediately moved in close and began fondling the sagging breasts of the shortest of the unsteady feminine trio as he talked to her.

Farley, much subtler than his brother, was already using both hands to stroke the buttocks of the other two.

"M..My G...God!" Rodney was not only stammering again, he was so honestly shocked, he didn't even realize he was attempting to communicate with a pig. "Th...They're mo... molesting those old women! Th.. That's a criminal..."

Barney drunkenly nuzzled the stunned young man's arm and gave him a reassuring 'Oink.'

Evidently the pig knew what he was grunting about. The disturbed attorney watched with an open mouth as, through the windshield, he witnessed that, instead of being offended, all three of the molestation recipients seemed to be expressing their delight.

They began to shriek and giggle as Trux and Farley led them off toward the motor home.

Barney jumped from Rodney's lap and hurried to greet the new visitors as Trux and Farley helped them inside.

"Make yourselves at home, girls. Other than if you gotta' go, we got all the comforts. Shitter don't work so it's called go outside and play 'Seek and go squat' if the urge grabs you, but other than that we got ever thing," Trux said as he closed the door.

"This here's Barney. He belongs to my brother Farley here. He don't bite, but I ain't makin' no promises 'bout Farley. Young dude up front's Rod. You know what they say 'bout the younguns. Younger the Buck the stiffer the horn."

The women laughed hysterically while Rodney, terribly embarrassed, cringed in the driver's seat and attempted to brush the swine residue from the front of his trousers.

Farley nudged Barney gently aside with one knee as he gallantly seated the ladies whose rumps he had recently been stroking out side on the sidewalk.

The third woman remained standing in front of Trux. She attempted to introduce herself and her companions in a slurred voice. Her gray hair was short and curly and her green, bloodshot eyes were big and round.

"That's Irene and that's Jeannie."

Jeannie patted Barney on the snout and Irene reached up and gave Farley's beard a playful tug as both women chorused their hellos.

The short thing with the big green eyes leaned suggestively against Trux.

"And I'm horny," she said emphatically. This caused her two female companions to go into another giggling fit.

Trux's mouthful of teeth stretched into his wide grin. He barked a not unfriendly order to Rodney as he pulled the woman to him.

"Don't just sit there, Rod. Do a John Wayne and Move em' out! Get the hell off Main Street."

Rodney wasn't quite sure what a John Wayne was. He vaguely remembered hearing about an airport somewhere in the Los Angeles area by that name, but the rest of the command was clear.

He put the big machine in gear and began driving forward as Trux looked into the big green eyes of the inebriated lady in his arms.

"Your name's really Horny?"

"No, my name's Geraldine, but I'm really horny."

"Remember Geraldine," said Jeannie, the taller and thinner of the trio, whose features boasted an extremely long and narrow proboscis, "we don't make it with locals."

Next to her, Irene, the remaining drunken dowager, pulled Farley down on her lap.

"Hell!" said Farley, as he began tickling Irene's more than ample, exposed cleavage with the thick whiskers sprouting from his chin, "Me n' Trux ain't no locals. We're from Darwin at least a third of the time. And ole Rod up there's from way the Hell and gone! LA or some other damned place."

In the aisle of the moving motor home, Geraldine began rotating her sagging breasts forcefully in a circle against the lower portion of Trux's chest. At the same time the short, green eyed, inebriated wench did similar things with her hips to an even lower portion of his anatomy where, obviously with Trux, it really counted.

"Welcome stranger!" she cried, as she propelled him back into the bedroom area where poor Rodney had last seen his misplaced 'Slum Mobile' through the rear window during the hasty departure from Dirty Socks Lake.

Trux's grin was now so broad he may have had dimples in his earlobes. He pulled the tattered curtain closed and he and the determined little lady disappeared from sight.

Farley raised his shaggy face from the wide woman named Irene's cleavage and called to the driver as he rose to his feet.

He then moved to the icebox and the cases filled with liquor bottles along with a tall stack of plastic party glasses piled next to them. Barney was right on his heels.

"See that old piece of shit pickup up ahead on your right, Rod? Just after the gun shop? Hang a left up that dirt road this side of, it then head on out of town. I'll get these good lookin' bunnies a drink. What'll it be, Foxy Fillies?"

"Got any vodka? I love vodka!" Irene answered immediately.

"Rum if you got it!" Jeannie slurred affably, "Or just plain old whiskey if you don't. With a beer chaser. I'm not picky."

"Got em' all!" Retorted Farley, his deep voice booming with pride. "How about a little tad of each? That's how Barney likes it."

Barney practically held his breath, as above him, Farley began opening bottles. Once this chore had been attended to, the porker's bearded hero with the protruding belly poured a generous tad of each into the pigs own personal bowl.

Farley did this prior to filling the women's requests and it made Barney feel very special. Farley also added a whole can of beer to the mixture in the concave vessel.

This, for Barney, was what it was all about. He didn't really care about Uncle Trux and Daddy Farley's other additional activities. As far as Barney was concerned, it didn't get any better than this.

He'd worry about the hangover tomorrow. Every thing in its proper place at the proper time. Right now, as Uncle Trux would have undoubtedly said if he weren't otherwise occupied in the bedroom with the short human female with those big green eyes, "By God, Barney's in hog heaven!"

While Farley served similar concoctions to Irene and Jeannie, Rodney, obeying instructions, turned the motor home to the left and started up the dirt road.

The lumbering vehicle had traveled less than half a mile when the young lawyer saw a 'One Way' sign through the windshield. He was traveling in the wrong direction.

Alarmed, he quickly applied the brakes and called back over his shoulder. "We're going the wrong way!"

Jeannie sat on the edge of the old cracked leather seat with a can of beer in one hand. She held a plastic party glass filled with whisky, rum, vodka and an additional kind of hard liquor she couldn't quite distinguish, in the other.

The skinny lady with the long nose was obviously attempting to make up her mind as to which should be granted consumption priority.

Irene, still seated beside her, was making strange little noises. The ingredients in the glass she was presently pouring past her palate may have promoted these sounds.

Conversely, Farley, now kneeling in the aisle in front of her, with both his hands exploring the world beneath her skirt, was in all probability the true provider of the motivational moan factor.

The bearded man looked up at Jeannie as he continued to exercise his sense of touch toward the upper portion of Irene's substantial lower torso.

"What's that kid carry'n on about?"

Jeannie replied before finally making a decision and sticking her protracted proboscis into the plastic glass.

"He just seen the 'One Way' sign."

"Don't worry about it!" Farley called to Rodney as, beneath the material of Irene's skirt, the outline of his fingers could be seen continuing to creep their way up toward the beginning of the lady's generous thighs. "That sign's just for gravel trucks in the day time. Nobody gives a shit this time of night! Put the hammer down, Rod! Let's go up to them Alabama Hills and do some howlin! Moon out ain't quite full, but she's close enough!"

"He's a cute little shit," said Jeannie, referring to the young man behind the steering wheel as she tossed aside the now totally voided clear plastic container. "I'm gonna go see if he needs help getting off. Off to the Alabama Hills I mean."

Howling at her own joke, the thin woman rose to her feet. Holding her still nearly full beer can high to keep its contents from spilling, she staggered toward the young lawyer who was still driving forward, albeit with certain reservations.

Irene, still seated, handed her plastic party drink container that was now also empty, to the kneeling Farley.

"Gimme one more, barkeep," she said with a giggle. "Only this time, don't be so stingy with the booze."

Farley heaved a deep sigh as he reluctantly withdrew his roaming hands and rushing fingers from beneath the material of her skirt.

Struggling to his feet, he took the disposable glass from her outstretched hand.

"As the feller in the song says, on one condition. You gotta tell me what them under drawers of yours is made of."

As Farley lurched toward the libation supply, Irene's look betrayed the fact that his question had temporarily taken the woman with the wide set of hips slightly aback.

92

"Spandex!" she replied. "And my underwear's none of your damned business!" she added, as she lifted her broad behind up from the old leather seat.

She then began peeling the embarrassing malleable garment in question down over her flaccid thighs. She was evidently determined to keep her elastic bloomers from being the object of further discussion for the remainder of this romantic excursion.

In the front of the rig, Jeannie leaned over the back of the driver's seat and offered her beer to Rodney.

"Buy you a drink, Sailor?" said the thin lady with the pronounced protuberance, sounding very seductive.

The young lawyer was about to explain to her, politely as possible, that he didn't drink. Then he discovered she was attempting to slip her free hand down the front of his shirt.

He suddenly got the same uncomfortable feeling he'd experienced back in the Century City outer office when Miss Wayling refused to stop looking at his crotch. Fortunately for him, his tie temporarily deterred the intended grope.

Granted, this woman, in spite of her nose was not quite as unattractive as the masculine faced secretary for the law firm of Herkimer, Herkimer, Herkimer, Herkimer and Van Aukin. Nonetheless, she was still much too old to be even thinking of doing such things with a man as young as Rodney.

The very act of any possible invasion to his body beneath his clothing by a woman who could well be twice his age, was unthinkable. It disturbed Rodney so much, in fact, that he suddenly needed a drink of that beer very badly.

Keeping a firm grasp on the steering wheel with his left hand, and his eyes on the headlight illuminated dirt road through the windshield in front of him, he reach back with his right and took the beer.

Raising the can to his lips, he drank every drop of its contents in one long gulp. Quickly, he handed the now empty aluminum container back to the woman, hoping to give her something else to do with her touchy feely hands.

"I..I'm s...sort of busy right now," he said, trying to control his stammer, while at the same time hoping to appease any injured feelings. "Gotta do like.. like the man shed... I mean, said...Gotta put the...."

However limited the alcohol content in the beer may have been it had all immediately gone straight to the brain of the young man who had foregone drinking.

The road in front of him began to swirl and, for the life of him, Rodney couldn't remember the term Farley had used. Some kind of tool.

"Screwdriver down!" he finally blurted out in a loud voice as he pressed his foot down hard on the accelerator.

A huge cloud of dust rose up toward the moonlit sky as the HOWDY HOSS shot forward at an alarming rate of speed through the peaceful tranquility of the wee hours of the rural morning.

As the speeding recreational vehicle passed a gigantic boulder, any and all heretofore mentioned tranquility came to a screeching halt. A marked police sedan, its siren howling and bright blue and red lights flashing, streaked into sight from behind the natural formation, hot on the motor home's tail.

The combination of air rendering, high pitched noise from outside and the blinding multicolored lights in the rear view mirror, threw Rodney's already obfuscated mind into a total state of panic.

He gripped the steering wheel even tighter and kept his foot pressed down hard on the gas pedal. The young lawyer honestly couldn't remember what one was supposed to do when confronted with such unlikely circumstances.

Behind him, Farley, who had obviously been in the act of pulling down his pants when his moment of questionable intimacy was so rudely interrupted, was pulling them up again over his narrow hips.

Irene, still on the old leather seat in front of him, was pushing her skirt down over her wide ones. At the same time, she looked around frantically for her elusive Spandex under garment.

Jeannie stood in the middle of the aisle of the rapidly moving vehicle. Her elongated thin features expressed a great deal of alarm as reality seeped in through the alcohol soaked crevices of her inner cranium.

"Holy shit!! It's that asshole!!" exclaimed Farley. "That piece of puke Arty!!"

"Dear God!" wailed Jeannie as the sound of the siren continued to penetrate the walls of the motor home. "If Arty catches us in here, we can kiss our good reputations goodbye, Irene!"

"Kiss our tires goodbye, we don't get our asses outa here quick!" Farley shouted as he lurched toward the front of the rig past Jeannie. Behind him Barney was crawling under a seat opposite the icebox.

"What do I do?" cried Rodney, sounding extremely helpless as he continued to drive forward with the law enforcement vehicle still right behind him. From outside, a loud 'Bang!' mingled momentarily with the sound of the siren.

"He's shooting at us!" Screamed Irene as she attempted to wiggle into her Spandex. "Turn left!"

Rodney turned the steering wheel sharply to the left. Irene tumbled off the seat headfirst with her expansive rump up in the air. The spandex apparel now held her firmly around the knees.

"No! Turn right! Turn right!" yelled Jeannie, who had careened against the cases of booze. Bottles spilled out in every direction, many of them breaking.

Rodney twisted the wheel back to the right as the sound of another shot from outside pierced its way in again through the song of the siren. The two women fell against the bulkhead next to the seat Barney was hiding beneath. The pig looked out at the ladies and gave each a look of sincere sympathy.

Farley, retaining his own footing expertly, moved up beside the panic stricken young lawyer and grabbed the steering wheel.

"Piss on this! Gimme that!"

Outside, the police car was forced to come to a halt to avoid colliding with the HOWDY HOSS as the old motor home fishtailed, then went into a spin.

The vintage vehicle leapt off the road and somehow righted itself before its front bumper plowed into another boulder.

Inside, Farley cursed while Irene and Jeannie screamed and tried to crawl out of the way as Trux and Geraldine came tumbling, end over end from the back of the motor home.

Down the aisle they rolled, their au naturel bodies wrapped in nothing but a blanket and each other.

When the vehicle at last quit vibrating, and the awful noise of the siren finally faded away, Trux was lying face up beneath the dashboard with the short little woman on top of him. It was apparent, due to the totally unclothed exposure of both, that neither had incurred any damage whatsoever from the broken glass in the aisle behind them during their tumbling act.

While it was quite obvious that Geraldine found no humor in the moment, her big chinned partner in bedlam was convulsed with hysterical laughter.

"Now that's what I call 'Ass over Teakettle,'" Trux quipped, when he was finally able to speak. He looked up at Rodney who had somehow managed to retain his seat behind the steering wheel.

"Well, Rod," said the broad shouldered red neck, giving the terrified young man from the city his best Stienway grin. "Now you been trollin."

The side door slammed open and Sheriff Arty Dubs stuck his head in from outside. He held the Magnum in his left hand ready.

His upper lip curled into a viscous sneer above his overhanging incisors as he gave the situation a speedy, professional surveillance.

"You low life, trashy, scum suckin' preverts!" he said in voice filled with nastiness and superiority, as he looked directly at the Maynard brothers. "Good thing my mamma ain't in here!"

He then addressed the entire group.

"All you true believers better give your heart to God, cause right now, your ass belongs to me!!" Arty announced, trying very hard to look and sound just like Clint Eastwood.

CHAPTER EIGHT
FAT BOY FROM BUGTUSSLE

Reverend Brother Roy Ogles the Pastor of the Lone Pine Devotion to Divinity Community Church, had never really doubted the existence of God. Unlike Agnus Wayling, the mistress of secretarial sexual manipulation back in Century City, he had always known the Creator was up or out there somewhere. It had just taken him until he was almost eighteen to make firm contact.

He had been born with the name 'Leroy' in the small town of Bugtussle, Oklahoma and subsequently raised there while patiently awaiting that connection.

The overweight boy's initial social standing during the high school years had been somewhat similar to that of Miss Wayling's.

He was also immediately ostracized by his more talented and infinitely more attractive peers. No student in Bugtussle High wished to be seen hanging out with a fat kid named Leroy.

About the only attention he did received when some of the more uncouth boys in school would chase him down and rip off his trousers.

He also had to be careful when walking around corners. On more than one occasion he ended up receiving a dishpan full of fresh chicken manure in his face procured from a hen house on one of the student's father's farms.

However, instead of taking the proverbial bit in his teeth and creating a niche for himself as Agnus had done, he accepted this as God's will and waited for the moment when He would come and right all wrongs. The wait proved to be a long one..

In the meantime he developed a perverse pleasure from destroying the property of others whenever possible.

His father, a hard working local mill worker named Earnest, hated only two types of men on this earth, pimps and preachers. Earnest was convinced that both professions performed the same function. Each took advantage of the weakness of mankind, which when combined with what they represented, lined their own pockets with unearned profits.

Therefore the youth, then known as 'Fat Leroy' was never allowed to even go near any church in Bugtussle. Leroy was certain this added to the delay.

The lad's obesity was inherited from his mother who seemed never to have had any thoughts of her own. Her maiden name was Hogg. Ernest Ogles had married the woman shortly before the rest of her small family left Oklahoma for the silver mines somewhere in California.

Entering into wedlock with the Hogg girl was a decision Ernest came to regret more and more each day as she continued growing in front of his very eyes. Since it had been a preacher who officiated this legally binding ceremony, his hatred of the clergy was only strengthened.

Only one child was brought forth into the world through this union. The senior Ogles, after taking his first look at the extremely large baby less than an hour after its emergence from the womb, vowed never to make the same mistake again.

Fat Leroy was never made aware of this. In all probability the boy couldn't have found room within his confused and cluttered mind to worry about it anyway.

He was usually much too busy consuming food when he wasn't waiting for God to show up to think of anything else. Staying out of the other kid's way and avoiding having chicken manure spread all over his face took up any remaining time.

Ever since the boy had been weaned from his mother's enormous breast, he had become extremely carnivorous. However, if meat was not readily available, any food would do. One worked up an appetite while waiting for the Lord.

On his seventeenth birthday he received a small pocket knife as his only present. Leroy loved it. Slashing the tires of football player's hot rods then became his other pastime as he remained in readiness for his audience with the Almighty.

Aside from the churches, which he longed to enter, but was not allowed to go near, the town boasted a movie theatre, known as the Lyric, and the usual assortment of boring stores. The small metropolis had little else to offer a young man nobody his own age wished to be seen with.

There was an old Civil War era courthouse in the town square that held his interest periodically. At least on Saturdays, things happened there.

He would feed his young fleshy face and watch with fascination, as the sheriff would bring in the bootleggers to be locked up. Later, the portly boy got to watch with all the other citizens who expressed interest as the moonshine was ceremoniously poured down the only drain in town.

On many of these occasions, his father would join him. These may have been the only times the youth and the senior Mr. Ogles ever really were seen together in public after he reached high school age. Ernest didn't like to be seen hanging out with a fat kid named Leroy either.

He enjoyed these sessions. To the youth this was some sort of communion. It gave him a sense of belonging and made him feel like the Lord was moving closer to him. He only regretted some sort of prayer not being spoken while the sickening odor of the illegal liquor being discarded down the drain wafted through the crowd.

One sweltering summer Saturday, during his fourth and hopefully final year in high school, Leroy found himself sitting in the Bugtussle's only motion picture theatre, the Lyric.

He had just finished watching an afternoon showing of an old released film entitled *The Ten Commandments*.

Fortunately the boy wasn't prohibited from going to the movies that day because his father wasn't familiar enough with the Bible to know this was a film of religious significance.

Earnest assumed all matinees to be Hopalong Cassidy cliffhangers. That's what they had been when he was a lad.

While the C. B. De Mille epic had moved young Ogles deeply, he felt certain that the man named Moses hadn't made it down that mountain with all the tablets. Surely God intended a lot more things to be forbidden.

He sat there munching on his popcorn and hot dog as the rest of the audience filed out. It would be a few minutes before the new crowd entered. He wanted to avoid any of the bullies that might be attending the movies on this particular day. There were other reasons too, why he wished to be alone.

As soon as the fat kid found himself to be so, he quickly devoured his edibles and pulled forth his cherished pocket knife.

The blade of that instrument had caused many a hero of the Bugtussle high school athletic program to walk home on various evenings. It was also the reason several of the cheerleaders, although they would never admit it, were still virgins.

On this particular afternoon it was used to carve a few additional commandments that had not made it to the screen, but really belonged, on the back of the seat in front of the young overweight movie critic. Among the suggestions were, 'Thou shalt not smear chicken shit on the face of thy neighbor.'

'Thou shalt not slash tires' was not among the offerings. Neither did the large round young man carve any rule against overeating in the back of that theatre seat.

He did however, slice up the upholstery of a few more just for fun after searching beneath them for enough loose change to buy more popcorn. As people started to enter for the second show, he pocketed both the money and his knife and left the exhibition building of cinema displays.

As the huge flabby lad, not to be known as Leroy much longer, had emerged from the movie house that afternoon, he heard sounds in the distance. It took a while for him to figure out where this noise he found extremely pleasant to his youthful ears was coming from and what it represented.

About five miles out of Bugtussle was a rundown community called Vinegar Hill. In that dilapidated settlement there existed a tabernacle. The young man with the God fixation had, of course, heard of it. However, even though he had lived this close to Vinegar Hill he had never really seen it.

The tabernacle was a huge building that would seat hundreds. Inside and up front, was what was referred to as a Moaner's Bench. The interior of the structure built for the sake of salvation, also boasted a repentance pit complete with sawdust, a large pulpit and a bandstand.

The building had been closed for some time even back then. The last minister to hold services there had been chased out of town just avoiding an old fashioned ensemble of tar and feathers.

Leroy didn't quite understand exactly what had happened. He had heard that the man of the cloth had been chased all the way to the Oklahoma border because he insisted that the original King James Version of the Bible was not written in English.

Adding insult to injury, this same man who claimed to be a spokesman for God claimed Jesus and all his disciples were Jews. Since nobody in that particular area of Oklahoma in those days had ever met a Jew, the elders and laymen of various other protestant denominations had called around.

The decision by those holding religious local power was that Jews should be hated, as were Catholics. Therefore if they were to continue loving Jesus as the Bible they read said they should, the Son of God could not possibly have been a Jew.

For that reason, the minister of the tabernacle in Vinegar Hill had been forced to depart and the house of worship had remained vacant ever since.

Contrariwise, it seemed that on that special Saturday, while the Lyric theatre in Bugtussle showed reruns of *The Ten Commandments,* the tabernacle in Vinegar Hill was no longer vacant. At least not on that particular afternoon and night. The old house Of worship was indeed sporting a show of its own.

This information was given to the boy named Leroy who grew not only up, but out, until he eventually became the revered man known as Brother Roy Ogles, by an old timer in front of the theatre. He was responding to the obese teen's inquires regarding the sound in the distance he now recognized to be the of pounded drums and shaking of tambourines.

According to the senior citizen of Bugtussle, a religious organization from Tennessee who called themselves 'Friends of Jesus' had rented the place. He went on to inform the young man that supposedly, people were coming from miles around to have their souls saved by some famous evangelist.

To this day, the overweight son of the man who hated pimps and preachers couldn't remember the name of the evangelist. Notwithstanding, never would the time that saver of souls from Tennessee's trip to Vinegar Hill, Oklahoma, be forgotten.

The Ogles boy was not allowed to attend any religious function in Bugtussle. However, since the family never went anywhere, the subject of such in another locale being forbidden had never come up.

The chubby eighteen-year-old knew this to be a sign. Five miles was a long walk for a youth at least eighty pounds overweight. It was, however, a journey that must be taken if that same overweight teenage boy was to realize his life's ambition and meet God.

Darkness was close to settling in when the youth finally reached his destination. It didn't matter. The glow of the crowd enhanced by a multitude of lighted lanterns cast as much light around the tabernacle as was needed.

The boy, then called Leroy, could feel the joy in the air. There seemed to be hundreds of the fanatically chosen 'Friends of Jesus' filing into the old edifice. The boy held back.

He wanted to enter but he knew some of the local teenagers of both sexes in the crowd. He had come to find God, not lose his trousers and end up going home with a face full of bird feces. He stayed hidden in the shadows as much as his wide girth would permit.

He was sure if he could get inside he would finally get to meet God. However, he was not confident that even if he were to manage sneaking in unnoticed, he would be welcomed by strangers. Why was it so difficult to meet and talk to the Lord?

He looked around, trying to make up his mind about what was to be his next move. The atmosphere was more like that of a carnival than a religious gathering.

The 'Friends of Jesus' had with them, cages of venomous snakes to handle, crushed glass to eat and cases of Drano to drink.

These were supposedly brought along prove that Jesus would give them the strength to overcome poisons ingested while they went into their trances.

There were many parts of that evening not mentioned when, years later Brother Roy related the experience to his own congregation in Lone Pine. The snakes, crushed glass and the drinking of Drano were among them. Now that his own relationship with God was solid, he felt certain that even though he hadn't seen any real disasters, some of those friendships with Jesus might not have been as firmly ingrained as initially imagined.

It was never a chance Brother Roy wished to have taken by any of his flock once he had control of his own church. A dead or even very ill member of the congregation adds nothing or at the most, very little to the collection plate.

Brother Ogles also failed to go into many other details regarding the night that had cemented his own relationship so solidly with the Creator.

When retelling the story he never mentioned how those outside pilgrims, in addition to the previously mentioned items, had also brought with them a sizable influx of pretty, ripe, albeit ragged young girls. The function of these sweet young waifs seemed to be encouraging the local onlookers to enter and join them.

The overweight lad from nearby Bugtussle who wanted so desperately to meet God, nearly fainted when one of these young urchins had pressed her nubile body against his fat one and urged him to follow her. Follow he did.

It was the very first time he had experienced the feeling of lust and maybe the last. For the moment the young man forgot not only all about God, he wasn't even thinking of food. The two things that had always controlled his mind seemed never to have existed as, eyes glued to her buttocks, he moved like a zombie behind the girl as she disappeared into the old tabernacle.

Once inside he never saw the maiden again. Years later, as he would secretly relive the moment, he thought it more than possible she was an angel sent by God who obviously required his presence. If this were the case, she was undoubtedly pulled back up to heaven as soon as she had completed her mission.

Immediately upon entering, young Leroy was grabbed by two strong men and carried forward to the front of the tabernacle's interior. There he was flung down of top of the 'Moaner's' bench.

Out of the corner of hie eye, in the sawdust pit of repentance next to the bench he saw the wife of a Bugtussle neighbor. Her name was Eunice Gilliam. Eunice, along with some other women he knew, was writhing about and talking in tongues as she attempted to accept the Savior.

The terrified tubby teen had no time to say hello. He was frantically attempting to scramble to his feet and get his fat posterior out of there.

He lost his balance and fell, landing flat on his beefy back atop the bench. At that precise moment, a flock of shrouded old crones had converged upon the struggling fat boy from every direction, pinning him down. They were also talking in tongues.

The crowd of crones parted as the evangelist whose name Brother Roy still cannot remember, surged forward. Both hands of the man of the cloth held live, hissing copperheads.

Leroy, rolling away from the hissing revolting reptiles, tumbled awkwardly off the bench. He landed once again on his back. This time he found himself in the sawdust pit where Eunice, the neighbor's wife, still writhed about.

The possessed lady was on her feet now and he was directly beneath her. The boy's eyes were wide and full of total terror as he looked up.

Suddenly, a calmness fell over him. He was no longer afraid.

The Bugtussle neighbor's wife had either failed to wear any underpants on that day or they had somehow been lost in the turmoil of becoming a 'Friend of Jesus.' Whatever the previous scenario, there were none to obstruct young Ogle's view as he gazed up between her splayed legs.

Were a qualified doctor of medicine to have been afforded the same view at exactly the same precise second, he or she would have undoubtedly diagnosed the woman as being in the process of having an orgasm. That would have been the scientific explanation, but the fat kid from Bugtussle knew immediately what was really going on.

God had finally made an appearance. It was the moment he had longed for and dreamed about. Leroy Ogles had at long last, communicated with the Supreme Being. It could be nothing else.

The hefty man-child had such an air of serenity on his face as he rose, that all within the tabernacle backed away from him in awe. Even the copperheads in the evangelist's clutches began to cower.

He had entered that building as a timid boy. He walked out as a man with purpose. At that moment he changed his name to Roy.

Brother Roy Ogles knew now what he was destined to do with this life. He knew now that you talk to God. God does not talk to you. If God hears you He will send a sign.

The message he had received while lying in the pit of repentance couldn't have been more clear. God had seen fit to commit his energies to Roy Ogles. For that reason, Roy Ogles must return the favor.

Some of the teenagers who loved to do awful things to the Ogles boy were gathered around the tabernacle entrance as he walked out into the night air. There was something about his new demeanor they had never seen before. None could put a finger on it, but all backed away and let him pass without incident. The days of losing his pants and the other awful pranks were over.

Much to his father's dismay, his son Leroy, who would now only answer to the name Roy, through literature obtain from the 'Friends of Jesus' gathering, managed to locate a seminary in northern California.

The institution regarded devotion to the Lord the predominate enrolment prerequisite. A high school diploma was all that was required in the way of formal education to satisfy the laws of the state. His grades in the academics didn't really matter as long as he was a graduate and those in power at the seminary were convinced those who wished to devote their lives to the Supreme Being were sincere.

After receiving a letter from the young man, the seminary officials were so impressed they even agreed to waive tuition. In spite of his failing marks, the teachers of Bugtussle High, not wanting to put up with the fat kid another

102

year had already decided he would graduate anyway. God had cleared the path.

The following spring, Roy Ogles, carrying with him an extremely close personal relationship with the Holy Father, went west to become His personal messenger.

In California, the young man not only answered his calling to walk hand in hand with God, he also discovered Fruit Loops. A nourishing food not nearly as bulky as hamburgers, hot dogs or slices of pizza. They were especially delicious with gravy, but they could also be carried about and munched like popcorn and were not nearly so messy.

Shortly thereafter, his biological father, Earnest, so ashamed of what his son had elected to do with his life, had first shot his wife and then himself.

Both were found dead by their neighbor, Eunice Gilliam whose husband was unaware she had ever been to a place called Vinegar Hill.

Brother Roy had taken his parents' demise as another positive sign from God. In spite of his father's rejection of the Supreme Power, the good Lord, in his forgiving way had seen fit to take both the man and Roy's mother into his embrace and escort them both off to that far better place anyway.

In His infinite wisdom, the Creator had seen fit to perform this miraculous task even before their scheduled time. What could be more wonderful?

He didn't return to Oklahoma, even for the funeral. Upon fulfilling the requirements that made him a full-fledged messenger of God in the state of California, he had headed for the Owens Valley. Ogle's now deceased mother had relatives there.

For a short time he had stayed with his cousin Heffaroid Hogg in their shack above Dirty Socks Lake. The shabby dwelling was below the borax mine Heffaroid had been attempting to operate since all the silver mines in the area had shut down.

That had not been a pleasant experience but through the grace of God, the pastor of Lone Pine's Devotion to Divinity Church soon had a heart attack. Brother Roy had immediately moved into the parsonage behind the house of worship. He had been tending this flock ever since.

While he wasn't actually loved, he was feared and respected by the Devotion to Divinity congregation.

Gone forever was the fat boy from Bugtussle with whom nobody wished to be seen for such a long a period of time. Brother Roy Ogles was considered now by those who attended his church a man who not only preached the word of the Lord, but one with almost uncanny direct contact with the Supreme Being.

They marveled at his ability to communicate so freely with God. It was as if Brother Roy had enjoying personal conversations with the Creator ever since he was born. Those who believed in him yearned to share his secret.

The monstrous man of the cloth was not about to divulge the clandestine knowledge gleaned in that tabernacle years ago in Oklahoma. He was aware he had learned the secret to the Divinity's most admirable trait but he was not about to share it. If God meant for others to know, they would be informed by God, not Brother Roy Ogles. The Reverend truly believed this was in keeping with His wishes.

The secret is simple. God never talks back. He only listens. This knowledge in itself, gave Brother Roy tremendous superiority. Others waited for their answer from the Divinity before making another request.

Their gigantic pastor always kept on moving forward, still talking, asking for more. It was only logical to assume he had already received his missive while they, in turn, were placed on hold.

There was no doubt in Brother Roy's head that God did listen to him more than others. He had witnessed far too many signs for this not to be true.

Granted, there were times when Brother Roy wished the Lord would have acted on the advice given to him by the large man who was now an established Lone Pine leader of religion in a more orderly and speedier fashion. However, the pastor knew God had a lot on His plate and he forgave Him.

Brother Roy just took great comfort in the fact that he and the Holy Spirit were on the same side. Considering the Lord's limitations, while all other creatures on this earth were definitely inferior, the good Reverend felt that he and God were relatively equal.

Brother Roys' jovial, flabby face resemble a condescending, yet gracious, huge flesh colored meringue pie above his white clerical collar as he smiled and shook hands with his handful of parishioners before they entered his small house of worship. The long, flowing, deep purple robes that covered his immense body consisted of more material than the fabrication requirements for three Boy Scout pup tents.

A bell beneath the steeple of the small structure behind him rang out welcoming support to his actions as he greeted the people of Lone Pine.

He wished there were more of the towns population who had enough sense to realize that the word of God and the word of Reverend Ogles were one and the same.

He'd begun holding two Sunday services instead of one. Even though most attended both, the collection plate had still been a little light lately.

The entire town seemed to be filled with the melodious ringing sound, as was customary on Sunday mornings. In reality, Lone Pine did not boast an over abundance of churches; those existing just seemed to possess very loud bells.

Brother Roy resented the interference of those hollow metallic devices in the belfries of the other Lone Pine houses of worship scattered about town. His was the only church for true believers. The large pastor had engaged in more than one conversation with God on this very subject.

The lord knew the condition of his collection plates. He really needed to do something about it. The other centers of prayer for the misguided and obviously naïve, for some reason, still remained open for business.

The Reverend knew, however, that this was only temporary. God moved in mysterious ways. When the day of overdue reckoning did arrive, Brother Roy would be ready to assume his small town position of superiority.

In the meantime, he was still in possession of his pocket knife. Sometimes, for old times sake, he would roam the streets of Lone Pine late at night and slice into the tread of an occasional tire belonging to the automobiles of rival clergymen. This gave him comfort until the time arrived when he would be duty bound to take over everything.

Brother Roy was fully aware of this upcoming divine duty and he was ready to assume command. He felt certain there was no other ordained minister of Christianity anywhere to whom God had sent his first message from between a pair of female legs. The only exception might have been the personal Son of the Creator, Jesus Christ Himself.

The fleshy face of the pastor of Lone Pine's Devotion to Divinity Church broke into an even broader conglomeration of pleased, oversized fatty tissues as he looked beyond the small crowd in front of him.

His first cousin, Heffaroid Hogg and his sweet sisters with whom he had lived for a short time years ago when first arriving in the Owens Valley were in town. He could see them climbing out of a dilapidated relic, that at onetime, may have been referred to as a truck.

The decrepit, mutilated machine had evidently just arrived at the curb of the street beyond his church. The Reverend's relatives had obviously come to hear his sermon this morning. That didn't happen every Sunday and their presence on this one pleased him very much.

Brother Roy murmured a soft 'Thank you' to his Good Buddy above for keeping the engine in the old Hogg truck from falling apart during the trip.

Catch Pen and Squeeze Chute, whom Brother Roy always referred to as his own darling nieces, even though in reality they were also his first cousins like Heffaroid, still lived in that shack with their brother near the Hogg Borax mine above Dirty Socks Lake.

The same humble dwelling which they had, at one time many years ago, been gracious enough to share with him, cramped though the quarters were. His sweet nieces were but little girls then. Time does fly when you work hand in hand along with the Lord.

He moved forward to greet them. While all four shared certain facial similarities, the resemblance in size alone was uncanny. There would be no room for Brother Roy in that shack now.

The collar button and its corresponding hole of the freshly washed, albeit stained and wrinkled, white shirt Heffaroid was wearing, failed miserably to meet beneath the man's multitude of jowls.

Nonetheless, the big borax miner from Dirty Socks Lake was sporting a tie for this special occasion; most of which was tucked into the bib of his tight fitting, faded and patched faded blue Duckbill overalls.

His sisters' extremely full figured bodies that had been so prominently displayed in the altogether at the lake the evening before, were now totally covered.

Each wore a long shapeless shift that started just beneath the triple chins of their firm, pretty round faces and billowed downward. The garments of each concealed even the bottoms of their plump ankles.

Both large young women avoided Brother Roy's eyes as the pastor met them in the middle of the churchyard.

"Happy Sabbath, Cousin Heffaroid!" Brother Roy said heartily, as he thrust his ham like hand forward to be shaken by Heffaroids, which seemed to be of equal size.

"Glad you and my sweet little nieces could make it to hear His words and mine."

The eyes of the giant in overalls registered absolutely no pleasantry as he gave his two sisters a look of open shame.

"It's because of my sisters we're here, Cousin Brother Roy. They done somthin' awful yesterday. They let the Maynard brothers see em' nekid. Some other fella too. You gotta pray up somthin' to make it right."

Brother Roy quickly pulled the mammoth trio away from the others entering the church. He desperately hoped none of his parishioners had heard his cousin's words. News traveled fast in the Owens Valley. Recounting this particular kind of current event could have an effect on the collection plate.

"The Maynards are sinful disciples of Satan himself!" said Brother Roy, lowering his voice in spite of the fact that he was speaking with a vengeance. He was looking directly into the reddening, ashamed faces of Catch Pen and Squeeze Chute. "The fact that they travel about openly with a cloven hoofed creature, created exclusively by Him Above to be slaughtered and eaten, symbolizes their devotion to the Devil," the Reverend continued.

It was rare when spouting the ways of the Lord that Brother Roy didn't somehow manage to bring up the subject of food. It was also not the first time that the Reverend had made it known that he, personally, would delight in being the chosen one to devour Farley Maynard's curly tailed companion.

The one time fat boy from Bugtussle was infuriated every time he saw anyone making a pet out of anything that God had meant to be eaten.

"The Maynards are destined to burn forever in the fires of Hell!!" Brother Roy concluded.

"I was thinkin' on more of maybe a punishment for em' here on earth. Fore that time comes, Cousin," said Heffaroid.

"We'll talk of this later. After my sermon. After I've passed the plate and the others have returned to their homes," replied Brother Roy as his eyes lit on two old lady late comers walking up the path from the street.

He reached into a hidden pocket of his large flowing robe for the stash Fruit Loops he kept there. One so large needed constant nourishment when constantly carrying out the wishes of himself and the Lord.

"Go inside and be seated. May God have mercy on your dear sweet souls!" He added to his round, embarrassed nieces as they headed into the church.

The three large bodies became temporarily wedged in the doorway as all tried to enter at the same time.

Above the struggling trio, the bells in the church of Brother Roy's belfry kept right on ringing.

CHAPTER NINE
REALITY SUCKS

The bells above the Devotion to Divinity House of worship continued to peal, combined with those of the others. Even after Heffaroid and his sisters made it through the doorway, the instruments kept right on calling out to all residents of Lone Pine so their souls might be saved.

This metallic ringing could not only be heard outside all over town, but also inside many buildings. Especially one particular structure in a different neighborhood.

This edifice boasted neither bells nor belfries. However it had been erected originally long ago for much the same purpose as those that did.

Under ordinary circumstances, Rodney would have found the melodious ringing pleasant to his ears. On this particular morning, he hated them.

They were responsible for waking him up and revealing reality to his suffering soul. The memory of what he desperately wanted to be just another egregious nightmare had actually happened.

He, Rodney Van Aukin, the young attorney with such a promising future, was incarcerated. Any doubt that he might really be elsewhere was totally erased as he looked up and saw outside sunlight drifting in through thick, steel vertical bars.

This particular assemblage of hideous lack of liberty barriers was embedded in the frame of a two feet square window built into the wall above the foot of the uncomfortable concrete slab he had been told was a cot that he was now lying on. He was locked up behind not only these bars, but also those on the far side of this above ground dungeon. There was no way out.

The other bars looked like those he'd seen imprisoning animals at the zoo. They reached from floor to ceiling and seemed to go on forever. Their function was to separate the rows of awful cells such as the one he was now sharing with the Maynard brothers and the pig, from a long corridor that led onward between the caged cubicles for common criminals.

Those poor women were also locked up in one of these human vivariums somewhere down that dismal hallway. He tried not to think about the ladies. Right now Rodney had himself to worry about. Although he was trained to get other people out of places like this, he wasn't quite sure what to do when he, himself was the victim.

Even if it hadn't been Sunday, he wouldn't have the nerve to call either of his immediate superiors in Century City. How could he explain to them how he managed to end up in this unthinkable dilemma, when even he couldn't figure it out?

He supposed that eventually he would have to call Louise, although he had no idea what he could possibly say to her when he did. Poor Rodney was a man of far too many questions right now with absolutely no answers.

He had been able to persuade the sheriff to let him bring along his briefcase when they had all been arrested and marched out of the motor home. It was now somewhere in the frontal interior of this dreadful institution of confinement along with his other belongings except for his clothing, which he was surprised they allowed him to continue wearing.

He'd had visions the night before of being forced into some sort of prison uniform when he was literally thrown into the police car shortly after they were arrested. He probably shouldn't have told that county sheriff his profession. It really hadn't seemed to impress the official.

An unpleasant aroma hung over everything around him. The odor was growing increasingly more predominant as the day outside, and consequently, the inside of the cell, grew warmer. How much of that foul scent belonged personally to him, Rodney wasn't certain.

The sheep stench and cologne residue from the day before were both still very much with the young lawyer. He felt positively filthy from the top of his head all the way down to the soles of his feet. He desperately needed to bathe and his teeth felt as if each one were wearing grimy little corduroy jackets.

Actually, the smell in spite of its undeniable loathsomeness, didn't seem to bother him nearly as much as his other problems. Perhaps deep depression desensitized the inner organs of the nose.

Rodney struggled up to a sitting position on the jail house cot. He now sat with his back to the cell's outer wall facing the rest of the caged enclosure. The first thing he saw was Barney.

The pig's whole body seemed to be shaking as he drank from the lidless commode. This facility for human waste disposal was the only one present inside this particular perimeter of the wall behind him and bars in every other direction beyond. It was filthy and situated in the corner of the cell nearest where the depressed young man was sitting.

The sight of the pig drinking out of the toilet bothered him much more than the smells. He was fortunate not to be feeling the aftermath of that beer that had put his brain into such a tail spin last night, but now, looking at what Barney was doing, his stomach was becoming more than just a little queasy.

Obviously the inner organs down in that portion of his body hadn't undergone any form of desensitization. He needed to think about something else, and quickly.

He began to take stock of the condition of his other companions of confinement. Strangely enough, he began to feel slightly better in comparison. Even the tremendous mental anguish he was suffering, combined with the mild revulsion in his digestive system, couldn't be that much worse than the obvious, severe physical discomfort they were experiencing.

Rodney had suffered through just enough hangovers in his short lifetime that he could not only readily recognize, but also remember all too well, the symptoms. He'd hate to have that misfortune added to his already insurmountable list of miseries this morning. He felt thankful that he hadn't really joined in on any of the previous evening's astounding alcohol consumption.

It had definitely been one of his more intelligent decisions when he'd made up his mind never to drink the stuff again in any great quantity, since the day after he arrived in Los Angeles from Boston.

Of the three, Barney appeared to be in worst shape. The poor porker, evidently finished slurping the disgusting commode water for the moment, staggered to the front of the cell next to the large, locked barred gate leading out into the corridor between the rows of cages.

With a plaintive grunt, that sounded more like a groan, the creature with the round pink snout and the cloven hooves flopped down on its belly. Mercifully, he seemed to go to sleep immediately. In reality, it hurt too much for the pig to keep his eyes open.

In the other two bunks across from Rodney's, the globular organs of Trux and Farley were not only open, they were glazed and bloodshot. Both stared vacantly up at the ceiling. Outside, most of the bells had ceased to peal, but at least two in the distance continued to ring.

Prior to being hauled away to the slammer from the wrecked motor home the night before after his aisle acrobatics, Trux had been allowed to dress. Possibly he should have kept his clothing off. His apparel hadn't exactly looked like something out of Esquire Magazine before, but now, like those of Rodney and his brother, his garments were wrinkled and grungy.

His square jawed face also looked as if it had been slept in. It was more than apparent the man was hurting. Still, he seemed not to be feeling quite as much pain as was his brother.

Almost nothing could have possibly made Farley appear more miserable. The bearded man moaned pathetically as he gingerly rubbed the top of his shaggy head with a trembling hand.

"Will you shut up?" Trux finally spoke, giving his brother a dirty look. "I'm tryin' to listen to the damned church bells!"

"Fuck off and die! You oughta hear the bells inside my head!" lamented Farley.

Barney finally risked opening an eye. With much effort, he rose to his feet again and moved on all four unsteady legs toward Farley's cot. Once there, the pig laid his own aching head on his moaning master's salient stomach.

Beyond the barred window beneath where Rodney remained sitting, the bells finally stopped tolling. Another sound immediately replaced the first.

This one was high pitched and squeaky. Rodney seemed to remember hearing it earlier before he was fully awake.

The noise continued, echoing inward from the corridor beyond the bars, growing louder until it was directly in front the cell of egregious suffering. All occupants looked toward the source.

The squeaking came to an end as a uniformed red headed man, who appeared to be about the same age as Rodney, brought the rusty wheeled, metal cart he had been pushing to a halt beyond the tall gate.

A tall thermos jug and two large aluminum kettles rested on top of the squeaky wheeled contraption. Next to these were other items consisting of a stack of dingy looking crockery plates, some spoons, a long wooden handled ladle and three bent and battered tin cups. Hanging from a rung near the top of the cart's surface was a long greasy pair of metal tongs.

"Mornin' Trux. Mornin' Farley. Sure am sorry to see you boys in here again," Jiggs called in though the bars.

"Especially you, Barney," the Deputy added as his eyes scanned the cell, looking to see what kind of mess that pig had left for him to clean up this time.

Sure enough, a small pile of runny manure was undeniably visible in the far corner of the cell opposite the commode. The young assistant lawman felt fairly certain it hadn't been left there by either of the Maynard brothers or the other guy.

Behind the bars, Rodney followed the lawman's searching gaze. As he saw what Jiggs was looking at with his own eyes, he silently added one more definite component to the mixture of odors permeating the jail house atmosphere.

"I better clean that up before I feed you folks," Jiggs sounded none too happy as he started to unlock the gate.

"Hell with that! First things first!" said Trux emphatically. The broad shouldered Lone Pine City Jail detainee dismissed Barney's telltale mess with a nonchalant wave of his hand.

"Whatcha got?" he asked as he rose to his feet and lumbered to the barred gate.

Jiggs heaved a sigh of at least temporary relief as he turned and picked up the lid of one of the kettles on top of the cart with one hand. He lifted the pair of tongs from the rung on the contraption with his other.

The deputy then stuck the separated ends of the tongs inside the big open round metallic vessel as he answered the big chinned Maynard brother's question.

"Just like always, Trux. We got umbrella steak, then we got umbrella steak. The ladies Arty brought in here with you last night said it made em' wanna puke, so it's all yours."

Rodney didn't hear the last part of Jiggs' retort. He'd quit listening when he heard the word steak. A good steak just might settle the queasiness in his stomach. He hoped whoever had prepared the piece of meat hadn't overcooked it. Then he looked through the bars again.

Outside the cell, Jiggs, with the tongs, was withdrawing two greasy, pathetic fried and buckled slices of bologna which he proceeded to slap down on one of the plates. He repeated this action until four plates were covered with the nauseous looking processed luncheon meat.

"Umbrella steaks!" Trux's deep voice held a tiny note of enthusiasm in spite of his hangover.

"What the Hell! At least you're still servin' somethin' fit to eat in this shithouse! Hurry it up Jiggs! A man could starve to death the way you fuck around."

Rodney continued to stare through the bars in disbelief at Jiggs. The redheaded lawman now was dipping the wooden ladle into the other pot which he had rendered lidless. The large spoon resurfaced filled with a thick and slimy lumpy substance which Jiggs proceeded to pour over the pathetic greasy slabs of bologna on the plates.

"Gravy looks good this mornin," said Tux before looking back and calling to his suffering bearded brother.

"Best move your scrawny ass and get your fat gut over here Farley!"

Rodney looked at the pile of swine feces in the corner of the cell as Farley struggled to his feet and moved gingerly, with Barney beside him, to the front of the caged enclosure to join Trux and Jiggs.

He then turned his head and looked at what had been referred to as 'Umbrella Steaks' on one of the plates Jiggs was now handing through the bars. The concoction looked disgustingly similar to the manure.

Barney evidently failed to share the young barrister's opinion. As the pig reached the bars, he stuck his snout eagerly between his Daddy Farley and his Uncle Trux and grunted. He wanted to make sure Jiggs didn't forget him.

Barney knew that with rising prices, the county couldn't afford to buy bologna with pork or beef in it. They always served turkey bologna in the Lone Pine jail.

As a rule, Barney never ate the flesh of any animal, but turkeys were different. Daddy Farley had convinced his beloved four legged companion long ago that it was okay to eat them. Turkeys had no souls.

He didn't consider what other animal flesh ingredients might be mixed in with the gravy. A hungry pig with a hangover, only recently awakened in a jail meant for humans, can't be expected to think of everything.

"Come on Rod. You gotta eat," Trux called over his shoulder. Farley, still looking very much like he was ready to attend his own funeral, bent over and placed an overflowing plate in front of Barney before accepting one for himself. His hands continued to shake.

"I'm not very hungry," the unhappy young man replied as he twisted about. He was trying very hard to find something to look at in these surroundings that might take his mind off both the food being served through those bars and the gooey lumps of excretion lying in the corner.

They were the first words he'd spoken since awakening in this dreadful place. He had to count his blessings in spite of everything. At least he hadn't stammered.

"That's bullshit!!" said Trux, walking toward him from the bars with another of the filled plates and a tin cup containing a murky black liquid.

"Here. Take this un'. See how the boloney bucks up like that when its been fried? Looks a little like an umbrella don't it? That's how come they call em' 'Umbrella Steaks'. That oughta' appeal to a guy like you from LA. Hangin' out at the beach and all."

Rodney could only stare. He had no comment. The detailed etymology regarding how that mess in the plate Trux was offering him came by its name, made it no less disgusting .

"Gottcha' some coffee too. I'll get some more for my own self. Like I said. Gotta eat," he continued as he placed the plate, spoon and cup in Rodney's hands.

"Long as you ain't got no buzz goin' to fuck up, that is!" The well meaning red neck added over his shoulder as he returned to the gate and the still waiting young man in uniform who waited behind the bars with yet another dish filled with the day's delicacy.

The youngest prisoner in the Lone Pine jail that morning, looked and, indeed felt like he might well vomit at any minute.

Fighting down the revulsion welling up from inside, he carefully set the cup on the cot's edge between the metal and the mattress.

Averting his eyes and holding the plate at arm's length, Rodney somehow managed to stand. He then also mustered up both coordination and strength to cross on unsteady legs to where Barney was in the process of gobbling down his first helping. The pig gladly accepted a second as the suffering young man set it down in front of his round, pink snout. The animals curtly tail waved about as he grunted in gratitude. Barney was well on his way to recovery.

The incarcerated barrister with the flip flopping inner organs then handed the unused spoon to Jiggs through the bars.

Staggering back to the mattress covered concrete slab, he managed to despondently reseat himself. He reached down and picked up the cup. The brown stuff inside it didn't taste much like coffee, and it was only lukewarm. Rodney placed the remainder beneath the bunk.

He stared off into space, calling on all his available mental facilities to will his intestines to cease dancing the rumba.

"Say, Trux," Jiggs said, attempting to sound casual as he prepared the cart for its return trip back to the main part of the sheriff's station. "I been thinking…"

"That's the kinda shit'll get ya in trouble, Jiggs," Trux responded amiably over his shoulder while he and Farley returned to their own cots, balancing full plates, spoons and tin cups in their arms. Somehow both reached their destinations without spilling too much. They sat down, preparing to eat breakfast.

Jiggs laughed and hesitated for a second. Then he called back.

"Arty'd be pissed if he knew I done it, but I called Irene's mamma for her a little while ago…."

"Who the hell's Irene?" asked Farley who looked like it was painful to even open his mouth wide enough to get the spoon in, let alone find it, with his trembling hand.

"I think that's the name of that sweet young thing you fell in love with last night, Farley," Trux informed him.

"Oh her," said his brother, groaning slightly as he forced the spoonful of gravy soaked fried bologna in past his teeth after he was able to get the food up to his mouth. "I forgot. I ain't been well, ya know."

"Anyway," Jiggs said. The Deputy was beginning to look none too sure of himself, as he attempted to continue his original train of thought. "I could do the same for you boys. I mean, if you wanted me to call Arthell, I'd….."

Inside the cell, the Maynard brothers, both their breakfasts totally forgotten, turned and looked at the Deputy at exactly the same time.

"You got her phone number?" asked Trux. All friendliness was gone from his voice.

"You carryin' it around in your damned pocket?" Farley's gravely tones sounded even less amicable than those just passed between the lips of his brother.

"Of course not. I don't have her number. Why would I? I only spoke to her once. That day you were all at the county fair. I just thought if you wanted to give it to me, I'd…."

"Trux just told you about that thinkin' crap!" Farley interrupted. "Don't you never bother her. She ain't got nothin' to do with this shit!"

"She ain't got nothin' to do with you neither!" chimed in Trux. "She's a nice girl!"

On the other side of the bars, Jiggs was obviously regretting he'd ever broached the subject.

"I know that, Trux. I wasn't just thinkin' her anyway. About her only I mean. Who I was really thinkin' of callin'…. ," Jiggs winced. He'd used that word again. He'd used it twice. "Forget I brought it up," the embarrassed red young official with the red hair finished lamely.

"We'll do that! You just remember not to never even think about callin' her no more!! Or nothin' else neither!" Trux snapped.

What the angry lantern jawed red neck had just said made absolutely no sense to Rodney.

However, Jiggs, the other young man present seemed to know exactly what the older man was talking about. He also looked like he was fully aware that the subject, whatever it may have been, was closed and should remain that way.

"Guess I better get back to work," the much-humbled uniformed Deputy replied quickly.

The loud squeaking noise filled the corridor and all the nearby cells again as he began pushing the cart back toward the main part of the sheriff's station. He mumbled an additional awkward farewell as he made his hasty retreat.

"I'll be back for the dishes and spoons in a little bit. I'll try to bring you some more coffee if there's any left. Oh, I'll clean up Barney's mess then, too."

"I'll talk to Barney. See can he have another one ready for ya'. Make it worth your while," Farley called after him. The cranky tone in the bearded red neck's voice seemed to vanish as rapidly as it had materialized. His last comment sounded almost jovial and he turned immediately back to his fried bologna and gravy.

Evidently the short surge of adrenaline caused by brief irritation, had a positive effect on his nervous system. His hand no longer shook as he lifted the spoon.

Trux seemed to have also forgotten the issue already as he chewed away at his breakfast. It still looked like hog manure to Rodney.

The young lawyer couldn't quite figure what had just happened. He thought for only a second, about asking whom this person Arthell might be, but too many other things weighed heavily on his mind at the moment. The name seemed to have an unsettling effect on both of them anyway.

Trux looked at Farley between mouthfuls of umbrella steak and the dark brown stuff in the tin cup. He shook his blond curly head sadly.

"God. Farley, you really do look bad. If I'd known you was gonna live this long I'da took better care of ya."

"I never dreamed this simple assignment would lead to jail," Rodney had made the statement to himself. He didn't even realize he had spoken out loud until Trux responded.

"Ain't bad as jail goes," said Trux. "You oughta do a couple days in the Darwin slammer. Right Farley?"

"Fuckin right! This sum bitch is a regular Motel Six compared to that shit hole!" Farley was definitely doing better.

Rodney looked at the runny manure, the food the Maynards were eating, and the bars, which seemed to be everywhere. He inhaled the foul air.

"I can't imagine how anything could be worse than this disgusting place," he said with an involuntary shudder.

Trux put his now empty dish and the dirty spoon on his bunk next to his already drained cup, before emitting a loud belch. He rose and began unzipping his fly as he walked in front of Rodney to the commode.

"Believe it Rod," the big chinned Maynard said, suddenly becoming very serious as he began to urinate loudly. "That Darwin jail's built on skids. Sucker's got a wagon tongue in 'er. I ain't shittin' ya. Goddamn wagon tongue. Back in the old days when they still had law there, the marshal used to hitch up a team of mules to that old jail and pull it down the street...."

This was the second time in less than twenty-four hours the Rodney had been forced to move quickly if he wished to avoid being splashed by this man's urine. The young attorney looked past the corridor bars down the dingy hallway as he got up from the cot and backed away.

The women were down there somewhere and they wouldn't have any walls either. Even if they couldn't see what Trux was doing, they would surely hear and know. He was mortified.

Trux continued both with his dissertation and the business of voiding his bladder. As the big man with the mouth full of teeth kept painting his very graphic verbal image, Rodney forgot the women and what was being done in front of his very eyes.

Although he really didn't want to, he started to recall his own terrible recent visit to the town Trux was speaking of and began to, at least partially, believe him.

"That ole marshal. Mean muthafucka he was too. He'd throw the troublemakers in that ole jail, then haul em away with them dumb assed mules. Man. Woman. God damned beast. Your plumbin' didn't make no difference. They all went into that fuckin' jail. Then he'd haul em' out in the hot, cocksuckin' desert. No water and the sun beatin' down on that tin roof... They cooled off! Took the pepper outa their pee pees! Bet your ass on that!"

Farley gave out with a humorless laugh as he stood. "Trux oughta know. Me too. We both been throwed in that sum bitch!"

"Got my first piece of ass in that old jail." Trux said proudly as he replaced his private equipment before zipping up and pushing the flush lever on the commode.

"Caught the clapp too, as I recall," Farley replied in a matter of fact tone as he began unzipping his own fly while moving in front of Trux to take his turn visiting the porcelain goddess.

Trux snorted. He rolled his blue eyes that were becoming remarkably clear as he moved away. He spoke to Rodney again as he indicated his brother with a jerk of his thumb.

"Don't pay no attention to Needle Dick the Bug Fucker there. He only went to school one day in his life. That was the day the teacher was out sick."

Rodney was in no mood for even the slightest frivolity. The young man wouldn't have been able to laugh at a joke had he even been aware Trux was attempting to tell one.

He walked to the front of the cell. He took hold of the bars of the locked gate with each hand and just stared out into the corridor.

He was wishing he could be dead if he couldn't be elsewhere. To make matters worse he'd just remembered that the items 'Bail' or 'Fine' weren't even listed on his expense account sheet.

Farley did get the witticism, and even though he had heard it before, the bearded man still found it to be very funny. He broke into peals of laughter as he stood looking down into the toilet bowl.

"You sum bitch!" Farley managed to blurt out between guffaws, "You make me piss on my hands, I swear I'm gonna wipe em' all over your big ugly chin!"

If the threat worried Trux, he gave no indication. Instead, he stretched his arms toward the ceiling and grinned.

"You know I'm feelin' a whole lot better," he announced. "Bout time to figger on how to get outa this pigsty. No offence, Barney."

The pig was now standing beneath Farley's cot, lapping the dregs of turkey bologna and gravy from his master's plate. He gave his Uncle Trux a look that clearly indicated that no offence was taken.

In spite of the fact that they served a mean umbrella steak right in your room, Barney didn't care much for this hotel either. The bathroom accommodation situation was lousy for pigs. There was also no place in the joint a creature with cloven hooves and a curly tail could get a decent drink.

Trux started to say something else to his brother, but suddenly, all attention was diverted.

The voice of Arty Dubs himself floated in from beyond the corridor bars where Rodney still stood. It sounded hollow and distorted.

The grating, metallic opening of the outer door coming from the direction taken earlier by Jiggs when he wheeled away the food cart obscured the sheriff's actual words.

Trux, along with Farley, who was finished and now attempting to rapidly zip up, hurried to join Rodney at the bars.

In the corridor beyond them, the sheriff was leading a weathered old lady, who appeared to be in at least her late nineties, forward from the big steel door, past the cells.

Both the lawman and the senior citizen pointedly ignored Rodney, Farley and Trux who were looking out through the bars at them. Arty ushered the newcomer past the cell they occupied and continued on down the long hallway between the equally long rows of more bars.

In the very last cell on the right, the ladies from the previous middle of the night HOWDY HOSS incident looked up through their own set of vertical barriers as the lady and the sheriff approached.

The pathetic trio, no longer feeling, and definitely not looking like the party animals they thought themselves to be the night before, rose sheepishly from their respective cots. They hung their heads and tried to put themselves together. It was a losing battle.

The shame faced, bedraggled feminine group inside the cell spoke not a word to each other. They remained silent, yet extremely respectful, as they gratefully acknowledged the presence of the woman much older than any of them, now standing with the sheriff outside their cage.

The humorless eyes of the stern faced wrinkled, mature lady peering in through the bars, focused exclusively on Irene, as the uniformed officer began unlocking the gate between them.

"Irene, you and the girls can go home now," said Arty, sounding very official. "Your Mamma's paid the fines for all of you."

The ancient woman continued to stare at her middle aged, wide hipped daughter as the latter hastily attempted to hide her Spandex support under garment beneath her arm. It wasn't being worn at the moment because she had actually considered strangling herself with it after she had asked Jiggs to make the phone call. When she found she lacked the necessary intestinal fortitude, she'd been so depressed she forgot to put it back on.

Avoiding her mother's accusing stare, Irene stepped out of the cell into the corridor. The others shuffled forward through the open gate behind her.

Irene's mother stepped back beside the sheriff to let the other women precede her on the long walk down the corridor of cages toward the big steel door that led to liberty.

Geraldine was the last to leave the cell. Her short gray hair was no longer curly. Instead, it stuck out straight in a variety of directions from her head. She was also missing the heel of her left shoe.

The short little green-eyed creature looked as if she might be doing a very unflattering imitation of Quasimodo as she and her partners in crime moved past the other cells.

The members of the small, sad parade proceeded onward the end of the hallway and the large steel portal, which was now open. The waiting Jiggs stood framed in its doorway.

All were extremely careful not to even glance in the Maynards' direction as they hurried by them.

Irene's mother, however, did look in through the bars at the brothers. The old lady even stopped in front of their cell as she and Arty brought up the rear of the procession and spoke to them.

"You're the Maynard boys aren't you?" she asked in a sweet, frail voice. "Trux and Farley Maynard?"

Inside the cell both of them grinned. They were obviously proud that their reputations had preceded them.

"Yes Ma'am," they responded in unison.

The senior citizen's voice had lost both sweetness and frailty when she spoke again.

"If either one of you no good filthy bastards ever comes within ten miles of that big assed, dumb shit daughter of mine again, I'm going to take my late husband Threon's gun and blow the balls off both of you!"

Without uttering another word, Irene's aged mother turned and swept down the corridor after the others who were now no longer in sight.

Trux stuck his big chin through the bars and watched both the woman and Jiggs disappear as the deputy pulled the big door shut. The broad shouldered man then turned his attention on Arty, who remained standing outside the cell.

"She just threatened me n' Farley's lives, Arty! You gonna let her get away with that?"

"Sounded more like a promise to me. Hope she keeps it. Ten miles ain't much of a radius for ole Irene. That girl gets around."

Trux turned back to find Rodney finally using the cell's lone facility now that the women were gone.

"Hey Rod! You're the hotshot lawyer. Don't what that old gash just said constitute a threat?"

Rodney was only thankful that he had nearly finished before the others realized what he'd been doing. He kept his back to them as he completed what else needed to be done before closing his trousers.

"I..I'm sorry. I wasn't really listening."

"Some God damned lawyer you are," spat out Farley. "Whose side you on anyway?"

Fortunately for the terribly uncomfortable young man, Arty Dubs came to the rescue.

"Enough of this bullshit! You know the drill. You get one God damn phone call. It's now or never, slime suckers. I'm a busy man!"

"Okay! Okay!" said Trux. "Shouldn't be that big a deal. We'll just pay the God damned fines. How much cash me'n Farley have on us when we checked in here last night, Arty?"

"You kiddin'? You was flat broke. Like always."

"Gotta be somethin' wrong here," said Trux suspiciously before turning to his brother. "You couldn't of spent no two hundred dollars on booze."

Farley kneeled to scratch the pig on its nose. "Nah, I think it was more like two hundred and two and maybe fifty five or fifty six cents. Billy Bob over at the Booze Barn said he'd float us for the extra, so I wasn't payin' too much attention."

Trux seemed to relax. "Well, so long as Billy Bob ain't gonna be on our backs for the balance..." He turned back to the sheriff. "How much of that booze was left?"

"Anything wasn't broke, I had Jiggs pour it out," replied Arty, obviously eager to answer the question.

"You really are a first rate asshole, Arty."

Arty seemed to take the square jawed prisoner's observation on his character as a compliment.

"I try Trux. You're just lucky I didn't impound that piece of shit you and your spinached-mugged brother drive around in. I would have if Larry's wrecker hadn't been tied up pullin' some numb nuts outa the ditch up Bishop Way. Still will, it ain't pried loose from that boulder fore sundown. Ole Larry'd love to get his hands on that rig of yours after you pricks ripped him off for that tank of gas."

"Larry Peterson's one of the biggest God damned thieves in the Owens Valley. He's always fuckin' somebody. Sellin' em' shit they don't need. Puttin' parts in their cars that don't work. He's done it to us even. Me n' Farley was just fuckin' im' back."

"Might even throw in an extra ticket for defacing public property to boot," Arty continued, as if Trux hadn't spoken. "How's my asshole status doin' Trux? Improvin' I hope."

"Well shit!" Trux said, trying to figure things out. "How the Hell we gonna get anything done if we don't even have a lousy dime for a fuckin' phone call?"

"You're a dinosaur Trux," said the sheriff. He shook his head in wonder.

The man on the other side of the bars from him was truly ignorant. "Phone costs a quarter these days. Why don't you hit up your partner there? The big time city shyster? He's got enough money to cut you all loose in an envelope out there. Looks like he might be just stupid enough to do it."

Lights suddenly flashed in both of Trux's blue eyes. He wheeled around toward Rodney who was holding his hands out awkwardly; having discovered there was no place to wash them. Farley also rose to his feet and turned to look at the young lawyer.

"Shit! I'd forgot! For all practical purposes that's our money anyway, ain't it?" Trux asked Rodney.

"I....I guess it is. After you sign the papers in my briefcase, of course." It was ironic. They were about to go free because of the money in his envelope. Rodney, however, would still be behind these bars.

At least he was about to accomplish his mission. Surely the Herkimers would take that into consideration. No matter how disappointed they might in him as a lawyer, surely they would come to his aid when they found out what he had been forced to go through before he ended up in this awful place.

Trux tuned back to the bars and the sheriff, who was growing visibly impatient beyond them.

"You heard the man!" Trux barked. "Bring him his God damned briefcase!"

"Just a minute, Trux," said Farley. "I ain't sure we oughta' do no business in jail."

"What crawled up your ass?" Trux responded, now nearly yelling at his brother. "You wanna stay in this puke palace?"

"You know I don't, but it don't seem right somehow makin' a deal in the slammer."

"It ain't right! And it ain't gonna happen!" announced Arty, taking command. "I think it's illegal, and if it ain't, I know it's un-American! I don't know what this is all about and I don't wanna'. Don't make no never mind. I'm tellin' all of you, right here and now, ain't nobody walkin' outa my jail with more money than he come in with! City dude's stupid enough to loan you two deadbeats the bread that's a different story. But you ain't signin' no deals in my jail! Now I'm getting' tired of this shit!" He called past the Maynards and the pig to Rodney.

"How about it Mister? You gonna bail em' out?"

"I'm sorry. I can't even use that money to bail myself out." Rodney felt totally deflated. For a fleeting moment he'd thought he was making progress. Now he was back to square zero. "It wasn't entrusted to me for that purpose."

"What the Hell you talkin' about?" demanded Trux.

"I can't spend money that isn't mine." Rodney attempted to explain. "I do have a little of my own out there with the rest of my property. I know I can let you have enough for that phone call you were just...."

"Kiss my ass!" said Trux. The punk had eighteen hundred dollars in an envelope out front with his name on it and here he was talking chump change. He turned to his brother. "Can you believe this shit?"

Farley seemed not to hear. The slightly older, bearded Maynard was looking at Rodney, giving the young man what seemed to be a very pensive appraisal.

Rodney heaved a deep sigh. Nobody understood his position. He looked past the angry Trux and spoke to the sheriff. "I would like to exercise my right to make my one phone call now, please."

"Asshole!" said Trux.

"Maybe not Trux," Farley mused quietly. His voice was so soft that only his brother could hear him. "An asshole'd get hisself out and leave us in here. Maybe he's just an honest dumb shit. That don't make him a bad person. The world could use a few more honest dumb shits."

Trux hated it when Farley threw tidbits of logic into the middle of one of his tirades. Especially when they required too much heavy thought for a snap judgment.

His expression remained surly, but the hatred was gone from his blue eyes as he looked at the lawyer again.

"You can make the call in here if you want," said Arty. "I'll have Jiggs bring in your fancy cell phone if..."

Rodney never gave the sheriff a chance to finish his sentence. He walked quickly toward the barred gate.

"No! I'll use a pay phone. And I'd like to wash my hands if I may."

Arty shrugged and unlocked the gate. Farley called after the confused young man as he walked out into the corridor and the sheriff re-locked the hinged and barred barrier. "Rod... Would you mind bringin' Barney some water back?"

"Sure Farley," said Rodney. He turned back immediately. He was not only thankful that at least one of the brothers was still speaking to him, he really did think fresh water for the pig was a good idea. He then addressed the sheriff. "Do you have some sort of a bowl or...?"

"Oh Jesus Jefferson Clinton!" Arty fairly exploded. "I'll have Jiggs bring the God damned pig some God damned water! Now get your sissy city shit together and come on, or I'm gonna throw you back in there and you can shove your phone call up your ass!"

"Pig don't need no water," Trux said, attempting a sneer that didn't quite make it as he thoughtfully watched Rodney being led away by Arty. "Been drinkin' outa' the crapper all night."

122

Barney looked up at the big chinned Red Neck. Humans often said one thing when they were thinking something else. It was a rarity for his Uncle Trux, but then he too, was only human. He couldn't help it.

Both Uncle Trux and Daddy Farley knew how to get them out of here. One of them would end up doing what they always did when they ended up in these kinds of places.

It was something neither of them wanted to do. Their reason for avoiding the obvious until they explored all other options which never worked wasn't clear to Barney. It was tied into something they both called manhood. The pig didn't quite understand. But then that's probably because he was indeed a pig and not a man. However, they would get out of here. Of that he was certain. In the meantime, until they made up their minds, now that he felt better, maybe he could get some decent sleep.

CHAPTER TEN
QUEEN OF HEARTS IN A DECK OF JOKERS

"While you're back there, take that stupid pig some fresh water."

Arty stood behind the booking desk of the outer office of the sheriff's station. He looked disgusted with himself for even having made such a statement.

Rodney's briefcase, the envelope, still filled with hundred dollar bills, the young attorney's wristwatch and another small pile of cash including some change lay in front of him.

Rodney himself was still behind bars, although this part of the building's interior looked far less dismal and ominous than his recent surroundings. At least before he'd been placed in this newest cage, he'd been allowed to go into a decent restroom and wash his hands.

The young attorney now occupied a holding facility in full view of the counter the sheriff was standing behind as the official gathered up Rodney's belongings and proceeded to put them back into a large envelope. The owner of that property, in turn, was putting money into a pay telephone attached to the wall within the cage he now occupied. He seemed to be experiencing difficulty getting the correct coins into their proper slots.

Jiggs turned back toward the sheriff from where he stood in front of the big metal door leading into the jail itself. He held a pooper scooper and a long handled broom beneath his right arm. In his left hand was a large plastic trash sack.

"He's not really that stupid, but he sure can be messy," Jiggs said in response to Arty's order. The deputy shifted the sack to his right hand, still managing to retain his hold on the other two items. He then picked up a galvanized pail from a nearby shelf as he moved toward the door marked 'Rest Room' to fetch the requested water.

"Don't you go givin' them no phone change now when you go into their cell. Ain't allowed. Prisoners in this jail don't get no help from the law," Arty called after him.

Once again, Jiggs turned back toward his superior.

"You know you're gonna end up lettin' em' go. You always do."

Arty avoided the deputy's eyes and his lips formed a small, irritated pout around his prominent teeth. He spoke over his shoulder to his subordinate as he turned to place Rodney's property into a big safe resting next to a computer behind the booking counter.

"You watch your mouth, Jiggs," he mumbled. " And keep yer nose outa other folks beeswax. Otherwise you just might end up havin' to find a job somewhere you gotta pick up shit permanent. Nothin' says I can't make their lives miserable as possible in the meantime. Now do what I told ya. I ain't got time for no small talk."

Jiggs nodded and made a mental note to heed the sheriff's advice. This was the second time today the deputy had nearly let his anal cavity override its oral counterpart.

The born and bred native son of the Owens Valley never intended to offend anyone. He also liked his job, even if he would be back rolling tires for his boss to shoot at the following morning. At least that conjured up a more agreeable image than a full time future routine of feces cleansing.

Jiggs turned away from the sheriff without another word. He tried to avoid dropping the pooper scooper, the broom, the sack or the bucket, as he headed into the restroom for the water.

In the holding area, across the sheriff's station outer office hall from the restroom, Rodney was finally having some luck with the pay phone.

He heard a ringing sound in the receiver he now held up to his ear. It was undoubtedly also being heard in Louise's apartment at the same time. He still wasn't sure what he was going to say to her, but he had made up his mind to explain the situation as well as he could and beg for her help.

In the bedroom of Louise's Beverly Hills posh apartment, the phone was indeed ringing. Louise was also present, but she wasn't ready to pick the instrument up at this moment.

The Beverly Hills Princess was sleeping. She had traveled to Palm Springs the evening prior, with some of her wealthy friends. There, they had all attended a fashionable affair at the very exclusive Palm Springs Country Club.

It was quite late when she returned to Beverly Hills, and like Rodney, she hadn't retired until the wee hours of this morning. Unlike the poor unfortunate young man, four hundred miles away, she had gone to bed in comfort.

Her face was covered not only with the latest fashionable beauty cream, but a huge sleeping mask as well. A thin line of drool from the corner of her mouth had carved a tiny trail though the thick substance on her chin downward toward her neck.

The communication instrument on her bedside table continued to ring. She turned her back to Edison's noisy invention by rolling over on the waterbed. She pulled her pillow over her tousled head to shut out the sound.

In the holding tank of the Lone Pine sheriff's station, Rodney's face lit up as he still held the receiver to his ear.

The ringing on the other end of the wire had finally discontinued and was replaced by the voice of his fiancée. Never had it sounded so beautiful to the young man.

"Hello. This is Louise…."

Rodney was so overjoyed he interrupted her immediately. "Louise! Thank God I reached you. The most awful thing…."

He stopped talking when he realized the other voice had not really picked up.

"I'm not in at the moment. However, if it's Saturday, I can be reached at the Palms Springs Country Club….."

Rodney bit his lip. It was her answering machine. He nearly drew blood as the voice continued. He realized he would have to wait until Louise's accounting of where she could be reached came to an end, before he could leave a message of his own.

"…I'm not exactly sure what the number is there, but .. ah.. well… You can look it up, or call information…Monday through Friday, between nine thirty and ten am, I'm usually at the Beverly Hills boutique having my nails done…"

Rodney dug into his pocket with the hand not holding the receiver. He withdrew two quarters.

It was all he had left from the money the sheriff had signed out to him. There was more in his property envelope now resting in that safe beyond the bars but the official had assured him this would be enough. Now, as Louise's voice droned on, he became doubtful.

If her message ran much longer and he were required to insert more change in the telephone's coin box, there was a very good chance the sheriff's calculations would turn out to be incorrect. He wouldn't have enough change in his immediate possession to keep the line open.

The incarcerated young attorney really didn't relish the thought of repeating the previous routine with the disagreeable local lawman to obtain more and start all over again. As he ground his teeth, the strident tones continued in his ear.

"Of course if I can't be reached at one of those places, you can always try calling…."

The young barrister's face twisted in frustration. He realized he was dealing with an inanimate object on the other end of his connection, and it was beyond his power to speed it along. He ground his teeth again, waiting for Louise to sign off. Praying for the beep.

"…You can't find me around home at noon. I usually hang out at Carlos and Charlie's…. That's on the strip… I don't have that number, but…"

Without warning, Louise's metallic voice was replaced by another. One of AT&T's finest was bringing Rodney's fears to fruition.

"Thank you for using AT&T," said the newest voice. It too was feminine, but much more professional and infinitely less damaging to the ear. It was also another recording.

"Your three minutes are up. Please deposit four dollars and twenty five cents, then continue talking...."

The frantic young man looked down at the two lone quarters now in the palm of his hand not holding the receiver. He turned toward the outer office seeking assistance. Neither the sheriff nor his deputy was anywhere to be seen.

Rodney quietly hung up the phone and waited for someone to take him back to that awful cell where he expected to rot before he would ever be rescued.

*** *** *** *** *** ***

"How'd it go Rod?" called Farley as Jiggs unlocked the gate and the despondent young lawyer walked back into the cell.

"Not worth a shit from the looks of things," said Trux when Rodney walked to his cot without responding to the other Maynard brother's question.

Jiggs had obviously been in here while the unhappy young man was attempting to communicate with the outside world. The place had definitely been cleaned up.

The manure pile was gone and Barney now rested near Farley's bunk with a pail of water next to him. Rodney didn't even care.

He moved to the window facing outside. Through the bars he could see a distant range of snow capped mountains at what he assumed to be the end of the desert. They were beautiful. Unfortunately, in his present state of mind, the sight only served to remind him how really ugly were his immediate surroundings.

In the corridor, Jiggs had already locked the gate and was proceeding back toward the big steel door that led to the outer office. The deputy paused as Trux called after him.

"Hang on a minute will ya Jiggs?" the broad shouldered man with the big chin now spoke to his brother as Jiggs waited on the other side of the bars.

"Whaddya' think?"

"I think it's called shit or get off the pot."

"We wouldn't have to do this if you hadn't made such a big deal 'bout not signin' them papers n' gettin' Arty all excited."

"I just didn't think we should. Still don't. Not in here. Not till we get a chance to look em' over real careful."

"I really gotta be getting' back Trux," Jiggs called from the corridor,

"Arty comes lookin' for me, my ass is grass."

"Just one more second Jiggs," Trux said as he rose from his cot and walked to Rodney who still stood looking out the window. As he moved, he spoke once more to Farley.

"Think she'll be pissed?"

"'She never is," was the bearded brother's reply.

"Say Rodney," Trux said to the younger man as he walked up beside him. "You got any change left over from makin' your phone call? You do, I'd like to take you up on that offer you made before 'bout loanin us enough to make one."

Rodneys' hand automatically went into his pocket as he turned from the window toward the other man. "I've got two quarters. You're welcome to both of them. Ah... This is my own money.. Not like...."

"Aw shit. You don't have to explain. Like Farley says, You ain't an asshole, just an honest dumb shit. Just one of em'll do. Still can't get over the some bitch costin' more'n a God damned dime," Trux added, as he took one of the quarters from Rodney and hurried toward the corridor where Jiggs stood waiting on the other side of the bars.

"I'm ready to make my phone call now, Jiggs," The broad shouldered man called to the deputy.

"I'm gonna do it," he said to his brother as he waited for Jiggs to unlock the gate.

"Looks that way," was Farley's nonchalant response.

At the gate, Jiggs hesitated. "I dunno," he said. "Maybe I oughta' go get Arty. He already give you one shot. Better make sure it's alright."

"The man's entitled to his one phone call! When he decides to request it, is his decision!"

Rodney didn't realize he had even spoken, let alone so loudly until the words had already tumbled past his lips.

"I'm sorry," he said apologetically, as he walked past the seated Farley and the pig to the gate where Trux stood facing Jiggs through the bars. "But that is the law. You could get in real trouble if you refused it to him when requested."

The young man wasn't quite sure why he suddenly felt this imperative need to defend Trux. Maybe somewhere deep inside, his legal training had received a wake up call. Perhaps it was really just the guilt he felt for not being able to overcome his unreasonable set of ethics.

Trux's features were filled with surprised respect as he turned to him. The red neck's tone matched his look

"You talkin' straight shit here, Rod?"

"Straight shit," Rodney repeated, shocked that he could even say the last word. He hadn't even stuttered.

"You sure I don't have to ask Arty?" asked Jiggs.

"All I'm saying is, if it ever came to court…" Rodney began, but Jiggs interrupted him. The deputy knew the other young man was a lawyer. He'd seen his identification.

"I sure wouldn't want anything like that to happen. Come on Trux."

Trux's big shiny teeth seemed to make the dreary surroundings brighter. He showed nearly all of them as Jiggs unlocked the gate.

"Don't worry about a thing, boys. One quick phone call and we'll all be someplace else in less'n two hours. We'll be shittin' in tall cotton. Sippin' a tall one and laughin' n' lyin'. You too Rod."

Rodney tried to give him a reassuring smile through the bars as Jiggs locked up again.

"You just try to get yourself and your brother out. You don't have to …."

Trux didn't let the young man finish. He called back sounding very happy as he followed the deputy toward the big metal door. He obviously now felt very good now about what he was about to do, even though he hadn't wanted to do it in the beginning.

"I said all of us. You and us still got business! We ain't lettin' you go. Least till we decide to turn ya down! Besides, me'n Farley like honest dumb shits. 'Specially when they're 'bout half smart. We kinda' lean about three fourths of the way in that direction ourselves."

"Tell her I love her," Farley shouted after him.

"She knows that!" Trux responded with equal projection.

The broad shouldered man's optimistic voice echoed throughout the cellblock as he and Jiggs disappeared into the front of the building.

Rodney turned back to Farley. "I hope he has better luck than I did. Unfortunately, I just found out the hard way how it feels when these things don't work out."

"Oh, it'll work out alright," Farley replied with confidence. "Me n' Trux always swear we'll never call her if we ever get in trouble again. Course we always get in trouble again and we always end up callin' her. The Argus Queen never lets us down!"

"The Argus Queen?" asked Rodney.

"A very special Lady. Tell you all about her when Trux gets back."

*** *** *** *** *** ***

"That's what our daddy always called the Argus range," said Trux, as he pointed beyond the bars of the window in the cell facing the outside wall of the jail cell. The broad shouldered man was referring with his gesture to the

129

majestic mountains Rodney had observed earlier.

They were still locked up in the Lone Pine criminal facility, and Trux's prediction of freedom in less than two hours was almost to an end. Both the Maynards had assured Rodney, however, that termination of this particular incarceration period was now only a matter of minutes.

They stood on either side of the younger man now, as they all gazed out at the pulchritudinous, magnificent work of nature.

"An Argus Queen is a lady that's as old as them mountains and still just as beautiful," Trux continued.

"Thelma sure is beautiful all right," commented Farley with quiet conviction. "Always has been. Always will be."

"Thelma?" asked Rodney, "You mean the lady you said was coming to bail you out? Her name's Thelma?"

He had heard Jiggs mention another name during the deputy's slight confrontation with the brothers earlier. The young attorney had assumed that was the name of the lady they had finally decided to call. He was obviously wrong.

"That's her name alright! 'Thelma'." affirmed Trux. "Best woman on earth. And the most beautiful. But she won't be puttin' up no bail. Not Thelma."

"No bail?" echoed Rodney.

"Thelma gets you outa jail, all the charges get dropped. Ain't quite sure how she does it, but that's how ole Thelma operates," Farley informed him.

Trux turned back toward the interior of the cell from the window. "Cause Arty can't say no to her, dumb shit. Nobody can."

Trux suddenly began to snicker as a new thought hit him. "Maybe she's got a picture somewhere of ole Arty fuckin' a goat."

Barney, who had been standing behind the trio, suddenly gave out with a series of very concerned grunts. Both Rodney and Farley turned to the obviously disturbed animal. The latter kneeled beside the pig and began stroking his head in reassurance.

"Uncle Trux was just makin' a funny, Barney. He didn't mean it."

Farley looked up at Rodney as the pig immediately calmed down.

"Gotta be careful what we say sometimes in front of Barney," explained Farley as he returned to a standing position. "Way he figgers, if it's goats one day, next day it might be pigs."

"I was just bull shitin' Barney," Trux said to the pig. "But even if I wasn't, you'd probably be safe seein' as how you're a boy pig. 'Spite of all his other faults, I'm purty sure Arty ain't no queer."

Farley got a big laugh out of that one as he moved toward the front of the cell.

130

"Yes Sir!" said the bearded prisoner, when he was able to talk again. "Any minute now, Thelma's gonna come walkin' through that big ole iron door. Sure am glad you finally took my advice and called her, Trux."

"Your advise? You didn't wanna call her neither, you fuzzy faced Ferret!" Trux said, as he walked up beside the other Maynard.

Farley ignored his brother's disparaging reference to his whiskers and beckoned for Rodney to join them.

"You'll see Rod. If she ain't the most best lookin' thing you ever did see, I'll shit in your hat, by God."

Rodney, having already witnessed on two previous occasions, the Maynard brothers' taste in the opposite sex, was thankful he didn't wear a hat.

However, he didn't wish to be rude. No matter how physically unattractive he was sure the person in question would turn out to be, he was certain she had a beautiful soul. The possibility that she might be really able to help free him from this place also had to be considered.

"Well," began the younger man, sounding extremely polite as he moved up behind the other two men. "If she's anything at all like the rest of the women I've seen you with, I'm sure she's...."

Rodney stopped in mid sentence as the big metal door at the end of the corridor beyond the bars opened with a tremendous clank. The attorney just stood there with his mouth totally agape. He looked as if he might have gone into some sort of hypnotic trance.

Coming up the hallway of bars toward him, with a very unhappy, subdued Arty Dubs by her side, was a tall woman with absolutely stunning natural blond, long flowing hair. She was about forty-five years old.

The curvaceous body belonging to this fabulous female making her entrance was absolutely unbelievable.

To say this woman's anatomy would have made all the sex symbols throughout history, including Marilyn Monroe, Raquel Welch and Lonnie Anderson, during their prime, green with envy, would be an understatement. It would also, undoubtedly have the same effect on the egos of the current crop of contemporary lusted after bombshells, not excluding Jennifer Lopez.

She turned to mummer something to Arty. The sight of her derriere, most of which was quite visible beneath the tight fitting and extremely brief faded denim cutoffs covering it, was breathtaking. Her shapely legs, extending downward for a considerable distance to a pair of well turned ankles, created a similar phenomenon.

These wonderful attributes were only overshadowed by the wondrous things the front of the gorgeous lady's bra-less upper torso did for the T-shirt she was wearing.

Thelma was the proud possessor of the most pulchritudinous pair of mammary glands in not only the entire Owens Valley, but also probably the world and she was fully aware of it. She also knew the definition of the adjective and could pronounce it.

Her perfectly placed, extremely attractive intelligent eyes danced with laughter. Her sensual mouth formed a beautiful smile on her totally flawless face as she and the sheriff reached the gate of the cell.

"I run into you boys in the darndest places," said the Argus Queen to Trux and Farley.

"Hello Barney," she added as she looked through the bars at the pig. "Can't you keep these two out of trouble?"

The animal rushed to the barred gate, obviously overjoyed to see the beautiful lady.

"It was all Barney's fault," said Trux pushing his square jawed face through the bars.

"I'm sure it was," Thelma replied, rolling her lovely eyes after giving Trux a truly loving kiss on his lips.

"You're lookin' awful good, Darlin. You got no idea how good!" Farley exclaimed in earnest as he stuck his own furry face through the bars.

"I'll bet you say that to all the girls who get you out of jail," Thelma replied after Farley had received his own affectionate gesture of obvious genuine affection on the mouth with her own.

"How many years have I been doing this for you two?"

Farley stepped back and scratched his beard, trying to come up with an honest answer. "I dunno... Think about twenty three years maybe...could be twenty six.." He turned to Trux. "How many you figger Trux?"

"Who gives a shit? You gonna unlock that gate or not, Arty?"

On the other side of the bars Arty began to bristle. The blond woman gave Trux a look of affectionate reproach before turning to the uniformed, grumpy looking man beside her.

Arty heaved a reluctant sigh as her eyes met his. The sheriff of Lone Pine began muttering in low, terse tones as he stepped forward and inserted a big key in the lock.

"Okay! It's against my better judgment, but the lady's talked me into droppin' all the charges on you guys. Now move the Hell out 'fore I change my mind!"

Trux, Farley and Barney hurried out into the corridor as the gate swung open. Farley called over his shoulder to Rodney.

"You heard the man Rod. Lets go!"

Rodney hadn't moved since he had caught his first glimpse of the beautiful woman and he didn't look capable of doing so now. He looked like an unkempt statue as he continued to just stand and stare.

Trux chucked, "Thelma, this is Rod."

Thelma swept into the cell and gave the young man a hug, pressing her wonderful breasts against his soiled and wrinkled vest.

"Hello, Rod."

He continued to just stare at her as she took his arm in hers and led him out of the cell.

"Let's go home," she said in the sweetest voice that he could ever remember hearing.

*** *** *** *** *** ***

Of all the various places he, Daddy Farley and Uncle Trux called home, Thelma's house was by far Barney's favorite. The pig happily led the way.

The strange procession, consisting of the Maynard brothers, the bedraggled young man in the soiled rumpled three-pieced suit, and their lovely savior, all zigzagged through the side streets of Lone Pine following behind the merry spirited swine.

The local citizens they encountered, the majority dressed in their Sunday best, responded with the utmost courtesy as the beautiful woman greeted them.

If any regarded her choice of company as the least bit heterodox, such sentiments certainly were well concealed, even to one another. Not even a word regarding the subject was whispered after the lady and her entourage passed by and were well out of earshot.

Nobody in Lone Pine had anything bad to say about Thelma Houston. Almost all talked despairingly about the Maynard brothers and their scandalous erratic escapades at one time or another. However, neither name was ever despairingly mentioned in connection with Thelma. Even those who despised both, treated each with utmost respect while in her presence.

The populous of the Owens Valley was famous for its degrading gossip. With the exception of a handful of folks in some of the farthest outlying areas, Thelma was exempt.

Even Brother Roy Ogles, who damned everybody from time to time, was careful never to use her name when launching into one of his frequent self righteous public tirades.

Most had known her since she was very young. They remembered when she had been their very first Avon lady. That was before she had invented her own beauty products that were said to be far superior.

The gorgeous lady, with the help of a small chemical laboratory in Bishop, had developed these exclusive aids to attractiveness into reality many years ago. She had been distributing them personally all over the territory ever since.

She was also highly respected for her intelligence. She had been one of the first persons, male or female, to purchase a computer in the Owens Valley and was considered an expert with its technology.

While Thelma claimed this to be a gross exaggeration, her one-woman business ran much soother than probably any other of those, multi managed or otherwise by either gender, in the entire area.

She made an excellent living. Every woman in the Owens Valley felt that if they applied her secrets to their bodies and faces, they were sharing at least a little part of the voluptuous creature's secrets and hopefully, even a little of her intellect.

Added to her reason for success, was the simple fact that no husband of her customers ever refused her entry to their homes. Neither were they heard to complain about their spouses' extravagant purchases when Thelma came calling.

It was common knowledge that she had been contacted by some big city cosmetology corporation with an offer to expand her business and leave Lone Pine, but had declined. This made the local citizenry feel very special, but then, Thelma had that effect on almost all people without any help.

Rodney was unaware of any of the breathtakingly beautiful lady's biographical data. He just knew she was the reason he was finally a free man and she was also absolutely charming.

Already she knew his name was really Rodney and where he was from. She hadn't even asked how they came to be in jail. The pretty woman didn't seem to care. It was obvious that both Trux and Farley adored her, and apparently she held the same affection toward them.

Under ordinary circumstances the strange relationship would have made Rodney more than slightly curious. At the moment, however, the young man was enjoying the simple pleasure of being allowed to walk about outdoors with no locks or bars in sight.

It was absolutely amazing how the same afternoon sun that had been such a source of misery the day before, could bring him so much comfort just twenty four hours later.

There was no room in his mind for even the slightest detail pertaining to anything else right now. He still had terrible problems, but, maybe for the first time in Rodney's life, worry was on hold for the moment.

Thelma laughed merrily at the off colored quips offered by Trux and Farley as the promenade of misfits and the dazzling lady continued onward between the humble Lone Pine dwellings.

Suddenly, Barney, still in the lead, let out an excited squeal. He began racing toward a sizable, extremely well maintained house situated on the nearest corner.

The excited porker let out yet another squeal of delight as he reached the front lawn of the house where he skidded to a halt on his four short legs. Tossing his head in what appeared to be sheer delight, the pig turned to give those still behind him a look of triumph.

"By God, Barney's glad to see the old homestead," said Trux, laughing.

"We all are," he added as he put his arm around Thelma.

"Any place would look good to you guys after a night in the Gray Bar Hotel," replied the beautiful woman, as she craned her neck slightly upward to plant a kiss on the man's oversized jaw.

"Barney's just hopin' you got some cold uns' on ice," was Farley's comment as they all hurried toward the front door of the house where the pig was waiting impatiently on its steps.

Thelma moved close to the other brother. She put her arm affectionately on his. Farley received a kiss of his own from the gorgeous lady as they all continued to move forward.

"I've got a feeling Barney doesn't have an exclusive on that hope," she said. "You know I do. At least a case. Don't I always?"

The pretty woman turned back to Rodney who was lagging slightly behind. They were at the door now and Barney looked up in delighted anticipation.

"Come on in and make yourself at home, Rodney. Trux and Farley will show you around. Beers are in the box. I'll fix you boys something to eat, but first I've got to change out of these shorts. Pardon my French, but they're crawling right up the crack of my ass."

CHAPTER ELEVEN
APPARITION OF AN ANGEL

Thelma was now wearing what appeared to be nothing at all except a long blue silk robe tied together at the front of her tiny waist with a nylon cord. The cord threatened to come untied at any second. She now stood in front of the stove in her exceptionally clean looking kitchen preparing bacon and eggs.

The bacon was a turkey product of course. She wouldn't consider serving any other kind with Barney in the house.

Rodney, Trux and Farley sat behind her around a very handsome wooded table adorned with a cheerfully colored cloth which matched the mood of the rest of the room's merry décor.

Barney lay contentedly beneath the chair Farley was sitting on. A bowl of beer rested on the floor very close to his snout. Both Trux and Farley held cans filled with the same beverage in their hands. It was Blue Ribbon, their favorite.

A cup of coffee, looking far more appetizing than the brown murky liquid he'd attempted to drink in jail, rested in front of Rodney. He still wore his entire three-piece suit that looked much worse for the wear. The gracious lady had suggested that he at least remove the jacket and tie, but he had declined.

Granted, the young barrister was uncomfortable, but now that the first wave of freedom had passed, he had to get back to business. Rodney was from Boston where the two words comfortable and business were simply not synonymous. In spite of where he may have been forced to spend the previous night, image was still important.

Next to the coffee cup, was his now open briefcase. Its prior contents, including the cellular telephone and the envelope of money, were spread out on the tabletop in front of him. He was having difficulty keeping his eyes off Thelma's lovely natural cleavage and on the document he was attempting to show the Maynards.

"I really wish you'd look at these now," the young man said. "I'm sure it's all in order and you'll realize the people my firm represent are making you a fair offer. I don't want to rush you, and I appreciate all you've done for me, but there's so much I have to take care of before I start back. My car…"

Farley, being very careful not to disturb Barney, pushed back his chair and rose to his feet after setting his can of beer on the table. He moved to the stove to join Thelma.

The sexy woman now had the burners turned off beneath the two skillets on top of the stove and was transferring the food into dishes, which rested on a counter top next to the appliance.

"Never do business on an empty stomach!" the bearded man said, before Rodney could finish. He draped an arm around the lovely lady, nearly causing the front of her robe to come totally open.

"I'm starvin' baby," he continued in his deep, low voice as he pulled her to him.

She carefully finished distributing generous amounts of turkey bacon and eggs from the pans to the plates. That remaining in the skillets was for Barney.

The Argus Queen then turned and wrapped both of her arms around the affectionate mans' thick waist.

"You've been starving since I met you," she told him, as she nuzzled her beautiful face against the front of his filthy shirt.

"And you smell!" she added with a smile as she pulled back her head. "Somebody needs to get you in the bathtub and wash you all over."

"As I recall, you said the same thing the day we met. Probably how we got together," said Farley, sounding somewhat philosophical.

He turned back toward the table, addressing Trux. "Whadda' think Trux? She look as good as when we first met this purty little thing?"

A mischievous gleam appeared in Trux's blue eyes. His face stretched into the wide grin. His multitude of teeth gleamed as he carefully sat his own beer can down on the table. He then got to his feet.

"Put on a couple of pounds maybe," Trux said, perusing her magnificent physical structure as he moved from the table to the couple and threw his arms around her from behind. The gorgeous woman with the long blond hair was now locked completely in the clutches of both of the brothers.

To Rodney's amazement Thelma made no attempt to wiggle her way out of the two man embrace. She was obviously enjoying it. The beautiful woman smiled as she snuggled both the front and back of her curvaceous body against each of theirs.

Trux looked around the back of Thelma's head at his brother. The gleam remained in the broad shouldered man's eyes.

"Farley," he said attempting to sound solemn. "How long has it been since me n' you chewed the fat?"

Now Thelma did begin to squirm.

"Come on you guys. I've got biscuits in the oven!" she protested, trying very hard to suppress the giggles welling up inside her throat.

"Too long!" Farley's teeth weren't nearly a plentiful as those of Trux's. His grin, however, was just as wide as the brothers wrestled the exotic woman to the floor and began chewing all over her gorgeous body.

The room was filled with the delighted laughter of all three as they rolled around on top and beneath each other. The beautiful lady's light blue silken robe managed to keep at least part of her beautiful body covered some of the time.

Barney rose rapidly and ran to an interior open doorway leading to the living room. The pig just wanted to be on the safe side, as the trio of torsos tumbled in the direction of the table.

Rodney was also now on his feet. The young man in the soiled and rumpled three-piece suit couldn't believe what was going on. He was shocked and disgusted. In addition, a strange feeling of excitement was creeping into the two other emotions. That didn't make him feel any better.

He backed away to the living room doorway and joined the pig. He started to avert his eyes from the indecent scene on the floor, but suddenly, he saw whips of smoke drifting into to the kitchen from around the corners of the stove's closed oven door.

"Fire!" called Rodney, the other activity suddenly losing its importance.

The playful cavorting that was now beneath the kitchen table came to an abrupt end. The eyes of all three participants turned toward Rodney who could only point to the stove and the smoke coming from its oven.

"It's the biscuits!" Thelma exclaimed, starting to laugh again, as she untangled her marvelous looking limbs from those of the Maynard brothers. She scrambled to her feet and rushed to the stove.

"I told you!" said the shapely lady, attempting to wrap the robe back around her attributes of nature, turn off the oven and open its door all at the same time.

"Today we are serving biscuits a la burne le crispe," she announced in a very bad accent meant to be French while managing to butcher the language at the same time. Thelma was a woman of many talents, but imitating foreign accents was not included in her repertoire.

The lady plucked a rag hanging from a rack attached to the wall above the stove. Using the cloth to protect her hand, she pulled the pan of dark, smoking baked bread from the oven.

"And the first one to complain does all the cooking from now on!" she added as she waved away the smoke and sat the smoldering pan down beside the already filled plates of food.

"I like my biscuits well done," said Trux amiably, as he and Farley reseated themselves at the table.

"Like mine charred," was Farley's following comment.

Unnoticed by anyone but Rodney, Barney's ears went up. The pig nearly knocked the barrister off his feet as it dashed toward the kitchen door.

"You'd eat dog shit," said Trux still on the prior subject and insistent about getting one up on his brother.

Suddenly, Barney, now at the door, began to squeal loudly.

Trux turned to the noisy animal. "I said dog shit, not hog shit, Barney. Stop bein' so damn sensitive."

The man with the big chin returned his attention back across the tabletop to his brother and lowered his voice. "You better get his ears checked."

Thelma was now looking out through the kitchen window over the sink. From outside came the sound of a car door opening.

"It's Arthell," she said.

Rodney looked at her. He'd heard that name before. He thought it was the one mentioned by Jiggs back at the jail when the brothers had become briefly upset.

The focus of both Trux and Farley was on the door now, as Thelma turned back to them.

"About time. She was at a friend's house when I found out I had to go get you guys. I called her and asked her to stop at the store for some groceries. And something to drink of course."

Both Trux and Farley were on their feet again. Neither looked happy.

"What friend?" asked Farley.

"You let her drive your car?" Trux asked almost at the same time.

"Amy Lou Sandler. Royce Sandler's daughter. She came home for a visit. She's leaving today. And yes, I let her drive my car. Would you go give her a hand with those bags?"

"Long as the friend weren't some horny young stud!" said Farley. "And you shouldn't be lettin her drive, Thelma! Not by herself! "

"Arthell shouldn't be nowhere by herself! She ain't but a child!" exclaimed Trux vehemently.

Curiosity had overcome Rodney.

"Who's Arthell?" he asked timidly from where he still stood in the living room doorway.

At the kitchen portal, Barney was practically going crazy trying to get the attention of anyone possessing the thumbs and fingers required to turn that complicated knob that would open it.

"My God, Trux, Arthell's twenty-two years old! Get used to it!" said Thelma.

Apparently she hadn't heard Rodney's question. He asked it again, speaking somewhat louder.

"Who's Arthell?" They heard him this time.

The three other people in the room turned and looked at him. In spite of their own personal tiff that was obviously still in progress, they all beamed with pride as they answered in unison.

"Our daughter!" said Thelma, Trux and Farley.

Due to the fact they were all speaking at once, Rodney wasn't quite sure he'd understood them correctly. What the young attorney thought he'd heard didn't make sense. On the other hand, he realized he probably should have stopped trying to make sense out of anything a long time ago.

Thelma spoke to him all by herself this time.

"Rodney," she asked sweetly, "would you open that door before Barney breaks it down and go out and help the poor girl with those bags? I can't seem to get these two to do anything anymore."

Rodney nodded numbly. He moved to the door and opened it. Barney practically flew outside with a delighted squeal.

"Damnit, Themla! It ain't safe to let a nice girl roam around out there alone! Me n' Farley oughta know. Do you have any idea what...?"

Those were the last words Rodney heard from inside Thelma's kitchen as he followed the pig through the door.

As he stepped over the threshold, he nearly reverted to the same catatonic state he had experienced when he first laid eyes on Thelma.

At that time, the young man who had been sent from Century City to buy a mountain had been convinced beyond any doubt that the lady, who had arrived to free them from their state of incarceration, was the most beautiful woman in the world. Now, he was looking at another who was making him rapidly reconsider his prior convictions.

She was squatting down in front of the open passenger door of a late model cream colored compact and scratching a very happy Barney between his ears.

She was absolutely exquisite.

The pretty, fresh Twenty-two-year-old blond beauty looked up at Rodney and gave him a wonderful dazzling smile that nearly stopped his heart. A bag of groceries, this newest outstanding beauty had obviously been in the process of unloading before the pig came out, sat on the vehicle's seat just inside the door. Another sat on the driveway pavement, slightly behind her.

"Hi," she said in a voice that sounded more melodious than any piece of music Rodney had ever heard.

"You must be a friend of Daddy Trux and Daddy Farley's. As soon as Barney came out to meet me, I knew Mamma must have gotten them out of jail. I'm Arthell."

Rodney attempted to smile back as the vision of loveliness gave Barney a pat on his rear.

She rose up to her feet displaying a perfect set of legs as she stood there in the cutest little short skirt he had ever seen. The pig trotted back toward the house from her side.

It jumped up on the back step in front of the kitchen door as the smitten young man crept unconsciously forward.

Barney gave out with a soft grunt of contentment as he sat down. He felt it was time for these two young people to get to know one another, now that he'd properly received his own greeting.

Rodney was suddenly aware that his teeth needed brushing and he hoped he didn't smell as bad to this angel as he did to himself.

"I'm Rodney," he somehow managed to say his own name without stammering. He knew she hadn't stopped his heart from beating after all. It was now thumping so loud it threatened to burst through his eardrums.

"It's really great to meet you Rodney," Arthell said, as she turned and reached into the compact for the other sack of groceries.

He hurried forward to help her.

As he moved in behind the fantastic looking young lady, a roll of toilet paper tumbled from the top of the bag she was attempting to pull from the car's passenger seat. The item fell down onto the floorboard.

Arthell was forced to bend over to reach for it. The attorney nearly swooned at the wondrous sight.

"Let me get that," he said, attempting to recover.

She gave him that smile again as she straightened up and stepped back to allow Rodney access to the automobile's interior.

"I'd really appreciate it," she said in an honest, sweet voice that made firecrackers explode some where deep in his brain.

He reached in and managed to retrieve the elusive roll of toilet paper. The bedazzled young man in the soiled suit wasn't able to see the fabulous twenty-two-year-old femme fatale's favorable appraisal of his own posterior.

It was just as well. Those firecrackers would have undoubtedly become skyrockets, exploding the poor fellow's head, which he bumped only slightly as he raised up.

He placed the toilet paper back in the sack of groceries and turned to hand all items now intact, to the vision of all fantasies.

She reached out for the bag. Their hands touched. At the same time their eyes met. This world suddenly seemed to stand still for both young people, spinning them off into a universe all their own.

"What the Hell's goin' on out here?"

The couple immediately returned to earth as they turned to see Trux's broad shouldered body framed in the open kitchen doorway.

The big chinned red neck eyed Rodney with much more than just a hint of suspicion. Barney still lay on the step, now directly in front of the man's big feet. The pig looked up and grunted.

What the animal was trying to tell its Uncle Trux, wasn't quite clear. Trux wasn't paying any attention to Barney at the moment anyway, so it didn't really matter.

Arthell released her hold on the bulging grocery sack and ran to Trux. The pig was between the toes of both sets of feet now as she leaned forward and hugged the man. She was obviously delighted to see him.

"It's so good to have you home Daddy Trux! You just don't know!"

A softness came over the roughshod man that almost totally contradicted the rest of his character as he returned the tender embrace.

"Good to be home, sweetheart." For a minute it looked as if his blue eyes were about to mist over, but any trace of this vanished as he looked down at Barney.

"Barney, for God's sake! Move your ass 'fore you trip somebody! Go take a crap or something!"

The pig heaved a deep sigh as he rose and complied with the man's wishes. Nobody had to hit Barney over the head with a sledgehammer. He could tell when he wasn't wanted. Besides, Uncle Trux had a good idea and Barney liked privacy when he was so disposed.

The pig trotted off around the corner of the house, heading for some bushes, without so much as another grunt.

Trux watched Barney's departure for a second and then turned his attention back to the beautiful young girl he still held in his arms. He smiled gently as he released her.

No gentleness was visible however, in the following glare he gave to Rodney as she returned to help the young man with the groceries. He started to speak again, then, evidently changing his mind, backed into the kitchen, closing the door.

Rodney was about to lose his grip on the grocery bag. Arthell walked up and stabilized the cumbersome sack before moving past him to pick up the other, still resting in the driveway. She closed the car door before doing so.

Suddenly, as she started toward him with the sack in her arms, she looked down at a clump of bushes just beyond the driveway and made a face.

"Ugh!!" She grunted, sounding just a little bit like Barney.

Rodney held the bag in his own arms tightly; praying that he wouldn't drop it. He moved as quickly as he could back to her side. In spite of his concern for what was bothering her, he couldn't help but think she was the probably the only girl in the world that could make a face expressing disgust and still remain so devastatingly beautiful.

"What's wrong?" he asked.

Arthell inclined her head toward the bushes. A big ugly, wart covered slimy green frog was hopping away from them toward a puddle created by a leaky lawn sprinkler head.

"I know it's silly but I can't stand frogs," she said. "I even like lizards. And I don't mind spiders. I even think some snakes are cute. I can't stand frogs. I'm not afraid of them, I just don't like them. They're slimy. Silly, Huh?"

Rodney couldn't believe his ears.

"Not as far as I'm concerned," he said. "I'm not that fond of frogs, myself."

"Really?"

"I'd cross my heart but I'd have to put this bag down. Trux looked like he thought we really better get this stuff inside."

They both laughed. It was comfortable laughter. Something the young man couldn't ever remember experiencing before.

"Is Trux Maynard really your father?" asked Rodney as he and the lovely girl started toward the house together with their burdens.

"It's either him or Daddy Farley," she replied cheerfully. "Mamma won't say for sure. Says she doesn't want to disappoint anyone. It really doesn't matter. One of them is, and I love them both. They're the two neatest guys in the world. Crazy, but that's what makes them so neat. Were you in jail with them?"

Rodney was torn between answering the question and expressing his shock. The kitchen portal opened, saving the young man the necessity of making a decision.

It was Farley who now stood in the doorway. Arthell squealed happily and threw her arms around the bearded man as he took the sack of groceries from her.

"Daddy Farley! I was wondering where you were!"

Farley gave her a quick kiss on her pretty cheek. "And we was wonderin' where you was." He said in his deep gruff voice, as he looked directly at Rodney who stood just beyond the step, still clutching the other bag.

"Sure is takin' a long time to bring a couple pokes of grub inside. Man could starve to death 'round here if your mamma hadn't already made breakfast."

Farley turned his attention back to the girl as they entered the kitchen together.

"So," he began, sounding overly casual. "How's my sweet little virgin today?"

The last part of his question was not so casual. "You are still a virgin ain't you Arthell?"

She laughed as she skipped into the house with one of the men who might be her father. "Of course, Daddy Farley," she answered, sounding not at all embarrassed.

Rodney decided the best thing for him to concentrate on at this very moment was trying not to trip as he followed behind them.

*** *** *** *** *** ***

Barney was on the back step outside the kitchen door again, enjoying the afternoon sun.

Inside the kitchen itself, everyone was now seated around the table. All had finished eating except Rodney and Arthell. The young people dawdled with their food as they stared at each other. They seemed to be feeding off each other's vibrations.

Rodney's briefcase, now closed, rested on the seat of a vacant chair between the young lawyer and Thelma.

The older of the two beautiful women present, now seemed to be deeply engrossed in the property purchase agreement, which she held in her hands. The other items from the briefcase previously strewn about on the tabletop, including the envelope of money and the portable telephone, were now on top of the briefcase.

Trux and Farley were watching the exchange of gazes between their daughter and the young whippersnapper from the city. It was quite obvious that they'd both seen more than enough.

One of them was the father of the sweet little girl at this table. Neither was about to let another man even think about doing to their daughter, what they did to other men's daughters. Such was the way of the red neck.

Trux finally broke the silence. The broad shouldered man's voice was much louder than necessary as he rose to his feet and reached for the document in Thelma's possession.

"Okay! Everbody's been fed! Let's get our asses down to business! Bring us a pen, Thelma. Time we signed this paper and collected the rest of that money in Rodney's envelope! No since wastin' anymore of his time! Let's get this shit out of the way and get his car for im' so he can be on his way! Kid's got a life to get back to!"

"Yessir! We kept him away from the neon lights and all them fancy night clubs with all them purty women an' their big cars an' swimmin' pools too damn long," chimed in Farley, also speaking with more volume than usual.

"Not to mention all them fags in the fast lane!" Trux added.

"Oughta be ashamed of ourselves!" Farley said, continuing the thought as he managed to stifle a burp.

"Always ready to do business on a full gut! Tell me where the pen is, Thelma, I'll get er!" he announced while pushing his chair back from the table in an exaggerated fashion.

"I'm not sure you and Farley should sign this paper, Trux," said Thelma, holding the document out of his reach.

"What the Hell you talkin' about, Thelma?" Trux reached again for the item, but Thelma was on her feet now and moved away from her broad shouldered lover as she addressed Rodney.

"Rodney, why this mountain? There's really nothing on it except old rocks and rattlesnakes. No timber. The ground's unstable from what I've been told. It would be almost impossible to build on. Who are these people, the H. and H. Holding Corporation?"

"Come on, Thelma! Don't you go killin' this deal for us! Gimme the damn thing!" Trux was almost whining as her pursued her for the paper.

She kept dancing out of his way around the room, whirling around with the grace of an elusive ballerina. Her silk robe opened just below the waist, flaring out behind her displaying the woman's magnificently proportioned thighs and a great deal more.

Whether she was wearing anything beneath the garment was no longer open for debate. This seemed not to be of concern to the woman. She was waiting for Rodney's answer.

When the young man spoke, he was honest, if not terribly informative.

"I've never really met the clients personally. The senior partners at my firm handled all that. I'm just authorized to make the purchase."

Rodney suddenly realized just how unimportant his function really was, and even worse, sounded. He glanced quickly in Arthell's direction to see if she was thinking the same thing.

Her smile said she didn't care. The girl was absolutely amazing. And she didn't like frogs.

Farley saw that smile. "I'll find a pen!" he declared, as he quickly got up from the table and hurried into the living room.

"Come on Thelma! Give me the Goddamned paper!" demanded Trux. "You're gonna talk us outa eighteen hunnerd dollars here!"

"I gotta pen!" called Farley, as the bearded Maynard brother with the big tummy and very little rear end returned to the kitchen almost immediately. He waved the writing implement in the air.

On the other side of the room, Thelma stopped twirling. She heaved a deep sigh and handed Trux the contract.

"I wish you'd find out a little more about why somebody wants it," she said dubiously, as she pulled the robe together. "I just think you should dig a little deeper before you sell it, but it is yours. Go ahead."

Trux gave the beautiful lady a quick kiss before hurrying to the still seated Rodney's side.

Farley was waiting on the young man's other side. The pen was poised in his hand. Trux pushed the attorney's plate that was still not quite empty, out of the way and laid the document down in its place.

"Gimme the pen," he said to Farley.

"I went and got the God damned thing. I oughta' go first," complained Farley.

"Who gives a shit?" Was Truxs' response. "Just do it! Rod has to get on the road. Right, Rod?"

Before Rodney could answer, or Farley had a chance to exercise his requested right as first signee, Arthell reached over and snatched the instrument from the hand of the latter.

She began speaking before either of her fathers' had a chance to comment on her behavior.

"It's Sunday! You both told me people should never do business on Sunday."

Trux and Farley looked at each other over Rodney's head.

"One of us said that?" asked Trux.

"Not that I recall," was Farley's answer. "Don't sound like us."

"You both said that!" Thelma declared as she moved forward and joined the conversation.

"When Chance Wilson was still county supervisor, he offered you two that job as watchmen up at the dam on weekends. The reason you gave for turning him down was because you both said it wasn't right to work or do any business on Sundays."

"That's what you said. And that's what I've always believed," the adorable Arthell chimed in.

"Because that's what you told your child," added Thelma, making sure the men she loved got the point.

Rodney looked from one person to another as Trux and Farley pondered the hole they'd some how dug for themselves.

Some time in the past, they hadn't wished to give up their Saturday nights and had used Sunday as an excuse. Right now, of all times, that little white lie they'd told a sweet little girl who believed everything they said, so long ago they didn't even remember telling it, had returned to haunt them.

"Besides," said Arthell, taking advantage of the pause to make an announcement that had just popped into her pretty head.

She'd never felt this way before, and she wished to explore the feeling, before the recipient of these new found emotions walked out of her young life.

"I was going to invite Rodney to church. Would you like to go, Rodney?"

"Church?" Trux shook his head. "Church's over. Sun'll be down in three or four hours. It's damned near nighttime. Church is Sunday mornins."

146

"One church has two services. One in the morning and one in the early evening. It's close to here. We could walk," Arthell came back quickly.

She didn't mention the particular church to which she was referring, happened to be The Devotion to Divinity house of worship. Farley hated its pastor, the overweight Brother Roy Ogles.

"Would you go with me, Rodney?" she asked again.

Rodney wanted to go anywhere with this beautiful creature that she wished to take him. He knew, however, he that he simply wasn't presentable enough in appearance to accept the invitation.

He could almost hear his own heart breaking as he looked down at his dirty clothing, and gave her a very apologetic answer.

"I'd really love to. I mean that, but I can't. My clothes are filthy. I left my suitcase in my car back at... When I arrived to talk business with your fathers, I had to leave it, before we..."

Farley jumped in, deterring the young man from furnishing more information than either he or Trux felt was needed right at the moment.

"You're right Rod," he said, even though he was looking at Trux. Turning to Arthell, he spoke in exaggerated sympathetic tones.

"Kid ain't got nothin' to wear," said Farley. "Looks awful. Church ain't really a bad idea now that I think on it, but he couldn't never go lookin' like that."

"Not only that, he smells bad," added Trux. The big chinned man turned to Rodney.

"You know I didn't say nothin before, but did anybody ever tell you, you smell like sheep dip?"

Much to her daughter's relief, 'Super Mom' flew to the rescue.

Thelma swooped in behind Rodney. She pushed both of the Maynard brothers aside as she reached down to feel the material of the young man's suit jacket.

"No trouble. We've got lots of soap and hot water. That suit looks like it's wash and wear," she said. "You just hop in the shower and leave the rest to me. You'll be spending the night of course. I'll have a place fixed up for you to sleep when you kids get back from church."

Trux and Farley gave each other smoldering looks as Arthell began gathering up Rodney's things including the land purchase document, and putting them back into the briefcase.

"Careful with that envelope," Trux cautioned the beautiful girl. "Got a whole bunch of money in it with me n' Farley's names on it."

He turned to his brother and spoke in a sotto voice.

"This is all your fault! You hadn't come up with that stupid 'Honest Dumb Shit' theory, while we was still locked up, He'd be history."

"So I was wrong," Farley whispered back. "I ain't got no tattoo on my ass says, 'Farley don't never fuck up' do I?"

"Ain't room on your skinny ass for no tattoo," Trux hissed.

Thelma, ignoring both of them, pulled Rodney to his feet. She spoke to Arthell who was about to place the cellular phone into the briefcase along with the rest of Rodney's belongings.

"Better leave that out, Arthell. Rodney probably has to make a call and tell someone about his change in plans."

"I really should, I guess," said Rodney, looking at the instrument. "But if I reverse the charges, do you have a phone I could use?"

Thelma gave him a curious look. Quickly, he came up with an explanation for the request.

"Probably wouldn't get very good reception way out here on that," he mumbled while halfheartedly pointed to the instrument in question; thinking at the same time just how lame he really must be sounding.

"You'll get great reception," Thelma assured him. "I've got one and I use it all the time."

The young man was suddenly filled with concern for this beautiful woman with the even more beautiful daughter.

Trux and Farley continued to whisper to each other as they moved to the sink. Both shot occasional dirty glances at whom before had been just another likable young jerk, but had transformed into a slimy, slick sophisticated big city wolf, when they saw how their daughter looked at him.

"Aren't you afraid of getting a brain tumor?" Rodney asked Thelma. The subject of the deadly telephone was still very much on his mind. He felt duty bound to make her aware of its deadly dangers. "I've read lots of articles…"

Thelma smiled. She now knew the young man's problem.

"Rodney," she said before he could finish with what she already knew what he was about to say, "You know the old saying, 'Don't believe what you hear and only half what you see'? I believe the first part goes for what you read too. I think it's the people who write that kind of garbage that give other people brain tumors."

She saw his dubious reaction and lightened her tone before continuing.

"But that's only my opinion and you're welcome to use my phone. There's one in the hall outside the bathroom. Arthell, make sure you show him how to work that shower. There's a new toothbrush in the side cabinet. Don't forget to bring me his clothes. Better hurry."

Rodney happily took the briefcase and cell phone from the exquisite young lady and followed her through the doorway leading to the living room and beyond. He was about to become clean of body once more. Trux and Farley moved forward from the sink to the middle of the room. Both had blood in their eye.

"You let em' go to the bathroom together!" Trux said accusingly to the Argus Queen.

"And you two are next!" she answered, ignoring his implication. "Shame on you! Telling that poor boy he smelled like sheep dip!"

"Well, he does. And that ain't the point!" Trux shot back. "What's this shit about him spendin' the night?"

"You're the ones who don't do business on Sunday. Where else would the poor boy spend the night?"

"He ain't gonna need nowhere to spend no more God damned nights! I'm gonna kill the little cock sucker right now!" Farley declared, as he headed for the doorway.

Trux, his fists doubled, was right behind his brother. Thelma, displaying amazing agility, moved in front of them both, barring their way.

"Stop it right now!" she said in a very firm voice. "Just stop it! Leave those two kids alone! Because of you two, no young man within a hundred miles around, will even speak to that girl. She wants a date for church this afternoon, and by God, she's going to have one!"

The beautiful woman smiled sweetly as she finished her edict with what sounded like an innocent question.

"Do I make myself clear?"

Both disgruntled red necks lowered their eyes. "Thelma, she's a good girl," Muttered Trux.

"I know she is Trux," Replied Thelma, her tone becoming quite merry.

"Now that we've got everything settled," she continued, as she began picking up the dirty dishes from the table. "Let's get this kitchen cleaned up. Farley, you dry. Trux, you wash."

Trux grumbled as he and Farley trudged obediently toward the sink. "Farley always gets to dry."

"I do not," said Farley. "I washed last time."

Trux mumbled beneath his breath as the two red necks reached their destination.

"He tries anything on Arthell, by God, I'm gonna...."

"What was that?" asked Thelma as she arrived by his side and placed the dishes into the sink.

"I said Farley always gets to dry," replied Trux as he turned on the water and picked up a dishrag.

*** *** *** *** *** ***

Horace Herkimer was certain his Latino maid must have dried his martini glass with her filthy immigrant underwear.

The water spots on the expensive piece of crystal he held with the impeccably manicured fingertips of his right hand were totally disgusting.

The slightly flabby partner of the prestigious Century City law firm sighed as he reached beneath the wonderfully crafted walnut bar in the den of his palatial Bel Air apartment for a napkin.

The miserable woman responsible always took Sundays off. She was not only unavailable to yell at, he'd have to rectify the deplorable situation himself. Not that her presence would have served any real purpose. She always pretended not to understand English.

He pulled forth the napkin and began making a face as he wiped away the residue before pouring his martini. Even prior to the water spot discovery, the executive had been in a foul mood.

His secretary had called him early Saturday morning, shortly after Van Aukin had departed for Lone Pine to announce she wouldn't be in the office on Monday. She hadn't even been that sure regarding Tuesday.

She had babbled something about going to San Diego. Some sort of an outing with her friend Harrington Fox to attend some sort of navel officer's graduation.

It wasn't the first time Miss Wayling had pulled a stunt like this. Sometimes the woman would just take off without even telling him. He knew there was nothing he could do about it. That's just the way Agnus was.

Her periodic self proclaimed holidays always made him nervous. One of these days Harold was going to ask why he didn't handle their employee with a firmer hand. He couldn't fathom attempting to explain his reasons for being unable to do so to his brother.

Fortunately, so far, Harold always remained silent during Miss Wayling's absences, but that couldn't last forever.

Horace knew he had a day of reckoning coming some day regarding this subject he had nightmares about it. Whoever invented the vibrator should die a very slow, painful death.

Her absence at this time was also damned inconvenient. Horace had been forced to monitor the office answering machines himself for two days now, and it was driving him crazy.

Van Aukin had failed to check in from wherever he had been sent to purchase that property. There was no excuse for such a blatant lack of professionalism.

The stupid little jerk had both his and Harold's home numbers even if Horace had perhaps made some sort of error checking the office machine he was not really familiar with.

Horace and his brother stood to make a tremendous profit on this deal and it was imperative they should be kept abreast of its progress. Time was precarious.

The little twerp hadn't even called Louise. Not that he believed for a minute his daughter really cared. Horace couldn't imagine anyone in their mind really feeling that way about someone as stupid as Rodney, but the idiot really should have called somebody!

Horace Herkimer would be so glad when all this was over. The satisfaction of giving Van Aukin his walking papers, and the fact that he himself would suddenly become quite wealthy, was only part of it.

If all went well, he could tell his other two partners that traveled around the country helping the downtrodden, leaving himself and Harold to do all the work, what he had always wanted them to know. They could kiss his perfect, hemorrhoid free and only slightly vibrator damaged anal opening.

Horace Herkimer was sick of being just one more insignificant Herkimer in a long list of Herkimers.

His independence hinged on presenting those signed papers giving he and his brother Harold ownership of that mountain. They had to be presented by early Tuesday afternoon to the company that was offering the two million. If he and Harold couldn't deliver by then, their agreement of confidentiality would be void. Were that to happen, the company might well seek other representation.

That halfwit nematode he'd arranged to have his daughter sleep with just in case any thing went sour, better get back here with that document on time. If he didn't, the whole deal could fall apart.

The fancy French style telephone on the bar next to him began to ring as he finally poured himself a martini.

He took a sip of the divine substance as he considered letting his personal answering machine pick it up. Horace didn't really wish to talk to anyone right now.

On the other hand he wasn't exactly proficient with that piece of mechanical equipment either.

He had a habit of erasing the messages while rewinding them back before he got a chance to hear them. That was why he was always very careful to give his personal home number to only a select few who knew if he didn't answer, they should call the office.

There was an extreme long shot that it might be the nematode. Maybe he had tried the office number and somehow the message hadn't gotten through.

He was extremely dubious, but if indeed such a thing had happened, it was slightly feasible that Rodney might eventually come up with the good sense to call Horace at home.

There was also the remote possibility that it might be Agnus calling to say she was cutting short her San Diego trip. He was doubtful that the ringing represented either, but he couldn't afford to take a chance it didn't.

Horace took one more sip and lifted the phone receiver from its cradle. Pulling it up to his ear, he spoke guardedly into the ornate instrument's mouthpiece.

"Horace Herkimer. What? Who?"

Suddenly, he formed his testimony to flawless dentistry into a perfect smile and his tone became insipidly jovial. It was indeed the nematode on the other end of the wire.

"Of course I'll be happy to accept the charges!" Why in the hell was the idiot calling collect?

"Hello Rodney! Great to hear from you my boy! Where are you? On you're way home with every thing wrapped up?"

Rodney was totally nude except for a towel which was wrapped tightly around his trim waist as he stood in the hallway just outside Thelma's bathroom in her Lone Pine home.

He had just finished showering, and his teeth were finally free of those little corduroy jackets, as he talked into the telephone to Horace Herkimer.

"Not exactly Mr. Herkimer," he said as he looked in the hall mirror. He still couldn't quite believe it.

He'd undressed in the bathroom and handed his clothes out to Arthell through the door that he was careful to keep as closed as possible during the exchange. After he made sure she was gone, he'd finally looked at himself in that mirror expecting the worse.

The face that had stared back at him then, was the same one reflected in the hall mirror now. The skin had not peeled as he had been so certain it would.

Instead, it had turned quite tan and there was not a blemish in sight. There was no sign at all of the skin condition that had plagued him since the age of twelve. It was like a miracle.

"Actually, I'm still in Lone Pine, Mr. Herkimer. I know it's Sunday, and I shouldn't be calling you at home, but I wasn't able to check in last night…"

In Bel Air, Horace Herkimer was about to ruin his perfect dental work as he ground his expensive caps together.

"Rodney, please. Don't tell me what I already know. Tell me what I don't know! Did you contact the Maynards and get their signatures?"

"Made contact with them sir!" Rodney stood in the hallway of the Lone Pine dwelling, still wrapped in only the towel.

He marveled at the fact he hadn't stammered once since this conversation started. He thought back for a fleeting second before speaking into the telephone again. He hadn't stammered since he'd been in jail. Surely he hadn't discovered a cure for speech impediments.

"Yes sir. I'm still here," He said in answer to the question coming through the receiver. "No, they haven't exactly signed yet, but they're ready. Seems they won't do business on Sunday, Mr. Herkimer."

In his upscale den in Bel Air, Horace Herkimer did not look happy as he spoke again into the telephone.

"I've never heard of anything quite so ridiculous! Well, do what you have to do. Just make sure you're on the road back early tomorrow morning. We have a schedule problem here, Rodney. You were aware of that before you left."

"Well, it's not quite that simple Mr. Herkimer," Rodney said, as he looked up and saw the beautiful Arthell walking down the hallway with his freshly laundered and ironed clothing.

"I've got a little problem of my own. Car problem," he added quickly as Arthell moved up to face him.

She stood there, openly admiring the exposed portions of his body as she laid the clothing carefully on the hall table next to the half nude young man talking into the telephone. She had changed for church and, if it was possible, she looked even more exquisite.

"But I should be on my way by the afternoon. The following day at the very latest."

"The following day is unacceptable Rodney!" Horace was beginning to lose patience with this upstart he hadn't liked anyway from the beginning anyway.

"You start out in the morning with those signed papers if you have to rent a car or walk!" Realizing he may have sounded just a little too harsh, the Century City executive decide to take another route of persuasion.

"Besides," he said in more soothing tones, "You have to think of Louise. You shouldn't keep the girl you're going to walk down the aisle waiting."

The tones of solace in the executive's voice transcended into more of a veiled threat.

"There are an awful lot of young men who would like to be in your position right now Rodney," he said into the mouthpiece of the fancy French communications instrument.

"I'm sure there are," Rodney replied into Thelma's ordinary hallway phone as he watched Arthell's fantastic behind disappearing down the hallway.

"Bet on it young fella," There was more than veiled commination in Horace Herkimer's voice now.

"Tomorrow morning, Rodney, come Hell or high water! Fax me that purchase agreement the minute you have it signed. A copy will buy us some time, but I need that original in my hand as quickly as possible. Call me before you leave. Understand?"

"I'll do what I can Mr. Herkimer. Can't promise anything more. Good bye, sir," Rodney said, before hanging up the phone.

The young attorney in the towel didn't have time to talk anymore. He swept up the clean clothing from the top of the hall table and hurried into the bathroom to dress. Rodney had a date with an Angel!

Back in Bel Air, his superior was not exactly thrilled. It was just possible he hadn't picked the perfect patsy after all. The way Rodney had just signed off really bothered him.

Horace Herkimer poured himself one more martini. Then he reached for the fancy telephone again. He dialed a number After he finally heard an answer on the other end of the wire, the uneasy executive began speaking into the instrument.

"Harold? Horace. We may have a problem."

"No, I'm not talking about Agnus not coming in on Monday!" he said after taking a deep breath.

"That's an inconvenience. I'm talking problem here, Harold. Please pay attention! I just talked to Rodney."

Horace listened to the voice coming through the receiver. His artificially tanned face showed obvious strain as the self-important man struggled to keep from losing control. His own voice sounded only slightly sarcastic when he spoke again.

"Harold, if he were back in town, then we wouldn't have a problem, now would we?"

He took another breath, then continued. His tone changed to an almost conspiratorial whisper.

"I don't mean to create any panic, but just in case, we should be ready to move in a more personal direction if it becomes necessary. I know that might pose a problem if Agnus isn't back in time. If it comes to that, we'll improvise, Harold. The point is, no matter what, we must be ready to move!"

CHAPTER TWELVE
CYCLONE COURTSHIP

"Move your scrawny ass! I can't see!"

"If my ass is so God damned scrawny, you shouldn't have no trouble lookin' around it."

"Just get out of the way!" Trux grumbled as he pushed Farley aside and peeked around the rear of the station wagon he and his brother were hiding behind.

The Maynard brothers were in the tiny parking lot of the Lone Pine Devotion to Divinity Church, keeping a vigilant eye on the house of worship.

Thelma had a late afternoon beauty product delivery. Barney had expressed a desire to tag along.

Consequently, the Maynard brothers getting out of the house to make certain that little bastard Rodney didn't try anything unspeakable with their daughter, hadn't been a problem.

The Argus Queen had insisted they bathe and clip their toenails before she left. While the results of the latter undertaking was not visible, they did indeed appear much more presentable. Both were also wearing clean clothing.

Nonetheless, the red neck brothers still looked totally out of place crouching behind a vehicle in the church parking lot sharing a pint bottle of whiskey.

Both were impatient. They knew time was limited.

When Thelma returned, she was going to take them to pick up the motor home. Arty had told them it had to be removed from where it was now against that boulder on the road leading up to the Alabama Hills tonight or he would impound it.

The Argus Queen could probably talk the sheriff out of that too, but she didn't seem so inclined. It didn't matter. They needed the rig anyway to get the little son of a bitch that was with Arthell right now back to his car. Once that was accomplished, he'd have no reason to be with her ever again.

The brothers' immediate mission was to see that Arthell returned home immediately after this church service.

They would then take Rodney with them on the motor home excursion. Such an act would further insure less chance of child molestation on his part, and manslaughter on theirs.

"What the Hell's goin' on in there?" asked Trux.

He was holding up his hand to shield his blue eyes from the late afternoon sun that was about to disappear behind the steeple, trying to get a better view of the building beneath it.

"What do you think?" responded Farley as he pulled the opened half-full pint bottle up to his whisker surrounded mouth.

"Same old shit," he said after he took a generous swallow of the glass containers' ingredients and smacked his lips in appreciation.

"Fat fucker's in there tellin' how everbody's gonna end up shovelin' coal for the Devil if they don't do everthing like he says and think the same way he does. And of course, give him all their money. Why in the Hell would Arthell bring anybody here? You know I ain't got nothin' again' religion, but Brother Roy Ogles shouldn't even be allowed in a church, let alone be runnin' one."

Trux kept his eyes fixed on the building in question as he reached back for the bottle.

"You just don't like him 'cause he's Heffaroid Hoggs' cousin."

"I don't like him 'cause he wants to eat Barney! And I hate the way he talks the old ladies in this town into turnin' their social security checks over to him. He's a real scum bucket!"

"You don't suppose that little son of a bitch snuck out the back way with her, do you?" Trux said, returning to the reason he and his brother were hiding in the church parking lot behind someone's station wagon in the first place.

Farley looked over Trux's broad shoulder as the other man drank from the bottle.

"Looks like it's over. Either that or some of em' got tired of the bullshit. There's folks comin' out. Yep! It's over. There's the fat fucker all dressed up in his stupid lookin' bathrobe now!"

"And there's our baby and the little asshole. Quick! Duck down! We don't want her to think we're spyin on em!" Trux exclaimed, pulling his brother and the pint of whisky back out of sight behind the station wagon.

On the church steps, Rodney and Arthell let the small crowd file out of the building around them. They didn't even seem to realize there was anyone else present as they looked into each other's eyes. Thelma had been unable to remove the stains from his vest and tie, but the young man looked quite comfortable without either. This new casual look seemed to become him.

Brother Roy Ogles stood a few feet away from the young couple, in his enormous flowing robe, shaking hands with the individuals that made up his departing flock. The Mammoth man of the cloth was not in a particularly good mood. The news regarding the Maynards' escapade with his innocent nieces this morning had disturbed him deeply.

The fact that the collection plate hadn't exactly been overflowing this evening didn't make the big man feel any better. Brother Roy held two services every Sunday for a reason that was somehow escaping his parishioners. He needed to have a chat with God regarding this subject. There had to be a subtle method of making them more aware of their financial obligations without being led to believe he was after their money.

One old lady coming out of the church headed straight for the parking lot. She may have left something simmering on her stove at home, possibly taken a laxative about to kick in, or simply didn't care for the sermon. It could well have been a combination of all three.

Whatever her motivation, she got into her automobile and immediately started its engine. Unfortunately for the Maynard brothers, she was the owner of the station wagon they were hiding behind.

It was gone before they had time to realize she even was in it. Trux, Farley and the remainder of the whiskey were left totally exposed to the churchyard and all those standing in front of the Lone Pine house of worship.

Rage began welling up from the very depths of Brother Roy's gigantic body as he saw the two red neck brothers squatting in the parking lot of his church, with the now, nearly finished bottle of whiskey.

He nearly choked on the handful of Fruit Loops he had just secretively shoved onto his face for solace. Swallowing hard, he pointed a banana-sized finger at both.

Once the last Fruit Loop passed a point within his throat that allowed him to speak again, the furious fat follower of God let forth with a bellow of majestic fury.

"Desecration! Spirits in the front yard of God! I'll not have it!"

Trux and Farley, both slightly embarrassed, struggled up to a standing position. Farley held the pint behind his back as the gigantic pastor, his robe billowing out behind his gargantuan rear, charged toward them.

"I'll put the wrath of God on you both!" the large fellow screamed. "You are not to bring your evil ways to the Lord's front door!"

He was up in their faces now as he continued to rant and rave. He pulled Farley's hand into sight and snatched the bottle from it.

The glass container shattered with a loud crash as it struck a concrete wall at the back of the parking lot when the reverend flung it aside.

"Sinners!" Brother Roy boomed. "Sinners who make friends with the creature of the cloven hoof!"

"You leave Barney outa this! And there was a good two shots left in that jug!" Farley spoke up defensively on both issues.

Brother Roy continued to rave, repeating they same words he had spoken to his poor misguided nieces only this morning.

"The creature of the cloven hoof was created to be eaten to show the…."

Trux had heard enough. "Get fucked Preacher!" Were his exact words.

"And shut your hole! That bullshit must be comin' straight outa' your ass! Your mouth's gotta know better!"

The huge man let out an almost inhuman roar. Before Trux could even react, Brother Roy's huge hands were around his neck. The reverend began shaking the broad shouldered man about like a rag doll as his ranting and raving continued.

"I'll not have such vile words spoken in front of the domain of the Lord and my innocent flock!"

Back in front of the church, the small gathering watched the confrontation with quiet interest, patiently awaiting its outcome. It was obvious that none had the slightest inclination to become involved.

Rodney started to move forward from Arthell's side to make his way beyond the apathy.

"Somebody's got to help him!"

Arthell pulled him back.

"No!" she said. "They'll get out of it. My fathers always do. They'd be embarrassed if you got involved. Just stay with me. Believe me. They'll work it out."

Rodney stated to protest, but as the beautiful girl took his hand and squeezed it tightly, he obeyed her request. How could a lowly lawyer with his name listed last on a door, argue with the wisdom of an angel?

At the edge of the church parking lot, Trux was beginning to turn bright red. He was being nearly choked to death by the two ham-sized hands totally encompassing his entire neck and there seemed to be nothing he could do to prevent it.

"God damnit!" he managed to gasp in his brother's direction. "Do somthin' Farley!"

Without warning, Farley let out with a banshee howl and ducked beneath Brother Roy's arms. Almost quicker than the eye could follow, he rose back up between the angry pastor and the man he was strangling.

Farley was now face to face with the aggressor who still had both hands occupied with the damage he was inflicting on Trux.

The bearded man with the tiny buttocks and protruding tummy reached forward. He wrapped both his own free arms around Brother Roy's neck and pulled the big fellow's head to his.

He then pressed his mouth to that of the reverend's, sticking his tongue directly down the other man's throat as far as it would go.

Wild eyed and retching, Brother Roy released his hold on Trux's throat immediately.

The pastor's whole oversized body began to convulse in horrified repugnance as he frantically attempted to extricate himself from Farley's lip

158

lock. Farley hung on.

Finally, after what seemed to Brother Roy an eternity, the huge preacher managed to fling the persistent bearded smoocher away.

"Awarrg!" cried the orally assaulted spokesman of the Lord, retching as he staggered backward. Farley, who had landed in a heap at the feet of his brother, sprang up immediately.

"Come on preacher! Just one more! You're so damned cute! Makes my dick hardern' a ten pound poke of nickel jawbreakers just lookin' at ya!" Said Farley, his arms outstretched as he moved toward the gagging man.

"Pervert! Sodimizer! Stay away from me!" screamed Brother Roy as he tripped on his robe and fell back onto his leviathan rump. He kept his huge hands in front of his face, cowering and whimpering as he clambered awkwardly to his feet.

The large man then turned and ran screaming back into the church past Rodney and Arthell who were both biting their thumbs to keep from breaking into wild guffaws of absolute hysteria.

"Dear Lord Jesus! I've been defiled!" wailed Brother Roy, as he disappeared from sight.

Now that the show seemed to be over, the members of Brother Roy's flock began going their separate ways as if nothing out of the ordinary had just happened.

Their laughter would come later when they were far enough away from sacred ground and their pastor to retell the story to others.

Rodney and his angel remained behind attempting to stifle now, what they too, would laugh about another time.

Farley wandered back to the edge of the parking lot, wiping the inside of his mouth with the sleeve of his clean shirt.

"Damn! I wish he hadn't broke that whisky jug. I could sure use somthin' to gargle with about now," he said as he sputtered and spit. His brother followed him.

Trux thought he'd seen every thing up until now. The big chinned man was simply appalled.

"How the fuck could you do that?" He asked with a visible shudder.

Farley shrugged. "Had no choice," he explained between additional spits. "Either that or hit im' and he's too damned big! And you're fuckin' welcome by the way! Bat piss! I wish he hadn't broke that jug! God! I hate the taste of Fruit Loops!"

"Oh, shit! Here comes Arthell and Jerkoff! Act like nothin' happened."

Farley stopped spitting as Rodney and Arthell, still trying to keep straight faces, and walking hand and hand, came up to the bearded man with the bad taste in his mouth and his brother.

159

All humor immediately drained from the young attorney's face as Trux glared at him. Rodney quickly released his hold on the beauty and stepped away from her.

If Arthell noticed this, she gave no indication and her good humor remained as he addressed the Maynard brothers.

"Can't you two stay out of trouble?" asked the lovely girl, in such a loving way, all three male hearts present skipped at least one beat. "What brought all that on?"

"Couldn't help it Darlin. We were just walkin' along, mindin' our own business and the big son of a bitch jumped us."

"Well, what really happened," Trux said, leaping into the conversation, "was he jumped Farley and I hadda' do somthin."

He looked Rodney directly in the eye.

"I can get real mean when somebody does somthin' bad to one of my family, ya know?"

Farley turned to his brother and started to remind him just who really save the day here, and to what sacrifice. When he saw what Trux was trying to do, however, the bearded man decided to drop who did what to whom in the Brother Roy incident and return to the problem at hand. He looked back at Arthell who was now gazing at Rodney.

He cleared his throat loudly to get the attention of both young people.

"Yeah. Me n' Trux both always been that way. Mess with the Maynard family, start pickin' out your tombstone! We laugh and joke a lot, Me n' Trux do, but comes to them we really care about we don't fuck around."

The last part of what he felt to be his pointed statement was also directed at the little moon eyed bastard standing beside his baby.

"Anyway it's all over. Gettin' late too," said Trux, squinting up at the sun that was hovering now just above the western horizon, about to disappear beyond it.

"We all better be getting back to the house. Your mamma's gonna take us out to pick up the HOWDY HOSS and we need Rod here, to give us a hand. Sooner we get it in runnin' shape, sooner we can get the kid back to his car and on his way."

"Come on, Daddy Trux. You and Daddy Farley are the experts," Arthell said with a little frown creasing her pretty brow. "You don't need Rodney to help you with that. He doesn't know anything about motor homes, do you Rodney?"

Rodney's answer was, if nothing else, honest.

"I can't even drive one very well," he said.

"That's for damned sure," Farley agreed grumpily. Trux glared at him. Would his brother ever rid himself of hoof and mouth disease?

160

"So, there you go," Arthell said brightly. "Rodney would just be in your way. You guys go on. This will be perfect. I promised him I'd show him around town."

"Ain't nothin to see in Lone Pine. Besides, he's already seen it."

"Daddy Farley, the inside of the jail doesn't really represent the town."

"To us it does," Farley replied. "Besides, the sun's almost down. You know how quick it gets dark this time of year once the sun goes down."

"Then we'd better hurry, huh?" was Arthell's speedy response.

She took Rodney's hand once again and began leading the young man away toward the main street area of Lone Pine. She called back over her shoulder.

"Tell Mamma we wont be late. I love you both."

"We love you too honey!"

It was all Trux could think of to say as he watched the couple walking away. As soon as the younger people were out of earshot, he tuned to Farley and spoke in low, terse tones.

"You think you can get the HOWDY HOSS runnin' by yourself?"

"I imagine. What you gonna be doin?"

"What the hell you think I'm gonna' be doin', shit for brains?" said Trux, as he moved away in the direction taken by Arthell and Rodney who had just turned a corner and disappeared from sight. "I'm gonna make damned sure all they do is walk!"

The sunset to the west, far beyond the boundaries of Lone Pine, was absolutely breathtaking. Rodney and Arthell stopped to drink in its beauty.

Trux, not far to the couple's rear flank, was forced to duck behind the trunk of one of few trees in town, except for those cultivated in the park, to avoid being spotted.

To him, this daily wonder of the disappearing heavenly body meant only one thing. It would be much harder to track the activities of the beauty and the bad guy once it got dark. Silently he cursed the structure of the universe.

Ahead of him, they moved on. As soon as he was certain it was safe, Trux ambulated forward, in cautious pursuit.

Even though it was still daylight, the neon and other artificial illumination of the business enterprise's on Main Street were already in full function. The young attorney and his fabulous female companion gained access to the moderately busy thoroughfare from the mouth of an alley.

As they walked up the sidewalk, looking in shop windows and making small talk, Trux peeked out from around a corner of the same passageway between buildings.

The broad shouldered self appointed individual of surveillance, started to step forward to follow, but his entities of scrutiny paused again. The broad

161

face with the lantern jaw and too many teeth, topped with a full head of curly blond hair, pulled back out of sight.

Arthell had brought the leisurely stroll she and Rodney were enjoying to a temporary halt to greet none other than Standing Up and Sitting Down. The same two individuals Rodney had encountered the previous day when they were sharing a bottle of wine outside the post office.

"Hi Standing Up! Hi Sitting Down! How you doing?"

The two men removed their broad brimmed hats with feathers protruding from the brims and let their long sleek black hair fall down over their shoulders. If either recognized Rodney, it was not apparent.

"Hello sweet Daughter of the Wind," said Standing Up, as he stood there with his hat now in one hand and a bottle of unopened wine in the other. "I'm just fine, but don't ever ask Sitting Down that. He might tell you. Believe me you don't need to hear his answers and there'll be a lot of em."

"Standing Up's been chewing peyote again," was Sitting Down's comment. "How's your Mamma?"

"Stupid question," Standing Up chimed in. "Her mother's beautiful as is the daughter. Give her my love. Excuse him. He drinks. He's trying to forget."

Arthell's laughter was genuine. It sounded like tinkling little silver bells to Rodney.

"So what is it you're trying to forget, Sitting Down?" she asked with a merry smile on her flawless young face.

"Give your Mamma my love too. Ask Standing Up. He's the one that knows everything."

"He can't remember," said Standing Up wisely, as he placed his hat back on his head.

"Go with the White Buffalo, Daughter of the Wind."

"I will, Standing Up," Arthell responded still laughing.

"He don't know nothin 'bout no White Buffalo," Sitting Down put his own wide brimmed hat back on his long jet-black hair.

"Now pink elephants, that's a horse of a different color."

Some of the dialogue he'd encountered with these two the day he arrived in Lone Pine was beginning to possibly make sense to Rodney. The attorney had to make sure.

"Your names are Standing Up and Sitting Down?" asked the young Lawyer.

"No. His name's Standing Up. My name's Sitting Down," said Sitting Down.

Rodney stood there for a minute. He just couldn't help himself. The young man had to ask.

162

"How did you come by such strange names?"

Sitting Down started to speak. He looked just a little offended. Before any words passed his lips, Standing Up began talking first. His voice was suddenly extremely deep.

"Old Indian custom, White eyes," he said. Doing an imitation of the old motion picture Native American stereotype. "Indian father names baby after the first thing he sees after the child pops out of the happy hunting bush!"

Sitting Down's eyes darted quickly in Arthell's direction to make sure the young lady was not offended.

Both he and Standing Up adored their beloved Daughter of the wind. Arthell was stifling a giggle as Rodney attempted an answer. It was a very old joke but knowing these two, it was certain to come out with a new twist.

"I see," said Rodney. "So when you two were born, the first thing each of your father saw was…"

"You got it!" Responded Sitting Down before the naïve young man from Boston could finish. "Our fathers saw the same thing. He saw two dog's humping. Same dogs."

"The dog Sitting Down was named for, was very lazy you see…" Standing Up left the explanation unfinished.

Arthell was laughing out loud now. The look on Rodney's puzzled face was funnier even than what the other two had done with the old joke.

"What's your name?" Sitting Down asked the young man from the big city. "Don't tell me, let me guess. 'Fat old pale face broad wearin' surgical mask', right?"

"My name is Rodney Van Aukin."

Standing Up looked at Sitting Down as he made a terrible face. The Native American then looked back at Rodney in mock sympathy.

"Damn! That must have been awful. I hope he got over it."

While the younger man was trying to sort this out in his head, Standing up turned to Arthell.

"Gotta' go. Can't let this wine age. Old wine ain't good for you."

"I'll remember that, Standing Up! See you guys!" said Arthell between delighted giggles. She waved to the pair who were already heading down the street toward Trux's hiding place.

Suddenly from somewhere within him, an unaccustomed guffaw came to the surface, escaping through Rodney's lips. The young man had somehow, finally understood the gag. The joke was on him and it was alright. It was also extremely funny.

He turned to the lovely young lady beside him. Tears rolled down the cheeks of both their youthful faces as together, they began to howl with laughter.

"That Arthell's an awful good kid." Sitting Down said to Standing Up, as the two men with the one wine bottle passed the alley in which Trux was lurking.

"Good influence too," responded Standing Up as he began unscrewing the top from the bottle. "Remember how bad that guy she's with smelled yesterday?"

"Think he's gonna try and get in her pants?"

"Don't talk that way! Somethin' wrong with im' if he don't."

Trux considered leaping out of the alley and starting the Indian wars again by punching the Native American in the nose.

He didn't have time. Arthell and Rodney were heading on up the street. He couldn't even bring himself to imagine what terrible fate might befall his innocent baby were he lose sight of them. He stepped out of the shadows and pushed onward, pursuing his objective.

Behind him, heading in the opposite direction, Standing up was cursing his companion in Kiowasua for taking the wine jug without permission. Sitting Down was retorting nastily in Rom.

"You're kidding! Those guys are really artists?" Rodney asked Arthell in response to a statement she had just made regarding the two men he had finally realized to be wonderfully funny. The girl and her escort for the evening had finally gained control of their laughter.

"Fine artists," she replied with enthusiastic conviction. "Standing Up's a painter and Sitting Down does the most fantastic things with silver. You should go out to the Reservation and see their work before you leave."

The laughter left Rodney completely and he suddenly felt a wave of sadness wash over him as the couple continued their stroll up the sidewalk.

Both young people were unaware that Trux was behind them and close enough now to hear their conversation.

"I'm afraid once I pick up my car tomorrow, I won't have time stick around to see much of anything. I have to go back to LA right away."

Behind them, Trux was carefully following in the exact footsteps of a very pregnant woman pedestrian whose girth kept him out of Rodney and Arthell's line of vision if either happened to look back.

In spite of the fact that he was forced to walk with his knees bent, because he was much taller than the woman in front of him, his wide grin returned. He liked the turn the conversation was taking.

Arthell not only felt Rodney's sadness, she would have shared it, had she not been taught only to dwell on the good of the moment. He was by her side now. That was good.

She didn't exactly change the subject, but attempted to steer the conversation in a slightly different direction as she maintained her cheerful mood.

"Where is your car anyway?"

Still trudging along behind the pregnant woman, slumped and with his knees bent, the grin on Truxs' face began to fade.

He knew Arthell didn't repeat things about himself and Farley to her mother. Even if she did, Thelma never cared about their escapades anyway. Nonetheless, being chased away from Dirty Socks by Heffaroid Hogg and his shotgun was embarrassing.

"I wouldn't be able to find it without help," Rodney replied in answer to the girl's question, trying not to offend the 'Honesty Monster' and still avoid saying too much at the same time. "Some place between here and Darwin."

Rodney wasn't terribly eager to share that terrible experience about being caught naked with those fat girls either, even if it hadn't been his fault. It wasn't exactly a story he felt would impress this girl he was so smitten with.

Behind the woman with child, Tux heaved a small sigh of relief as the young attorney did a little subject alteration of his own.

"It's a Karmann Ghia," said the young man.

"What?"

"My car. It's a Karmann Ghia. They don't make them anymore. It used to be really cute."

His voice became sad again as he thought of what the little automobile had looked like that last time he saw it.

"Actually, it doesn't look as great as it used to. You'd probably be ashamed to be seen it," he finished lamely.

The breathtakingly beautiful young woman abruptly stopped walking and turned to face him. Her unexpected action forced Rodney to also come to a halt.

In order not to be discovered, Trux had to immediately give up the shelter of the expectant mother's swollen body and seek something else to hide behind.

Fortunately for him, they were all now in front of a Burger King. The sneaky, nimble red neck was able to jump behind the far side of a statue shaped like a giant hamburger, without being seen by either Rodney or Arthell.

The latter spoke earnestly to the young man she felt so attracted to.

"Rodney, I don't care about cars. I care about people. If you ever decide to come back, I'll ride in whatever you happen to be driving, or we can walk, just like we're doing now."

"You don't care what kind of a car your..." He had nearly made an inappropriate verbal slip and said boyfriend.

He quickly amended the question. "Say you're with a guy. You wouldn't care what his car looks like?"

"If I were out with a guy…" Arthell began. She also was very careful to keep her words hypothetical. It probably wasn't a good idea to let him know just yet, that she'd never really been out on what anyone could really refer to as an actual date ever in her life.

Conversely, while she wasn't exactly plagued with the same affliction as Rodney, it still wasn't in the wholesome young lady's' nature to lie.

"Of course I wouldn't be thinking about his car or what it looked like," she continued, "it wouldn't be about what he looked like either. It would be how I felt about the guy."

She smiled and moved closer to Rodney, seemingly oblivious to the pedestrians being forced to walk around them.

"Although the guy I'm with right now looks mighty good and I think I like him an awful lot."

Behind the giant burger, Trux's usually wide blue eyes started to become extremely narrow.

"You really don't care that much about cars?" asked Rodney. "And you really don't like frogs?"

"I can take cars or leave cars. I can't stand frogs. What is this? Twenty questions? Why are you laughing?"

He nearly took her in his arms right there in front of everybody and told her all about Louise. At the last minute he decided the time was inappropriate.

"I'm laughing because I'm happy!" he told her. That was certainly the truth.

He looked around at the Burger King. "I'm also hungry. Your mother's bacon and eggs were wonderful, but I never got to finish breakfast or whatever it was. 'Post jailhouse blues brunch,' I guess."

"I didn't either," she said as she laughed. She loved his sense of humor. Arthell had no way of knowing Rodney was never aware until tonight, when, for some reason he found the funny in the pair of Native American artist's 'Two Dogs' routine, he had one.

The gorgeous girl took him by the arm. Still laughing, she began ushering the young fellow toward the line of people waiting to gain access to the fast food service window. "I better warn you. I don't like frogs, but I do love onions."

Rodney felt so wonderful at that moment; he was fighting back tears of joy.

"Guess what? Me too!" he managed to say, without making a total fool of himself.

"And ketchup too, I'm afraid. I'm just a red neck girl."

"I love ketchup!" responded Rodney in a joyous tone..

Behind the giant burger, Trux was having battles with several of his own emotions. However, none were joyous.

At least the horny little bastard hadn't told her how he lost his car or where it was.

In reality, neither Rodney nor the broad shouldered red neck knew the true location of the Karmann Ghia at this precise moment.

The little vehicle in question was bumping along over the unpaved ruts of a seldom traveled back road as it entered the outskirts the of Lone Pine.

If Rodney thought the poor little automobile looked sad when he last saw it through the rear window of the HOWDY HOSS, it was a blessing he couldn't see it now. Even in the growing darkness its overall appearance was absolutely pathetic. The current driver of the German feat of engineering did nothing to enhance its beauty.

Heffaroid Hogg had somehow managed to stuff his large body into the driver's seat behind the steering wheel.

Due to his enormous size, his line of vision was above the top of the windshield frame still bearing the battle scars of the chainsaw incident outside of Darwin.

The large proprietor of the small borax mine above Dirty Socks Lake couldn't remember when he didn't have some problems. Tonight they were becoming insurmountable.

The discussion with Brother Roy at church today had been good for his sisters' souls, he supposed, but his cousin had still sent them home without a solution. Heffaroid was sure Brother Roy, whom he knew held the ear of God, could come up with one if he would only concentrate.

The man named Hogg had no one else to whom he could turn.

Worming the little car with its groaning springs through the back streets of Lone Pine, he finally arrived at the parsonage to discover Brother Roy not to be home.

He drove on to the Church of Devotion to Divinity itself and pulled into the driveway beside the building built for worship. At the end of the strip of pavement, he made a sharp left turn and both he and the little car disappeared behind the holy edifice.

The place looked deserted except for one small light coming through a small window near the building's rear portal. Brother Roy had to be here. Heffaroid had already been to his cousin of the cloth's house, so he knew the reverend wasn't home.

Grunting and groaning, the obese fellow finally disengaged himself from the little car's front seat and, walking stiffly, panted and puffed his way to the back door and knocked.

When he received no immediate response, He knocked again, this time louder. Still getting no satisfaction, Heffaroid began pounding on the paneling with his huge fist. He started yelling at the same time.

"Cousin Brother Roy! I know you're in there! Open the door! It's me! Heffaroid!"

This particular method of announcing his presence brought immediate results. The door opened, but only enough for Brother Roy to peek out with only one of his eyes visible.

"It is that really you, Cousin?" asked the Pastor, ready to slam the door shut and bar the barrier, if the caller wasn't really who he said he was.

Telltale traces of Fruit Loops and gravy were evident on the lower, jowls of the pastor's fat face. Some, when they have trouble communicating with the Lord, turn to liquor. With Brother Roy, it was gravy with his Fruit Loops.

"Of course it's me, Cousin Brother Roy. Who did you think it was?"

The door opened wider. Just enough for Brother Roy to look out around his relative who was almost as big as he was.

He saw the Karmann Ghia and pulled the hinged barrier back toward him. Again, only one of his eyes could be seen from outside.

"Whose car is that?" the reverend asked with a hiss.

"That fella I told you was with the Maynards left it when I run em' all off with my shotgun. It's a puny little piece of pigeon puke, but my truck broke down today right after I come home from church…"

"Are you alone?" queried Brother Roy cautiously. Slowly, he began to pull the portal open once more.

"Yeah, I'm alone. I left Catch Pen and Squeeze Chute at the shack. I gotta do somethin' 'bout those two Brother Roy!" Heffaroid looked at his cousin's face.

"What's wrong with you anyhow?"

"I had a sign from God this afternoon, Heffy," he said, using the nickname he had given his cousin shortly after moving in with the Hogg family when he left the seminary to do God's work.

The name 'Heffaroid' was much too formal for family in Brother Roy's opinion. Especially when that member of the family was infinitely held such inferior standing in the eyes of the Lord.

Brother Roy's composure was returning. After the terrible thing God had allowed to happen to him this afternoon, the reverend and the Creator hadn't exactly been on speaking terms. Now, the powerful man of the pulpit was beginning to understand what it all meant. The door opened a little further.

Heffaroid spoke back in an almost frightened whisper. "You had a sign from Him?"

Brother Roy flung the portal open all the way. "From Him, Heffy! He

168

delivered a message to me! A very clear message! He agrees with you, my cousin!"

"Heffaroid retained the whisper that became even more reverent. "God agrees with me? Me? Hefforoid Hogg? Me?"

"Absolutly Cousin! It is the will of the Lord that the Maynard brothers should indeed receive grave punishment here on earth before their inevitable journey to the everlasting fires of Hell! Exactly what you asked him for this very morning. God hears those who call on Him, Heffy!"

"That's how come I'm here," said Heffaroid. His voice was louder now, but still filled with wonder.

"Of course it is. He sent you. Come in Heffy. Let us explore the Lord's options regarding unforgettable suffering during this lifetime for Trux and Farley Maynard together."

Trux was totally unaware of any 'Doom before Demise' scheme taking place in the Devotion to Divinity Church, on his and Farley's behalf.

There would have been no time to deal with something so trivial even if he were. He was busy looking out through a knothole in the wall of a wooden, outdoor men's toilet facility in the middle of the Lone Pine City Park.

He was very near the same spot where the man with the square jaw and his brother had argued over the edibility of a watermelon so many years ago. There was unquestionably more than a stolen watermelon at stake on this particular night.

It definitely could be considered dark outside now. The moon had not yet risen, but electric light spilled down from bulbs inserted in tall lampposts surrounding the perimeter of the tiny recreational area, providing sufficient illumination.

Arthell and Rodney occupied a bench, enjoying hamburgers with onions, and each other. Neither seemed to be aware of anyone else in the park, or the lone eyeball peeking through a hole in the side of the nearby restroom.

This single organ of red neck vision was watching their every move but the young man and woman had only eyes for each other. They sat in the middle of their own private world.

Inside the toilet, Trux was forced to back away from the knothole as a skinny man entered from outside and move quickly to the facility's lone urinal.

The broad shouldered Maynard brother pretended to be having difficulty closing his fly as he waited for the intruder to finish his purpose for being there and go his merry way.

Either it had been a long time between pit stops for the skinny man, or the poor fellow was suffering from some sort of prostate disorder. He seemed to

169

take forever.

When he did finally finish, the newcomer proved to be one of those individuals who believed in thoroughly washing his hands, examining both carefully, then washing them again. Trux gritted his extra large sized teeth and continued to fiddle with his fly.

When, at long last, he was once more the only occupant of the restroom, Trux immediately turned back to the wall.

He flattened his big chin against its surface, looking through the knothole again. The girl he felt certain to be his daughter and the sexual deviate he knew was bent on deflowering her, were now no longer in sight.

One poor citizen of Lone Pine was only out for a peaceful evening walk in the park when he'd been summoned by the call of nature.

The unfortunate victim of terrible timing went sprawling back onto the grass as the toilet door swung abruptly open, hitting him squarely in the face. Trux Maynard came storming out into the night.

When the man on the ground looked up and saw the look on the broad shouldered man's face, he decided the pressure on his bladder took precedent over that of manly satisfaction. He climbed to his feet and proceeded on into the facility. The maniac who had knocked him down, charged onward into the night like an angry bull.

Trux looked like a square jawed submarine periscope from the neck up as he stood in the middle of the small park surveying his surroundings.

Just beyond the ring of electric lighting, but still visible, due to the light of the moon that was just beginning to rise, he could see two pairs of shoe clad feet. They were protruding from behind a bush, and each set seemed to belong to a member of the opposite sex.

The male feet were pointed downward and were situated between those that appeared to be female. The toes of the latter were in turn, directed toward the sky.

Trux raced to the bushes to find a young couple in a state of semi undress locked in others arms with their lips pressed together.

With a mighty roar, the big chinned red neck reached down and pulled the boy from the top of the girl, using only one of his hands. The matching appendage was balled up into a huge fist as he twisted the young man around so that the offender could be struck appropriately in the mouth.

Suddenly, Trux froze with his cocked right arm in mid air. He had seen the youth he was now holding around town from time to time, but it certainly wasn't Rodney.

"Wh..what's your problem Maynard?" asked the frightened boy when the broad shouldered man released him.

On the ground, the girl, a flat chested teenager, looked up at the attacker through big round, brown eyes.

She felt certain that those muggers, whom she had only seen on big city television programs, were at last infiltrating the small town of Lone Pine. It wasn't safe to get laid in the park anymore.

"Mistake identity!" called Trux, as he raced away out of the park. "Good luck!"

Trux frantically began running up and down streets, alleys and paths, searching for the missing couple.

They were finally spotted back on the main street of town by the self-appointed undercover chaperone with the big chin and suspicious blue eyes. Arthell and Rodney were innocently looking in through a lighted shop window at Indian jewelry on display.

Trux watched the elusive couple as he flattened himself against the exterior of the same bar where he and Farley had talked Geraldine and the other girls into taking a ride with them the fateful previous night.

That was back when things were normal. Before Rodney had begun to cause all this trouble.

Suddenly, he realized where he was. Fearful that he might be recognized, and someone would call out his name, the Maynard brother with the curly hair, scooped up a discarded newspaper from a wire trash receptacle.

Holding the publication up in front of his face, he moved to the curb and seated himself on a bench. Trux had no idea he was holding the newspaper upside down as he peered over the top of it at the couple. He was determined not to let them out of his sight again.

Suddenly, a vision of loveliness blocked his view. Thelma was now standing directly in front of him.

"What the Hell are you doing?" she asked in an irritated tone as she took the upside newspaper away from him.

"You and Farley pick up the HOWDY HOSS?" It was all Trux could think of to say.

CHAPTER THIRTEEN
ABUNDANCE OF BUMPS IN THE NIGHT

"I don't know why Rodney can't sleep out here in the HOWDY HOSS!" Farley's deep voice held more than an indignant whine as he spoke to Thelma.

He, Trux and Barney were all standing beside the motor home now.

The big rig looked worse than ever, as it sat in Thelma's driveway behind her house in front of Thelma's also parked, cream colored compact.

The kitchen lights floating out through the windows with the help of the moon clearly illuminated the regrettable current disaster statistics of the much older and larger of the two vehicles. Its bumper was mangled, headlamps broken, and the front end behind both was crumpled.

Each brother held a can of Blue Ribbon beer in his hand. A cooler containing more sat on the threshold of the motor home's open side door.

In contrast, Thelma herself couldn't have looked more glamorous, as she lingered in the open back doorway of her own house. She was wearing a very slinky nightgown that left little to the imagination but did wondrous things for that small portion remaining.

Arthell and Rodney had returned shortly after the Argus Queen had drug Trux home by his proverbial ear. The brothers were both fairly certain that due to Trux's vigilance, the girl's virtue had not been compromised. However, tomorrow morning was still a long way off. Both were still very concerned.

"I say if it's good enough for Barney, it oughta' be good enough for Rodney," Farley continued. "And Barney don't mind."

"Ain't that much different between a pig and a lawyer anyway," said Trux.

Barney didn't look the least bit offended. Farley, however, definitely took his brother's statement to be derogatory.

"Ain't no reason to insult Barney just cause he don't care who he sleeps with."

Trux addressed his next statement to Thelma even though the fist part of it referred to Farley.

"I think Puss Gut here just made my point, Thelma. Ain't no reason the little shit can't bunk out here. It's only for one night, for God's sake."

Thelma gave them both a tolerant loving smile.

"He'll be just fine on the couch in my office," she said, while stretching her lovely upper limbs, which did marvelous visual things to her breasts beneath the sheer material of her nighty. The physical action did even more for the lower portion of her spectacular body.

"You guys coming to bed soon?"

Under normal circumstances the Maynard brothers would have been crawling over each other to get to the lady's bedroom. Tonight they had a real problem that even superceded sex with the lady they both really loved, at least in Trux's mind.

"I dunno. Maybe me n' Farley better stay out here in the HOWDY HOSS tonight. We gotta lot to think on."

She smiled. One of the multitudes of wonderful things that made up Thelma's unique personality was her undying patience. Having a pair of lifetime lovers like the Maynard brothers, this particular trait was undoubtedly a necessity.

"Suit yourselves. Just remember boys, when the Argus Queen's a snoozin, you're the ones a losin." She blew them both kisses then retreated inside, closing the door behind her.

The lights inside the kitchen were extinguished almost immediately. Farley's face, now illuminated only by moonlight, showed real concern.

"Ain't no sense in us stayin' out here, Trux. How come you said that?"

Trux gave his brother a disgusted look.

"Come on Farley, your dick ain't big enough to get in the way of what's right in front of your eyes, even when you gotta woody." He was trying to get Farley to recognize logic.

"That's our little girl in there. We can't afford no distraction till that sex freak's outa' here."

"Maybe he ain't, Trux."

"Ain't what?"

"What you just said. What we been thinkin' 'bout him. Me n' Thelma was talkin' when we went to pick up the HOWDY HOSS. He ain't such a bad kid."

"Farley, I love that woman as much as you do, but don't go lettin' her fill your head with no shit!" Trux looked his brother straight in the eye.

"Women don't understand how a man's mind works. We do!" The big chinned man's voice became low and tense, as he continued attempting to enlighten his brother regarding the danger ahead.

"What was you thinkin' when you was his age and seen a pretty young thing like Arthell?"

Farley didn't have to think long. The look of pure hate from earlier that afternoon returned to his eyes. Trux had to hold his brother back as the bearded man threw his half-full beer can away into the shadows of the night and started to charge the house.

"Evil little bastard! I'm gonna kill him! I really am! Little cock sucker!"

"We can't do that. We'd end up back in jail and even Thelma couldn't get us out then. Besides, she'd be pissed. We just gotta make sure, one way or another, the little son of a bitch goes home tomorrow. At least the HOWDY HOSS is still runnin. We can get his candy ass back to Dirty Socks and his car. Go tonight if we had lights and wasn't damn near outa gas."

Farley heaved a deep sigh of frustration as he headed for the beer cooler.

"What are we gonna do in the mean time, Trux?"

Trux stroked his big chin and pondered the situation as Barney nuzzled Farley's pants leg with his snout, hoping to get across the fact that he could also use a fresh, cold one.

Farley's thirsty four-legged friend seemed to give the broad shouldered man inspiration. He leaned down and scratched the animal on the soft part of its throat.

"Barney, when you get done with your beer, Uncle Trux's got an idea."

The pig looked up and gave the energetic red neck with the curly blond hair and blue eyes a friendly, yet reserved, grunt. He loved it when Uncle Trux displayed these rare signs of physical affection toward him, but Barney certainly hoped this new idea wasn't going to get them all thrown in jail again.

*** *** *** *** *** ***

The house was quiet and the couch in Thelma's office was certainly far more comfortable than the jail cot on which Rodney had been forced to spend the previous night.

Still, no matter how hard he tried, the young lawyer simply could not get to sleep. His mind refused to stop dwelling on the vision of whom Rodney was convinced was beyond the slightest shadow of any doubt, the world's most perfect young woman, lying in her own bed only two doors away.

Through the semi darkness, he could see Thelma's computer resting on top of her desk.

He was glad the monitor was covered. Back in high school when he had first been introduced to the world of these electronic marvels, he'd harbored a suspicion about monitors.

To him they always seemed to be the mechanisms big, large eye. One could gaze into those electronically developed video display devices and glean information about almost everything.

To young Rodney at that time, it had then stood to reason that the computer, in turn, through its cyclops organ of sight, could see into, and examine the brain of the person looking at it. Where else did all those facts and figures come from?

Rodney was an educated adult now, and he knew his original hypothesis to be unfounded. Nonetheless, he still felt better with the devise shrouded. The befuddled young barrister didn't want anyone or anything peeking inside any part of him right now, especially his brain.

His thoughts were an embarrassing tangled mess of totally illogical thought patterns. The inside of his head felt like it was overflowing with a gigantic complicated jigsaw puzzle. Too many pieces of that puzzle were either lost or misplaced. Maybe they just weren't meant to fit into one picture in the first place.

There were so many things he wanted to tell this absolutely wonderful person who had entered his life in the middle of such bizarre circumstances.

He longed to express the sensation of pure joy he experienced just looking at her, the thrill that went through him when she touched his hand. He wanted her to know that being with her made him want to laugh and cry at the same time.

Then, there were things that he didn't necessarily have a real desire to tell her, but he knew he must.

These would be details dictated as always, by that flaw in his character that he abhorred. His pesky honesty defect.

The information demanding disclosure by his personal perennial parasite would undoubtedly dampen those feelings of fondness she had already expressed toward him. In addition, it was certain to prevent new ones from nurturing.

Once he informed her about his situation with Louise, she probably wouldn't even care to listen to those other things in his heart he so desperately wished to share with her.

Right now he couldn't even figure out why he'd ever become engaged in the first place.

He did feel a certain affection toward the pretentious young woman back in Beverly Hills, but he knew now, he certainly was not in love with her. Neither Louise nor Rodney had really explored the emotion of love.

Everything that just seemed to happen, on and after, that first drunken night he arrived in Los Angeles, had been taken as a sign that they were destined to be together. The path of least resistance had been accepted by both as life's inevitable route of progress.

It was strange, the young man reflected, as he lay tossing on the couch across the room from the Argus Queens' computer, it had never occurred to him to equate the word life with being alive. That was probably because, until today, when he first laid eyes on this exotic young beauty who's family situation was so strange it couldn't even be fathomed, he had never known how it felt to really be alive.

He was thinking too much, and his thoughts were far too complicated. None of this material was ever covered in law school. He couldn't recall Norman Vincent Peale touching on it either.

He rolled over on the couch. Tomorrow, he would somehow get his car back and drive away from what he couldn't deal with.

He wasn't going back to Louise. He knew now his relationship with Horace Herkimer's daughter was not only something that should not have happened, but could never continue. Very likely, once she saw the condition of the Slum Mobile, he'd be sent packing from the Beverly Hills apartment anyway.

At least she wouldn't be alone. Louise would always have her frogs.

However, as he lay there, tossing and turning on the couch belonging to the mother of the girl that really held his heart, he convinced himself that he really wasn't worthy of her love. Arthell deserved better.

She had probably already come to that conclusion herself. He decided firmly never to bother her again. He would complete his business and leave, as soon as possible, the following day. The beautiful young woman's memory would become but a cherished dream.

Maybe after he closed the deal and gave the Maynards' their money, he would take the paper with their signatures back to Horace and Harold Herkimer, and resign his position.

Maybe he would then return to New England and enter a monastery in Maine. Joining the Peace Corps and traveling to Africa was another option.

Maybe the Peace Corps could use his legal training.

Maybe he could get some sleep if he lay on his right side.

Down the short hallway, in her own room, Arthell was also awake and thinking of Rodney. Her thoughts about him, while indeed deep, were not nearly so complicated as his.

As Thelma had stated earlier, every young available man in the delightful girl's age group within the entire Owens Valley, had been frightened to even approach her since she began blossoming into womanhood.

None wished to endure the wrath of either overprotective man who might be her father. This was something that never bothered the sweet young person who liked everybody and everything, except frogs.

Her mother had always told her that running amuck looking for romance was every bit as foolish as running away from it. When that pristine moment arrived, Arthell would know. Nature needed no push to proceed.

The other girls she had grown up with had either already thrust their way, or had been shoved into sexual encounters. Some had experienced sex even earlier than the age of twelve. Even though they boasted about these experiences, the underlying sadness of what they should have felt and failed to, was pitifully transparent.

There had never been the slightest doubt in Arthell's pretty head that someday her perfect young man would arrive. Today he had.

Except for one brief uncomfortable moment, when he had attempted to talk about his car, the evening had been flawless. He was so different from the local braggadocios young bulls she had so far encountered.

The pensive budding beauty was sure the young man lying now on the couch in her mother's office, must have a girlfriend back where he came from. It would be too sad if he did not.

She knew full well that jealousy was a monster of self-indulgence that only flourished upon personal invitation. To limit or place boundaries on love was a severe nullification of the emotions real meaning.

If two people really felt love for each other, the magic between the two of them was all that really mattered. Feelings on either party's part toward another, were totally different issues.

Should these sentiments bloom into something more physical beyond the beautiful connection of mind and soul, a blessing had been added. If not, the relationship was to be no less cherished.

She smiled up into the semi darkness of the room decorated with Native American art, polished driftwood and childhood memories. Her Rodney was like a little boy in so many ways. The young woman found these traits to be endearing.

He must look so very special at this moment, curled up in a ball on that couch in her mother's office. She felt a sudden urge to see him exactly that way.

Arthell rose from her bed. The short night gown she wore was not nearly so suggestive as the slinky sleeping garment adorning her mother's voluptuous curves on this night, but still displayed her healthy, fine young figure to its fullest.

She tiptoed through a shaft of moonlight drifting in from outside her open window to the closet for a robe.

Suddenly, the girl realized how silly such a garment would be on such a warm night. She only planned to peek in on the young man to watch him sleeping.

If for some reason, the boy she was so fond of wasn't deep in slumber, there was no reason why he shouldn't see her in her nightgown anyway.

She also realized that she might be slightly thirsty. Maybe while she was up, she'd go into the kitchen for a drink of water.

She turned and walked to the door leading out into the hallway and subsequently her mother's office. There was a purpose to her stride as she pulled the portal open and stepped out into the corridor.

Her bare foot landed squarely on top of poor Barney's sensitive, curly tail. The pig's high pitched, unearthly barnyard wail of pain and total shock echoed off the walls of every room in the house.

When Barney had been posted on sentry duty out side Arthell's bedroom door as insurance against after hour callers, the unsuspecting animal had no idea his newly appointed position could lead to such trauma.

Having your tail stepped on while in the middle of deep, peaceful slumber, was a horrible way for a pig to have to wake up.

Barney's scream of pain and panic pierced through the outer walls of Thelma's dwelling and in through those of the HOWDY HOSS. The Maynard brothers' organic alarm system had indeed proved to be functional.

Inside the battered and abused old motor home, all Hell was breaking loose. Farley, who had been sleeping up front, bolted straight up in his underwear.

Leaping toward the side door, he tripped over the old leather seat and crashed headfirst into the icebox. Cans of the day's prior purchase of Blue Ribbon beer tumbled out all over the bearded man.

Trux practically flew out of the rig's interior bedroom area. He nearly ripped the top of his head off as he tried to get out through the door.

The man with the big chin stepped back to collect his wits for only a second, then lowered his head and charged the exit again. This time he collided with Farley who was also attempting to make his own egress so he might flee to his endangered little girl's side.

After giving each other a terrible cursing, and being knocked off balance several more times, as they stepped on rolling cans of beer, they both managed to make it out of the motor home.

The red neck brothers raced through the night toward the sound of the still squealing pig. They charged into the rear of Thelma's abode to the rescue of their helpless, defenseless little daughter.

The hall lights were already on as well as several others in the house, as Trux and Farley came racing around the hallway corner in their unflattering underwear.

Thelma and Arthell, still wearing revealing nightgowns were already there. The sexy sleeping apparel of each now evinced much more, due to their present positions. Both were kneeling in front of Arthell's open bedroom doorway on either side of poor Barney, trying to calm him down.

Rodney, looking more bewildered than ever, was wrapped in a blanket as he stood in front of the portal entryway to Thelma's office. The higher education graduate, who was so proud of his excellent marks in courtroom procedure, looked much more like a frightened kindergarten kid on his first day of school after his mother had departed.

The Maynard brothers immediately leaped on the young man. Each grabbed him by an arm as they began pulling him toward the corner of the hallway toward the kitchen and the back door of the house beyond it

"Baby raping little cock sucker!" snarled Trux.

"We gonna' learn ya' a new four bit word! College crud! 'Castration'! You educated, ignorant asshole!" Farley cried out.

Barney began to squeal even louder. Arthell jumped to her feet to defend Rodney. She grabbed the young attorney by both shoulders and began pulling him to her, attempting to pry him away from Trux and Farley. Rodney now knew what it might feel lie to be a Thanksgiving turkey wishbone.

"He didn't do anything!" the pretty young woman screamed, partly out of anger at her unreasonable fathers, but mainly to be heard over the sound of the pig.

Barney continued to wail as Thelma rose and moved to her daughter's side. "Will somebody please tell me what's going on?" she demanded at the top of her lungs.

"Stay out of this woman!" Trux yelled back as he and Farley finally were able to wrestle Rodney away from Arthell. The blanket fell from the young man's body revealing all of him that wasn't covered by his Jockey shorts.

Trux reached beneath the arms of the wrongfully accused. Clasping his own hands together behind the lawyer's neck, the red neck began pushing Rodney's head forward, executing a classic Full Nelson wrestling hold to render his victim helpless.

In the background, the pig continued to squeal as Trux drug the young man back toward the open doorway of Thelma's office.

The broad shouldered man with the big chin and the blood in his eye, finished yelling at the Argus Queen before calling over his shoulder to Farley.

"We'll handle this! You and the girl go on back to bed! Get his stuff Farley! He's outa' here!"

Barney still howled to the heavens as Thelma yanked open another hallway door revealing a broom closet. She pulled out a long handled mop and charged the Maynard brothers. As the angry beautiful woman came up behind her pair of lovers, she began beating both severely about the head and shoulders.

The pig continued to scream as Trux released his hold on Rodney and both he and Farley beat a hasty retreat to the end of the hallway leading around the corner to the kitchen. They could think of no other way on the spur of the moment, to avoid further contact with the business end of the Argus Queen's mean mop.

"Farley!" yelled Thelma, holding the mop ready, like a member of the

Swat Team might do with his or her automatic weapon. "Turn that pig off!"

Farley, keeping his hands up in a defensive position in case that mop in Thelma's hands might go off again, sidled toward the squealing swine, staying close to the wall.

He kept his eyes on those of the dangerous woman at all times as he moved in front of her to the pig's side, using extreme caution.

When the bearded man finally reached his destination, he leaned down and touched Barney lightly on the tip of his snout.

Immediately the pig stopped squealing and looked benignly up at his master.

The sudden silence that followed was so shocking; a good two minutes passed before anyone said anything at all.

Thelma was the first to speak again. "I asked what was going on?" she demanded of Trux and Farley who now stood at opposite ends of the short hallway.

Trux was careful not to move forward as he peeked around the hallway corner from the kitchen.

"Do I have to draw you a picture, Thelma?" he asked.

"It's purty damned obvious what happened," Trux continued as he moved back into the hallway just far enough to point his finger at Rodney who had managed to pick the fallen blanket from the floor and was trying to cover himself again.

"He tried to break into her bedroom!"

"I did not!" protested Rodney.

"He'd a done it too!" stated Farley, growing just a little braver. He inched a couple of inches back toward the middle of the hallway. He was still very careful to keep beyond immediate range of that mop. "If we hadn't had Barney outside her door!"

The beautiful head of the household had a fleeting moment of fear. Was it possible that Barney's high pitched, prolonged squealing may have somehow affected her eardrums?

Thelma had been involved with both of these crazy guys for many years. She was never really surprised at anything they might end up doing no matter how outlandish, but surely they hadn't done what Farley just said they did.

She turned to the bearded brother. He was one of the men she'd always love even if she ended up killing both him and the other one she was just as much in love with, before this night came to an end. Thelma was hoping against all hopes that she hadn't heard Farley correctly.

"You didn't really put that pig outside my daughter's door?"

"Well, shit! She's my daughter too!" replied Farley defensively, not really answering the lady's question, but still telling her what she didn't really want to hear, by justifying the action

"Or mine!" asserted Trux. "And it worked. You heard him squeal."

"Yes I certainly did."

Thelma's face was a mask of disbelief. She wasn't sure what she was going to say next, but the odds were excellent that it would not be pleasant.

Arthell spoke up in a very tiny voice

"I stepped on the pig," she admitted, as she hung her lovely head.

All eyes in the hallway, including those of Rodney's turned toward her.

She assumed her normal voice again and focused her eyes on Barney as she moved past her Daddy Farley to the pig's side. The pretty girl's short nightgown rode up over her thighs as she squatted down beside the now docile animal.

"I'm sorry Barney," she said, really meaning it, as she stroked his snout.

Barney released a series of grunts to let her know not only was she forgiven, but also that he had a few apologies of his own to express. He regretted ever becoming involved in this mess.

"How come you to step on him, anyhow, Arthell?" Farley's tone was filled with a combination of confusion and suspicion.

He gave Rodney a quick glance to make certain the punk wasn't ogling those young nubile thighs. Although with that broom still in Thelma's hands, it wasn't quite clear in his mind what he and Trux could do about it right now.

Thelma had heard enough.

"Maybe she was thirsty! Maybe she wanted a drink of water! Or quite possibly she just wanted to walk around. She lives here!" The Argus Queen was a real advocate when it came to the right of privacy.

"Just in case your alcohol consumption has thrust you into a state of disorientation, you're not in Arty Dubs' jail anymore. This is my home!"

Trux and Farley remained silent. When Thelma brought out the mop and started using big words all on the same night, she was well on her way to becoming really pissed.

Arthell's eyes and her mother's met. The embarrassed girl marveled at the older woman's intuition. She had entertained the thought of a drink of water, even though that hadn't been the real reason Arthell was leaving her room.

Thelma knew her daughter's real thirst. She also trusted the girl's judgement. Her tone was sweet, yet sharp as she now spoke to the Maynard brothers.

"Both of you should be ashamed of yourselves. I really think you should apologize. And you should do it now!"

Trux hung his blond curly head.

"You're right, Thelma," he said, as he walked in front of both the

181

beautiful woman and her beautiful daughter to the pig.

"Sorry Barney."

Farley joined him. "Yeah, sorry Barney."

Thelma's voice was no longer quite so sweet, but it was loud.

"Not to the pig, damnit!" she snapped, while pointing to Arthell and Rodney. "To them!"

Arthell moved to the open doorway of Thelma's office that Rodney now stood in front of once again with the blanket wrapped around his nearly naked body. She clutched the young attorney's arm through the bedding material and they both waited.

It seemed to take at least a decade for Trux and Farley to walk down the length of the short hallway to face the young couple.

When at last they arrived, Trux mumbled something that might possibly have been an apology if anyone could have understood it. Farley's words were less distinguishable than those of his brother.

Arthell smiled as if both men had uttered eloquent words of contrition. No matter what they had done, she knew their love for her had been the motivating force behind the action.

"It's okay," she said.

"No harm done," Rodney said, as he pulled his right arm loose from the clutches of the divine creature beside him to shake hands with the brothers.

The blanket fell down to the floor again. Trux just watched with steely eyes as both the young lawyer and the girl scrambled to pick it up and cover him one more time.

Farley, clearly wishing an immediate change of scenery, turned and patted his leg for Barney to come to him.

The pig wanted out of there too. He quickly walked to the side of the bearded man with the potbelly.

"I gotta take Barney to the motor home," Farley announced, as he and the animal proceeded past the others toward the hallway corner that led to the kitchen and the rear of the dwellings interior. "He'll never get to sleep if we leave im' in here after bein' scared so bad."

"You come on back in here after you get him bedded down. And don't take all night," Thelma called after Farley as he and the pig disappeared around the hallway corner. "You and Trux are spending the rest of this night with me."

She turned to Trux who was still looking at Rodney.

"I invited both of you into my bed earlier." The Argus Queen said, using an extremely firm tone. "It's no longer an invitation. It's now an order! I want the two of you close by so I can keep an eye on you!"

"Good idea," said Trux, reluctantly tearing his eyes away from the attorney to give the lady who had just delivered the edict an affirmative nod.

Rodney's own eyes had become big as saucers. He was obviously aware that when the Maynard brothers and Arthell's mother were much younger, they had all three been involved in some sort of strange, triangular sexual activity. The proper born and bred young Bostonian had no idea that such a relation ship might still exist between them.

How could such an unspeakable thing still be happening at their age? He was simply aghast. There were no other words that could describe the young man's reaction.

Thelma put her lethal mop away and Arthell continued to stand beside Rodney while Trux stared again at the still stunned, young law school graduate.

"Pig may be gone," the man with the big chin said with meaning as he pointed with his thumb at Thelma's room at the end of the hall, "But I ain't. Gonna' be right down there in that room. Right there at the end of the hall!"

Thelma had turned off all of the lights except the one in the hallway where they were still gathered, when Farley, his underwear flapping, finally returned. The bearded man had a glass of water in his hand.

"We probably wouldn't really a' cut your nuts out," he muttered under his breath to Rodney, as he handed the glass to Arthell. "But you never know. Still better not try nothin."

Before anymore could be said Thelma took each brother by an arm and began ushering both down the hall to her boudoir. She called back over her shoulder

"Sleep well kids. I'll keep these dudes occupied so they don't bother you anymore tonight."

She herded her men into the bedroom and pushed the door firmly shut behind them all as they disappeared from sight.

Rodney could only stare at that door for a long moment while Arthell took a sip from the water glass Farley had given her.

When the young man with the puritanical upbringing could speak again, he was certain his stammer would return. It did not.

The tone in his voice, however, was an exact match for the appalled expression that did unflattering things to his features. Except for the sour look, Rodney's face was otherwise becoming much more attractive in masculine appearance, due to its lack of former blemishes combined with the deep tan that was continuing to develop.

"Your mother is really going to sleep with both of those old men?"

Arthell didn't exactly understand the question. She nodded and took another sip of water.

"That doesn't bother you?"

She was still slightly puzzled, but she thought she was starting to follow his thought pattern.

"They're in love Rodney," she stated the fact simply; feeling there was no more to say.

"But there's two of them!"

"Uh huh."

"That's really a little bit too unconventional, Arthell. Don't you think so?"

"My mother's a very unconventional woman," she said with pride.

Rodney looked at the closed door at the end of the hall again. Somehow he wasn't communicating.

"It's just not socially acceptable, Arthell, what they're doing."

The extremely attractive girl smothered a giggle. "My mom was pretty mad. They probably aren't doing anything right now." Her pleasant attitude continued. Then she added a more serious after thought.

"People really in love have to follow the rules of their own hearts. It wouldn't make any sense if they followed someone else's."

He had to make her understand.

"But even if that were true, even if it was okay, they can't really be in love with your mother. They cheat on her! And if you could see some of the women."

Arthell smiled. Now she understood his problem. She offered him the glass of water.

"Try some. It's really good."

He managed to keep the blanket in place as he took the glass from her. Her smile brightened as she asked him a question.

"Rodney," she began speaking slowly, wanting desperately for this young man she had grown so fond of in such a short time, to comprehend what she was about to say.

"My mother says that cheating is when you steal. You know, like when you use someone else's answers on a test or take something that hasn't been given to you? Trux and Farley Maynard share answers with those other women you're taking about. They give much than they take and never take anything that hasn't been already given. How can that possibly be cheating?"

He took a sip of the water. She was right about it being good. But she couldn't possibly be correct about the other thing. His mind raced. There had to be a million flaws in her limited logic. Why couldn't he think of at least one?

She waited politely for his response. When it was obvious none was forthcoming, the pretty girl continued with more philosophy from the independent mind of Thelma Houston.

"Mom says free spirits who have as much love in their souls as those two,

184

need the freedom to spread that love around."

When there was still no verbal riposte from the young man who was trained to debate issues, Arthell asked yet another question. She changed the subject only slightly.

"How many men have you ever met that can cram as much living into one day as my fathers?"

The young attorney couldn't think of a soul. He was regretting ever bringing the subject up. He would rather drink some more water.

He lifted the glass back up to his lips and drained it as the gorgeous girl continued. Would she never run out of questions he seemed to be incapable of answering?

"My mom's a very special woman. You agree?"

Finally, a question he could answer with no reservations.

"That goes without saying."

"Those two crazy red necks in there are pretty special too." She went on, indicating the closed door at the end of the hall. "And special people take on the world in their own special way. Can you understand that?"

He looked around for a place to dispose of the empty glass in his hand.

"I'm trying to," he said, really meaning it. The 'Honesty monster' wouldn't let him say so if he didn't. She took the translucent tumbler from him and walked past the young man wrapped in the blanket, into her mother's office.

At the end of the hall, the door to Thelma's bedroom started to open. It closed almost immediately as the voice of the lady herself floated firmly out into the corridor from behind it.

"Close the door, and come back to bed, Trux!"

Arthell was placing the empty glass on a small table next to her mother's computer as Rodney entered the office behind her.

"I think I'm really beginning to," he said, continuing the hallway conversation. "Understand, I mean. Arthell, could I ask you something?"

Her flawless young features were void of any apparent secrecy as she faced him.

"Of course, Rodney."

"Did you really step on the pig?"

She began to giggle as she nodded.

"And I wasn't really thirsty either."

They both began to laugh. It wasn't loud, but it was genuine and collective. At that moment it was as if the two young people were one person. Finally Arthell spoke again.

"Now it's my turn," she said. "What's she like?"

For a moment Rodney wanted to feign ignorance. He couldn't. That little demon, honesty was inside him, probing his heart with its pitchfork again.

"She's not at all like you," he responded at last. "She loves cars and frogs. I don't think she really likes me much, though."

"If that's really true, I feel sad for her," Arthell said. "I mean about not liking you," she added quickly. "Everybody's entitled to their own opinions about frogs and cars."

"When I go back, I'm going to tell her it's all over."

"That's up to you. You should know though, even if you don't, she has nothing to do with the way we feel about each other."

"I don't understand that." It was so easy to be honest with this girl. The pesky little parasite must be either turning cartwheels of approval or terrified it would have no further function if a relationship were to further develop between Rodney and his newfound angel.

She moved close to him and put her arms up around his neck. The girl, who seemed to be totally free of all guile, pulled his head down until their lips met.

The blanket fell to the floor for at least the fourth time that night as the couple shared a long, passionate kiss. Finally they released one another.

She called over the lacy night gown strap of her otherwise bare, sexy shoulder as she exited the office.

"You'll figure it out. Good night, Rodney."

He collapsed on to the couch and lay there grinning at the ceiling like either a carefree idiot or a young man in love. The two categories have been stated to be synonymous by some, but who cares when you have just been kissed by an angel?

Arthell came out of the office and flipped a wall switch downward, extinguishing the electric lighting in the hallway. She then skipped happily through the darkness to her own room and entered it.

As the girl's door closed, Thelma's voice could be heard, once again, from behind the portal of her own sleeping quarters.

"Trux! Get your eyeball out of that keyhole and your ass back in this bed right now!"

CHAPTER FOURTEEN
SANCTIMONIOUS MANEUVERS

At least another hour had arrived and departed since it had been so decreed where Trux Maynard's posterior was to be positioned for the remainder of the night.

The sovereignty of the Argus Queen was quiet and peaceful. Unfortunately, all periods of tranquility often signify approaching turbulence. This night was to be no exception.

A lonely overhead cloud had drifted in front of the moon. What looked like two gigantic, unidentifiable dark blobs stealthily approached the house, where inside, Thelma, her loved ones and the weary traveler were sleeping.

The cloud and the moon soon separated, revealing the features of Heffaroid Hogg and Brother Roy Ogles. They still looked like two dark gigantic blobs, but the blobs now had fat, unattractive recognizable faces and were indeed identifiable.

"You think it's safe, Cousin Brother Roy?" whispered Heffaroid. "It sure took em' a long time to shut off the lights."

"Those who cavort in the Devil's play pen keep late hours, Heffy. Patience is virtue. You must remember that." The large minister whispered back.

The two monstrous cousins tiptoed their collective weight of at least nine hundred pounds down Thelma's driveway toward the rear of the darkened dwelling.

By the time they reached the back portion of the cream colored stationary compact that could be seen sticking out from around the corner of the building, metatarsal strain became unbearable. The immense duo lowered their heels to the ground and shuffled silently onward.

A white clerical collar still encircled Brother Roy's immense neck but the purple robe no longer covered his huge fleshy frame. A flat crowned black hat with a slouching, medium sized brim now sat on top of his big head.

Side pockets of the too tight, matching black suit coat the man of the cloth was also now wearing, bulged out on either side of his already bulging body. Due to the lack of daylight it was not apparent just how small this suit really was for him as opposed to his flowing robe.

It had been some time since Brother Roy had paid a visit to his private tailor in Santa Barbara who was reported to be a retired sail maker. He'd put on a few pounds since that time, or perhaps his garments had been washed in very hot water by mistake.

The reverend's mind was not, however, on physical appearances at the moment. The large spokesman for Supreme Power's thoughts were totally focused on how close he was to entering phase one of the Lord's newest plan.

A preparation of punishment for two specific members of mankind.

The pockets of Brother Roy's snug jacket were filled with tools of the Creator to ensure his mission be successful.

Among these instruments of God were also a few handfuls of Fruit Loops. He planned on sharing them with Heffaroid when the two huge men finished what the Lord had sent them here to accomplish.

In the meantime, he occasionally sneaked out a nibble or two for himself. His cousin didn't need any distractions right now.

"At least they finally brought the pig back out and put im' in the motor home. There for awhile I was skeered they was gonna' let the filthy thing sleep in the house with em'." Heffaroid whispered again.

He and his cousin had been watching Thelma's household for quite some time and the large man from the borax mine above Dirty Socks Lake, was tired and hungry.

He was especially hungry. He really wished Brother Roy would let him have some of those Fruit Loops, although he was hesitant to say so.

This doing the work of God was new to Heffaroid. He was unsure of proper protocol.

Brother Roy's responsive whisper held a note of irritation as they rounded the corner of the house.

They paid no attention to the compact as they waddled past it. The focus of their attention was solely on the motor home parked in front of it which was now only a few feet away in front of the fat intruders.

"Don't make me tell you about the virtue of patience again. I, like the Lord, hate repeating myself. The creature of the cloven hoof is finally within our grasp. That is all that matters."

They stopped before they reached the closed door of the silent large vehicle that was obviously their destination. A few Fruit Loops fell to the asphalt as Brother Roy pulled a small bottle from one of the bulging pockets. Moonlight reflected off the glass container and the liquid inside it while the huge pastor began unscrewing its cap.

Heffaroid, his attention on the fallen Fruit Loops let a set of car keys he had been holding, slip from his fat fingers. They hit the asphalt beneath him with a loud clatter.

"What was that?" asked Brother Roy, continuing to whisper while he removed the cap from the bottle.

The pastor looked longingly at the tires of both the motor home and

Thelma's compact parked behind it. It was a shame he wouldn't have the pleasure of slashing at least one of them on this night. Such an act simply would not fit in with present procedure. Maybe another time.

"I dropped the keys to that fella's pukey little putt mobile," Heffaroid answered, when he finally figured out exactly what had fallen from his hand while he was watching the unfortunate display of wasted nourishment.

"Well, don't just stand there. Pick them up Heffy. And put them in your pocket. I need some help here. Even the Savior had the assistance of his apostles."

There was somebody out there. Barney knew it. He just wasn't sure who. He was certain it wasn't Daddy Farley or Uncle Trux.

The pig was all too familiar with the scent of the two brothers. He also knew it wasn't Sister Arthell or Mamma Thelma. He loved the way they smelled. This was not necessarily a pleasant odor.

Whoever was prowling around outside the motor home was somebody who had no business being there unless it was the young man from the trolling trip.

Barney didn't have Rodney's scent down just yet. It was possible that the pig's two dearest companions had finally won their argument and the pig was to have a roommate after all.

After the evening's previous fiasco, Barney didn't want to start squealing until he was really certain. If it was someone that didn't belong, Barney was ready for whoever it was. He had just enough booze in his system to feel feisty.

The plucky pig maneuvered his round body into position and faced the inside of the door. He lifted the upper lip of his snout and barred his tusks. He'd squeal all right if it wasn't the young man, and Daddy and Uncle Trux would come running.

However, Barney planned on getting a lunch from whoever dared to invade his domain before the Maynard brothers arrived to take their meal.

On the other side of that portal, Heffaroid was still nervous.

"What happens if he starts squealin' again, Cousin?" he asked the pastor who now was pouring the contents of the open bottle of chloroform he now held in one huge hand onto a large white handkerchief spread out over the palm of the other.

"We could hear the little bastard two blocks away."

Brother Roy's teeth gleamed in the moonlight as he smiled. He tossed the bottle aside and, holding the now soaked handkerchief in his oversized palm very carefully, he reached into yet another pocket with his free, fat appendage.

This time, the man who loved God, because the Supreme Being never disagreed with him, withdrew a long, tubular canister out into the moonlit night air. The devise had a silver spray attachment mounted on its top.

"That's where your part of carrying out His work comes to pass, Heffy." The preacher said, as the object was transferred from one large man to the other.

"What is it?"

"And on the eighth day, Heffy, The Lord created mace," the reverend whispered devoutly.

He crept onward toward the side portal of the HOWDY HOSS, still holding the soaked cloth in his hand. He motioned for Heffaroid to follow with the weapon of God entrusted to him.

The door to the motor home was yanked open.

It wasn't the young man he and Daddy Farley and Uncle Trux had spent the previous night in jail with. There were two of them and they were big.

Ignoring the size of the invaders, Barney started to leap forward. The spray of the incapacitating mace chemical ingredients hit him squarely in his face.

He felt a terrible stinging sensation in his eyes and throat. It was suddenly impossible for him to move. Everything, including his vocal cords seemed to be paralyzed. He was unable to even cry out for help.

The poor pig fell backward onto its haunches and a very large hand holding something white was thrust against his snout.

As Barney fell asleep for the third time that night, he heard the oratorical tones of a human voice seeming to be coming from hundreds of miles away.

"Pick him up, Heffy! I have to leave the Lord's message."

*** *** *** *** *** ***

The missive was crudely printed by the fat hand of Brother Roy Ogles on Devotion to the Divinity stationary.

It fluttered in the early morning breeze from its pinned position on the out side of the motor home door, and contained several spelling errors.

There was, however, no mistaking the message's intent that read as follows:

AT THREE O' CLOCK THIS AFTERNOON YOU ARE ALL INVITED TO A BBQ, OR A WEDDIN WHICH EVER COMES FIRST AT DIRTY SOCKS LAKE. MY CUZZIN BROTHER ROY OGLES WILL BE THERE. WE WILL BE CELABRATIN THE MARRIAGE OF MY TWO SISTERS CATCH PEN AND SQUEEZE CHUTE HOGG TO THE MAYNARD BROTHERS OR WE IS GOAN TO EAT THAT FAT PIG OF YORN AS

THE GOOD LORD INTENDED. P.S. YOU KNOW HOW MUCH MY CUZZIN LIKES PORK.

Even though he had not written the note, it was signed in scrawling, barely legible longhand, by Heffaroid Hogg.

"I come out to give him some orange juice and tell im' good mornin', and they was a bunch of birds all over. They was eatin' somethin' on the ground. I shooed em' off. Then I seen this!" wailed an extremely upset Farley, who wore nothing except his faded jeans.

He held a translucent pitcher, half filled with pulpy orange liquid while gesturing helplessly with his free hand toward the motor home.

Trux, Thelma, Arthell and Rodney were all crowded together in front of the side door of the HOWDY HOSS reading the note attached to it.

Rodney, was minus his customary jacket, vest and tie. Still, he seemed to be wearing more clothing as the sun peeked over the distant eastern horizon, than the rest.

Like his brother, Trux was also naked from the waist up, but he was wearing his boots and presumably, his socks. Arthell now wore the bathrobe she had decided against the previous evening, over her nighty.

Thelma was also attired in what might be called a robe, but she had evidently discarded her nightgown sometime during the time she finally retired and was summoned from bed due to this calamity.

This flimsy substitute she had thrown on in haste, displayed more of her fabulous physical attributes than the revealing gown ever had.

"Wonder how come they was able to get im' outa there with out him kickin' up a ruckus?" murmured Trux.

"Ole Barney usually don't take no shit from strangers."

Thelma, fighting to keep all of her well-endowed body from totally escaping her wrap, stooped over and picked up the empty mace can.

A smattering of fallen Fruit Loops remained on the surface of the driveway where the canister had been discarded. Evidently the birds mentioned by Farley had been forced to leave them behind when chased away by the anguished bearded man.

She tucked a large, absolutely breathtakingly beautiful, freedom-seeking breast back out of sight as she used her otherwise unoccupied hand to give Farley the recovered object.

Everyone else present was far too preoccupied with the tragedy confronting him or her to even notice the impromptu early morning peep show. Once she was semi covered, the pretty lady took the pitcher of juice from the distraught man now holding the canister.

The visible portion of Farley's furry face turned absolutely red with anger

191

in spite of his deep tan, as he examined the can and realized what it had recently contained.

"Those fat slimy mothafuckers!" His words of disgust and despair tumbled from his mouth like angry toads.

"Me and Trux had this stuff used on us once in San Diego. It's the fuckin' shits!"

Rodney spied the empty chloroform bottle and something else reflecting off the rising sun lying on the asphalt beyond the grieving Maynard brothers.

The apparently discarded items lay between the front of Thelma's still parked, cream colored, apparently unmolested car and the rear of the HOWDY HOSS.

The young lawyer moved to them and scooped up both. He read the label on the bottle out loud.

"Chloroform. They must have…"

Rodney didn't have time to finish before Farley really exploded.

"Those piss complected dirty rotten after births! Those cock suckers used that on him too?" The bearded man was beside himself.

"That's awful! They coulda' killed him! Maybe they did! By God I'm gonna…."

Trux moved forward and laid his hand on his brother's shoulder.

"Calm down," he said. "With all the different kindsa' booze you poured down that pig, little chloroform n' mace ain't gonna kill im. He's okay. Stop pissin' and moanin'. We'll just get the damned hog back."

Trux turned to Rodney who was now examining the shiny item he had picked up from the driveway along with the bottle. It was a small gold charm in the shape of a gavel.

"You're the God damned lawyer! Say somethin'!" demanded the broad shouldered man with the big chin.

Rodney looked slightly embarrassed as he showed the tiny gold charm to the others. "This came off my key ring. My car… They must have…"

"Fuck your car! Who cares about your piss ant God damn car?" Trux snarled. "What are we gonna' do 'bout my brother's pig?"

"Notify the sheriff of course," the answer was so obvious Rodney couldn't understand why the question had even been asked.

"You outa' your jack assed mind?" asked Trux. "Arty Dubs' ain't gonna help us! He hates me n' Farley's guts!"

"But he likes Thelma, and he did have Jiggs take fresh water to Barney when we were in… Ah ..Jail." Reasoned the younger man. Rodney hated the thought that Arthell knew he'd been incarcerated.

This stumped Trux for a minute. He didn't really know what to come back with. The Argus Queen's influence over the local sheriff had always been a mystery to him, but it was not to be denied. Maybe the kid was onto something.

Farley was ready to clutch at any straw. The grief stricken, bearded man walked up to Thelma. His right hand covered the lower part of his mouth in case his beard failed to hide his quivering chin.

"Do you think you could get Arty to help us, Thelma?" he asked in a pleading tone.

The owner of the missing pig was willing to consider all options if one might lead to the return of his beloved Barney.

Surely there had to be another way without marrying into the Hogg family. He knew Trux would never consider being a party to that plan no matter how fond anybody was of the kidnapped pig.

The invitation on the motor home door was clear. Barney's freedom was dependent on both of the Maynard brothers showing up for the ceremony of bliss.

The beautiful older woman turned and handed the pitcher to Arthell before taking each of Farley's hands in her own.

She wanted so baldly to tell him what he wanted to hear. In her heart, the Argus Queen knew she could not.

"I'm afraid the sheriff couldn't help you even if he were willing, Farley. Dirty Socks Lake is out of Arty's jurisdiction. It's in the next county."

She released one of Farley's hands and reached up to stroke his cheek.

The heartbroken man pulled away from her and, turning his back on the group walked to the far corner of the house where the driveway disappeared around the building as it continued on beyond the compact toward the street.

He was starting to cry and he didn't want anyone to see his tears.

Trux watched his brother walk away. He sneered and made a sound of disgust in his throat as he looked at Rodney again.

"Dirty Socks Lake is in the next county!" He said, repeating Thelma's words while he thought up some of his own.

"Some hot shot lawyer you are! That word 'Jurisdiction' too big for them educated dumb fucks to teach you in that stupid law school? Now look how you made Farley feel! You insensitive pile of college boy diarrhea dog shit!"

Arthell's pretty young eyes flashed with anger. She loved her Daddy Trux and she felt just awful over what had happened to Barney.

Nonetheless, nobody was going to get away with picking on Rodney when he hadn't done anything wrong. For a minute it looked very much like the side of Trux's face might become the recipient of the pitcher, orange juice and all, which was now in her possession.

Thelma was faster than her daughter. That was a perfectly good pitcher. She would hate to see it broken. She wasn't that concerned over its contents.

193

Immediately, she moved past Trux to take the young man's arm and, if necessary, his side.

She gave the caustic man with the prominent jaw that was thrust out further than usual at the moment, a look of reproachful warning. Thelma then began addressing the young lawyer in a gentle, yet noticeably sarcastic tone.

"Trux has a hard time expressing himself in the morning, Rodney. Don't mind him."

Trux started to retort. The fire in the Argus Queen's eyes told him he shouldn't. When he caught the look in Arthell's, he was further convinced.

The broad shouldered man gave Rodney one last look of contempt before striding away to join his brother who was standing in front of Thelma's car looking off into the distance in the general direction of Dirty Socks Lake.

"Did Daddy Farley and Daddy Trux do something to cause all this, Mamma?" asked Arthell. She was still holding the half filled pitcher as she walked up to face her mother and Rodney.

"Looks to me like Heffaroid finally caught your fathers skinny dipping with his sisters," Thelma replied.

She shook her head in slight exasperation as she pulled her pitiful excuse for a robe up over her lovely shoulder while stealing a quick glance at the gentlemen in question at the same time.

"I warned them this was going to happen someday. I never dreamed Barney would bear the brunt of the consequences though."

Arthell looked at Rodney. "Is that why you had to leave your car? You were running away from Heffaroid's naked sisters with those crazy Dads of mine?"

Rodney nodded shamefully.

"I wasn't wearing anything either," he confessed.

The honesty monster again. Why couldn't it go on sabbatical along with its stammer-inducing counterpart? No good could come from this confession.

Arthell didn't take the statement as a confession at all. The state of dress or undress on the part of this young man the sweet Lone Pine girl had grown so fond of in only a matter of hours, wasn't really the issue. She was having problems grasping the situation's outcome.

"So? Everybody was naked. What's the big deal? Why did that make Heffaroid so mad he'd take Barney and threaten to have Brother Roy eat him? How come he wants Daddy Farley and Daddy Trux to marry his sisters? I don't understand!"

Thelma felt a lump in her throat as she gazed into the open, honest curiosity in her daughter's eyes. This child of hers who could fathom only the good in people, had so many questions, and a mother with no time to furnish immediate answers.

"Sweetheart, I promise when there's time, I'll sit down and we'll have a long discussion about myopic vision. Right now we don't have time to worry about the 'Why.' We've got to concentrate on 'How.' There's got to be away we can save Barney and stop this absurdity."

She turned to the young attorney who was just as confused as Arthell.

"Rodney, I do think we could use your professional assistance here."

"I'm not sure what I can do, but I'll help anyway I can," Rodney assured the beautiful woman as he tried not to look at her body that refused to stay put beneath the skimpy piece of material supposedly meant to cover it.

Thelma realized his problem and smiled.

"If I promise to change into something more comfortable for you and less comfortable for me, could we at least go inside and talk about it? With your legal mind and my old body, surely we can come up with something. Arthell? Would you make some coffee?"

"Sure, Mom!" said Arthell. She took Rodney's arm with her free hand not occupied with the pitcher. She then began ushering the young attorney into the rear of the house behind her mother who was already leading the way.

Thelma called over a bare shoulder as her slippery habiliment threatened to expose all of the fantastic curves of her entire delectable left side before she disappeared through the open doorway of her kitchen.

"After you put the coffee on baby, would you call Mrs. Porter and Widow Jonstan and tell them I'll have to postpone their deliveries? I've got a feeling this is going to be a busy day."

Trux, still standing in front of the compact with Farley, called after the departing lawyer and the gorgeous young Arthell who looked quite shrouded in comparison to her mother.

"Arthell! You put some clothes on! And you keep your hands off of her, Mr. 'Big shot don't know shit, shyster'!"

Farley realized he was also wearing very little when he discovered he had no sleeve with which to wipe his tears away. He did the best he could with his fingers and hairy forearms.

"What we gonna do, Trux?"

"You heard Thelma. She's gonna' come up with a plan. We'll get your pig back!" his brother said with confidence. He continued with even more conviction.

"We got to! I can't stomach the thought of bein' married to one o' them bank mules the rest of my life! You get us into more shit Farley!"

"Me? You're the one said, 'Let's go get some fat ass!' You know it was you!"

"Bull shit! Since when are you so particular? You ain't never culled nothin' but a horse mule and a stove pipe!"

195

"I wouldn't a' done it if I knew we was puttin' Barney in danger," said Farley.

He turned away from his brother.

"He shouldn't have to get et for what we done!"

Trux just looked at him. There was really nothing more he could say. The tough talking red neck would never acknowledge to a living soul that he was nearly as fond of that pig as Farley was. He didn't even like admitting it to himself.

There had to be a way out of this without becoming Heffaroid Hogg's brother-in-law.

He was certain the little asshole that was so determined to get the girl he thought to be his daughter in the rack, wouldn't contribute anything to assist their plight. He wasn't smart enough.

On the other hand, Thelma was the most intelligent person he'd ever met. That was something else Trux Maynard would never say out loud to any person alive. However, he knew if anyone could make everything all right again, that anyone would be Thelma.

He looked at the grieving Farley once more, then walked to the motor home. Trux went inside to get a beer for himself and his brother.

While he was there, he searched around to see if one of them had by chance hidden any whisky some place they might have forgotten about. He was always able to think better after a shot.

His search was futile. He even entered the bed room area and looked under the mattress. Nothing!

Damn Arty Dubs for dumping all that good hooch!

Damn that little punk inside who wanted in his little girl's pants! Damn him for ever being born! Damn the punk's mamma! Damn Brother Roy's fat ass! Damn his own cock! Damn! Damn! Damn!

As he looked around the interior of the HOWDY HOSS, everything began to remind him of Barney. He picked up a shirt lying on the bed and struggled into it. He then quickly moved from the bed room area to the cooler and withdrew two beers.

After opening one, he stepped over the other cans on the floor as he exited the rig. He emerged from the old motor home to find two small birds on the driveway picking at the Fruit Loops left behind.

They flew away to avoid the toe of the big red neck's boot. The asphalt was free of Fruit Loops now. Trux gave the feathered creatures a disgusted look before walking to Farley's side and offering him the unopened beer.

Farley accepted the full container without a word. The bearded man clearly wasn't speaking to his brother. He opened the can and began to pace up and down the driveway.

196

Trux returned to the motor home and perched his behind on the side portal threshold. Both brothers looked up as they heard the back door of the house open and Thelma stepped outside.

Her hands were behind her back as she attempted to zip up the very fashionable black dress she was now wearing.

"Okay you guys," she said. "Come inside and get dressed."

Trux looked up at her in bewilderment. He reached up and pinched a piece of the material of the shoulder of his shirt.

"I am dressed," The man with the big chin said, wondering why anyone would care.

"You can't wear that to your wedding," Thelma replied as she succeeded in zipping up her own garment.

"Arthell laid out those two suits I bought you guys last year when we went to Barstow. Those suits neither one of you ever wore? They're on my bed. Hurry now! We don't have much time."

Trux rose to his feet with a look of total disbelief on his square jawed face.

"Are you outa' your cotton pickin' mind, woman?" he asked in disbelief.

"You mean we really gotta marry Catch Pen and Squeeze Chute, Thelma?" asked Farley, finally speaking up.

"You couldn't figger no other way?" He was clearly afraid of her forthcoming answer.

"Not if the plan Rodney and I came up with works," The Argus Queen replied. "But we really should hurry."

Trux snorted. "The day that asshole comes up with a plan...."

He stopped in mid sentence as Farley tossed away his can of beer, then walked to face Thelma.

"Is this plan gonna keep Barney from bein' et?" The bearded Maynard brother looked extremely serious as he asked the question.

"Like I said, if it works," Thelma answered. "But you will have to show up for the wedding. Don't worry, I'm not ready to give you two up just yet. I said, show up, nothing else. It's a good plan. Rodney came up with a lot of it."

"That tears it!" sneered Trux. "I pass on the piss ant's plan. He's too dumb to think up an thing 'sept getting' our asses in bigger slings than we already got em."

"Thelma said it was her plan too, and she's plenty smart. She just said she don't wanna lose us," stated Farley, as he turned back to his brother.

"What's your plan, Trux?" asked the bearded man giving his sibling an unwavering look.

Trux shifted his blue eyes away from both those of Farley and Thelma.

"I ain't come up with one just yet," he finally admitted.

197

Farley turned back to Thelma

"Do we gotta' take a bath 'fore we put on them suits?" he quieried.

Thelma laughed. "I don't think that's necessary."

Farley looked back at Trux "You are comin' with us to save Barney, ain't you, Trux?"

Trux took a drink of his beer, then another as Thelma and Farley stood in the open kitchen doorway watching him. At long last, he lifted the container up to his lips and drained it.

After bending down and placing the empty can carefully on the motor home threshold, he slowly walked forward and joined two of the three people, and four of the friends, he loved most in the world.

"You and that damned pig!" grumbled the big tough red neck as he walked in through the kitchen door ahead of them both.

*** *** *** *** ***

At that same exact second, the 'Damned pig' to whom Trux was referring, was doing some grumbling of his own.

He stood in the middle of a four by four foot steel mesh cage looking out through the opening of the small squares of sturdy metal strands.

The objects of the unhappy animal's attention were the two large inhuman humans who had whisked him away from the comfort of the HOWDY HOSS the night before.

Heffaroid and Brother Ogles stood just beyond the barrier. Both were chewing Fruit Loops

Barney had attempted to escape several times by hurling his body against the sides of the cage, but he had since given up. The steel was much too strong.

The pig was starting to become frightened. In addition to the feel of fear, he also felt physically ill.

The pig was a veteran when it came to hangovers, but this was no ordinary morning after condition.

Never had the poor animal experienced anything that compared to the discomfort of the brutal, painful aftermath of the chemicals previously induced into his system by these two brutes.

Barney continued to grunt his disdain for those responsible for his terrible state of circumstances. Neither Brother Roy or his cousin seemed to care. The two obese men just stood there beyond the crisscrossed barriers looking in at him while they munched away at the last of the Fruit Loops.

Barney turned away from the disgusting pair. He was sick enough. Looking at them just made him feel worse.

A few feet beyond the cage and its prisoner, the topless, dirty and scarred Karmann Ghia, sat parked on a fairly large alkali ledge.

Above the abused little German made machine was a falling down four room wooden shack. Girlish giggles could be heard coming out through one of the windows facing the lake.

Beyond that structure, were several more. Extremely crude looking shanties were embedded in the dingy yellow and greenish brown rocks and earth.

These ugly structures dotted the even uglier mountainside that, totally void of any vegetation whatsoever, towered over the shack that served as the Hogg dwelling.

The primitively constructed edifices built into the side of the soft surfaced, multicolored land mass that did boast a variety of minerals and other geological components, were the conglomeration of what was laughingly referred to by the local gentry as The Hogg Borax Mining Enterprises.

Barney didn't know this. The incarcerated porker would not have cared if he had.

He did show interest in the large lake that could be seen beyond the Karmann Ghia in the valley below, where the only sign of any plant life of any kind could be seen for miles.

He knew that place. It was where he and Daddy Farley and Daddy Trux had swum many times in the warm, smelly water with the fat women.

He had always considered the fat women as friends. Now they, along with the two awful fat men who had brought him to this place in the middle of the night were the enemy. Barney didn't understand.

Where were his beloved human companions now who seemed to have been replaced by these extremely large evil ones? Why was he being kept in this cage?

"Good lookin' cage, Cousin. How'd you come by it?" asked Brother Roy Ogles between mouthfuls of Fruit Loops as he looked in through the steel mesh in satisfaction at the trapped, complaining creature of the cloven hoof.

That pig was good for the main course of at least three meals. The man of the cloth planned on eating Barney whether the Maynards showed up or not.

If they did, the pig's demise and the subsequence devouring of same, was only a matter of postponement.

"Picked it up down Keeley way. Figger it fell off one of them government wildlife trucks. Must have been built to trap and pack around lizards in. Just picked it up. It was free. Never know when free shit might come in handy," replied Heffaroid.

He wiped the Fruit Loop residue from his fat chin with some apparent satisfaction as he glanced up at the shack responding to the girlish giggles still coming from inside it.

"My sisters sure are excited. What we gonna' do if them Maynards don't show, Cousin Brother Roy?"

"Then we do His will, Heffy," answered the pastor, practically drooling as he looked at the unhappy Barney through the steel mesh squares. "We eat the pig."

Both large men turned as Catch Pen stuck her round, overly made up face out through the window of the shack above them. She called down to her brother in her high nasal voice.

"Heffaroid? Could you come up and help hold the cheeks of Squeeze chutes' butt down while I pull her pantyhose up over em'? Neither one of us ever wore panty hose before, but Aunt Alma sent us some for last Christmas, and we wanna' wear em' for the weddin. They're an absolute bitch to pull on!"

"Be right there!" Heffaroid called back. He turned to Brother Roy.

"Got anymore Fruit Loops, cousin?"

Brother Roy shoved a hand full of the just requested delicacy into his mouth and talked around them as he shook his head.

"All gone I'm afraid, Heffy."

Heffaroid nodded. Attempting to hide his disappointment, he turned and began waddling up the hill. Catch Pen was calling his name again.

He looked back over his fat shoulder as he kept puffing his way up the incline toward the shack.

"Yessir! Them girls sure are excited! Me too if you wanna' know the truth. With some extra free labor in my mine, I might just start makin' it pay off! Sure am gonna' be thankin' you if all this works out, Cousin."

Brother Roy reluctantly tore his eyes away from the creature in the cage he had been mentally digesting. Still chewing on the last of the Fruit Loops, he lifted his large face toward the blazing morning sun.

"Thank Him, Heffy. I am but the poor servant obeying His Wishes. Thank the Lord by putting something extra in the collection plate! Contrary to what you may have been told Cousin, money is only the root of all evil when it doesn't go to the Lord and His messengers."

CHAPTER FIFTEEN
STRATEGIC INITIATION

"Mind if I take just one more look at that money?" asked Larry Peterson.

The short round man still wore the same greasy coveralls that had been his attire the previous Saturday morning when Rodney had first visited this location to purchase gas for the Ghia.

The service station and garage owner was now standing on his tip toes, looking up at the young attorney. Rodney was now seated behind the steering wheel of the battered HOWDY HOSS, leaning out through the open driver's window.

The motor home was parked between the gas pumps while fuel was automatically being transferred through one of the individual aspirate device's hoses into its tank.

Arthell, looking absolutely exquisite, in a frilly white frock, could be seen through the window, occupying the jump seat in the big rig beside Rodney.

"I know you showed me before, but I'd kinda like to check it out one more time." The man who was famous in Lone Pine for selling people auto parts they didn't need, continued as he craned his neck upward.

"Like I said, I thought it would be a cold day in Hell, 'fore I ever gassed up this son of a bitch again after what Trux done to me last time. But, since you're gonna make that good and you're payin' for this tank full too, I guess it's okay considerin' how much bread you got in that there envelope. I would like to see it again though, 'fore I collect my share."

Inside the motor home, Rodney accepted the envelope from Arthell who was holding it in her lap. The young attorney's briefcase sat on the floorboard beneath her feet.

He opened the top of the envelope and riffled the corners of the hundred dollar bills inside it as he held it out the window for Larry to see.

Behind the young couple Trux and Farley could be seen. Both looked extremely uncomfortable in their new suits complete with white shirts and ties, as they sat on the bed in the rear of the big vehicle.

The spiffed up Maynard brothers were engaged in a sotto conversation with Thelma, who still wore the stunning black dress as she stood in front of them. Trux, in particular, did not appear to be happy.

"Boy! That sure is a lot of money!" said Larry, nearly losing his balance as he continued looking up through the driver's window from outside.

"I did tell you Trux's bill he burnt me on, come to fifty eight dollars didn't

I?"

Only minutes ago it had been forty-eight. When Rodney had first broached the subject with the station owner after driving up to the gas pumps, the sum was thirty-five. At this point, the young attorney wasn't really counting.

"Fifty eight, plus whatever this bill comes to. I told you to fill it up and tell me the total, including both," he said, nodding in affirmation.

"They're in there ain't they? Trux and that filthy assed brother of his, don't never shave?"

Again Rodney nodded

"Shamed to show their faces. Low life trash! See they banged up this old piece of crap even more. Sheriff told me all about it. Wish to Hell they'd do everbody a favor and just kill em' selves and get it over with."

In side the motor home, Arthell, still seated beside Rodney, started to bristle. The young lawyer gave her a wink.

She immediately regained her composure as Rodney looked out the window at the short round man and nodded yet another time.

Directly out side, Larry remained on his tiptoes as he changed the subject.

He was trying to figure out a way to get his hands on more of that money in Rodney's envelope.

"Whatever happened to that other car you was driving?"

"I had a little trouble with it," replied Rodney, as he closed the envelope and handed it back to the smiling Arthell.

"Told you it needed a new water pump," declared Larry. "You bring it in. I'll give you a good deal ! I mean it!"

"I might just do that," said the excited young attorney. Rodney was having a tough time keeping his mind on this mundane conversation.

Not only was the great looking girl beside him a distraction, he had a lot of other things on his agenda right now. Some of it, he wasn't quite sure he had what it was going to take to accomplish.

It was a decided relief when he saw Larry finally lower his squat body off its toes and walk back to the gas pump.

"I still don't see why Rodney's drivin!" Grumbled Trux, as the conversation in the rear interior of the motor home became louder. "I don't even wanna' be under the same roof with the little fucker! And how come Arthell's sittin' so close to him?"

"You want to wake up looking at Squeeze Chute Hogg, the rest of your life, Trux?" asked Thelma.

Trux's lack of response indicated he did not. The beautiful lady turned her attention on Farley.

"You want Barney back, right Farley?" she asked.

"Damnit, Thelma, that's a dumb question. Course I do."

"Then it's time to end this dumb conversation and let us handle things. It's all part of the plan."

"Is it too much to ask what the God damn plan is?" Trux wanted to know.

Before Thelma could answer, something outside through one of the side windows nearest the street caught her attention.

Through the glass, the sheriff's marked patrol car could be seen pulling up and parking beyond the gas pumps. The uniformed Arty Dubs opened the driver's door and began exiting the official vehicle.

"What the Hell's he doin' here?" asked Trux, as Thelma hurried toward the motor home's side door, which now faced the police car.

"I called him and asked him to meet us here," the Argus Queen responded, as she opened the portal preparing to exit the HOWDY HOSS.

"Why in the name of Horse Shit Harry, Would you do that? You're the one pointed out the pig's in the next county, for Christ's sake!"

"Trust us Trux, it's all part of the plan," said the exquisite looking woman with the natural blond hair in the black dress, as she stepped out of the motor home.

Trux fumed as he turned to his brother who was tugging at the tie around his neck.

"What's the God damned plan?" he demanded, in spite of the fact he knew the other man didn't know either.

"We gotta trust her Trux. She ain't never let us down yet."

Outside, Thelma walked up to Arty who stood waiting beside the driver's door of his vehicle.

"I come as soon as I got your message, Thelma. Me n' Jiggs was down at the dump doin' a little target practice. What's so urgent?" asked the lawman as he eyed the HOWDY HOSS with open suspicion.

Thelma reached into her cleavage and extracted the note from the motor home door. Arty obviously enjoyed watching her tug the missive to freedom.

He watched with less interest as she unfolded the piece of paper before handing it to him.

"Read this," the lady requested.

Attempting to look very official, the sheriff took the paper and started to read. Almost immediately his stern façade of authority gave way to a broadening grin.

"I'll be damned!" Was his first response to the reading material in his hands.

"You're shittin' me!" Was his second.

"The Hogg sisters?" Arty was starting to giggle now. He began to double up with unbridled laughter as he continued reading.

Composing himself, he tried to go on.

"You know how much my Cuzzin' likes pooork!!!" Arty lost it on this one. The uniformed man screamed hysterically.

Thelma's serious reaction finally brought the howling, duly elected head of Lone Pine law enforcement back to reality. It still took him a while to assume a straight face before speaking to the lady again.

"Sorry Thelma. Ain't a thing I can do. Dirty Socks is outa' my jurisdiction. You know that."

On the other side of the motor home, the HOWDY HOSS was now all gassed up and ready to go.

Larry walked up to the still open driver's window once again and called up to Rodney.

"Okay! All filled up with my best high test! That'll be one hunnerd forty dollars and sixty eight cents countin' what I got burned outa' before."

Inside the motor home, the moment for Rodney had arrived. Could he do this?

He took a deep breath as he held out his hand to Arthell, who occupied the jump seat beside him. Instead of the envelope full of money, the pretty girl handed him a quarter that evidently had been clenched in her fist for quite sometime.

Rodney took the coin and leaned out the window to his left as far as he could. He flipped the quarter up into the air.

It took two hands, but he managed to catch it before it spiraled down to Larry's feet where the owner of the station was trying to figure out what was going on. The young attorney looked first at the coin, then down at the round man in the greasy coveralls.

"Heads! You lose!" he said, with a joyous cry before tossing the coin to Larry and pulling himself back in though the window.

He gripped the steering wheel with both hands, started the engine, put the old rig in gear, slammed his foot down hard on the gas and peeled out of the station in an amazingly short span of time.

Larry, who had taken the time to catch the quarter, was momentarily befuddled as he watched the big rig's speedy departure.

Inside the HOWDY HOSS, Trux and Farley who had been pulling beers from the icebox, were thrown forward onto the floorboards.

"What the fuck do you think you're doin?" screamed Trux as he pushed Farley away, who had landed on top of him.

Arty stood by his patrol car, alone now, watching the speeding motor home heading out of Lone Pine.

Larry came running up to the distracted lawman. The short, round man was yelling at the top of lungs.

"Arty! They done it to me again!!"

"Done what?" Arty yelled back, as he looked around, trying to figure out where Thelma might have disappeared.

"Fucked me outa the gas again! Go get em' Sheriff!"

Arty jerked the driver's door of his vehicle open and leaped behind the steering wheel.

The law enforcement sedan was out of the station with siren howling and lights flashing before he even closed the door.

Inside the patrol car, Arty drove with one hand while he finally managed to get the driver's door closed with the other. Only then did he look to his right.

The lawman nearly lost control of his official vehicle as he did a totally involuntary double take.

Sitting in the passenger seat beside him was Thelma, already strapped in. She smiled sweetly and said nothing.

It only took Arty seconds to recover.

Driving with his right hand, he began fumbling with his left, trying to get his big Magnum unsheathed. After much swearing and more fumbling, he finally managed to extract the big weapon and pull it up in front of him.

"They've pulled this shit in my town for the last time, Thelma!" he yelled over the scream of the siren. "You ain't talkin' me outa this one!"

Again, the Argus Queen only smiled as the sheriff pushed down hard on the accelerator. They zoomed out of town in pursuit of the perpetrators.

Inside the speeding motor home, Arthell had her beautiful eyes glued on the review mirror and the reflected image of the police car with its flashing lights, not that far behind them.

"Mamma's in there with Arty!" she exclaimed. "What are we going to do?"

"Don't worry Angel," Rodney assured her.

The young man gripped the steering wheel with both hands and concentrated on the two lane multicolored highway in front of him, continuing to drive the HOWDY HOSS forward.

The old motorized beast was speeding away from Lone Pine at maximum mechanical swiftness.

The usually subdued city boy was definitely exercising time honored reckless red neck tradition by keeping the pedal to the metal.

"It's all part of the plan!" he said with a confidence that sounded foreign to his own ears. Rodney was finding it difficult to associate himself with the majority of his current activities right at the moment.

He couldn't believe he had just spoken the name aloud to this ravishing beauty sitting next to him that he had secretly given her in his heart.

Even more formidable to fathom was the fact that he had just committed the very first illegal act of his life time, back at that service station, without intervention from within.

Maybe it was because his little Honesty Monster knew the man Larry to be not a nice person who cheated people on a routine basis and deserved retaliation.

Perhaps the little demon had not interfered because it knew how important it was to save Barney's life. It could have been because Thelma promised she would personally pay for this tank of gas once they had gone through with the plan.

There was also the outside possibility, the power inside the young man from Boston that had always kept him on the stringent straight and narrow, was unable to interfere because it was too busy laughing.

Whatever the reason and who ever he was right now, Rodney was filled with a sense of elation he had never before experienced.

Trux, behind him, was trying to keep his equilibrium, watch the sheriff, who was rapidly gaining on them, through the rear window of the rig beyond the open curtains of the bedroom area. At the same time, he was trying to open a can of Blue Ribbon beer.

The big chinned man in the new suit did not seem to hold shares in Rodney's stock of exuberance.

Farley, who had already accomplished the latter task, was hugging the back of the old leather seat with one hand, while he held his beer up to his beard surrounded lips with the other. He seemed to be attempting to take this unexpected turn of events in stride as best he could.

"What plan?" snarled Trux, after he had finally managed to open his beer and turn back toward the front.

"Somebody better tell me something, damn it!" he practically screamed. Suddenly, his blue eyes grew wide with alarm.

"And watch out for that guy on the tractor!" Trux did scream this time.

Rodney turned the wheel sharply to the left and managed to miss a poor soul who was driving his piece of farm equipment down the highway from one poorly irrigated reclaimed piece of desert to another.

The HOWDY HOSS, however, had to actually leave the road in order for this to happen. Rodney did not slow the big machine down as he continued to manipulate the steering wheel and the gearshift.

In the middle of the motor home aisle, the ingredients of the can that was no longer in Trux's hand as he tumbled to the floor once more, spewed all over Farley's new suit.

"Damn you! You young shit!! You're gonna kill us!" yelled Trux as he attempted to regain his footing. He promptly fell against his brother as the motor home jumped a ditch running parallel to the highway.

Outside the screeching of tires competed with the howl of the siren. The HOWDY HOSS jumped the ditch once more as the attorney steered it back onto the road in front of the speeding sheriff's car.

The official sedan had also just managed to miss the farmer and his machine. It was now Arty's turn to hit the ditch.

Instead of leaping the irrigation abyss, as had the larger rig it was chasing, the law enforcement vehicle was only able to gain partial access to the other side.

The engine of the cop car was sill running but it was now stuck, with its rear tires still in the ditch, spinning in place.

Inside the sedan, Arty Dubs ground his protruding teeth as he tried to get the vehicle free of its encumbrance while, at the same time, watching the motor home through the windshield.

The HOWDY HOSS was back on the highway again and evidently, its driver had it under control once more. The distance grew between the battered old utility rig and the sheriff's ditched automobile with its wailing siren and spinning wheels.

Still seated beside the frustrated lawman, Thelma continued to smile serenely.

Inside the motor home, Farley was on his knees retrieving a rolling bottle that said 'Fighting Cock Kentucky Whiskey' on its label, from the vehicle's floor.

It appeared to be about half full. The bearded man called toward the driver's seat.

"Purty good drivin' there, kid."

"Shit!" was Trux's comment as he disentangled himself from the bedcovers in the rear of the rig.

Behind the steering wheel, Rodney's face was ashen in spite of his new tan. However he continued to operate the controls of the valiant old utility rig like he had been doing this sort of thing all his life.

Arthell, still occupying the jump seat beside the frightened young man, leaned over and kissed his cheek.

"Oh, Rodney. You were so cool!" she said, obviously very impressed. Immediately, all color returned to the face of the boy from Boston.

Trux lurched forward from the bedroom area of the still speeding vehicle. His eyes were now on his brother, in the beer stained suit. Farley was perched in the old leather chair again while he unscrewed the lid from the bottle of whiskey.

"Where the Hell did you get that?" demanded the disgruntled Maynard with the oversized jaw.

"I looked all over this place this mornin' for whiskey, and couldn't find shit!"

"Got no idea." replied Farley who had now removed the cap from the round clear glass container.

"Come rollin' out from underneath somethin' when the shit hit the fan back there. Want some?"

"Is a pig's ass pork?" Was Trux's response as he snatched the bottle from the bearded man and pulled it up to his own lips.

Only after he had managed to pour a goodly portion of the lethal liquor down his throat, did he see the look of pain on his brother's face and realize what he had just said.

"I didn't mean nothin' by that. I was just runnin' my big mouth," Trux told the other man in way of an apology.

Up front, Rodney, who was obviously not privy to the moment, called back.

"I don't think it's a good idea for you guys to be drinking while we're driving. There's an open container law in California, you know."

"Rodney, you know so many things. You just never fail to amaze me," exclaimed an honestly impressed Arthell as she reached out and touched the driver's arm.

Trux was screaming again as he responded to the young man's unsolicited advise.

"Your God damned head's gonna be an open container, you don't keep your eyes on the road! And stop touchin' him, Arthell!"

He turned back to his brother, offering him the remainder of the whiskey.

Farley was no longer interested. He was too busy thinking about Barney's horrible dilemma.

*** *** *** *** ***

In the mean time, Barney was also thinking of Farley. The pig was really frightened now.

He was still secured in the cage but the location was no longer the same. He really didn't care for the way the day was progressing.

The Hogg party had now moved to the shores of Dirty Socks Lake. Barney's steel meshed coop of incarceration with the sad swine still inside looking out, now sat at the edge of the water near a freshly dug BBQ pit. A small fire burned within the hole in the sand.

Near the flames, sat an old wooden picnic table on which rested six loaves of bread, a large salad of some kind, a dozen raw turnips and an unmatched variety of eating utensils. What appeared to be at least a half-bushel of really big potatoes wrapped in tin foil sat roasting in the middle of the fire, at the bottom of the pit.

Between the bread and the turnips, sat an unopened half-gallon jug of BBQ sauce.

This and the marriage certificate along with a hand printed prenuptial agreement, assigning all of the Maynards' personal property including livestock, to the brother of the brides, were Brother Roy's contribution.

These two legal documents were tucked away in his Bible, which rested on the very end of the table, furthest away from the fire and nearest the water. Brother Roy's black suit coat lay in a rumpled wad next to the book of Holy Scriptures. No meat or anything to drink seemed to be present.

Barney wasn't used to anyone stocking up for a party without at least having a case of beer or two on ice.

The poor curly tailed prisoner had already been informed by the large man of the cloth, that if Daddy Farley and Uncle Trux failed to show up, he, Barney, was to furnish the meat.

The pastor still wore his hat. He also was wearing the black trousers that threatened to momentarily burst forth from his ballooning buttocks and whisky keg legs.

A very extra large plus sized T-shirt covered the upper part of his overflowing blimp facsimile torso. Over this, Brother Roy was wearing a black dickey attached to the clerical collar still around his elephantine neck. The dickey only concealed part of his fallen chest and none of his enormous stomach.

The false shirtfront was tied in the back with ribbons that all but disappeared into the folds of his fat as they wound their way around his swollen sides.

At first glance, the reverend might well have been mistaken for an obese penguin moving about in reverse, wearing a little black hat with a large, round cartoon pie face painted on the back of its head.

He stood over the table, sharpening a very large carving knife with a whetstone as he looked hungrily at the pig in the cage. As far as the reverend was concerned he was ready to rectify the gathering's lack of protein at any time.

The pig would be his to devour, if not this day, another soon. Once the Maynards entered the dictatorship of the Hogg family, the creature of the cloven hoof would be Heffaroids' property. Therefore, his present activity was in no way, wasted time. He only wished he hadn't run out of Fruit Loops.

Catch Pen and Squeeze Chute looked almost ravishing in their wedding dresses.

Each held a little nosegay of sagebrush in their pudgy fingers as they stood where the HOWDY HOSS was parked on the fateful day that Rodney had entered the lives of the condemned pig and the Maynard brothers.

The rotund sisters watched the road leading up to the lake intently.

The girls giggled as they softly conversed with each other and waited for the motor home and their future spouses to show up.

They didn't really care about who their prospective, legal bed partners were to be, they just wanted husbands, and Trux and Farley Maynard were the best that Heffaroid had been able to come up with.

Heffaroid himself stood a few feet away from his sisters next to the parked Karmann Ghia. He had utilized the little vehicle to bring Barney, in the cage, down from the shack. The steel mesh coop had been tide on top of the spot behind the seat above where Rodney's suitcase still rested on the little car's floorboard.

The barrels of the old shot gun had been since repaired from their recent explosion after being jammed into the lakeshore.

The obese, protective brother of the girls watching the road, held the once again, functional weapon in one huge hand. His other appendage was busy at the moment brushing a blue bottle fly away from his nose.

He also watched the road. He was glad Brother Roy and the Lord had decided to hang onto the pig and eat it later.

The massive miner was looking forward to the feast. However, first things had to come first. Catch Pen and Squeeze Chute needed to get married.

Trying to keep tabs on those horny sisters of his had nearly driven him crazy lately. He could also really use some extra labor he didn't have to pay in his borax mine.

In the cage, Barney's nerves were almost worn to a frazzle. He sure could use a drink right now.

He was also hungry. In spite of the fact that there was food present, Brother Roy knew one did not feed an animal on the day it was to be butchered. God willing, prayed the massive minister, this could well be that day.

The pig had examined the latch on of the outside the small gate of his cage. It didn't have a lock on it, but was secured with a sliding bolt he wasn't capable of operating. To free him, somebody with thumbs would actually have to come right up to the water's edge past all of the Hogg family to the cage itself.

Barney had no doubt that his Daddy Farley and his Uncle Trux were on their way to save him, but one of his large captors had a gun. The other was armed with a knife.

He was beginning to worry if his rescuers could succeed, even when they did show up.

Barney's rescue team was still on the highway. The HOWDY HOSS had not yet crossed the county line, but it was drawing nearer.

Unfortunately, Arty Dubs had finally managed to maneuver his official sedan out of the ditch. The sheriff's vehicle was coming up behind the speeding motor home, gaining on it fast with the siren screaming full blast.

Inside the fleeing big rig, Arthell had her eyes on the rear view mirror again. She had obviously been watching the sheriffs' recovery and now his subsequent progress.

"He's gaining!" she informed Rodney who still drove the motor home.

"No problem," the young attorney replied with that same confidence tone which up until today had been foreign to his nature. "I can see the county marker up ahead."

Arthell looked at the boy she was rapidly falling more in love with by the minute, possibly even the second.

"Rodney," she told him, "You have eyes like an eagle. And you're so in control."

Trux, kneeling, on the bed in the rear of the vehicle with his brother as both looked out the back window, called toward the couple in front over his broad shoulder.

"Don't get too God damned cocky punk! Arty Dubs may be a dumb shit, but they is one thing he's good at…"

"Shootin' out tires!" Farley finished for his brother. "With that big fuckin' Clint Eastwood .44 Magnum pistol of his! And the son of a bitch is getting close enough to do it, by God!"

"Worse thing that ever happened to this county was him seein' that damn movie, *Dirty Harry*!" Trux had to raise his voice now, to be heard over the sound of the siren that was now filling the interior of the HOWDY HOSS. "Now the son of a bitch shoots out tires!"

"I never saw *Dirty Harry*. Before my time I think," Rodney called back from the driver's seat. He was trying to make the old rig go faster, even though he knew it could not.

"I never saw it neither, but Arty damned sure did!" Trux yelled as he continued to peer through the glass at the rapidly approaching sheriff's sedan now directly behind them.

"Shit! We've had it now! He's got that fuckin' cannon pointin' out the window! And that big sucker's aimed right at our God damned rear tire!"

Inside the pursuing vehicle, Arty's Magnum was indeed in his left hand pointing out the window while he steered with his right. As Trux had already reported, the large pistol was aimed directly at the left rear tire of the battered old HOWDY HOSS.

"Your ass is mine now peckerheads!" he shouted.

He would have rather whispered like Clint Eastwood, but then he wouldn't be able to hear himself. The siren was too loud.

Thelma was no longer strapped to the passenger seat. The beautiful woman moved quickly and reached around the sheriff.

She grabbed the elbow of the hand holding the gun and it exploded harmlessly into the desert air.

"Put that stupid gun down Arty!" cried Thelma. "Arthell's in there!"

Arty shoved her away. "Turn me loose woman!" he yelled.

"I ain't gonna hurt Arthell! You know I wouldn't do that! All I'm gonna do is shoot out a tire! That's what Clint would do!"

The sheriff of Lone Pine, once again held the steering wheel steady with his right hand and once more took careful aim out the driver's window with the Magnum in his left. The motor home was right in front of them now.

Thelma Houston had learned at a very early age, that with exception of lifting heavy objects or writing ones name while urinating in the snow or sand, women were far superior to men in every way.

She knew without a doubt that the wisest man in the world did not possess even half the intelligence potential of the most ignorant woman. The problem with the majority of women in the world is that most are unaware of this superiority.

Men lack the power of simple reason and basic logic. To attempt reasoning with a male member of the human race, without taking the time to spell out every detail, as one must with small child, was, is, and always will be, futile.

Brother Dave Gardner, known to many as a night club comic of the nineteen fifties, and to the mentally adept as one of the world's greatest philosophers, once said, "Women have to be superior to men. Otherwise men wouldn't spend over seventy five percent of their time trying to get some of what all women got."

One might fault the late Mr. Gardner's grammar, but never his wisdom. There exists only one expedient method available to any woman needing access to any man's mind in a hurry.

Miss Wayling, the secretary of Herkimer, Herkimer, Herkimer, Herkimer and Van Aukin back in Century City, who might still have been in San Diego at the moment, was not cognizant to female intellectual superiority. She knew only of the sexual manipulative power held over men by her gender.

Had the lady who had launched her life exercising this ascendancy many years ago in the back seat of a vintage Chevrolet been aware of the unlimited boundaries of her intelligence potential, the outcome of her life might have been vastly altered. By now Agnus would probably be the owner of the company that made the car.

Thelma Houston of Lone Pine, did not even know of the masculine faced Agnus Wayling. It is doubtful she would have condoned the other woman's lifestyle or her methods if she had.

Agnus had discovered the puissance of oral copulation followed by that of her pudendum. She had concentrated only on perfecting that power, neglecting further intellectual growth.

Thelma advocated the use and exercising of the superior female brain whenever possible even though the process sometimes took great effort. To her, sex was to be enjoyed, not a tool of manipulation.

Thelma Houston and Agnus Wayling were quite different. Both, nonetheless, were women.

There are times when the 'Wayling Method' is the only method, no matter how smart the woman may be.

Poor Arty Dubs never knew what hit him. Before he could squeeze the trigger of that powerful Magnum, his fly was unzipped and that beautiful blond head was buried in his lap.

It is doubtful that Arty Dubs even knew about that former democratic President decreeing this not to be considered Sexual Activity.

That occurrence was some time ago and Arty never did watch much television. Anyway, like his hero Clint Eastwood, the lawman wasn't a democrat.

Whatever Thelma was doing at that moment certainly felt like sexual activity to the sheriff of Lone Pine, California.

All blood drained downward from his upper head to the lower one.

The outside spotlight just in front of the driver's door of the lawman's car was shattered by the Magnum bullet. The official law enforcement vehicle and its siren came to a screeching halt at exactly the same time on the shoulder of the road.

On the highway ahead, the HOWDY HOSS crossed the county line and continued onward toward its destination of Dirty Socks Lake. So far the plan was working, and everything was right on schedule.

CHAPTER SIXTEEN
CALCULATED RISKS

A crudely fashioned rusty iron spit had been erected over the pit near the shoreline of Dirty Socks Lake. More fuel had been added to the fire to make its blaze much higher.

The baked potatoes, still in their shiny, yet charred wrappers lay in a huge pile on the old wooden tabletop next to the other previously placed items of food and tarnished silverware. This exposed edible matter, combined with the growing stench of the minerals within the lake water beside it, was responsible for a tremendous gathering of flies.

Barney, who hated to go to the bathroom anyplace he was compelled to stay near, had finally been forced to succumb to nature. The poor abused animal had done the best he could under the circumstances.

He had tried to back up against the solid steel wires as snugly as possible to keep it all outside, but he hadn't been totally successful. Some of the pig's manure had stuck to the steel strands that made up the rear wall of the cage.

This had also beckoned the flies. The insects swarmed around poor Barney. He couldn't remember ever being quite so uncomfortable or unhappy.

The T-shirt beneath Brother Roy's still exposed dickey was soaked with perspiration. Small rivers of the same salty substance rolled down the many folds of the Devotion to Divinity's singer of psalm's fleshy face as he stood next to the cage.

He wrinkled his flaccid nose as he looked in through the metallic mesh and the swarm of buzzing flies at the mess behind the poor imprisoned pig. With a grunt of disgust, the grossly overweight preacher brandished the big carving knife in the air toward the surface of the warm water lake.

"Filthy Heathen! Don't you worry, you cloven hoofed devil. After I cut your miserable throat, we'll just chuck you in the water and get your carcass all clean, before we start slicin' you up. Times almost up succulent swine! You may be servin' the Lord's purpose for allowing you to temporarily walk upon His earth very soon, now!"

The pastor held the blade of the knife up so that the hot overhead sun could reflect off its freshly sharpened metallic edge as he continued ranting and raving.

"If not, you're still gonna feel my teeth gnawin' on your bones and the wrath of God, soon enough. You have my solemn promise as His loyal servant, pig! Oh, am I gonna enjoy sayin the blessing over you!"

Barney was trying to ignore both the big man in the black hat and the tight fitting clothing of the same color, and the flies. The rude human had been saying things even more terrible all afternoon.

He looked once again toward the road leading from the distant highway to the lake. There was still no sign of Daddy Farley or Uncle Trux. Barney knew if they didn't come to save him there had to be a good very reason, but he was beginning to give up hope.

At the side of the lake nearest the road and next to the Karmann Ghia, Catch Pen and Squeeze chute were also getting anxious.

They too, were staring to worry about the arrival of Trux and Farley Maynard. The reason for the fat girls' anxieties was different than those affecting the pig, but they were just as apprehensive.

The large girls were rapidly reaching a melt down stage. This condition was partially due to the hot afternoon sun, but mainly because of their unaccustomed apparel.

Pantyhose stretched over the lower half of an extensive bulbous body, combined with a layer of ruffled petticoat skirts beneath a wedding dress can be extremely uncomfortable to one of that size not accustomed to such finery.

To the sisters' left, and closer to the lake, their even larger brother, Heffaroid, was scrunched down on his broad behind beneath the shade of a piece of scrub brush. The shotgun lay across his wide knees.

At that particular moment, the huge fellow was preoccupied in a personal feud with a swarm of gnats. The tiny insects seemed insistent on sharing one of the few shady spot at the odorous water's edge.

Back at the cage, Brother Roy turned from his flow of continual verbal abuse directed at the captive creature of the cloven hoof to tend the fire and get away from the flies.

Barney's ears stood straight up as something caught the pig's eyes beyond the Hogg sisters' vigilance stations away from the lake.

Beneath the shade of the scrub brush, Heffaroid swatted more gnats away from his nose. He also looked in the direction of the road.

Using the stock of the shotgun as a temporary tool of leverage, the big girls' bigger brother began the laborious task of rising to his feet.

In the near distance, the HOWDY HOSS was creating a cloud of dust on the small hillside beyond, as it slowly made its way downward toward the lake.

"Forget the pig and grab your Bible, Cousin! They're a comin!" Heffaroid shouted to Brother Roy as he lumbered with his weapon toward his sisters.

Catch Pen and Squeeze Chute were already pointing and jumping up and down with glee as the battered old motor home with its broken headlamps and otherwise mutilated front end continued its approach.

215

Barney alternated his attention between his oncoming saviors and the fat minister who somehow was able to struggle into his jacket without bursting the seams. Picking up the Bible as per request, the pastor made one last comment to the pig in the cage, before waddling away to join the rest of the overweight welcoming committee.

"Only a stay of execution, symbol of Satan! You still gonna end up in my stomach like the Lord intended. His will shall be done!"

As the motor home drove closer, Trux could be seen clearly through the big rig's windshield as he sat behind the steering wheel operating its controls.

"It's Trux!" squealed Squeeze Chute, as she continued hopping up and down in delight. Heffaroid moved up beside his joyous jumping sibling only to have he come down hard on his foot with one of her own. The fat man screamed in pain.

"Shut up and calm down," he said in an angry injured tone as he hobbled about, doing some jumping of his own, while trying not to lose his grip on the shotgun. "You're both actin' like a couple of heifers in heat."

The HOWDY HOSS pulled up directly in front of the group. As the old rig shuddered to a halt, Brother Roy and his Bible waddled up to join the rest of the larger than life reception committee.

"I shudder when I think of what the kids is gonna look like. Look at the chin on that ugly sucker!" Heffaroid muttered to his cousin.

Roy said nothing as he and the other large man watched Trux, in his suit, still behind the windshield, rise from the driver's seat of the motor home. The red neck's image became blurred beyond the glass as he moved back into the interior of the rig.

The side door of the HOWDY HOSS opened and the two Maynard brothers stepped out into the blazing sunlight. The suits both were still wearing no longer looked new.

Arthell, maintaining her image of loveliness in the pretty white dress, exited the utility vehicle behind them.

Rodney was nowhere to be seen.

"Oh! They look so handsome in their suits! They dressed up for us, Catch Pen!" Squeeze Chute cooed in exited nasality.

"And they even brought a bridesmaid!" exclaimed Catch Pen, Just as excited, but not quite so nasal. "How thoughtful!"

"I still wish I knew what the fuck was goin' on," Trux whispered to Farley as the two brothers stood awkwardly with Thelma's daughter in front of the motor home's open side portal.

The huge sisters could stand the waiting no longer. The wilted sagebrush nosegays went flying.

Arthell stepped quickly aside to avoid being crushed by the stampede as the big girls broke away from their brother and charged Trux and Farley.

The Maynard brothers became the recipients of many hugs and slobbering kisses as they were hurled helplessly back against the side of the motor home.

Brother Roy heaved a deep sigh of disgust, then trudged over in a huff and pried the cousins he called his nieces away from the two prospective grooms. Heffaroid moved in with his shotgun to join them.

"All right. Let's get this delightful event over with," said the preacher, obviously disgruntled that his feast of pork had been temporarily postponed.

He lifted his Bible and withdrew the license and the prenuptial agreement from between its pages. Holding all those objects in one fat hand he dug in the loose pocket of his tight jacket with the other. Finally, the fat man produced a ballpoint pen.

"Sign these!" he ordered Trux and Farley as he shoved both documents at them.

"We ain't signin' shit!" snarled Trux as he tried to back away only to find both new barrels of Heffaroid's old shotgun only a few inches from his head.

"You sign it first!" Heffaroid ordered Farley. "Or I'll blow off his big ole chin! I swear I'll do it! You don't believe me, just start fuckin' around."

"There is no need for that kind of language, Heffy! This a day for rejoicing with God," Brother Roy admonished.

"On the other hand. If they refuse to realize their obligations, and don't feel the need for rejoicing, there is still no need for foul language, but...."

The pastor let his last sentence go unfinished. It seemed apparent that neither the minister or the Lord with whom Brother Roy claimed to share such close contact, seemed to have any other gripe regarding the reverend's cousin's current conduct.

Both Farley and Heffaroid took this as a sign that everything else taking place at that moment was consonant with both. At least in the eyes of Brother Roy Ogles.

"My apologies to you and The Almighty, Cousin Brother Roy," said Heffaroid in an almost reverent tone. "What's it gonna be Maynard? You're brothers chin, n' maybe your balls, or a weddin'?"

The visible portion of Farley's face above the beard showed great concern. This was no time to argue religion. He reached out and took the papers and the pen from the preacher.

"Turn around Trux," he said, in a tight deep voice, as he prepared to write on his brother's back.

"What the Hell you doin' Farley?"

"I'm gonna sign em' Trux, and so are you. We wont be no help to Barney if we're dead. Now turn around."

Reluctantly, the obstinate red neck with too many teeth turned back toward the HOWDY HOSS. He looked at Arthell who didn't appear to be that happy herself.

"Really great plan your asshole friend come up with!" said Trux, as Farley placed the first paper against the upper part of his back between his broad shoulders.

Near the water's edge, Barney looked at the strange proceedings next to the motor home through the steel strands of the cage. The pig wasn't sure what was going on over there but it didn't look good.

Suddenly, he heard a sound in the water behind him. The pig turned to see Rodney's head, hair plastered against his face, emerging from beneath the surface of the lake.

Back at the motor home, Farley had finished signing the marriage certificate and was now pressing the other paper against Trux's back.

"Let's get this over with and get on to the 'Dearly Beloved's'!" said Brother Roy, impatiently.

It was obvious by the looks on all the members of the Hogg family that they concurred. The expressions on the faces of Arthell and the Maynards', especially Trux's showed clearly that they did not.

Behind them, next to the fire, the table and the water, Rodney, soaking wet and wearing only Jockey shorts, crept forward to the cage. The young man slid the bolt back. Barney was free at last.

The pig charged out of his steel mesh prison. He bared his tusks and let forth with his famous ear-rendering squeal.

In front of the motor home, all activity stopped. Every head turned toward the battle cry of Barney as the mighty swine raced forward. Rodney ran behind him, unable to match the four-legged animal's pace.

Trux spun around and knocked the shotgun from Heffaroid's huge hands. Both barrels exploded into the air.

The kick of the powerful old weapon knocked its large owner off his feet. The firearm flew from his hands, landed on a large rock, then bounced into the sand.

Trux grabbed Arthell and began propelling her back into the motor home. The Hogg sisters scrambled out of the way as Brother Roy slipped his Bible into one of his jacket pockets, then lunged at Farley.

A loud ripping sound blended with Barney's squeal as Farley went falling backward with the large minister on top of him.

The good reverends' trousers had finally endured too much stress. They were now split up the back from crotch to belt line.

There may be ecclesiastic laws regarding how many layers of cloth a man of the cloth is required to wear. If there are such rules and one them happens to dictate the presence of lower underwear, Brother Roy was clearly in violation that day.

His exposed, jumbo buns looked like two big round, pink beach balls as they thrust upward toward the sun. They made prefect targets for Barney who galloped up snarling and began taking several angry bites out of each.

Screams from Brother Roy replaced Barney's squeals. Rodney raced past the pig and his assault on the pastor's rear echelon to the beginning of the assaulted reverend's alimentary canal.

The young man in the Jockey shorts began pulling Farley out from beneath the screaming preacher's heavy body. Rodney's heart was pounding so loudly in his ears that he didn't hear the mighty roar of Heffaroid Hogg drowning out his cousin's shrieks of pain.

The irate brother of the two fat girls whose characters' he felt to be besmirched was now standing directly over the semi naked young man from Boston. Having found his shotgun, once again, to be no longer useful as a firearm, Heffaroid was now grasping the broken weapon by its double barrels, turning it into a lethal club.

He held it high in the air over his own head as he prepared to bring the old scatterguns' heavy wooden and metal stock down hard on that of Rodney Van Aukin.

Barney, however, had heard Heffaroid's stentorian bellow. The pig took one last bite out of Brother Roy's behind, then scrambled up over the reverend's exposed and mutilated manatee mounds to dart between the threatening, gigantic borax miner's distended shanks.

The speeding swine grabbed a mouthful of one of the big fellow's overall pants legs as he streaked through the swollen denim covered arches.

Heffaroid was thrown off balance as his left, tree trunk sized, lower limb was pulled back and out from under him. The shotgun flew out of his hands and up into the air as he tumbled forward onto his fat face.

It was only a matter of fleeting seconds when the defective firearm clattered down on top of his skull.

Trux, having propelled Arthell to safety, was outside the motor home again.

The broad shouldered man grabbed the dazed Farley from Rodney and began dragging his brother to the shelter of the HOWDY HOSS. Rodney, unaware that Barney's troubles were not yet over, scooped up the fallen marriage certificate and ran after the Maynards.

In the mean time, Catch Pen and Squeeze Chute were charging Barney. They knew nothing of their pastor cousin's plot to eat the pig after their marriage. They only knew there would be no wedding if the pig were allowed to escape.

The two colossal lasses lunged at Barney from either side of the much smaller creature. Like a shot, the pig leaped out of the way at the last second.

The leviathan torsos of female flesh collided as Barney zoomed into the motor home just ahead of the young attorney wearing Jockey shorts, who had executed his initial liberation.

Inside the HOWDY HOSS, Trux sat behind the steering wheel once again. The engine was already running as he called back to Rodney who was, with Arthell's help, hurriedly pulling the side door of the big rigged closed.

"Stop fuckin' around and close that damned door!" yelled Trux. "And put some clothes on for shit's sake! There's a lady present! Stay away from him Arthell! Lookin' at somebody nekid can get ya' in trouble!"

In order to immediately depart these premises and get back to the highway, Trux had to turn the motor home around. He slammed the shift into reverse and began backing up as fast as he could.

In the rear of the big utility rig, Farley sat on the floorboards. He was hugging Barney and trying very hard to fight back his tears of joy and relief.

Outside, all of the large people, including Brother Roy Ogles, with the busted britches and the butchered bare buttocks, were on their feet again.

They charged en masse toward the HOWDY HOSS like a thundering herd of rhinos as the rig completed its short, yet necessary backward jaunt. The transmission screamed as Trux jammed it into low gear, preparing to move out immediately.

Inside the battered old vehicle, Trux let out the clutch and stepped on the gas pedal. The engine roared but the motor home didn't move.

"What's wrong with this son of a bitch?" Trux asked nobody in particular as he frowned and pressed harder on the accelerator with his right foot.

Outside and directly behind the vintage recreational rig the Hogg family and the pastor of the Devotion to Divinity Church all had a firm grip on the rear bumper. The bevy of behemoths dug their heels into the ground and pulled back with all their collective might.

Beneath the sea of double, triple, and in Heffaroids' case, quadruple chins, the tires of the HOWDY HOSS were spinning. The old rig, however, was powerless to move forward.

Farley's bearded face appeared above them, looking out through the glass of the motor home's rear window.

"That bunch of lard asses has got us by the back bumper!" Farley yelled across the length or the vehicle interior to Trux, from his now kneeling position on the bed.

"Floor it Trux!"

"It is floored!" Trux called back, addressing the rearview mirror as the frustrated man with the square jaw practically stood on the gas pedal.

"Try a lower gear!" shouted Rodney, who stood in the middle of the aisle wearing only his underwear.

"Ain't no lower gear, you dumb shit! And put some clothes on!"

Arthell was still standing beside the near nude young barrister while Barney jumped up on the bed to be with Farley who continued looking out through the rear window at the gargantuan group responsible for the delay. She called to Trux in a defensive tone.

"He left his clothes on the other side of the lake! He doesn't have any!"

"Me n' Farley's got some shit either in the crapper or the closet back there! Just cover im' up! I got my own troubles right now!" Trux replied over the sound of the revving engine of the HOWDY HOSS.

He tried second gear, which failed to bring any satisfactory results.

"Move mothafucker!" he hissed through his many teeth, as he jerked the gearshift back into low and kept the accelerator pedal pressed to the floor.

Behind the running, yet stationary vehicle, the overweight people closed their eyes as sand and clumps of earth kicked up by the continual spinning tires sprayed their fat faces.

A determined lot, they all stubbornly retained their grip on the bumper. The tremendous weight pulling against it continued to prevent the big vibrating recreational vehicle from its intended departure.

The complaining engine of the HOWDY HOSS was so loud now that Rodney was terrified it was about to blow up. Something had to be done.

He had no clue from whence it came, probably bits and pieces of conversation from the Maynards earlier, but suddenly he had an idea. He leaned past Arthell who was digging old clothing out of the closet and tugged at the pants leg of Farley's soiled suit.

The bearded Maynard brother wearing that particular pair of trousers still kneeled on the bed with his attention on the humongous hostile herd beyond the rear window and the beloved pig beside him.

"You need somthin'?" Asked Farley without turning.

"Where's the sewage dump on this thing?" shouted the young man in his Jockey shorts, hoping to be heard over the motor and Trux's loud curses coming from the front.

Farley did turn now as he pointed to the toilet facility door opposite the closet Arthell continued to rummage around in, despite the current catastrophe.

"Black knob in there on the right over the shitter. But it won't do you no good. Shitter still won't work. I wouldn't go and …."

Whatever Farley was advising against went unfinished as Rodney jerked open the indicated portal and surged inside the small enclosure.

He grabbed the black knob that was exactly where Farley said it would be and pulled it toward him.

The huge foursome with the death grip on the rear bumper began to slip and slide as the waste from the inside toilet facility began pouring out beneath the rear of the old rig, making a long overdue egress.

The old motor home began to inch forward. The strength of the fleshy four prevailed. In spite of the slippery footing, they managed to retain their bulldog grips on the bumper, preventing their fugitives from gaining any real headway.

"We're moving!" cried Rodney as Arthell handed him an old pair of Farley's jeans. "Try second gear again!"

"Stop tellin' me what to do n' put them pants on!" Trux yelled back at him, while taking the young lawyer's advice.

The old vehicle was finally at its breaking point. It hunched up and emitted a huge belch of smoke. This was followed by a tremendous metallic ripping sound as the bumper came free from the rest of the machine.

The die hard determined detaining committee bearing the collective weight of well over sixteen hundred pounds, retained their hold on the large metal bar that was no longer a part of the HOWDY HOSS.

All, including the bumper, tumbled backward into a colossal heap. What remained of the old recreational vehicle finally made its getaway.

As the motor home departed in a cloud of dust, the Hogg family and Brother Roy finally managed to untangle themselves from the bumper and each other.

The pastor was the first to strenuously pull his massive frame up to a standing position. Squeeze Chute looked up and made a distressful nasal wailing sound as she pointed at the man of the cloth's posterior.

"Oh, Cousin Brother Roy! Your bum's all over bloody and it's all hangin' out!" she whined with great concern as she struggled to her own feet.

She raised the skirt of her wedding dress, exposing big rents in the pantyhose stretching over and around her more than ample thighs. She started to rip off a piece of her petticoat.

"Let me put a bandage on it, Cousin Brother...."

The reverend reached down with his huge paw and took hold of the material she was offering him. With one tremendous tug, he ripped the entire petticoat from beneath her skirt and wadded it up.

Brother Roy shoved the makeshift bandage down what was left of the seat of his pants and pulled Heffaroid to his feet.

"We can't let that pig... I mean them, get away, Heffy!" shouted the large pastor. "Hurry Heffy! In the name of our Lord!!"

Squeeze Chute, now minus her petticoat, pulled Catch Pen up from the ground as Brother Roy pushed the still dazed Heffaroid toward the little Karmann Ghia.

Inside the rapidly moving HOWDY HOSS, Rodney finally had something on other than his underwear. A pair of Farley's old jeans covered the lower portion of his lean torso. The worn denim trousers were far too big for the lanky young man in the waist, but the fit was fine in the seat.

He stood in the rear of the motor home that was finally not only surging forward, but also traveling at a rapid clip over the bumpy road leading away from Dirty Socks Lake.

The delayed reaction of fear regarding what he had just been through was beginning to set in as he attempted to secure the loose fitting pair of pants around his lean waist with a piece of rope. Arthell had found it for him somewhere in the closet or under the bed.

The pretty girl, herself, now stood behind him, balancing herself against the moving vehicle's motion, as she slipped an old threadbare long sleeved shirt over his shoulders. She looked at him with great concern.

"Rodney! You're shaking. That water's warm. You couldn't be catching cold."

He finished tying a knot in the rope around his middle and lurched forward to the old leather chair. The shirt fell from his bare shoulders.

"I'm scared!" he admitted as he sank down into the seat. "I didn't get scared while it was happening but I sure am making up for it now."

Arthell's heart skipped a little beat as she bent over to pick up the shirt. Never had she known any man to be so honest.

"You were really brave. I don't mind telling you I was plenty scared while it was all going on. Here, let me help you put on this shirt."

"He's a growed man for the sake of skunk shit! He can damn well dress hisself!" Trux called from his position in the driver's seat.

"And sit down Arthell! But not with him! Sit some other damned place!"

Arthell started to retort, but decide not to. She placed her cute little behind on a seat across the aisle from Rodney who was trying to keep his fingers from trembling long enough to get into the shirt.

"How's everthing fit there?" asked Farley. The grateful bearded man now sat on the bed facing the front of the rig's interior with Barney snuggled up against his legs. Farley had wiped the filth from the pig's hindquarters with an old burlap sack he had since tossed out of sight into the toilet area. The animal, now presentable and once again with his loved ones, was happily chewing away at an apple his Daddy had given him.

"They'll do Farley. Thanks," said Rodney in response to Farley's question regarding the borrowed clothing.

"Never dreamed when you had us drop you off 'fore we drove on in, without you, that you'd be showin up 'thout no clothes," observed Farley. "Course I didn't really know the plan."

"Wasn't really part of the plan," Rodney admitted. "I just couldn't think of another way to come up from behind with out any body seeing me. That's why I ended up swimming under the water. Good thing you insisted I leave my wallet with my I. D. here in the HOWDY HOSS with my briefcase, Arthell. I'm sure there was a better way to execute that part of the plan, but like I said, I just couldn't think…."

"I think it was a brilliant decision," said Arthell, her eyes shining and her voice filled with conviction.

"Shame I ain't got no shoes to fit ya," the bearded Maynard brother's attitude toward the young man he had wanted to castrate the prior evening had improved greatly. Barney had been rescued and he and Trux were no longer in danger of becoming bridegrooms. Little things meant a lot to Farley.

"I've got an extra pair in my suitcase," replied Rodney, still trying to stop shaking.

"But yer suitcase is in yer car, boy," said Farley, giving the younger man a strange look. Maybe the ordeal had been too much for this city boy.

"And yer car's still back at the lake," the bearded man continued gently.

"Not if the rest of the plan's still working," replied the young attorney. He wasn't shaking quite so badly now.

"There's more to this here plan?" asked Farley looking slightly confused. He'd heard of such a thing as water on the brain.

"I'll be go to Hell or some other big city!" Trux called back from where he sat driving as fast as he could over the uneven road and looking in the rearview mirror at the same time.

"Those two fat fuckers, Heffaroid and the preacher are comin' after us in that pussy little car of dipshit's!"

In the rear, Farley looked back through the window. Sure enough, the Karmann Ghia, raising a huge cloud of dust for its small size, was indeed behind them. Heffaroid was at the wheel with Brother Roy stuffed in beside him.

The departure of the two desert whales had been slightly delayed while they crammed their oversized bodies into the front of the tiny topless German made machine. However, never underestimate the wrath or determination of two fat men scorned.

They had overcome the impossible. Now they were in hot pursuit and gaining on the escapees.

The bearded Maynard brother turned from the rear window of the motor home and looked at to Rodney.

"I'll be damned!" was all he had to say.

The pig looked up and grunted his agreement. Anybody who had saved him from being served with baked potatoes and turnips was all right in Barney's book. He just hoped that now that he'd finally been fed, instead of being fed to someone else, one of these good friends of his in this moving motor home, would suggest breaking out the beer.

"Head back for Lone Pine," Rodney called to Trux, as Arthell looked at the lawyer through absolutely adoring eyes.

"Bull shit!" Trux yelled back. "Arty'll be lookin' for us, we go that way! I'm gonna' make a left turn up here and lose em' on the back road to Olancha!"

Arthell rose and started up the aisle toward Trux.

"Please Daddy Trux, listen to what Rodney says. He's the one that has the plan."

"I got his plan between my legs!" Trux responded as he negotiated a bend in the rough dirt road that made the beautiful girl fall back onto Rodney's lap.

"And get offa him for shit's sake!"

Farley rose and helped Arthell back to her original seat. He called up the aisle to his brother as he did so.

"You done that Trux! I know we're in a hurry, but you oughta be more careful. Oughta do what the kid says too. Remember that it ain't just his plan, it's also Thelma's. To my way of thinkin', it's workin' out so far. We got Barney back and we ain't married. I ain't really sure what's comin' up next any moren' you, but you really should do like he's tellin' you."

Before Trux could respond, Arthell was calling to him again. The usually sweet girl was beginning to sound just a wee bit cranky.

"Please stop being so bullheaded and give Rodney a little credit! Go back to Lone Pine!"

Trux looked in front of him through the windshield. The turn to Lone Pine was right in front of him. He looked in the rearview mirror.

The Karmann Ghia with the two crazy fat men was right behind him. He had to make a decision.

At the last minute, the HOWDY HOSS, somehow managing to remain upright, made an abrupt right turn toward Lone Pine. The Karma Gail behind it fishtailed, then straightened out and headed after the speeding old utility rig.

Except for some rhythmic, fairly subtle, up and down motions, back at the county line, the official Lone Pine sheriff's sedan was going nowhere. It still occupied the exact same spot on the shoulder of the road.

The vehicle hadn't moved an inch since it had come to its previous sudden stop. Exactly at the same time the misguided Magnum had blown apart the cop car's spot light instead of the rear tire of the HOWDY HOSS.

Only one occupant could be seen through the windshield of the parked vehicle. Arty Dubs, still wearing his hat, and the uniformed shirt with the gleaming badge, starred straight ahead through the glass. His eyes appeared to be almost of the same substance as the windshield.

Occasional soft female and male moans of ecstasy coming from within the car mingled with exterior calls of desert birds and distant coyote howls. Otherwise all was quiet.

Slowly, the sheriff's eyes began to focus on something ahead of him on the highway. It took him a moment or two to locate his tongue.

"I'll be go to Hell!" he said in a husky voice. "Them dumb shits are comin' back this way! I don't believe it!"

Thelma's pretty blond hair was tousled and there was absolutely no doubt whatsoever where her tongue had been. She raised up beside him to take her own look through the windshield.

The returning motor home, being chased by the Karmann Ghia was still slightly over a mile away. Nonetheless, both vehicles were coming straight toward the sheriff's car and its occupants, at a very high rate of speed.

"It's about time," the beautiful lady whispered, as she attempted to catch her breath.

Thelma was not the kind of person to relate personal activities. Especially that which had kept her continually busy since she convinced the leading law enforcement official of Lone Pine to pause in his efforts to blow apart tires.

Had she been, the Argus Queen would undoubtedly still go unchallenged in the Guinness Book of World Records to this day.

Even Agnus Wayling on her best day had never even come close to matching this feat of time, endurance and overall longevity.

The HOWDY HOSS was almost across the county line now. The Ghia, with Heffaroid and Brother Roy still stuffed in its front, was right behind it.

The little car was only a few feet from where the bumper used to be on the battered old RV. Both vehicles maintained their breakneck speed.

Inside the old motor home, Rodney called from the back of its interior to Trux who still operated the controls of the big machine.

"Trux! Stop! Hit the brakes. Hard!"

Up front, Trux started to give a negative reaction to the young lawyer's assertive suggestion from his position behind the steering wheel.

Suddenly, Farley and Arthell were standing in the rear aisle on either side of Rodney. All three shouted at the driver in unison!

"Stop! Stop now! Hit the brakes!"

"Ah, fuck it!" muttered Trux as he hit the binders. The rest of the passengers of the HOWDY HOSS, including Barney, came tumbling down the aisle toward him.

Inside the sheriffs' car, Arty was attempting to untangle his effervescent bright blue boxer shorts and his uniform trousers from the top of his western style boots. He looked up past Thelma to see the motor home skid to a complete stop.

It was just past the county line now and right next to the passenger seat window of the official automobile.

As the big rig was brought to its rude unceremonious halt, the sudden shift in gravity lifted the rear end of the HOWDY HOSS temporarily upward.

It came immediately back down on top of the front end of the Karmann Ghia, which Heffaroid had failed to stop in time to avoid crashing into the motor home.

The little car was now wedged beneath the backside of the much larger vehicle all the way to its windshield, which somehow remained intact. Heffaroid and Brother Roy too, seemed to have come through the ordeal miraculously unharmed.

However, both were now totally trapped in the wreckage. They were also now inside Arty's jurisdiction.

The sheriff's effervescent shorts were in place now, but his pants still hung down around his ankles, as he exited the driver's door of his own vehicle. Holding the big Magnum in his left hand, he hobbled around in front of the sedan. The lawman seemed unsure exactly where he should be pointing the weapon.

Thelma exited the passenger side of the cop car as Trux, Farley, Arthell and Rodney climbed out of the side door of the motor home.

Rodney looked ridiculous in the old shirt and the jeans wrapped around his waist with a rope. He looked no more so than did the Maynard brothers in their all but ruined suits and ties.

Barney stood in the open doorway behind them, marveling at this entire strange human and mechanical behavior.

Both Trux and Farley began snickering and pointing at Arty's loud underwear which was quite visible beneath the tails of his official Lone Pine sheriff's uniform shirt.

"You always wear them kinda' shorts, Arty?" asked Farley.

For the first time since Trux became suspicious of Rodney's intentions toward Arthell, the famous multi toothed grin returned to his square jawed face. He gave his brother an elbow jab in the ribs.

"Look a little like Thelma's drawers, don't they?"

Arty reached down and began pulling up his trousers with his hand not holding the pistol. He backed around the front of his car to shield himself behind its hood.

While the dignified sheriff of Lone Pine was pulling his pants up, Thelma, flashing a triumphant smile, making her flawless features even more beautiful, walked past the others to greet the pig.

"I'm so glad you're alright, Barney!" said Thelma, as she bent down and hugged the animal around the neck. The pig emitted a grateful grunt and she straightened up to face Rodney who smiled at the beautiful woman.

"Great plan!" the young lawyer said.

"Beautifully executed!" she told him.

The Argus Queen and the young man from Boston gave each other a high five, then walked together toward the rear of the motor home to survey the damage. Arthell beamed with pride at the two people she was so proud of, and followed.

Trux and Farley pointed and giggled at Arty one more time, who was still partially hidden behind the hood of the police car, pulling his trousers up into their proper place. The brothers then trailed after the pretty girl both thought to be their daughter.

Barney remained in the portal opening of the utility rig. He was hoping that soon, somebody would realize it was dangerously past cocktail hour.

Heffaroid and Brother Roy glowered up from their entrapped positions in the seat of what was left of the sad looking little Karmann Ghia, as the group rounded the rear corner of the motor home.

"They still look intact," Thelma said to Rodney. "Can't say the same for your car, though. I didn't plan on things turning out exactly this way."

"Don't worry about it. I've got insurance," Rodney said.

He couldn't believe his own attitude regarding what had just happened, but he liked it.

"Piss on the car lady!" said Heffaroid. "We coulda' been kilt! Get us outa' here! My cousin here needs a doctor! His butt's all over boar bites!"

"A little case of do unto others, Pastor Ogles?" Thelma asked Brother Roy in a very innocent tone.

"You know nothing of the Lords' work!" replied the huge, trapped reverend, with a disdainful sneer.

"I am Gods' messenger! A mere mortal like yourself is not qualified to judge me!"

Something inside Rodney began to boil. "You are the most despicable person I've ever seen!" he cried as he stepped forward. The words of righteous anger kept on flowing forth.

"You should be ashamed of yourself! How dare you blame God for the awful thing you tried to do? The God I pray to wouldn't even want you for a pimple on His ass!"

The young lawyer couldn't believe those words had just passed his lips, but they sure tasted good. The Honesty Monster wasn't so bad after all, when it and Rodney were in sync.

His remark received favorable response from all present except Heffaroid and Brother Roy. Even Trux gave the younger man a look of grudging respect until Arthell moved up beside Rodney and kissed his cheek.

"Oh, Rodney!" she exclaimed. "You and mom are so neat!"

Trux surged forward to separate the young lady from the lawyer in Farley's jeans, but was pulled back.

Arty grabbed the red neck with the big chin by his broad shoulder as the sheriff rounded the rear corner of the utility rig.

The Lone Pine law enforcement officer was fully dressed now. His Magnum nestled in its holster attached to the gun belt now strapped around his waist.

"I don't know what's goin' on here," said Arty as Trux turned to face him. "But I'm gonna' get to the bottom of it if I have to have to lock up ever dumb red necked peckerwood here!"

"Rodney's not a dumb red necked peckerwood!" Arthell spoke up defensively.

The sheriff ignored the young lady's remark and expanded his attention to include Farley.

"To start with, I'm arresting you two assholes for stealin' Larrys' gas!" He announced as his left hand drifted toward the holstered weapon on his gun belt.

"I've about had it with your name callin' Arty!" said Trux, pushing his own face up close to the law man's bucked toothed one.

"You call me n' Farley somthin' bad again, I'm gonna' shove that gun so far down your throat, you gonna' have bullets comin' outa' your bunghole!"

Thelma moved in between the two men.

"Oh, just stop it! Both of you! Arty, I'm paying for the stupid gas. I would have done it already back at the service station, but you were in such a hurry to leave I never had a chance!"

This stumped the sheriff. He looked around. He was sure he was being had in some way, but he wasn't certain how.

Rodney, pulled out the wallet he'd had the foresight to leave behind in his briefcase, from the pocket of Farley's ill fitting jeans. His tone sounded very official as he addressed the confused, elected official.

"Sheriff, I'm very glad you happened to come on the scene," said the young lawyer as he withdrew the registration for the Karmann Ghia. He handed it to Arty with one hand while indicating Heffaroid and the other overweight, immobile occupant of his mutilated little car with the other.

"I'd like to formally press charges on these two men for stealing my car."

"That's your car?" asked Arty, as he seemed to see Heffaroid, Brother Roy and the remains of the Karmann Ghia for the first time.

"I believe that document will bear out the facts," said Rodney, in his best lawyer voice. Arthell gazed at him with an expression of total admiration.

"He's right!" said the sheriff after looking at the registration, and walking around behind the Ghia to check its license plate.

Arty drew his gun as he moved from the rear of the little German manufactured machine to the still seated and trapped, alleged car thieves.

"You're both under arrest! The man's got the duly registered title!" He said reverting to his best Clint Eastwood whisper. "The car is his! Now both of you step out of that vehicle with your hands in the air."

Brother Roy and Heffaroid did indeed raise their hands. It became obvious even to Arty, that neither could move anything else.

Trux chuckled as he moved in beside the sheriff. Arty was having a tough time trying very hard to think of a solution to this situation not covered in the law enforcement manual.

"Gotta' cuttin' torch in the HOWDY HOSS, Arty. Me n' Farley'll get em' outa there for fifty bucks. Right Farley?"

"If we give it to Thelma to pay for the gas we used to save Barney," Farley said.

"Boy howdy! You can't hang onto money worth shit!" Trux told his brother.

"Okay, I guess."

He spoke to the sheriff again. "You want us to cut em' out for ya' or not?"

Arty thought for a moment, then nodded.

"You'll have to fill out a county voucher, I've got a couple in my car. Soon as I read em' their rights and put some cuffs on em', I'll pull one out for ya'."

Rodney reached into the rear space behind the colossal captive carjackers and would be pignappers. The attorney pulled out his suitcase while Arty read the borax miner and the preacher their rights. He then handcuffed them as best he could under the circumstances.

The suitcase felt good in Rodney's hand. It would be good to wear clothing that fit him again.

Arthell started to follow as the young man headed around the rear corner of the rig to enter the vehicle and change. She stopped as Trux spoke up in a sharp tone.

"Hang on there, Missy. You helped him get dressed already once today and that's too damned many times. You stick with me n' Farley. We're gonna need your help filling out them fancy forms of Arty's."

"Why don't you and her handle that, Trux?" asked Farley. "I'm gonna' get Barney somthin' to drink. He's gotta have a thirst worked up by now."

Trux nodded. Farley followed Rodney while Arthell reluctantly lagged behind. Arty, finished with his ritual, turned to Thelma.

"Mind keepin' an eye on my prisoners while I take care of some official business, Thelma?" he asked.

Thelma looked at the helpless, hefty Heffaroid and his cousin. They now looked like manacled, whale sized sardines in a crumpled can. She shrugged.

"I doubt very much that they'll be going anywhere, but okay, Arty."

Arty gave the preposterously plump pair one last superior look and indicated for Trux and Arthell to follow him with a jerk of his cowboy hat covered head. Trux and the girl trailed behind the now swaggering lawman.

When the trio reached the sheriff's car he opened the driver's door and reached in. He withdrew a book of forms and handed the item to the pretty girl.

"Fill this out while I get Jiggs on the horn and give im' the skinny," he ordered. The sheriff then reached in and turned on his two-way radio before plucking its microphone from its cradle near the right of the steering wheel. Arty leaned on the open driver's portal as he pushed the button on the mike and began speaking into it.

"Jiggs? This is Dubs!" he said trying very hard to sound just like Clint Eastwood again.

"I'm coming in with a couple of prisoners. Grand theft auto. You read me?"

Jiggs voice came back over the speaker inside the sedan immediately.

"I've been tryin to reach you for at least two hours, sheriff. You have your radio turned off?"

Arty's eyes narrowed. "I'm the sheriff, Jiggs. You're the deputy. That means I talk and you listen. Just a minute."

He turned and accepted the evidently already filled out forms from Arthell. The sheriff then gave Trux a nod, indicating for him to go fetch his torch and earn his fifty dollars.

As the big chinned red neck and the stunning young lady walked away, Arty spoke into the mike again. He began reading the information off Rodney's registration that was still in his possession.

"The vehicle in question is registered to a Rodney P. Van Aukin. Van Aukin is here with me right now."

Again, Jiggs voice came floating out from the radio speaker inside the official vehicle.

"Van Aukin's with you, sheriff?"

"That's affirmitive!"

"That's the reason I been tryin' to contact you sheriff." Jiggs' voice continued. "Two guys flew into the airport in a private plane today…"

In the booking office of the Lone Pine sheriffs' station, Jiggs sat with his back to the counter as he continued talking into the radio mike.

Behind him, on the other side of the tall flat surfaced barrier, stood two men wearing flowered Hawaiian shirts beneath their expensively tailored sports jackets.

Horace and Harold Herkimer did not wish to appear over dressed during their first, and hopefully only visit to the Owens valley.

Both listened with stern faces as the Deputy Sheriff continued talking over the station radio system.

"These Herkimer fellers, they already got a warrant from Judge Hanley. Guess they got some big time L. A. judge to call ahead. Paper says to arrest Van Aukin and bring im' in for questionin'. Somethin' about embezzlement's, what it says," Jiggs told Arty over the radio as he looked at the official paper in question.

CHAPTER SEVENTEEN
INDELICATE DISCLOSURES

Sheriff Arty Duds was not a happy man. He seemed to have totally lost control over his own turf. That motor home the Maynards called the HOWDY HOSS, which now looked worse than ever, was parked directly in front of his sheriffs' station with a pig in it.

The owners of both the animal and the horrendous mechanical eye sore were not back in his jail where Arty was convinced they always belonged. Instead, they were right here in his outer office. Adding insult to injury, both were being treated like royalty.

The outer office itself had been turned into a conference room with out anyone consulting him. Two big city lawyers had just taken over the place as if he, the sheriff was no more than some public servant.

Jiggs had drug out a desk from God knows where, and placed it near the holding tank. Horace and Harold Herkimer sat facing Rodney who had the contents of his briefcase, including the cellular telephone spread out on the desktop.

The Maynard brothers stood next to the desk with Thelma between them. Arty had only been asked to stand by in case these big city lawyers decided they wanted Van Aukin put in a cell. He felt totally left out in his own bailiwick.

He'd arrested the man at their request and now he wasn't even able to lock him up. He needed their permission. Arty didn't quite understand all the legalese. He was a lawman, not a lawyer.

It had something to do with that warrant they'd evidently pulled some fancy legal strings to obtain. The document gave them the liberty of deciding if they still wished to press charges.

He found this out after he'd gone to the trouble of bringing in the suspect they had asked him to arrest in the first place. It didn't make sense to Arty.

To make matters even worse, one of the people he had already locked up was a local clergyman with a perforated posterior. The sheriff had already been forced to spend county money bringing in a doctor to have the pastor's butt sewn up. The town had to be buzzing about that one.

Already, one old lady from the Devotion to Divinity Church had looked at Arty as if he might be the Devil himself. He had received this glare of accusation and disgust when the sweet old soul had arrived at the station shortly after the doctor.

She had with her with a pair of extremely large replacement pants for her pastor and a box of Fruit Loops. Jiggs hadn't been out front at the time, therefore the duty of telling the senior citizen of Lone Pine she couldn't see the reverend right then and why had fallen to the sheriff.

He knew as she departed, he would never get her vote when he ran for reelection.

Jiggs had since emerged when the doctor departed. He'd taken the Fruit Loops back to Ogles but the deputy had somehow, in all the confusion, forgotten the pants.

Arty hadn't realized this until he'd loudly put Jiggs to work cleaning up the outer office when he returned from the cell area. The lawman was trying to show the group of invaders who the boss was around here.

Now the kid was sweeping and the sheriff was holding a gigantic pair of trousers. In the meantime, a conference he wasn't involved with, was being conducted not ten feet away from him. Right in the middle of his turf!

Arty's Clint Eastwood image was going to Hell in a hand basket fast.

The sheriff stole a glance in Jiggs' direction who was now pushing his broom near the main entrance to the premises. The little son of a bitch better not be laughing at him.

The red headed deputy, however, seemed to be concentrating on the motor home sitting out front which could be seen through a window. He may have been thanking his lucky stars that the pig was out there and not in here. More probably, the young assistant's thoughts were on Thelma's lovely daughter who had remained in the dilapidated rig to keep the pig company.

If indeed that was the direction the younger man's mind was traveling, Arty couldn't blame him. The child really had grown up to be not only a looker, but also a really nice kid.

"Jiggs! Get your ass over here!" he ordered.

Jiggs looked up like he had just been caught with his hand in a cookie jar. The deputy tucked the broom beneath his arm and hurriedly moved back to the tall booking counter to face Arty. His superior handed him the preposterous pair of britches.

"You forgot to take these back to Ogles. Do it now!" said the head of Lone Pine law enforcement, as he handed the gargantuan garment to the young man in uniform.

Jiggs nodded. He took the trousers and turned. He then paused to steal a glance at the conference still going on near the holding tank, prior to heading to the rear of the station to do his superior's bidding.

The sheriff gave his deputy a dirty look, then turned his own attention back to the activity at that damn desk and those damn people, neither of which belonged where they were.

At the moment Rodney, wearing his own clothing again, which consisted of a sports shirt and a pair of slacks, was counting out the cash from the envelope before turning it over to the Herkimers.

He looked nervous. Still the young man appeared to be in much better control than when he had last faced these two gentlemen back in the big office in Century City and first received the same envelope.

"Well, as I told you, it's all here except for the two hundred dollars I advanced the Maynards." Rodney said, as he pushed the cash across the desktop to Horace Herkimer.

"And there's thirty dollars of my expense money I didn't spend." The young man from Boston hadn't stammered once, but he was obviously not impressing the Herkimers.

"That's still one hundred and seventy dollars short," said Harold Herkimer. "And I see no receipt from the Maynards here for any two hundred dollars. Unless there really is a deal in progress, you are still guilty of embezzlement, Van Aukin!"

Horace ignored the money and looked up at Trux and Farley.

"Did you agree to sell your land and accept an advance from this man?" he asked.

Trux's blue eyes were guarded.

"We didn't agree nothin'! And if this dude loaned us some money, I don't think that's any of your business," he stated flatly.

Harold Herkimer looked up at the rough-hewn man with the oversized chin.

"I would say if it were our money, that would make it our business," the lawyer said, using a slightly haughty tone.

"Your money, sir?" asked Thelma. "I was told you represented someone else, and it was their money."

"Of course! That's what Mr. Herkimer meant, Madame," said Horace Herkimer, speaking up quickly. "I'm sorry, I didn't catch your name."

"Her name's Thelma and don't you go callin' her no Madame!" snarled Farley who was beginning to bristle.

Horace took a deep breath. Things weren't going as smoothly as he had planned. He gave Harold a 'keep your mouth shut,' look and flashed his artificial teeth in what he had hoped to be interpreted as a charming smile.

"I assure you gentlemen, I meant no offence. I am merely attempting to determine...."

"And don't you go calling us names neither! Let's wade through the bullshit and get to the bottom line here. What's goin on?" said Trux, interrupting.

"It's really simple, Trux," Rodney spoke up. "Under the law, you and

Farley accepted two hundred dollars in good faith as a down payment on your mountain, and now Mr. Herkimer is ready to pay you the balance."

"I don't recall nothin' bout no down payment," replied Trux. "Me n' Farley said we'd think about it! That's all!"

"But when actual cash is accepted during a period of…" Rodney paused in an attempt to remember the exact wording of the law he was attempting to quote. He never got that far. Horace Herkimer interrupted him.

"Just be quiet Van Aukin! You have no idea what you're talking about!"

The young man was correct of course, and Horace knew it. However, such a ruling might have to be taken to court and a judge could well ask questions Horace and Harold weren't prepared to answer.

In addition, there simply wasn't time. He turned to Trux who seemed to be the spokesman for the pair of landowners.

"You said something to the effect of 'Cut to the chase,' sir. I'm in total agreement. I'll tell you what. Forget the two hundred. That's between you and Van Aukin. The offer is two thousand. I'll write you a check for the difference. Are you ready to turn over the property at this time?"

"Let me get this straight," said Trux. "Me n' Farley sign that paper and take your money, Rodney here don't get throwed in jail and took back to LA?"

"You have my word, sir," Horace was beginning to purr now. He had his fish on the hook and was adroitly reeling the sucker in.

"You transfer that mountain to H. and H. Holding corporation right now, and Rodney is a free man to go and do whatever he desires."

"Then we ain't signin' or sellin' shit!" Trux stated emphatically. "Come on Farley!"

Farley glanced at Rodney. The bearded man looked like he was about to speak up in protest, but seemed to change his mind when Trux took him by the arm and began pulling him toward the main exit of the sheriff's station.

"Trux!" Thelma called after him, as the broad shouldered man and his brother with the undersized buttocks reached the egress.

"I don't wanna' discuss it!" Trux called back as he and Farley walked out the door. Thelma followed as far as the portal and looked out of the window next to it. The stunning woman seemed to be deep in thought.

Back at the desk, both Herkimers were stunned.

"What happened?" Harold Herkimer whispered to Horace Herkimer.

Horace's face was turning slightly pink. He had obviously made a wrong choice. It was going to take some time to rethink things, and he didn't have much.

The Los Angeles executive rose to his feet. He called to the Sheriff whose back was to the rest of the big room now.

236

"Sheriff!"

Arty was now bending over the computer behind the booking desk.

"Hold your mud! There's one of them email things comin' in!"

Actually the sheriff knew absolutely nothing about that computer or what it did. But he had just heard that stupid disembodied voice tell him he had mail. He looked around toward the front entrance. Thelma knew all a bout this stuff.

Thelma was gone. She must have left when nobody was looking. Probably out trying to talk the Maynard brothers into changing their mind. Arty didn't really care much one way or the other.

He was glad she hadn't been there to help him with this computer business. He wasn't aware that she knew how ignorant he really was, therefore he didn't want her to know.

"Sheriff! I'm talking to you!" said Horace Herkimer.

"And I told you not to get your balls in an uproar! I'm busy here!" snapped the sheriff. His wording had become slightly more graphic now that he knew there was no longer a lady present and the dude was beginning to bug him.

He looked again at the monitor. Whatever it was, it would just have to wait. He'd tell Jiggs about it as soon as the deputy returned from his mission of mercy.

The sheriff did continue studying the screen for another second though, just to show that big city loudmouth Arty Dubs had better things to do than cater to the likes of him.

Finally, the barrel chested uniformed official turned around slowly after making a face at the little dude who was somewhere inside that stupid computer telling him again what he'd already told him.

He spoke in almost a whisper as he addressed the man on the other side of the counter who had yelled at him in such a rude manner.

"Somethin' I can do for you?"

"Sheriff Doobs, Mr. Herkimer and I will be pressing charges. Lock this man up. I'll start the extradition process as quickly as I can. You do understand what I'm talking about?"

Arty gave the man in the sports jacket and the flowered shirt a scathing look.

"The name is Dubs, and I understand a lot of things. Like the fact that he should have already been locked up in the first place."

Before Horace could answer, Jiggs entered from the rear metal door leading back to the cells.

"Sheriff," he said, "Heffaroid Hogg back there's sayin' he's willin' to sign somethin' takin' all responsibility for stealin' Van Aukin's car and the reverend's demandin' to be cut loose."

"First things first, Jiggs." The sheriff was trying really not to sound as tired and irritated as he really felt.

"We got us an email back here. Check it out and let me know what's goin' on."

Jiggs nodded and headed for the little gate that would give him access to join his superior behind the booking counter. The sheriff continued issuing orders as the deputy did so.

"Then we gotta' lock this guy up. It's finally okay. Take his property, n' throw im' back with Hogg and the reverend. After you take care of that, get Heffaroid's statement down on paper and we'll see about turnin' the preacher loose. Then, you get done with ever thing I just told you, I want you to tote that damned old desk back where you found it and don't never rearrange nothin' in here again 'less I say so!"

The deputy nodded as he reached the other side of the booking desk and sat down behind the sheriff at the computer to take care of his first assignment.

Still seated at the desk that didn't belong next to the holding tank but nonetheless was, Rodney heaved a deep sigh. He remained in his chair as he began putting the items he hadn't turned over to the Herkimers, including the cell phone back into his briefcase.

Behind the booking counter, Jiggs looked up at Arty indicating the message that was now on the computer screen.

"It's for them," said the deputy as he jerked his head toward the Herkimers who were huddled a short distance from Rodney involved in a whispered conversation with each other.

Arty sucked at his buck teeth with his lower lip. "Might of known. They've took over everything else."

"Want me to print it up for em'?" asked Jiggs.

"Hell no! Just tell em' what it says. Get your ass out there and get Van Aukin's property, then lock him up."

Jiggs nodded and manipulated the mouse in his right hand to click on the actual message. As it came on the screen, a puzzled look came over his young face.

The expression turned into more of a frown as he read the message. He took a deep breath then read it again.

It was probably sheer coincidence, but both names in that missive on the screen were familiar. They brought back a memory that made him slightly uncomfortable.

Before Arty could yell at him however, he was on his feet with a property envelope and slip in his hand.

Quickly the deputy headed out from behind the counter toward Rodney and the Herkimers. He still had the strange look on his face as he reached them.

"You got an email, Mr. Herkimer."

The heads of both Harold and Horace turned toward the young subordinate official.

"Which Mr. Herkimer?" they asked in unison.

"Both of you I guess," replied Jiggs. "From somebody named Harrington Fox."

Jiggs had that strange look on his face again.

"What did she have to say?" Horace asked impatiently.

Jiggs reacted as he heard the word 'She.'

"This Harrington's a woman?" he asked.

"Maybe Agnus is ready to come back to work," Harold whispered to Horace. "It's about time."

Jiggs overheard him.

"That exactly what she did say," he said. "The message was 'Leaving San Diego. Had a wonderful time. Agnus will be back to work this afternoon'."

For the first time Rodney took an interest in the conversation. He had no idea Agnus wasn't at work right now.

"Fine! Fine!" Horace said briskly. "Thank you Deputy. Now take this man back there and lock him up. Mr. Herkimer and I …."

"Harrington's a strange name for a woman. I met a woman named Harrington once. Last name was Fox, too," said Jiggs, interrupting the blustering big city attorney. "She was with another woman named Agnus too." Continued the deputy screwing up his face as his mind meandered back into time. "Agnus Wayling. I think it was. Yeah! Wayling was the other old chick's last name."

Now Rodney really was interested. The deputy lowered his voice. He knew he shouldn't be talking about this but seeing those two names together after all this time had him rattled. He wasn't thinking clearly.

"They were both kinda' old, but they sure didn't act their ages. Neither one of em'. It was right after I got out of high school when I was working for the forest service youth firefighter's brigade. There was this fire outside of Tahoe…."

Rodney couldn't help but notice that both Herkimers were beginning to turn red.

Over at the booking desk, Arty was tired of people talking when he couldn't hear what was being said.

"What the Hell's goin' on over there Jiggs? I thought you were gonna' lock that guy up!"

"I'm on it Sheriff!" Jiggs called back becoming very official. The Tahoe story was obviously destined to remain unfinished. He turned to Rodney.

"Better gimme all your stuff"

Horace Herkimer reached into his pocket and pulled out a small square of cardboard with printing on it and handed it to the deputy.

"Put this with Van Aukin's property!" he commanded. His color was returning to normal by the time he turned his full attention on Rodney.

"It's a storage claim ticket." He informed the young man who used to work for him that he was now sending to jail.

"If you ever get out of prison, that's where you'll find any belongings you may have left behind at my daughter's apartment. She wants nothing more to do with you! You are never to attempt contacting her again."

Rodney was still trying to figure out what Miss Wayling and the friend he'd never heard of till now, had done to make them such a memory in Jiggs mind.

He was also wondering why his ex superiors blushed when they found out the deputy knew the women.

Horace's announcement brought him back to the moment at hand. He breathed a deep sigh of relief. At least he'd received one piece of good news from the big city along with all the bad.

He closed the briefcase and handed it to Jiggs along with his wallet, as he stood up from his chair.

"You want to make your phone call now?" asked the Deputy, indicating the pay telephone that could be seen through the bars of the holding tank.

"I don't seem to have anyone to call "

Rodney's statement was simple as he walked toward the booking counter to go through proper arrest procedure prior to being escorted to that awful place in the back of the building.

A location which, unfortunately, he was all too familiar with. He was anxious to ask Jiggs more about Miss Wayling and Tahoe, though.

The main door opened at that moment and Thelma reentered the building. She hadn't gone all the way to the motor home to talk to Trux or Farley. She'd stepped outside to think. She was still deep in thought as she moved slowly back toward the center of the enclosure.

Something was terribly wrong here. She knew the law concerning the acceptance of partial monies in a land transaction and Rodney was absolutely correct. Trux had even acknowledged receiving it.

Why weren't these two esteemed members of the California Bar Association aware of this?

The lovely woman hated seeing Rodney locked up again when it was only a little over twenty-four hours since she'd been responsible for his release from the very same jail. However, before she leaned on her beloved Maynard brothers to get him out of there, which might turn out to be detrimental to their interests, certain other things had to be investigated.

"Excuse me, Mr. Herkimer," Thelma said politely, as she walked up to Horace and Harold. The big city siblings were still standing next to the out of place desk near the holding tank as they whispered to each other again.

Across the room at the booking counter, Arty decided that if Thelma had come back to keep him from locking Rodney up again, she would have said something by now. At least somebody was going to let him do his job.

He watched his assistant law enforcement officer with the red hair, inventory poor Rodney's property before taking him back to one of the cells.

Horace and Harold turned toward this mysterious beautiful woman.

"Yes?" responded Horace guardedly. He still hadn't figured out where she fit into this puzzle, but it was obvious she had a certain amount of influence over the people whose land he desperately needed.

"I think I can handle this problem, given some time." Thelma told the two attorneys. "I'm sure you want what's best for all concerned."

"How much time?" asked Horace, totally ignoring the second portion of the great looking lady's statement.

"If I could have at least until tomorrow evening before you start any extradition procedures, I think I can guarantee Trux will look upon your offer in a brand new light. His brother too."

The Herkimers exchanged a glance. Harold nodded before Horace turned back to Thelma. The latter was having a rough time keeping his eyes off her beautiful breasts. They seemed to be screaming to be freed from the confines of her tight black dress immediately.

"Granted my dear. But please do bear in mind, the firm of Herkimer, Herkimer, Herkimer, Herkimer has no time to waste." Horace's eyes of lust won over his educated mind as he continued.

"If you'd like, we could discuss this in more detail later over dinner."

Thelma gave the man a coy smile as she thrust out her ample chest even further.

"The members of my firm have no time to waste either. Thanks anyway Mr. Herkimer."

She nodded to the other Mr. Herkimer and called to Rodney before turning and sweeping out through the main entrance of the Lone Pine sheriffs' station.

"Hang in there Rodney!"

Harold Herkimer looked after the departing vision of perfect female anatomy and shook his head in wonder.

"Did you see the size of those?" he asked the other Mr. Herkimer. "They

241

have to be plastic."

"My compliments to the plastic surgeon, if they are." replied Horace. He looked up to see Arty who had wandered up during their conversation.

"What's that old sex pot's connection to those idiots anyway, Sheriff?"

Their was no friendliness whatsoever in the eyes of the sheriff of Lone Pine when he answered.

"You can trash the Maynards all you want, but I'd watch my mouth sayin' anything at all 'bout that lady. She happens to be one of the most respected people in this whole valley. Her connection with anything or anyone is strictly none of your damn business! You understand, Mr. Herkmanure?"

Horace started to respond. Whether it was in apology or to point out that the sheriff had mispronounced his name or otherwise, was never to be known.

All of his words were completely drowned out by the anguished cry of a young female voice coming from the front entrance of the station.

"Rodney!!!" screamed Arthell.

The young hero had assured her that nothing could go wrong in his meeting with the Herkimers. The pretty young person had therefore remained behind in the HOWDY HOSS with Barney.

She really had no idea what had been going on inside this building, even after Trux and Farley had returned.

Only when her mother had finally come out, had she learned the fate that had befallen the man she was so in love with.

Trux especially, had been unhappy when she announced they could all go home with out her.

The motor home, however, could be seen departing the law enforcement premises through the open door as she ran across the large enclosure. Tears ran in torrents down her pretty cheeks.

The frantic beauty grabbed onto Rodney just as Jiggs was propelling him through the portal leading back to the cell area.

Sobbing, she hung onto the young man, refusing to let go. Jiggs didn't know what to do.

Finally, Arty strode across the room and attempted to pry the young lovers apart.

After finding the task to be impossible without hurting someone, the sheriff heaved a disgusted sigh and escorted them both back through the door leading to the jail proper. The red haired deputy just stood there with his mouth open.

In the middle of the big booking area, Horace and Harold Herkimer were also reacting to the spectacle.

"Now I see the problem, Mr. Herkimer. Our messenger fell victim to the flesh," observed Harold.

"Disgusting!" replied Horace. "Thank God my sweet daughter will never know what a terrible choice she almost made."

Harold lowered his voice much like Jiggs had done when he started to talk about Tahoe. Actually the younger Herkimer brother had the same subject on his mind.

"What do you suppose happened between that deputy and Agnus, Horace?"

Horace froze. Was it possible Harold somehow knew about he and Miss Wayling and the runaway vibrator? He turned to face his sibling. His voice was also very low.

"Have you developed a special interest regarding Miss Wayling's private life, Harold?"

Harold swallowed hard. He saw something quite disturbing in his brother's eyes. Surely Horace didn't know about his bout with Agnus and the amil nitrate. He wouldn't know how to handle that. He could feel his face start to turn red again.

"No. Of course not. I could care less," he said.

Horace was breathing easier. Harold knew nothing. It was time to change the subject.

"Then perhaps we should concentrate on something we do care about. Covering our collectives financial asses. Money equals freedom, Harold."

Harold nodded his head vigorously up and down in agreement. Obviously Horace was ignorant about his little fling with Agnus. It would be best never to bring her name up again except in business.

"Right Horace," said Harold. "Let's get the Hell out of this hick jail and see if we can salvage what that little moron fucked up!"

In the long corridor between the cells Arthell continued to wail. The distraught beauty also refused to release her hold on Rodney as a very unhappy Arty Dubs ushered the young man accused of embezzling one hundred and seventy dollars down the hall.

He paused with the miserable looking young man and the screaming, clutching girl in front of a cell.

It was next to the one occupied by Heffaroid Hogg and Brother Roy Ogles who were sharing the box of Fruit Loops delivered by the widow earlier. The pastor of the Lone Pine Devotion to Divinity Church was wearing the trousers that came with them.

For some reason, now that they covered the lower half of his ballooning lower torso, they no longer appeared to be nearly as gigantic as when the sheriff first received them.

The bloodied remains of the ripped and ruined pants were now wadded up with the remnants of Squeeze Chute's petticoat. The rumpled, soiled heap lay forgotten on the floor next to the commode behind the mammoth munching jailbirds .

The Pastor called out through the bars.

"Sheriff! I'm glad you're here!"

"That makes one of us, Reverend!"

Arty was forced to shout over the girl's cries and pleas as he unlocked the gate next to the cell with the two oversized men.

"Heffaroid's willing to take all responsibility for the stolen car!" yelled the fat pastor. "You've got to let me out of here! I have the Lord's work to do!"

"We all got our jobs, Reverend. Jiggs told me all about it," retorted the sheriff in a loud voice as he managed to pry the young couple apart long enough to push Rodney into the cell and lock him up.

Immediately, the sobbing beauty pressed the front of her blossoming young body against the bars, reaching for the young man beyond them.

"Does the fact you're puttin' him in here, mean me n' Cousin Brother Roy get out anyhow?" Heffaroid called out through a mouthful of Fruit Loops from the cell he shared with the other obese man.

Arty kept looking at the grief stricken girl for a minute. Then he called back to Heffaroid.

"Fraid not Heffaroid! This is somethin' different. You still got to face car theft charges even if the guy you stole it from's in jail hissown self."

The conversation was becoming absurd and Arty knew it.

The fact that Arthell wouldn't stop crying and reaching through the bars after the man he'd just locked up, wasn't making matters any better.

"Didn't steal it!" Heffaroid said, "I just borrowed the damned thing 'thout permission! Little piece of shit ain't worth stealin'! And anyway, both this kid and them scum suckin' Maynards seen my sisters neked!! "

"I don't wanna talk about it! That's up to you and this man here and the judge! The reverend right Heffaroid?"

Arty continued yelling over the young girl's loud sobs that were really starting to do strange things to the strings of the sheriff's heart.

"You willin' to sign a statement coppin' to the whole thing with the car, yourself?"

In the cell, Heffaroid looked at Brother Roy. The latter fat man offered him some more Fruit Loops. The borax miner took a huge handful from the box, then nodded.

Arty looked once again at Arthell locked in embrace with Rodney through the bars. He decided to leave her there.

"Okay, Reverend," he said as he walked back up the corridor toward the door leading out of the jail area.

"I'll have Jiggs come back and get your cousin to sign somthin'. Since the

Maynards didn't press the pig stealin', if Heffaroid does that, I guess you're outa' here! You'll still have to show up in court if this thing goes to trial. On the other hand, who knows? Guy got the car stole might be extradited by then."

The sheriff paused before opening the big metal door and looked back.

Arthell continued to clutch Rodney through the bars and Heffaroid began screaming about something to eat. The Fruit Loop box was empty.

Brother Roy was condemning the young couple to Hell for their disgusting display of public affection, and thwarting his attempt to carry out the Lord's plan for the pig. He was also complaining about the stitches in his wide rump and holding the young lovers directly responsible.

The place resembled a loony bin and the sheriff was sure the inside of his own head probably looked no different.

Arty opened the portal and walked through it. With the exception of the time he had spent alone in the car with Thelma out at the county line, this had to have been one of the worst days of his life.

Once the sheriff gained access to the front interior of the station, he closed the big door shutting out the mayhem still going on in the cells behind him. He stood for a minute watching Jiggs struggle with the desk the deputy was now attempting to drag away from the holding cell. Everything was in such a mess.

He muttered beneath his breath as he moved toward the booking counter.

"I'll bet Clint never had to put up with shit like this!"

CHAPTER EIGHTEEN
FAMILY FEUD

"Shit! It's gonna be a great day!"

Trux delivered this remark with gusto as he completed the finishing touches on a big wooden plank on the back of the HOWDY HOSS which now replaced the abused old utility rig's missing rear bumper.

The morning sun shone down on the vintage vehicle as it sat once more in Thelma's driveway near her kitchen door. Farley sat on the steps of the dwelling's rear portal scratching Barney's ears while the pig happily lapped away at the beer in his bowl.

"Ain't sure it's that great for Rodney," replied Farley.

"Come on!" said Trux, as he walked around the motor home to where his brother was sitting. He shifted a hammer he'd been working with from one hand to the other.

"We did what we hadda' do! We hadda' think of our little girl. Arthell's happiness comes first, Farley, you know that!"

"She didn't look that happy last night after Thelma went down an drug her away from the jail, Trux. She didn't look happy at all."

"Kids don't know what's good for em'. It's up to us that do to make the right decisions for em'. I'll bet she's over that little shit already. You don't see her mopin' around the house do you? She went off with her mamma to make deliveries like nothin' ever happened this mornin. We done right, Farley believe me. Anyway, I was thinkin...."

Whatever Trux had on his mind at the moment was interrupted as Thelma's compact came around the corner of the driveway. The tan vehicle pulled to a stop behind the HOWDY HOSS.

Farley rose to his feet. He, Trux and Barney all walked to greet the lovely lady as she exited the driver's door of her vehicle. She was wearing shorts and halter on this particular morning, that, combined with the body beneath it, would have quelled the worst road rage on any freeway or turnpike in America.

Farley was first to reach her.

"Have a good mornin' baby?" The bearded man asked after he gave her a hug and a kiss.

"Fine," Thelma answered as she reached up and gave Trux his kiss before reaching back through the open doorway of her automobile for her shoulder bag.

"Mrs. Stockham out in Keeley exhausted my inventory. She's got five sisters, four daughters, and a mother-in-law she's determined to make into ravishing beauties before her family reunion next winter. I'm either going to have to make a trip to Bishop this week or arrange for a delivery."

Trux began to frown as he looked inside the car.

"Where's Arthell?" he wanted to know.

"We dropped by the jail to see Rodney when we got back to town. She decided to stay with him for a while."

"What?" roared Trux, as he tossed the hammer aside onto the driveway.

"Exactly which word didn't you understand, Trux?" asked the Argus Queen, looking at the man with the big chin from beneath arched eyebrows. "I said we dropped by the...."

"I heard you damnit!"

"Well, that's a relief."

Trux looked like he was about to explode. "I don't want her near him while he's still in this town!"

Thelma rolled her eyes at Farley before responding.

"Now I believe I'm the one that isn't hearing correctly. Would you like to explain how she could possibly be near him after he's left town? Or are you suggesting she leave Lone Pine too?"

"That ain't what I meant and you know it! What I'm tryin' to say is, 'Outa' sight outa' her head'! It's an old saying. Means it's just a passin' thing! Don't walk away! We gotta' talk about this!"

"I haven't got time," Thelma replied.

She leaned down and gave Barney a pat on the head before walking past both brothers and the motor home toward her kitchen door.

"I've got things to do. I'm expecting some email responses and I've got to arrange for that delivery. I'll see you boys later. That includes you, Barney."

The pig grunted in gratitude of his acknowledgement as the gorgeous, busy woman disappeared into the house. Trux turned immediately to Farley.

"What the Hell's wrong with her? I'm right ain't I? Everthing's worked out fine! We got rid of ole fat Heffaroid. Ogles is off our backs. We got gas in the tank. Arthell's safe from that city turd and..."

"I'm glad about everthin' ceptn' Rodney, Trux. He ain't really such a bad kid. He took all our shit and he still jumped right in and helped save Barney..."

Trux's voice began to rise in anger.

"Don't you go gettin' candy assed on me Farley!" he demanded. "He just wants to get in our little girl's pants. He'd break her heart, then leave her! You know that, damnit!!"

"No, I don't know that!"

"Then you're a dumb shit!"

"Maybe you're the dumb shit!"

"Don't you go callin' me names, God damnit!"

Farley should have known better, but he decided to try reasoning with his irate brother whose stubborn chin was now protruding so far it required a red flag.

"Could be he really loves her, Trux!"

"Yeah! And could be you got a twelve inch pecker!"

The bearded man elected to ignore the slur on his own manly endowment that could not be defended, and pursued a subject he felt warranted the effort.

"We don't know he don't, Trux. Love her I mean," he went on before the conversation could be brought back to the size of penises again.

"And we know she damn sure thinks she loves him! Maybe it's time we let her court, Trux. God damn! She's a growed up woman."

Trux could not believe what he was hearing from this man who almost never disagreed with him.

"Godamnit, Farley! Just imagine somebody takin' off her clothes! You think about that! Think about somebody doin' to our little girl what we do to women!"

"Stop that! Don't you go sayin' nasty things about Arthell! She wouldn't do nothin' like that!" Farley was almost as angry as Trux now.

"Besides that, he saved Barney!"

On the ground beneath the bickering brothers, the pig had been trying very hard to stay out of this argument. However, he had to give a grunt of agreement on this point.

"Fuck you!" Trux told the pig. He then turned on Farley as he went into what promised to become a total tirade.

"Fuck this pig! You think more of this God damned hog than you do about our own daughter!"

"I do not!" came back Farley.

Barney tried not to pass judgement on this statement by his beloved master. The pig was mighty fond of Arthell too.

"Whose side are you on?" Trux demanded of his brother.

"Well now, Trux, don't put it that way!" begged Farley. "I been thinkin' on this and…."

Trux raised and extended the middle finger of his right hand and shoved it in front of the bearded man's face.

"Think on this, bug fucker!"

"If you're gonna' put it that way damnit!" Farley's temper was starting to do a little flaring on its own. "If you're gonna act like an asshole, then I'm on

Rodney's side, by God!"

Trux literally screamed.

"He want's to violate our daughter!"

"He's in love, Trux. I bet he wants to marry her!"

"Bullshit! He's in lust! And you believe anything else, you ain't no brother of mine!"

"Well I do! Otherwise I wouldn't of said it!"

The brothers were nose to nose now. Both had their fists doubled. They stared at each other in total silence for at least two minutes.

Barney turned away and crawled beneath the motor home. If this dispute actually came to blows , he didn't want to watch.

Finally, Trux turned and began walking away down the driveway. The hurt and angry red neck kicked the discarded hammer beneath the motor home as he strode past it. He continued onward beside the compact, headed toward the corner of the house and the street beyond .

"Fuck you!" he said with out looking back. "I'm gonna take that fifty dollars I got from Arty for cuttin' Heffaroid n' the preacher outa' the piss ant's car, down to the Double L. and get drunk! N' you ain't invited!"

"You was supposed to give that money to Thelma for the gas!" Farley called after his angry brother.

"I found a better use for it! You pussy faced, puss gutted butthead!" Trux yelled as he disappeared totally from sight around the corner of the Argus Queen's dwelling.

Farley just stood there. The bearded man was also angry and hurt. He turned to Barney whose pink, round snout was poking out from beneath the under carriage of the HOWDY HOSS.

Farley kneeled on the driveway asphalt and held out his arms. The pig wiggled his body from beneath the motor home and crawled forward on its belly, grunting.

"Don't worry 'bout it Barney," Farley told the disturbed animal as it snuggled up against his chest. "Uncle Trux'll just get drunk and stupid and probably puke. Them things'll make a fella feel a whole lot better."

The pig grunted his understanding, then looked behind Farley as the backdoor opened and Thelma came out of the house. She had several computer readout sheets in one of her hands as she surveyed the scene in her back driveway.

"Sounded like World War Three out here. Where's Trux?"

"Me'n him had us a disagreement. He went to the Double L. to get shit faced," replied Farley as he and the pig both rose to their feet and moved to face the fantastic looking woman.

"Trust Trux to always turn to the sensible solution. Probably why he's one of the men I fell madly in love with," said Thelma.

"Rodney and Arthell were the subject of disagreement, I assume?" she asked, even though she already knew the answer.

Farley nodded.

"Might be the best thing," he said. "Him getting' drunk, I mean. Maybe we can go down after he's downed a few an' get him to sign that paper when he don't know what he's doin'."

"Speaking of that paper," said Thelma, as she sat down on the back step in front of the kitchen door, "I've been collecting a few pieces of my own. I had an email acquaintance of mine run a check on that H. and H. Holding Corporation the Herkimer firm represents. Took a while, but my source discovered it to be a one person California corporation owned by none other than Horace Herkimer himself."

Farley and Barney seated themselves on either side of the lady.

"How come he don't come right out and make the offer his ownself then?" asked Farley.

"I'm not really sure, but there's something rotten in Lone Pine, baby. Tell me about that mountain that seems so important that Rodney could go to prison over it."

"Well, Hell, ain't much to tell. Just an old mountain Daddy come by somehow and never was able to get rid of. I'd sell in a minute if…"

A light went on in Thelma's beautiful eyes.

"Does that old man that still know all about minerals still live out in the old saloon with his daughter in Darwin?" she asked.

"Old Henderson? Yeah, he's still there. Don't make much sense no more. He's usually so crazy or drunk or both, he can't shit in his hat. Nobody in maybe the world knows more about minerals though."

"Before you make any decisions regarding that mountain, I really think you should have this man Henderson look over the property."

"Ain't sure he'd do it for me," said Farley. "Might do it for Trux. Old Henderson really likes Trux."

The Argus Queen stood and looked down at the still seated man and pig.

"Did both you and Daddy Farley take a bath this morning, Barney?"

The pig looked up, grunting in affirmation.

"Good!" responded Thelma as she reached down to pull Farley to his feet. "At least that'll make three of us. Let's go get Uncle Trux. If he's had enough to drink to make him listen to reason, we'll all take a little ride in my car!"

*** *** *** *** *** ***

"Bend over and give yourself head!"

Trux Maynard was obviously not yet ready to listen to reason.

The Double L. was one of the many Lone Pine Main Street bars. However, This particular drinking establishment opened each day several hours ahead of all the others.

The establishment catered to those who needed a head start on the state of inebriation.

Due to its earlier welcome to the public, the Double L afforded escape from reality shortly after they awakened until it was time to pass out when this watering hole, along with all the rest in Lone Pine, closed their doors at two am the following morning. The clientele requiring these conditions were many, and Trux fit right in.

At the moment he sat perched on a barstool attempting to toss down his eighth straight shot since his arrival and Farley was annoying him.

Thelma stood in the bar's open doorway leading out into the street, letting in daylight. To Trux, her presence wasn't exactly welcome either.

"I can't talk to him when he's like this!" Farley's deep voice held an indignant whine as he turned back to Thelma.

The Argus Queen ignored the catcalls and whistles as she took a step in Trux's direction.

"Trux, please listen…."

The broad shouldered red neck who felt his values had been totally ignored by those he thought up until now, he could trust, almost fell as he rose from the barstool. Somehow, he managed to remain upright as he wheeled toward the woman.

"And you can go play squat tag in a God damn cactus patch!" he said, as he staggered toward the jukebox. "Get the fuck away from me, both of you! All either one of you wants to do is turn my daughter into a whore."

Thelma and Farley were shoved aside by more local patrons in a rush for morning fixes, as they conversed with each other in low tones.

"Well, forget him for the time being," Thelma told Farley. "We'll just have to go out to Darwin and talk to Old Henderson ourselves."

"I told you, I don't think he'll talk to us," the bearded man replied in a sotto voice. "His mind's gone south."

Another poor man sitting on a barstool nearest the establishment's main entrance, poured his shot of Old Grand Dad down his shirt front with his shaking hand, as Thelma adjusted the halter top adorning her fantastic bosoms.

"Then maybe I can make it go north!" she stated, before calling to Trux who was attempting to read the song titles on the jukebox.

"Trux, Farley and I are going to Darwin!"

"Go to Hell for all I care!" Trux called back as he continued looking at the song titles. "I hope you both end up nekid in a nest of Mojave Greens!"

Thelma took Farley by the arm and ushered the unhappy bearded Maynard brother out of the bar.

Outside, they walked to the pretty lady's compact parked at the curb with the waiting Barney inside, pressing his snout against the window.

Neither saw the two Herkimers standing at the end of the street.

The Century City lawyers had changed their attire since the prior day's conference in the outer office of the Lone Pine jail. Both now looked like they had taken a wrong turn on their way to the Beverly Hills golf course.

"I believe the man Trux is our key," Horace Herkimer said to Harold Herkimer. "I'll stick with him. You follow the other two."

Harold Herkimer nodded, then moved to a rental car parked not far away.

He hurried because Thelma's compact was already pulling away from the front of the Double L.

Horace moved toward the entrance of the same establishment. Yesterday, he had tried using Van Aukin as a bargaining chip. It hadn't worked. Today, he was going to try moving that very same chip in a different direction.

*** *** *** *** ***

In the Lone Pine jail, the young man in question had no idea he was still being used as any kind of a chip by the firm of Herkimer, Herkimer, Herkimer, Herkimer.

He did know he was clutching the hand of a beautiful young lady through the bars of his cell. He also now knew she loved him at least almost as much as he loved her.

In the caged enclosure next to him, Heffaroid Hogg was pouting. His mammoth body flowed over both sides of the mattress covered concrete slab he was lying on. Jiggs had evidently finally removed the remains of Brother Roy's tattered trousers and Squeeze Chute's petticoat from the cell.

Strangely enough, Rodney, who had lacked self-assurance all his life, was the one who seemed to be retaining his composure. It was Arthell who had never experienced an insecure moment that she could remember, who was in need of consoling.

"Rodney, what are we going to do?" she asked as a huge tear ran down her otherwise flawless face.

The young incarcerated attorney reached through the thick round perpendicular steel barriers and brushed away the tear with a gentle forefinger.

"We'll get out of this mess, settle down here in Lone Pine and have five kids," he told her.

Arthell felt more tears welling up inside her. She tried desperately to hold them back.

"But Arty says if that paper isn't signed, you'll do at least twenty years in prison."

Rodney didn't know where it was coming from, but suddenly he felt like giggling.

"What's so funny?" she sniffled.

"I was just thinking," he replied. "If I do have to be away for twenty years, when I come back, will you be my Argus Queen?"

She was crying now, but a big smile was visible through the tears as she pulled him close to the bars and planted her tender lips on his.

"Rodney Van Aukin, I'll be your Argus Queen forever. You'll never get rid of me."

In the next cell the cot Heffaroid was lying on was chained to the wall, but the whole apparatus nearly pulled free as the large fellow rolled off the bed.

He yelled at the sheriff who had just entered through the big metal door at the end of the corridor.

"Sheriff!" called Heffaroid, who was almost crying himself, "I gotta' have some food quick! All this puppy love is makin' me plumb sick!"

"Probably a real good reason why I shouldn't feed you nothin' Heffaroid," Arty called back. "Jiggs took the mornin' off and I sure don't feel like cleanin' up your barf!"

In his cell, Heffaroid gave the sheriff a dirty look and turned to face the wall.

In the corridor, Arty called to Arthell.

Rodney couldn't help but notice how the ordinarily arrogant law man's total demeanor changed when he talked to the young lady. Arthell seemed to cast her spell on all that gazed upon her.

The young lawyer couldn't help but feel a surge of pride. He was in love with someone very special, and she had made it known that she was more than fond of him.

"Arthell, your mammas callin' for you. She's somewhere out on the road, callin' on that cell phone of hers!"

Arthell blew Rodney a kiss through the bars. She called over her pretty shoulder to the young man as she then moved willingly toward the awaiting sheriff.

Arty continued to stand just inside the big metal door that led to the telephone in question where Thelma was waiting to speak to her daughter. He was casting some very strange glances it the direction of both the young people as Arthell spoke.

"I'll be right back. I'm glad she didn't call while I was still crying. I feel better now. We've got to get you out of here, Rodney. I love you."

The expression on Arty's face remained as the girl stepped up to him, ready to walk through the door.

"You comin' back here after your call, or you goin' on home?" he asked her in a low, earnest voice that said he really wanted to know.

"I'm coming back here, of course," she told him as she disappeared through the big doorway.

Arty then focused his full attention on Rodney. He watched the young man for a few seconds before he turned and followed the beautiful girl out of the corridor.

*** *** *** *** *** ***

The beautiful mother of that beautiful girl sat behind the steering wheel of her compact.

She was in the process of finishing the phone call to her daughter. Farley and Barney, through the car window beside her, could be seen walking out from behind a huge cactus patch several yards away.

The bearded man and his pig were headed toward where she had parked on the side of the road in the middle of this desolate, almost lifeless area of desert.

She had taken advantage of Barney's natural urges while en route to the old town of Darwin, which was not yet visible in the distance, to contact the girl.

It was really a good idea to let Arthell know what she was up to. Conversely, Thelma needed to know the same thing about her daughter.

"Arthell, you can't stay there at that jail all day. Well, maybe all day, but I know Arty will kick you out tonight. I'm just kidding, sweetheart. Hopefully tonight, we'll figure a way to get your young man out of there. Tell him to keep the faith, and I mean the real faith. Not the brand of Brother Roy Ogles. Bye, baby."

Thelma turned off her portable communication devise, and leaned over to put it away in the compact's glove compartment. As she was settling back into the front seat, the passenger door opened.

Farley reached in and pulled the back of the seat forward. He waited for Barney to climb into the rear, then returned everything to its proper position and slid into the car beside Thelma.

"I called Arthell," she informed him as he closed the door and she started the engine.

"We've simply got to get Rodney out of that jail, or she's going to move in."

254

"We shoulda' probably stayed at the Double L. till Trux got drunk enough to sign that paper," the bearded Maynard brother said, as the compact started moving forward in the direction of Darwin.

"The mood he was in, the drunker he got the more stubborn he was going to be," answered the Argus Queen, as she looked back at Barney.

"Besides, before either of you sign anything, we need to find out why Herkimer wants it so bad. So, Barney, how was it out there? The lizards and bugs let you do your business in peace?"

In the rear interior of the vehicle, Barney gave the pretty woman a grunt of gratitude for caring.

"He done fine," said Farley trying to make light talk with a heavy heart. The dispute he was having with his brother was really getting in the way of the bearded mans' usual humorous outlook on life.

"Least they ain't no Mojave Greens out here," he added for no apparent reason other than an attempt to make small talk.

"By the way," Thelma asked Farley as she continued to drive. "What is a Mojave Green?"

"What?"

"Trux said something about a Mojave Green too, when he was being so rude back at the Double L," she said. "What is it?"

"Oh," replied Farley. "He was just talkin' 'bout the rattlesnakes we been catchin' up on our mountain the last ten years or so."

"He wanted us to be caught in a nest of poisonous rattlesnakes?"

"Oh, you know Trux. He'll say anything when he's pissed. He didn't mean nothin'."

The bearded man spoke up quickly in defense of his brother in spite of their current differences, then continued with the subject.

"They sure as hell are poisonous though. Most poisonous snakes they is in America! Me n' Trux sell em' now an then over to the Naval base over to China Lake. They give us fifty bucks apiece for em'."

"Aren't you afraid of being bitten?"

"Nah," said Farley as he reached back and gave Barney an affectionate pat on his snout. "Barney here takes care of em'. He's a natural borned snake killer! Ain't ya Barney?"

The pig grunted. It was nice to have your talents not only recognized, but also lauded occasionally.

"Most pigs is," Farley went on. "But Barney's the best! We've told you all about how he got them scars on his face he's so proud of."

"I remember," said Thelma. "I'm just glad neither you or Trux have ever been bitten."

"Oh, Trux got bit by one of em' once."

"No!"

"Yep! He was drunk and I bet him he was chicken to kiss the ugly sucker. Well, He got down on his knees and stuck out his chin, an' that ole Green nailed him right on the button!"

"My God! You definitely did not tell me about that! What did you do?"

"Nothin!" said Farley, his bearded face still impassive. "I was drunk too."

Thelma digested this bit of news, then gave him a look of suspicion.

"You sure you're not putting me on?" she asked.

"You don't think he was borned with that chin do you?"

Now the corners of the bearded man's mouth began to twitch and his deep laughter followed. Thelma wasn't sure, but the pig in the back seat seemed to be laughing too.

Both man and beast were following the old adage set down over a decade ago by the incomparable Brother Dave Gardner. 'If you caint find the funny, you probably deserve the misery.'

It also told her, that even though Farley was really angry with his brother right now, he still loved the other man enough to poke fun at him. She felt exactly the same way and therefore had no choice but to join in.

It felt good. Humor was only one of the many reasons she had fallen in love with the Maynard brothers, but it definitely held high ratings.

She would be so happy when this mess was reconciled and they would all be laughing together again, the Argus Queen thought to herself as she continued to drive. She loved them both so much, even if she wasn't happy with one of them right now.

Thelma looked in her rear view mirror. Only one other automobile was visible on this desolate thoroughfare today.

She was glad she wasn't alone in the car, or for that matter, on the road. It was easy sometimes to imagine yourself the only one left in the whole world, when your destination was Darwin.

Behind the compact in the rental vehicle, Harold Herkimer wasn't happy with anybody.

The youngest brother of the Century City law firm found no humor whatsoever in his misery as he followed at what he hoped to be a safe distance behind the cream colored vehicle.

He had hoped that when the lady stopped she was going to end up turning around. She hadn't. She had started the damn car and driven onward, toward absolutely nothing.

His clothing was soaked with sweat. The air conditioning in the rental wasn't working and he was afraid to roll down the windows.

The Century City attorney was terrified one of those ugly insects that kept striking the windshield would get inside the vehicle and begin eating away

256

at his flesh. He also had a feeling the lady in front of him was going to drive off the edge of the earth soon.

If such a thing were to happen, was he required to follow?

He silently cursed his brother for assigning himself the easy job. Harold hated every inch of this country including that nauseous jerk water called Lone Pine where he and Horace had been forced to spend the previous night. Notwithstanding, he'd still rather be back in that bar with a bunch of boring yokels than out here in the center of nowhere. Who knew what could happen to a civilized person in the middle of all this desolation?

CHAPTER NINETEEN
INTEGUMENT INVESTIGATIONS

Horace Herkimer had never witnessed a gathering of so many uncivilized members of the human race beneath one roof at the same time.

He held a suspicion that no more than a fraction of the raucous daytime drinkers in Lone Pines' Double L. drinking establishment even qualified to be human.

The aspiring entrepreneur sat at a table in the back of the noisy room, nursing what may have been the worst martini that had ever passed his cultured lips. He would much prefer to have been elsewhere, but he had no choice.

The answer to his future was beyond this gathering of seated, babbling idiots and the swirling smoke around him. It was perched drunkenly on a stool over at that bar.

The success of the scheme he and Harold had worked so hard to bring to fruition and line their pockets, all depended on how this man Trux Maynard was approached and subsequently, handled. The first try had failed. There may not be a third.

Trux Maynard, who had no idea he was the subject of such scrutiny, was having a wonderful time at the moment. He was talking aloud to Trux Maynard.

The very inebriated broad shouldered red neck was so engrossed in the verbal exchange he was having with himself; he was totally oblivious to the presence of anyone else. This included an aging, unattractive and equally drunk older woman on the stool next to his.

The vintage female could easily qualify for the title of 'Crone' in the most indiscriminate of social circles, but she considered herself quite attractive. She was also feeling affectionate.

As Trux continued his one man conversation with himself, the woman was attempting to drape her misshapen, long neglected body over his.

"Things was fine! Just fine!" Trux babbled into his drink before he downed it and signaled for another.

"Fucking women! I hate em! God damned troublemakers is what they are! Even the good uns'! Didn't have pussies, wouldn't be no reason to talk to em'! That's what Farley's turnin' into! A fuckin pussy! I hate em'! Fucking women!"

The drunken member of the gender that seemed to be the topic of his private conversation with himself seated next to him had to investigate.

She wasn't sure if she had just been issued an invitation or a rejection. However, she was certainly going to find out.

"What's that about fucking women?" the old crone asked.

Trux was so deep into his own world, that he still had no idea there was anyone within twenty miles near him in any direction except the burly bartender, who placed another shot before him.

The man with the loose tongue and the big chin shoved some money from the rapidly diminishing pile that lay crumpled on the bar top between them, toward the other man. The purveyor of potations accepted the offered cash, picked up the empty shot glass, and moved on. Trux continued his one-person dissertation.

"Farley don't even know who his brother is! Usta' carry the little shit to school through twenty-eight inches of snow when my legs was only twenty-six inches long. Do I get any thanks? Hell no!"

"You got twenty-six inches, I wanna' see it!" said the persistent woman next to him. "Put up or shut up, asshole!"

Trux finally became aware of her presence. Under ordinary circumstances, the big red neck would have found the woman delightful. He would have been more than willing to find out exactly what she still had left to offer and would have done his best to make her feel young again, if only for a short while.

Today was not ordinary. Everybody he loved, including the young woman he thought to be his daughter, whom he was trying to save, had turned against him. It annoyed him greatly.

"Lady, would you mind takin' a hike?" he asked as he turned toward the intruder. "I'm tryin' to hold a conversation with myself, here!"

"Asshole!" cried the crone, repeating herself, as she took a swing at his big chin with her bony fist.

The blow glanced harmlessly off his alcohol-desensitized temple as Trux, still talking to himself, rose to his feet. The woman's arms kept flailing as he picked her up by the waist.

The crowd continued to converse with one another. However, they parted willingly as the broad shouldered man, holding the feisty female senior citizen at arms length, carried her to the back door.

He kicked the portal open stepped out into the alley. The withered wench struck his big chin one more time before he deposited the howling old girl, gently into a trash container.

It was not his intention to harm the aging, horny soul. The upset Maynard brother just wanted his privacy.

His task completed, he turned back and reentered the bar.

Horace Herkimer was sitting on the stool recently occupied by the woman now in the outside refuse receptacle, when Trux returned and reclaimed his own seat.

He gave the big city man a look filled with drunken suspicion.

"Where the Hell did you come from, buddy? Sling Shot Asia?"

Horace flashed his expensive dental work. "Don't you remember me, Mr. Maynard? I'm Horace Herkimer. Of Herkimer, Herkimer..."

"I remember your educated idiot ass. Save the two-dollar spiel! What the fuck do you want?"

Horace shrugged. "It looked to me like you needed a friend," replied the big city attorney.

Trux sneered at him. "When you're drunk, there's only three kinds of friends: one's that give you money, give you pussy, or give you whiskey. Which kind are you?"

Horace called to the burly bartender, who, as luck would have it, just happened to be within earshot.

"Excuse me sir," he said, sounding exceedingly benevolent, "give Mr. Maynard a double whatever he's been drinking and I'd like another of you're wonderful martinis."

The attorney almost choked on the last part of his speech, but somehow managed to retain his oily composure. He then tuned his attention back to Trux.

"Well. Now, Mr. Maynard, let's talk about money..."

In the Double L. drinking establishment of Lone Pine Horace Herkimer proceeded to launch into the topic of finance.

In the Lone Pine jail, the subject, much to the chagrin of Heffaroid Hogg, the theme of conversation for a short time had been sex.

Now it was food. The huge prisoner liked the newest subject much better.

Arthell had convinced the sheriff to have lunch picked up from a local chicken take out place today for the two prisoners and the young lady visitor.

It had taken her some time to sell the local law enforcement official on the idea, but somehow the determined lovely young lady had done it.

Either Arty or Jiggs had also been thoughtful enough to place a chair in the corridor so that the girl could sit facing Rodney through the bars while they dined.

The four empty cardboard buckets littering the floor in Heffaroid's adjoining cell obviously attested to the fact that Arthell had persuaded Arty to be generous while ordering.

Heffaroid liked food. He also liked to talk about it. Food was a much better topic than the one the kid who owned the piss ant car and the deputy had been involved in during the girl's absence.

While the persuasive sweet young woman had been out front convincing the sheriff to spring county funds for this repast, Jiggs had come back to the cell area to bring Heffaroid and Rodney some drinking water.

The large borax miner had been lying on that little miserable cot in his cell with his eyes closed. The two younger men thought he was sleeping but he wasn't.

He had heard the kid in the cage next to him ask the deputy about some women in Tahoe.

At first Jiggs had been reluctant but after some urging on Rodney's part the assistant lawman had been forthcoming. Heffaroid really wished he hadn't. He would much rather have really been asleep.

At that time the deputy had filled Rodney in on the previously mentioned Tahoe incident and the part Miss Wayling and her friend Harrington Fox had played in it.

At first, as the red headed young man had gone into graphic details, Rodney's eyes were wide with disbelief.

Then as Jiggs continued telling the story, bits and pieces within the law school graduate's mind began to come together.

According to the deputy, these two older women who happened to be prowling the Nevada mountains, had, one late afternoon, come upon a Forest Service camp.

The temporary shelter was filled with virile young men who had been imported to fight a forest fire in the Nevada mountains. The youths, mostly teenagers as had been Jiggs at the time, were digging a fire break in the crest of a hill in front of the trees above the camp. Their supervisor had been called away due to the beginning of yet another fire elsewhere.

Their mission had been to stay and stop the blaze if it reached this side of the mountain. Shortly after the two women arrived the fire break had been forgotten.

Miss Wayling and her friend Harrington Fox Had ravaged every young male body in the entire crew before the night was over.

In the morning the flames of the fire had indeed licked their way over the mountain top. However the young men whose job it was to quell the conflagration had been so involved with another kind of licking no one possessed the strength to do anything about it.

Since the blaze encountered no opposition, the fire had kept right on moving.

As the red haired lawman continued, the young lawyer began to think of certain things. Things he had really never understood.

According to the deputy, all ,including the ladies ,would have perished that morning in the burning forest of Nevada had not a fleet of helicopters arrived. The airborne machines had flown the exhausted youths and those responsible for their conditions to safety.

No one told what really happened. There wasn't a soul alive who would have believed it anyway

Rodney believed it now. The vision of the woman depicted as a sexual witch in the red headed fellow's story staring at his crotch back in the Century City office became vivid. He began recalling the rumors he hadn't thought credible. His thinking was rapidly undergoing total metamorphous.

He remembered the look last night on the faces of the two Herkimers. Certain ontological units that had always been fuzzy in his brain were now becoming clear to the young man from Boston.

When he had first found the Maynard brothers frolicking in the water with Heffaroid's naked sisters and subsequently been plunged into the 'Trolling' incident, Rodney thought he had been pulled from a world of civilization into one of decadence. He now knew he'd simply entered a world of honesty.

The same things had been going on all around him, probably even back in New England when he was still a child. They had just been covered up. He decided he liked this world a whole lot better.

Heffaroid, still pretending to be sleeping, hadn't enjoyed the story much at all. All he could think of was all those eligible young men up there in those mountains with just two old women.

The fact that the forest had burned down didn't bother him one way or the other. But the rest was disgusting.

At least two of those boys would have been much better off right here in the Owens Valley married to his two sisters and working in his borax mine.

Heffaroid hadn't gone through puberty. Puberty had gone through Heffaroid. The journey had been swift.

Other than a couple of nights with a Playboy magazine and one rendezvous with a sheep that really had brought him no satisfaction, all urges had left him. Almost immediately after making an appearance, they were gone.

He knew his sisters doted on every thing about sex, but Heffaroid wasn't really interested. The large man preferred the subject of food over fornication any day.

He was really glad to hear the deputy shut up upon Arthell's return with her announcement that chicken was on its way. He had been happier still when it had arrived. Immediately the enormous man had pretended to wake up. He had been further delighted after the deputy's departure when the young couple had insisted he share the food with them.

Now, as he gnawed at a drumstick, the big man managed to chew around the meat as he conversed with them through the bars.

"Good chicken! Sure do thank you."

"Thank the pretty lady. She's the one who talked the sheriff into having the chicken brought in," replied Rodney. "How did you work it anyway, Arthell? I'm impressed."

Arthell shrugged as she daintily tore off a piece of white meat with her thumb and forefinger.

"I just asked," she answered. "Ever since I can remember, Arty's always done almost everything I asked him to do. He's really very nice once you get to know him."

"Nobody could ever say no to you. I don't care who they might be," Rodney said.

He turned toward the bars of the next cell, bringing Heffaroid into the conversation.

"So, Mr. Hogg, you operate a borax mine?"

"Work my fingers to the bone tryin' to dig the stuff outa' the hillside, is more like it," grumbled the mammoth man as he dug another piece of chicken from the bucket in his huge hand.

"Can't afford no help. And without no help I can't really turn enough profit on it. Won't even be able to afford havin' it delivered to the mill, once the state starts puttin' in that new highway n' the guy who hauls it off for me starts rentin' out his truck to the Gumimint full time. Don't know what I'm gonna do then, lessin' I can some how figger a way to increase productivity so I can afford to pay more to have the stuff hauled off to the mill."

"New Highway?" asked Rodney. He wasn't sure why, but something, maybe the 'Honesty Monster' who had been keeping a low profile for most of this day, was telling him to listen.

For some reason, he was receiving a message from somewhere, that the big man in the other cell was giving him valuable information with out knowing it.

"Yeah. All the way to Spokane Washington from San Bernardino. Bring in a lot of money to folks maybe own some old lake bed property where they might be able to dig out some gravel or such. But it sure ain't gonna' do me nothin' but bad. Ain't nobody usin' borax on no stinken' highway, even once its made' into soap and the road gets dirty," answered Heffaroid, as he chewed all the remaining meat from the last chicken bone in his bucket.

"Say, you got anymore of that white meat? A neck'll do if you don't. I love to suck on them little bitsy bones. I can do a number on a chicken neck."

The young attorney smiled through the bars in front of him. Arthell smiled back and handed what was left of her bucket to him.

He then turned back to the adjoining cell and pushed the remainders of both his meal and hers, through the bars to the man who had commandeered and subsequently smashed the 'Slum Mobile.'

"You're welcome to the rest, Mr. Hogg. The lady and I are finished."

"Sure do thank you!" grunted Heffaroid, as he began wolfing down his new windfall of nutrition.

Rodney turned back to the young lady he loved. He still didn't know exactly what the information he had just received from the borax miner meant to his situation, but he did have an idea about how to begin finding out.

"Arthell," he said. "Do you think you could talk the sheriff into letting me put in a call to LA?"

"I'm sure I can," said the lovely young creature on the other side of the bars. She rose to a standing position.

"I'm sure either Arty or Jiggs will let you. Would you rather I asked them to bring your cell phone back?"

Rodney started to give a negative reaction, then stopped.

"Yeah! Good idea! Have em' bring my cell phone back. That way I'll have more privacy! And if I need to make more calls I'll have it handy. Really great idea if you can swing it."

He felt very proud of himself. Rodney Van Aukin wasn't going to let all those people who wrote that crap give him a brain tumor, by God!

He knew Thelma would be proud of him too. Besides he just might need to get in touch with that particular lady, once he'd made his call to LA.

*** *** *** *** ***

In the meantime the lady in question was driving her compact slowly up the spooky, eerie main street of Darwin toward the old saloon.

The afternoon sun cast an almost surrealistic glow on the ancient building as well as the several beat up pickups and other old vehicles now parked in front of it. The door to the old structure had been replaced since Rodney's previous visit. In spite of the heat and the fact that the place obviously had customers within, the repaired portal was closed

Inside Thelma's little automobile, Farley and Barney looked out the windows at what was to them just another one of the places within the vast Owens Valley they had always called home.

The reaction of their gorgeous driver, wearing the revealing shorts and halter outfit, was somewhat different.

"I've always hated this place," she remarked with a visible shudder. "I never understood how you and Trux could stand it."

"Oh, it wasn't always this bad," replied Farley as he peered through the windshield as they pulled up in front of the saloon.

"Yep! There's Old Henderson's truck. He's in the saloon. Peers they's quite a crowd in there today. Welfare checks musta' Come in."

Thelma parked the compact across the street. She turned back to Barney who remained in the rear interior of the little vehicle.

"Hold the fort, Barney. We'll be back, God willing and the creek don't rise. I'll leave the window rolled down for you."

The pig gave the wonderful lady a grunt of gratitude as she and Farley exited either side of the small automobile and stood looking at the foreboding old establishment.

"I imagine he's in there, but this ain't gonna be easy," observed Farley. "Old Henderson's daughter Darleen runs the saloon, don't want nobody talkin' to im', an she's meaner n' a stripped assed ape."

Thelma took a deep breath that did wondrous things to her already wondrous breasts and moved forward.

"Leave Darleen to me," she said. "God! How can anybody live here?"

Back at the edge of the old ghost town, Harold Herkimer was certain nobody did. He sat in the rental vehicle looking trough the windshield at the hand lettered sign that advised him to 'Keep the fuck out.'

The man from the civilized world wanted nothing more than to heed the warning and turn around and drive the other way. Horace had told him to follow the woman and the disgusting man in the compact. Harold usually did what Horace said. Today proved not to be an exception.

He eased the rental car's transmission into drive. The executive and the vehicle moved on into the decrepit old settlement as the hot afternoon wind began to howl.

*** *** *** *** ***

Inside the Double L., back in Lone Pine, there was a lot of howling going on, but it was the patrons, not the wind furnishing the noise.

The surrounding frolickers were past the first lap of their routine drinking day and well on their way to getting a good start on the still to come, evening stretch.

Horace Herkimer, who still sat at the bar next to Trux, was having a difficult time keeping the other man's attention.

"You see Mr. Maynard," the Century City attorney was saying, "if we were to pursue this avenue of events, I feel assured we both will reach a comfortable solution to our collective, individual goals…"

Trux shouted at him over the surrounding babble.

"You know, if you was to stop usin' all them four dollar words," the big chinned red neck said, enunciating his own syllables for emphasis, "I might be able to figger out what the Hell you're talkin' about!"

Before Herkimer could respond, a mountain of a man appeared. He had shoulders so broad, Trux looked like he had none in comparison. The imposing newcomer walked up and pulled the Maynard brother around to face him.

The man was at least six feet six inches in height, and his arms looked like redwood trunks. The veins in his bull neck pumping away like garden hoses indicated he might be upset about something.

"They tell me you're the one dumped my mamma in the garbage!" he said angrily.

Trux gave the much larger man an apologetic grin as he began climbing off the bar stool.

"Had to Paddy. Didn't have no choice. She was tryin to get into my drawers, and I didn't have no jumper cables to get the old clunker started."

The big fellow referred to, as Paddy, seemed to take offense to Trux's reference to his mother. He landed a hay maker punch on the Maynard brother's square jaw that sent the blow's recipient flying all the way across the room.

Horace Herkimer looked on in absolute horror as Trux's body slammed into the far wall of the establishment beneath a large, stuffed moose head.

Trux, somehow managing to remain on his feet, shook his head, then checked for missing teeth.

Satisfied he still retained far more than his share; the big chinned man reached up and tore the moose head from the wall. Holding the multi antlered long deceased animal's head out in front of him, Trux let out a blood curdling roar and charged back across the room at the big man who had just struck him.

As he reached his objective, the mad Maynard began pounding away at Paddy's head, shoulders and any other portion available on the front of the larger man's body, with the head of the long, deceased moose.

The horns broke away, and the eyes popped out, but Trux kept on pounding, driving Paddy against the bar. The gigantic fellow finally reached out and grabbed Horace Herkimer's stool just as the terrified man from Century City was vacating it.

Paddy was able to avoid just enough of the onslaught from the mutilated moose head to be able to lift the barstool up over his head and throw it at his attacker. Trux ducked and the stool sailed over him, just missing Horace as he dived beneath a nearby table.

Behind the bar, the burly fellow, who had, up until now, been serving drinks on the wide wooden counter vaulted over it. He held a very big, lethal looking club in his hand with which he hit Paddy very hard over the head as he landed.

266

The bigger man's eyes grew terribly red as he grabbed the business end of the club with one hand and backhanded the bartender with the other.

The server of booze flew back over the bar from whence he had just arrived. He crashed with resounding reverberation into an up until now, neatly stacked arrangement of cocktail glasses.

A customer then hit Paddy over the head with a chair.

Another customer struck the man who had just attacked Paddy.

Trux dove beneath the table with Herkimer as everybody within the drinking establishment's walls began hitting everybody else.

He reached over to console the big shot Century City lawyer who was now cowering and beginning to whimper like a new born baby.

"Relax!" he told Horace. "We're safe down here. One thing good about a fight. Sobers my ass right up!"

He pulled Herkimer out of the way of a flying beer bottle.

"Now let me get this straight," Trux continued, as the battle raged on above and around them. "You say you'll give us four thousand dollars and Rodney still gets his tail hauled outa' Lone Pine in chains, n' wont never be able to come back?"

"That's correct," replied Horace Herkimer.

He felt not only insecure, but also totally ridiculous talking business on his hands and knees beneath the table in the middle of this sleazy bar fight. "Technically this is a totally new transaction so Van Aukin would still be guilty of..."

"He goes to jail back in LA and can't come back! Right?"

"Right!" said Horace as a man crashed to the floor just beyond the underside of the table he and Trux were hiding beneath.

It was a lie. They would never be able to really charge Rodney with anything without disclosing his and Harold's intentions, but this yokel didn't need to know that.

"Let's move our asses! A man could get hisself killed in a joint like this!" said Trux.

He started to drag Horace out from under the table they were both beneath toward the back door of the establishment.

As Horace started to follow, the red neck then stopped and looked at the other occupant of the temporary shelter from the battle that still raged on above and around them.

"Gonna have to see your pecker."

"Excuse me?" Horace was sure he'd heard the man incorrectly.

"Never mind. We'll stop and take a leak on the way. Come on!" said Trux as he grabbed the big city conniver by the arm and resumed dragging him from beneath the piece of barroom furniture and across the floor.

They crawled over the prone bodies no longer active and beneath those still on their feet doing battle, toward the rear exit of the Double L.

"Let's go find Farley and get that Mothafucker signed. I heard him and Thelma say they was goin' to Darwin!"

While Trux and Horace Herkimer were crawling out of one of the many saloons in Lone Pine, Thelma and Farley were now seated at a table inside the only one in Darwin. Old Henderson was seated across from them.

Their reception was mixed. If the ancient mining engineer knew he had company, he gave no indication. He had his pile of rocks in front of him, and was picking them up one at a time as he looked beneath each.

Four miserable looking miners were seated at the bar. Two of them had been with Jake during the chain saw attack on Rodney that day out near the caves. They stared lasciviously at Thelma and her lack of any real clothing.

Darleen, behind the same bar, looked at the Argus Queen through eyes filled with undiluted hatred.

"He'll probably talk to us as soon as he's done there," Farley said in a low voice to Thelma as he indicated the old man seated across from them.

Henderson continued to ignore the couple as he kept right on examining the table top carefully beneath each of his rocks.

Finally, the wizened wrinkled miner from yesteryear lifted the last stone and looked underneath it. He gave a disappointed sigh and, at long last, turned his attention to Farley. He still did not appear to see the beautiful woman.

"What was you doin' there, Old Henderson?" queried Farley politely.

"Lookin' under rocks," replied the old man.

"For what?"

"Little bitty women," answered Old Henderson.

Farley was thinking this over when Darleen called in an extremely nasty voice from her station behind the battered old bar and the miserable looking foursome sitting in front of her.

"Leave him alone, Farley Maynard!" she said. " Get away from him! He don't want to talk to nobody!"

Old Henderson seemed to suddenly realize Thelma's presence for the first time. He rose gallantly to his feet.

"Please sit down, my dear sweet young woman," the old man said, as he looked her over.

"Oh, you are sitting down ain't you? In that case you can ask me to sit down," he continued, as he leaned forward practically falling into Thelma's marvelous cleavage.

"Please sit down, Mr. Henderson," she offered sweetly.

With trembling fingers, the old man managed to find his chair and reseat himself.

"Forgive me," he said, as he continued staring at her breasts. "I haven't seen tits that perfect since I left a place called Zorka. Do you have a pussy my dear?"

Thelma met him head on.

"You bet your ass I do!" she answered with a smile. "Can you still get it up?"

Old Henderson cackled. "I can still get it sideways," he announced proudly.

He wasn't sure who this woman with Farley Maynard was, but he certainly did admire her spirit.

"Then you're half way there for most, sir. All the way for the more creative."

Darleen was no longer behind the bar.

She came straight up to the table. Ignoring Farley and the other woman, she spoke directly to her father in her hard, brittle voice.

"Come on, Dad," she said. "You know you promised not to talk to anymore outsiders if I let the outhouse stay up."

Old Henderson glared at her.

"You better not let anything happen to my outhouse," he stated flatly. Then his tone took on a more reasonable timbre. "Farley's no outsider."

"Hell no!" affirmed Farley. "Me n' Trux both grew up here. You know that, Darleen."

"Neither am I, Darleen," Thelma turned her attention on the bitter rawboned lady who could really benefit with some of her beauty products. She was fully aware that the other woman's father was still ogling her breasts.

"I've been coming out here since I was fifteen. You remember the time I caught you with your head in my cousin's crotch? The back seat of that old Packard?"

Darleen gave the beautiful seated woman a look that went beyond hatred. She started to speak. Then, apparently changing her mind, she turned and with an extremely stiff-legged gait, headed back toward the bar. She seemed to have no more to say at the moment.

"My cousin's name was Edna," Thelma whispered to Farley before turning back to the salivating old mineral mining expert.

"Well, I'm a son of a bitch!" Muttered Farley. "No wonder all them years she wouldn't give me n' Trux no pussy."

"So, Mr. Henderson, tell me about this place called Zorka," Thelma said to Old Henderson whose eyes had never left her bosoms.

"Another planet. Other side of this galaxy," he responded.

"Lots of silver on Zorka. Women all had melons just like yours, but they

269

didn't have no pussies. I had to escape. I stowed away on one their spaceships when I found out they was takin' another trip down here to earth and when they touched down, I escaped."

"What was the alternative?" asked Thelma leaning forward to give the old man a better view.

"The what?"

"How did they make love?"

"Never bothered to find out!" the old timer responded quickly. "I found out they didn't have no pussies so I figgered a way to get my ass outa' there!"

"Sounds like a rush to judgment to me," Thelma said in a very serious tone. "You may have missed out on something very special."

"You know, I never thought of it that way," Old Henderson said after a moment's thought, during which, he continued to study the woman's fabulous breasts.

"They do come looking for me from time to time... Are those real?"

The Argus Queen flashed her dazzling smile. "You can feel for yourself," she told the delusional old man.

"Wonderful idea!" exclaimed the old miner, as he pushed the pile of rocks in front of him aside and leaned across the table, immediately taking the owner of those fascinating attributes up on her offer.

"Henderson, you wanna' go with me n' Thelma here, to check out me and Trux's mountain?" Farley asked him.

"Wonderful idea!" repeated Henderson as he held a breast in each hand. The old man didn't fondle or grope. He balanced each gently on his spread fingertips, as if touching precious jewels.

Suddenly, the door leading out to the street banged open and Jake pushed a very frightened Harold Herkimer forward into the interior of the old saloon.

"Found him sneaking around outside tryin' to look in the windows," said the man still wearing exactly the same clothing, including the hard hat that had covered his bald head while he was attempting to do Rodney in with the chain saw earlier.

He now jerked that metal covered hairless noggin in the direction of Thelma and Farley as he grabbed the totally terrified Harold in an arm lock.

"Says he's with them!" Jake announced to the others In the bar.

Darleen held the baseball bat in her hands this time, as she rushed out again from behind the bar.

"I knew these two meant trouble!" shouted the angry proprietor of the Darwin saloon.

"Henry! You n' Bobcat n' your buddies there, grab Farley. I'll take care of Miss Bitch with the boobs!"

The four miners at the bar dove on top of Farley before the bearded man had a chance to defend himself. He disappeared beneath their filthy bodies, as Darleen swung the bat directly at Thelma's blond head.

The Argus Queen ducked and leapt to her feet. She grabbed a handful of the other woman's hair. The baseball bat flew across the room and bounced off a wall as Darleen was thrown onto the floor.

"Please don't bruise the melons," pleaded Old Henderson.

Three more ragged miners entered the old establishment behind Jake and the captive Herkimer.

The new arrivals rushed forward and grabbed Thelma. The beautiful blond lady put up a fight and managed to inflict some pain on her aggressors, in spite of the fact that she was plainly over powered. It took much more effort than any of the three big rough men expected, but they finally managed to pin her helplessly against the wall near the entrance.

Darleen climbed to her feet and retrieved her baseball bat. Her smile was without mirth as she moved with the weapon toward the beautiful blond in the shorts and halter top.

That particular garment was now slightly askew and creating a distraction among Thelma's captors.

"Thought you'd get away with it didn't you bitch?" sneered the woman with the wind worn skin and the baseball bat.

"Everybody knows my dad's crazy. But we also know someday he'll remember where another vein of silver is! Then we'll have a town again unless he tells one of you outsiders where it is first!"

Thelma started to respond but was out shouted by the panicked Herkimer.

"This is all a horrible mistake! Please let me go! I can pay you! I've got money!" shrieked Harold.

"Please don't bruise the melons," begged Old Henderson to the men now holding Thelma.

"Shut up!" barked Darleen, sounding exactly like the bitch she was. The rawboned woman with the baseball bat called to two more miners who were just entering from outside, "Go get the jail!"

"Please don't bruise the melons," repeated Old Henderson.

He looked very concerned, as the angry mob began pushing those they called 'Outsiders' out into the street. At the same time they all took up his daughter's last command as a chant.

"Go get the jail! Go get the jail!"

As he was roughly propelled out of the old saloon into the warm, dry afternoon air by the mean looking man in the hard hat, Harold Herkimer felt like he was going to faint. He tried to swallow but his whole system seemed void of saliva.

The thin, big city attorney silently cursed his brother Horace for having ever talked him into becoming involved with this scam.

Oh, what he would give to be back within the secure, comfortable air-conditioned walls of that luxurious tall office building in Century City protected by its reliable and predictable layers of smog.

CHAPTER TWENTY
COLLECTIVE EFFORTS COLLIDE

Miss Wayling was on the fifteenth floor of that great big safe building in Century City.

She was at that same second, occupying that secure and comfortable edifice Harold Herkimer was dreaming of, as he was dragged totally without dignity into the street of the God forsaken desert town of Darwin.

The lady who controlled the men who ran the firm of Herkimer, Herkimer, Herkimer, Herkimer and until recently Van Aukin, was sitting at her desk. Neither of the previously repeated adjectives really seemed to fit in with her current emotions.

The masculine faced female manipulator of male debility was livid.

Just because she had taken a holiday from the firm with all most no prior notice did not mean her bosses had the liberty of doing the same thing to her. It was unheard of to go off and not leave at least one executive minding the store.

Heads would roll when her employers returned. This was no way to run a business. As a matter of fact, if they kept this up there would be no business to run.

Had the naval officer's party in San Diego not been raided by the shore patrol, she might well have stayed away longer and not called in for a few more days. If not for that stroke of fate, she might never have heard the message left on the answering machine. She had almost gone into shock when she heard Harold's voice saying he and Horace had run off to some jerkwater town in the middle of nowhere. That was when she asked Harrington to send off that email on her lap top. Agnus had come back immediately.

What could those two be thinking of? What would have happened if she had extended her vacation? They both knew she never called in until she was ready to come back to work.

Agnus had labored far too long and hard to get her bosses where she needed them to have everything go up in smoke. She tossed her bleached curls in indignation. She got angrier the more she thought about it. A light went on in the panel on her desk. She didn't sound that pleasant as she spoke into the microphone on her headset.

"Law offices of Herkimer, Herkimer, Herkimer, Herkimer. How may I help you?"

She hoped it was Horace calling from that place called Lone Pine. Agnus was ready to give him a piece of her mind. She might even mention the vibrator.

The incoming call was indeed from Lone Pine, but it was not Horace. Rodney Van Aukin was calling on his cellular phone from a jail cell in Lone Pine California, but Miss Wayling didn't know this. It was to be some time before she found out.

It had taken a while for Rodney was to regain possession of the advanced communications instrument. The sheriff had been called away to investigate a minor traffic accident on the road to Big Pine.

Jiggs was more than willing to oblige but Arty had given the deputy several duties to catch up on that had to be tended to. Finally, however, due to Arthell's insistence, the cell phone was pulled from Rodney's property and brought forth.

Now the young man from Boston held the phone up to his ear as if he had never heard of a brain tumor. Arthell, Jiggs, in the corridor beyond the bars and even Heffaroid in the adjoining cell were watching.

"Cut the bullshit Miss Wayling!" said Rodney into his cellular phone as Arthell, on the other side of the jail bars looked on in total admiration.

Jiggs was also impressed. Even Heffaroid had to admit the kid had sand.

Miss Wayling's voice became even more unpleasant.

"Who is this please?"

"I'll tell you who it isn't 'Agnus' dear," said Rodney as he gave Jiggs a wink through the bars.

"It isn't one of your fire fighting stud bunnies from yours and Harrington's favorite forest near Tahoe! I need to know the whereabouts of the president of the firm, Mr. Christopher Herkimer! And I need to know now!"

Outside the cage, Jiggs shifted his weight uncomfortably from one foot to the other. He hoped Rodney hadn't told Arthell about that terrible time outside of Tahoe.

He knew she was in love with the guy on the other side of the bars talking on the phone and he had no chance with her. The deputy was okay with that but still, there were some things guys just shouldn't tell girls about other guys. At least not nice girls.

The innocent look of curiosity on Arthell's sweet face as she looked at Jiggs told him that indeed Rodney had not spilled the beans. The redheaded deputy was starting to like the other young man more and more. He made a mental note to ask him never to tell her about Tahoe.

In the cell next to Rodney, Heffaroid, who had heard the story, hoped he wasn't going to have to listen to it again.

Back in Century City, Miss Wayling was losing her cool. She knew that tale only too well. It did not please her that others did.

Explaining to the authorities why she and Harrington just happened to be hiking in the woods that day with only sex toys in their back packs was not among Agnus's favorite memories.

"Mr. Herkimer is out of town at the moment," she said into her head set after a moment's pause.

"I didn't ask you where he wasn't! I asked you where he was! I need to get in touch with him right away!"

Miss Wayling didn't quite know what to do but she had decided whoever was on the other end of the line was somebody not to be trifled with.

"Who is calling please?" she asked, repeating the question she had already posed but in a much more civil tone.

When she got no immediate response, she decided she'd better give forth with the requested information.

"Mr. Christopher Herkimer and Mr. W P. Herkimer are actually in the air right now, but their executive helicopter should be landing in Phoenix in about five minutes."

"I really do need to know who's calling sir," said Miss Wayling, paraphrasing the question she had repeated at least twice already.

She had thought at first she recognized the voice of that wimp, Van Aukin, but she obviously knew better now and she wished to take no chances.

Back in the Lone Pine jail, Rodney shifted the cellular telephone from one ear to the other. This was fun.

"None of your damn business Miss Wayling! Just get a hold of Christopher Herkimer as soon as you can!" the young man said, as if he'd been ordering people around all his life.

"Have him call the sheriffs' office in Lone Pine, California! You got that? You'd better, Miss Wayling, otherwise you'll never give head to another Herkimer as long as you live!"

Jiggs looked at Rodney with grudging respect as he walked back toward the offices of the law enforcement facility. No wonder this guy had the prettiest girl in the Owens Valley in love with him.

When he'd first discovered Arthell's feelings for Rodney, the deputy had really wanted to punch the city slicker in the nose. He himself had worshipped the beautiful young lady from afar for so long. Then when he'd thought it over, he decided if Arthell liked him he must be okay.

That was why he'd decided to tell the guy about the old broads and Tahoe. For a minute there the deputy thought he'd made a mistake. He knew better now. The dude was okay. And was he cool! Jiggs filed away another mental note to approach the other young man for some pointers if he ended up sticking around town.

Rodney disconnected the cell phone and moved close to the bars where Arthell was waiting to kiss his cheek.

In the adjoining cell, Heffaroid turned away, embarrassed.

"That mountain's got to have something to do with the new highway," Rodney told Arthell. "I'm not sure exactly what, but you can bet that my ex future father in law doesn't have Trux and Farley's interests at heart or he wouldn't be in such a hurry to grab it."

"You're really very insightful," Arthell said, in open admiration.

"Years late and far too many dollars short I'm afraid," Rodney admitted.

The perennial prodding of the Honesty Monster wasn't needed anymore. The young attorney wanted to be totally candid with this woman he adored.

The psychological demon was now probably either sleeping, looking for a new vocation, or had departed to join the 'Stammer poltergeist' to haunt some other insecure soul.

"Until I met you, nobody believed in me," the young man told the beautiful girl on the other side of the bars.

"I was so busy trying not to do things the wrong way, I never took time to think about how to do them the right way. If I had, I certainly wouldn't have ended up in here."

A new thought hit him.

"But then, if I hadn't landed here the first time, I wouldn't have met you, right?"

"I'm awfully glad you did," smiled Arthell.

"Anyway, from what I've been told, this isn't bad as jails go. One of your fathers told me...."

Rodney smiled. He deepened his voice, and launched into a really funny imitation of Farley Maynard. "This sum bitch is a regular Motel Six, compared to that shit hole, the Darwin jail!" said the young man.

He stroked an imaginary beard and stuck his stomach out to make himself look even more like the man he was pretending to be.

Even Heffaroid got a chuckle out of this one. Arthell broke into honest laughter. There was no way for any of them to know that the very man whom Rodney had just imitated so humorously, and her wonderful mother were, at this very minute, about to be thrust into that horrible portable purgatory described in the parody.

*** *** *** *** ***

The Darwin jail looked even worse than Trux had described it.

A smoking, popping, vintage John Deere tractor towed it slowly down the main street of the decaying town toward the old saloon. A huge cloud of dust, created by two oversized rusting iron skids attached to the bottom of the old structure, billowed up from behind, as the metal rails cut through the dirt, gravel and decayed asphalt on the surface of the road beneath it.

In front of the ramshackle drinking establishment, Darleen was still in possession of the old baseball bat. She and the shabby miners still holding Thelma, Farley and Harold Herkimer watched and waited as the strange procession approached. So did their helpless captives.

The portable building was no more than four square feet wider in any direction than Old Henderson's outhouse. It was not, however, nearly so attractive.

All four walls were constructed of ancient rough-hewn logs. Each had long since lost all traces of bark and was at least two feet thick. These ageless timbers were greasy and grimy from being doused and soaked in creosote for countless years to keep the wood from rotting.

The roof of the hideous structure, consisted of twisted and rusted galvanized steel. Only one window seemed to be present. This single oblong opening, crisscrossed with thick steel bars, obviously forged decades hence, could be seen in the upper half of its thick, tarnished metal door.

There was now, or never had been, glass within that embrasure. The iron and carbon mixture making up the foreboding configuration of bars was sunk into the framework of the old incarceration edifice's only source of ventilation.

The gaunt ghost town resident, driving the old two-cylinder tractor looked like he had more space between his eyes than his shoulders. He brought the ancient machine and its grotesque, trailing burden to a halt in the middle of the street in front of the saloon.

As the popping sound of the tractor's simplified, basic combustible engine ceased, Darleen shouted to Jake and the other dirty, ragged men who held the three prisoners in their grasps.

"Throw em' in there! Lock it up and take em' out to the desert. They start stinkin' after a month or so, somebody can pull em' out and feed em' to the buzzards! Aint nobody comin' into Darwin and stealin' my dad's secrets!"

"Darleen," said Thelma, "We told you, we don't care about anything in the Darwin area. Farley just wants your father to…"

"And I told you, if I wanted any shit out of you, I'd pound it out of your perfect, plastic ass with this!" Darleen hissed viciously, brandishing the bat in Thelma's direction, before she shouted at the miners again,

"What are you waiting for? Get rid of these pieces of garbage!"

"This has got to be some kind of horrible joke!" exclaimed Harold Herkimer in a high pitched, trembling voice, as Jake and the other miners

277

began pushing he, Thelma and Farley toward the squat, ugly building hitched behind the tractor.

"You'll think fucking joke," muttered Farley through tight lips. "Yessir! You'll be laughin' your asshole right out through you're God damned mouth when they put us in this thing n' drag us out in the desert for a few days."

Thelma's compact was still parked across the street. Its pretty owner had been kind enough to leave the driver's window of the small automobile partially rolled down so Barney could get some air. Unfortunately, the pig now discovered she hadn't left enough space for him to crawl out. Since his particular species has no thumbs, he couldn't open the door.

The animal was going crazy. Daddy Farley and the beautiful lady they all loved so much were in trouble and he couldn't get out of the car to help them. Barney stuck his head out the window and pushed his weight against the remaining hindrance of glass with the rest of his body and all his might.

At the now open door of the jail, Harold had already been thrown inside. Jake turned to assist Bobcat and Henry who were having trouble with Farley who seemed unwilling to cooperate. He wasn't going in that structure behind the tractor if he could help it.

The other men and Darleen were having their own problems with Thelma. The Argus Queen lashed out with her shapely right bare leg and kicked one of her several unwanted male escorts squarely in the testicles.

Darleen moved in. Using both her arms she lifted the baseball bat above her head preparing to bring it down on the much more attractive woman's skull if Thelma didn't cooperate.

The rawboned proprietress of the Darwin saloon failed to hear the crashing sound of breaking glass, coming from the opposite side of the street behind her. However, she definitely did feel Barney's tusks sink into the flesh of her ankle, as the pig, covered with tiny shattered, translucent brittle amorphous particles, arrived on the scene. The bat flew from her hands over the back of her head, spiraling down onto the street behind her.

"The pig!" screamed Darleen, as she attempted to free her lower extremity from the mouth of the angry swine. "Somebody get Farley's God damned pig off me!"

Two of the miners holding Thelma released the gorgeous woman and leapt on the pig as ordered.

One of the aggressors stepped on the bat. His feet flew out from beneath him. The other went rolling away in a different direction on the surface of the old dirt and graveled street as Barney scrambled out of his grasp.

"In my pickup!" yelled Jake, who was now minus his hard hat with his dirty glabrous dome visible to the world.

The head gear had fallen off during his struggle with Farley. The stubborn bearded Maynard brother now had both of his palms pressed against either side of the old jail's door jam. He was pushing against the old structure on skids while Jake, Bobcat, Henry and another man attempted to shove him in through the opening.

The members of Darleen's posse were discovering that putting Farley inside the jail was proving more difficult than sticking a hair up the anal orifice of an angry wildcat.

"There's a tarp in the back of my pickup! Get the God damned thing out and throw it over the pig!" Jake continued to yell at the others attempting to subdue Barney as he tried to pry one of Farley's firmly planted palms free.

Darleen, hobbling on her injured ankle, grabbed hold of Thelma again. With the help of the remaining ragged miner, who had managed to retain his own two handed grip on the feisty beauty, Old Henderson's bitter daughter was finally able to make some headway. Together she and the man actually were able to start forcing the angry Argus Queen toward the jail where Farley was still pushing against both sides of the doorway, refusing to enter.

Barney dove at the man who had his hands on Thelma this time. His newest victim let out howl of pain as the pig's jaws clamped down on the fleshy part of the miner's upper thigh just above the back of his knee. Unfortunately for Barney, the two men whom he had dumped in the dust were now in possession of a wide tarpaulin procured from the bed of Jake's pickup.

Moving forward, each holding two ends of the large square, coarse and durable material, they threw it over the pig. Quickly, they began wrapping it around the aggressive, wiggling animal's body. Barney attempted to escape, but this time the ragged humans were too fast for him. He soon found himself enveloped, kicking and squealing, within the folds of canvass.

At the entrance of the portable jail, Jake finally was able to pry Farley's fingers loose from the sides of the portal entryway. The bald headed bully slapped the bearded man across the mouth before he and his companions began actually pushing their stubborn prisoner in through the opening of the private piece of Hell.

Beyond that doorway, Harold Herkimer could be seen whimpering helplessly as he cowered against the far wall of the claustrophobic, dank and dreary moveable dungeon.

Everyone else present was now shouting while the pig squealed loudly beneath the tarp. Nonetheless, a new sound drowned out all other noise.

"Take your filthy Goddamned hands off my brother!" Thundered the angry voice of Trux Maynard.

CHAPTER TWENTY ONE
PREVAILING FORCES

Trux looked very much like an outraged missile with a protruding chin, freshly discharged from a nuclear powered launcher.

He streaked forward toward the group of people and the portable jail beyond it from the HOWDY HOSS, which was sliding to a halt in the middle of the street only a few feet away from the jail.

Horace Herkimer sat behind the steering wheel of the battered big rig with both feet on its one brake pedal. The flabby Century City executive had been forced to leap into that position when Trux, who was operating the controls had vacated the motor home through its seldom used driver's door. The vehicle had been, at that time, still moving.

The enraged, broad shouldered Maynard brother charged through the throng of ragged vigilantes. He knocked at least half of them down like a bowling ball scoring a strike with ten pins, before reaching Farley's side.

Jake's nose became the unhappy recipient of Trux's fist. This blow was followed by one even more powerful to his stomach. The man with the filthy bald head tumbled backwards on top of his previously fallen metallic hat.

Trux wheeled about and hit Bobcat. He knocked the man into Henry who was already toppling to the ground after receiving a blow from Farley.

Darleen picked up the baseball bat and raced toward Trux. Thelma grabbed the questionably feminine self-appointed Darwin protector by the hair for the second time that day. The Argus Queen executed a forcible yank, and became the recipient of both a handful of hair and the wooden piece of old sports equipment in a matter of seconds. Darleen landed hard on her back against the surface of the Darwin street.

The fallen female victim of the swift maneuver attempted to reenact her breathing process as she stared up at the glaring afternoon sun.

Meanwhile, Barney had managed to crawl out from beneath the tarpaulin in time to attack two of the miners who looked inclined to come to Darleen's aid. Without hesitation, the pair changed their minds and elected to run off in other directions.

Harold Herkimer timidly stuck his head out through the doorway of the old jail to see Trux, Farley, and Thelma, still holding the bat, all now abreast of one another.

The pig, with the hair on his back standing straight up, was just slightly in front of his group of super heroes. All stood together with their backs to the open doorway through which Harold was creeping. Their eyes were on the bald headed Jake with his bleeding nose, Bobcat, Henry and the rest of the miners. All were now ignoring Darleen on the ground while they slunk away in various directions.

Some, like Jake, were nursing wounds. Others, more fortunate, obviously wished to remain so.

"Somebody want to tell me what this is all about?" asked Trux as he waited for the surging within his adrenaline glands to subside.

Darleen whimpered slightly as she struggled up to a sitting position and pointed in turn, at Farley, Thelma and Harold Herkimer.

The latter, like a wounded, terrified puppy, was trying to move to his brother's side who now lingered next to the stationary HOWDY HOSS.

"Him and this woman was tryin' to get my Dad to tell this outsider the secret of the Darwin silver!" whined Darleen.

"That's bullshit!" exclaimed Trux in disgust. "That guy and the other wimpy fart with him don't give a fuck about nothin' around here. They wanna' buy our mountain over above Little Lake."

By the motor home, Harold Herkimer whispered indignantly to Horace Herkimer.

"Did you hear what he just called us?"

"Sticks and stones, Harold," Horace whispered back as he continued to display his dental work. "Just be quiet. I've nearly sewn this thing up. While you were out here screwing around, I've been taking care of business."

Harold looked like he might explode.

"Screwing around?" he said almost crying. "Have you any idea what I've gone through?"

Horace kept smiling as he whispered once more out of the corner of his mouth. "Some other time, Harold," he said.

Back in front of the old jail and the John Deere tractor, Darleen was rising to her feet. Thelma and Farley now knelt on either side of Barney, telling him what a good pig he had been while they brushed the remaining minuscule shards of shattered glass from his back and sides.

The animal was just glad that Daddy Farley and Uncle Trux's beautiful lady wasn't angry with him for breaking her window.

At the same time, Trux was addressing Jake and the rest of the male citizens of Darwin who had been about to do harm to his brother and the woman they loved. The recipients of his attention were all watching him from a safe distance. Some were hiding behind their vehicles still parked in front of the saloon.

"What's the matter with you people?" asked Trux in a loud, bewildered voice.

"Me and Farley live here! We ain't gonna fuck nobody!"

He turned and called to Jake who was nursing his bloody nose behind the shelter of his pickup hood.

"You know that Jake!" Trux said. "When you broke your leg who was it brought you that load of wood and chopped it up and stacked it for you?"

Jake hung his head. "You and Farley did, Trux," the man with no hair and the injured nasal equipment mumbled.

"Even brought you jug of whiskey, as I recall," said Farley, reminiscing as he stood up.

Barney grunted. He remembered that.

"And you Bobcat," continued Trux, as he turned to one of the other two men who had personally been attempting to thrust Farley in through the doorway of the old jail, "when your wife got sick, didn't me n' Farley haul her to the Bishop hospital for you when your old jeep wouldn't start?"

"Give her a jug of whisky too, I believe," was Farley's comment.

Barney remembered that too.

Bobcat also hung his head. "Sorry," he said.

"And Henry!" Trux said as he pointed at the man standing next to Bobcat. "Did you forget when me n' Farley went all the way over to the navel base at Ridgecrest and fetched you back that black market jar of Blue Ointment so you could kill them crabs you picked up in that cathouse in Winamucca?"

"Also brung you back a jug of whiskey," said Farley

Barney gave out with another grunt, showing this was another incident he remembered well.

"My God! I don't believe this!" ranted Trux. He wheeled around to look at Jake again. "Especially you, Jake! Me n' Farley's done you more n' one favor!"

"So many I can't even count em," piped up Farley getting into the spirit.

"Damned right!" Trux went on as Jake truly began to look ashamed of himself while he held his nose. "Remember that time when me n' Farley was stayin' out at our caves and you come knockin' in the middle of the night huntin' for some clothes?"

The expression on the bald man's face said this was a time he would just as soon forget. Trux wasn't about to let him.

"You was passed out in that rig of yours on Lizard Road and someone come along and pumped the fly of your coveralls full of grease with one of them grease guns. You had gunk all over your tallywhacker, your balls, everthing. Even your ass was full of grease wasn't it Farley?"

"He was purty damned greasy all right," answered Farley, confirming the verbal picture his brother was painting for the crowd while Jake cringed.

"And didn't me n' Farley take you down to Dirty Socks in the HOWDY

HOSS n' help you get all cleaned off fore we gave you some clothes to wear home so that bitch you was livin' with at the time wouldn't know you'd been passed out drunk and come home with your pants fulla' shit steada' bein at work like you told her?"

"I think it was a jug of rum we give him that time. We was out of whiskey," said Farley.

Barney remembered this incident also. In addition, the pig vividly remembered it was Uncle Trux and Daddy Farley who had discovered the passed out bald headed man earlier. It was they who had pumped the grease into the man's fly in the first place.

Obviously Jake was not aware of this. He licked the blood from his lips that was falling downward from his nose and came out from behind the hood of his pickup. He spoke in a very small voice.

"I don't know what to say, Trux. We just got carried away. I swear I won't never to nothin' bad to you or any of your friends or family ever again."

"You damned sure better not! Now go take care of your nose fore you bleed all over everbody! And put on your hat for God's sake. You look disgusting. I've seen more hair on bacon."

Farley's eyes quickly darted in Barney's direction. He hoped his four-legged scrapping comrade had not been offended by his brother's euphemism. Barney hadn't. The family needed to stick together right now. This was no time for a pig to get petty.

Jake kept one hand on his afflicted nose as he bent over and picked up his hat with the other. Covering his hairless dome with the metal headgear he mumbled one last apology and turned back toward his pickup. He opened the driver's door of the vehicle and began climbing in behind the steering wheel.

The other men in the small crowd all began murmuring regrets for their actions. The Maynard brothers had done each and every one of them a good turn at one time or another.

Darleen stood alone now in the middle of the street. She knew she had lost the battle. She gave Thelma a hateful look as the other woman in the skimpy outfit moved to face her and offered her the baseball bat. After a moment, she accepted the object and turned away, limping into the old saloon all by herself. The others followed except for Jake who was now driving away.

Trux heaved a big sigh, then called to Horace who still lurked beside the motor home with Harold.

"All right, Herkimer," the big chinned red neck said, in a businesslike tone. "Get your ass over here with them papers."

Trux then lowered his voice as Horace started toward the spot where he and Farley were standing, and spoke into the ear of his bearded brother. "We stopped to piss on the way here, So I got the lookin' at his pecker bullshit outa' the way. Believe, me it ain't worth goin' through again."

"And take my word for it, I got the socializen' outa' way," Trux added honestly enough. "Lets just sign this shit so me n' you and Barney can go find a drink."

Farley, not knowing that Trux had made a new deal that would still get rid of Rodney, was overjoyed that the trouble between he and his brother had come to an end. Now life could return to normalcy. He put his arm affectionately on his sibling's broad shoulder.

"Good idea, Trux!" said the now smiling bearded man. "Me n' Barney could use a drink along about now. Right Barney?"

Barney looked up at his Uncle Trux, the pig was flattered to be included in the plan, but he knew the pretty lady Thelma, had other another agenda on her mind. He was not surprised when she spoke up to say as much.

"Not so fast," said Thelma, stepping up between the two sets of brothers when Horace followed by Harold, arrived with the requested documents. "I still think Henderson should look over the property first."

Trux attempted to push her gently, yet firmly out of the way.

"I think you've caused enough shit for one day Thelma," he replied. "Me n'Farley can handle this. Gimme a pen, Herkimer."

Horace was in the process of handing both the land transfer contract and the required writing implement to Trux, when a voice he had never heard before came from above. The attorney froze in place.

"That's no way to treat a lady, Trux Maynard!" said Old Henderson, whom everybody discovered to be standing on top of the cab of one of the dilapidated old trucks parked in front of the saloon.

He held the same pistol in his hand that had been in his possession the day he showed Rodney the caves just out side of town. It was pointed at the entire group including the Maynard brothers as he spoke again.

"No way at all!" the old man kept the group covered as he now addressed Thelma. "Would you be so kind as to help an old man down from here?"

Thelma smiled and hurried forward to honor the armed senior citizen's request. The old miner displayed amazing agility as the lady assisted him in his decent. He kept the gun pointed at his captive audience and continued to talk to the lovely lady during the process.

"Id'a never let em' go through with it my dear. Those purty melons would not have shriveled and died in that old hot hoosegow. I believe you and I have us a date on Maynard's mountain."

"I do believe you're correct Mr. Henderson," said Thelma, taking the old man's free arm.

Horace Herkimer started to protest, when it looked like Trux or Farley were not going to interfere with this interruption.

"I really don't think…," he began.

The big city executive's objection was stopped in mid sentence as Trux spoke to Thelma in a sarcastic tone.

"Go ahead Thelma," he said. "Spend a week with the old fart for all I care. Me n' Farley's signin' right now."

Horace Herkimer started once again to hand both pen and paper to Trux. They were pushed aside by Farley.

"I ain't signin' nothin' till Thelma say to, Trux."

Horace stood there with the objects in his hand. He looked in confusion from one Maynard brother to the other.

"Why you pussy whipped little pig lover!" Trux snapped at Farley. Immediately he looked down as Barney, below him, let out with an extremely offended grunt.

"God damnit, Barney, It was just a figger' of speech! You gotta' stop bein' so damned sensitive. Gotta' learn to be more like Thelma."

Thelma looked at Trux as she continued to hang onto Old Henderson's arm. It was impossible to read her expression.

Trux heaved a resigned sigh and shrugged at his brother.

"Oh what the hell? If it's gonna make everbody feel better," he said, before sidling up to Horace Herkimer and whispering in the big city lawyer's ear. Harold leaned forward to listen, trying very hard to find out what was going on and failing miserably.

"Might's well humor em," the broad shouldered red neck murmured. "Won't take long. We got a deal anyhow!"

"We'll take my truck!" Old Henderson announced as he shoved the gun in his belt. He then turned and opened the driver's door of the ancient vehicle he had only moments ago been standing on top of. He continued talking as he gestured for Thelma to slide in beyond the steering wheel before he entered.

"I took the liberty of sneaking a case of beer out of Darleens' refrigerator while everbody was actin' so damned stupid about the silver there ain't none of no more. It probably ain't too hot yet. Got an old empty lard bucket up front. As I remember, Barney likes a taste now and again."

This was enough for Farley and Barney. The pig and his master quickly hurried around the hood of the old truck toward its passenger side.

Once again, Trux shrugged as he looked at the two skeptical Herkimers.

"Looks like we got the back to ourselves, boys. Don't worry, I'll make Farley pass some of that beer back to us. One thing about my brother, he can be a hard head and a dumb shit. Ain't got enough ass to make a sick man a bowl of soup, but he ain't selfish!"

*** *** *** *** *** ***

The ancient truck bounced along an unpaved road through the desert that Old Henderson swore was a shortcut to the Maynards' mountain from Darwin. The shadow cast by the old vehicle was long as the sun slowly descended toward the vast western horizon.

In the rear of the truck, the Herkimers were holding on for dear life. Both were terrified they would be thrown out of the rig onto the sand and cactus where they would be devoured by the large lizards they saw scurrying about on either side of the bumpy thoroughfare, at any moment.

"Don't worry boys," said Trux as he sipped his beer. "Ain't no way nobody can look cool ridin' in the back of a pickup."

Either Trux was the only member of the trio of truck bed passengers that could stomach warm beer or the Century City lawyers didn't feel they could afford the extra hand needed to hold the can.

Inside the cab of the vintage vehicle designed for hauling heavy articles, Barney was enjoying his beer immensely. He sat on the floorboards scrunched up against the passenger door with his snout thrust inside the old lard pail promised by the antiquated driver as he slurped away noisily.

Farley sat directly above him, also imbibing from the can he held in his hand. The foamy beverage was warm and it wasn't Blue Ribbon, but it was wet and it was good.

Thelma sat between the bearded, beer guzzling Maynard brother and Old Henderson.

The latter was having a wonderful time reaching between the beautiful lady's shapely bare legs making unnecessary shifts as he operated the controls of the noisy, senescent machine. He was somehow managing to keep the truck moving forward without running off the road ahead of him, even though most of his attention was still riveted on Thelma's breasts.

"No sir," said the aging mining engineer. "You didn't have to worry. I would have never let anything happen to the best set of bazooms I've laid eyes on since I left the planet of Zorka!"

"I'm surprised you ever returned," said Thelma smiling. She made no move to hinder his extra shifting activity as she continued talking. "It seems silver and big breasts are your passion. You say this planet had both."

"That's a fact," Old Henderson responded. "But the women didn't have no pussies. Seemed important at the time, but you got me thinkin'. You know, you might be right. I shoulda' dug a little deeper whilst' I was there. Maybe there was a, what did you call it back in the saloon? An alternate?"

"Alternative," Thelma corrected him. "But close enough."

"Trouble with all of us, ain't it?" Old Henderson mused philosophically.

"We learn one way of makin' things happen, we don't even wanna' think about there might be another. Guess we're all guilty. I know them assholes back in Darwin, includin' that hard assed daughter of mine, are. Ain't a one of em' ever gonna' dig another penny's worth of silver outa' the ground anywhere near there, but they don't wanna' hear it. Don't wanna hear about me getting' picked up by the space ship, neither. Nobody ever even acted liked they believed me but you."

"Come on, Old Henderson," said Farley as he dug into the case of beer crammed into a small space on the floorboards between Barney's body and Thelma's feet. "I believed you. So did Barney."

"You're a good man, Farley Maynard, but you're also a liar by not callin' me one. Make sure you hand Trux back another one of those," Old Henderson said. The last part of his statement referred to the beer.

Farley nodded and dug two unopened cans from the crumbled cardboard case.

"You better not have another one till after we visit the mountain, Barney," he said to the pig before turning back with the two full containers in his hands.

He banged one on the rear window of the truck to get his brother's attention.

Beneath the bearded Maynard's feet and between his legs, Barney gave out a grudging grunt of acknowledgment. He really could use another, but he knew Farley was right.

"Then again maybe it is all a big ole' lie," said Old Henderson, returning to the previous subject, while he reached between Thelma's great legs again for the gear shift stick.

On the other side of the lady, Farley leaned out the open passenger window of the vehicle to hand Trux the beer.

"Could be they wasn't no space ship. Maybe I got hung up in a whorehouse up in Nevada and made up that story so Darleen wouldn't yell at me. Maybe then I found out if I stuck to tellin' that lie, folks'd leave me alone."

Old Henderson turned to Thelma and spoke again, this time asking her a question. "What would you say to that?"

Thelma retained her honest smile, and answered immediately. "I'd say either way, you not only had a fantastic experience, you should be applauded for a wonderful imagination," she replied. "I just hope you keep a firm grip on reality when we get up on that mountain."

Old Henderson chuckled. They didn't make them like the lady sitting next to him anymore.

"Don't you worry! If there's anything worth anything up there, Old

Henderson'll find it. You can bet those beautiful melons on that, and you know I wouldn't suggest anything that would even possibly put them no place 'septin' exactly where they are."

Thelma thrust the attributes in question out further toward the windshield so the old man could get even a better view.

"I take great comfort in that Mr. Henderson," she said with confidence.

"One hell of a good woman you've got here Maynard," Old Henderson told Farley as he drove forward.

"Me n' Trux know that, Henderson," replied Farley as he opened his own beer can now that his brother, in the rear of the moving truck, had his. "We screw around a lot, me n' Trux do, but we wouldn't even consider havin' no one else for permanent."

"The sentiments are mutual," responded the Argus Queen, as she put her hand affectionately on Farley's knee.

In the back of Old Henderson's truck, Trux, the third corner of Thelma's permanent love triangle, was squinting up at the sun. The hand not holding his newest acquired beer shaded his brow.

Maynards mountain could now be seen in the near distance beyond the front of the old truck's cab, looming up out of the desert into the sky. The tall natural landmass looked now as it had to Old Henderson and his father many years ago. It definitely resembled a gigantic woman's breast.

"We ain't got but another three and a half hours daylight left. Four tops, and this shit'll all be over with," Trux told the two other men sharing the bed of the aging rig with him.

"We wont be able to stay up on that mountain once it starts getting' dark, 'causa' the Mojave Greens. You'll be the owners of the property and back in LA, with the little dip shit locked up, by tomorrow easy."

"Mojave Greens?" queried Harold Herkimer, as he continued hanging on to the rack with both hands. He was forced to shout over the noise of the wind and the sound of the old truck that seemed ready to fall apart when it struck the next, seemingly inevitable bump in the road.

"What's that? Some sort of political environmental group?"

Trux started to laugh. For some reason, his thoughts drifted back to shortly after Rodney had arrived on the scene and had set he and his brother off into guffaws of laughter comparing fish to vaginas.

It was a shame Van Aukin had turned into such an asshole. Trux had liked him before he had started coming on to Arthell like a God damned gigolo.

"I guess you could compare politicians to rattlesnakes," he said, answering Harold Herkimer's question.

"Rattlesnakes?" responded Horace Herkimer in alarm. "There are rattlesnakes on this mountain?"

Trux cursed himself for talking too much.

"Just a few. Ain't no big thing. You ain't gonna back out on the deal and let Rodney outa' jail are ya?"

Ironically, Horace was, in turn, chastising himself for his own big mouth.

"No! Of course not. A deal is a deal! Right Mr. Herkimer?" he said, turning to his brother for support.

"Absolutly, Mr. Herkimer," agreed Harold. His voice reached a high pitch as the truck hit another bump in the road and he hung on for dear life. In reality, Harold Herkimer was sorry he'd ever heard of the miserable piece of real estate no matter how valuable it was.

"Anyway", said Trux reassuringly, after he drained the contents of the can in his hand and emitted a loud belch, "you don't have to worry 'bout the snakes. That's where Barney really struts his stuff. Long as it's still daylight and he can see em', them Greens don't stand a chance with ole Barney around."

The old truck pulled to a halt at the foot of the mountain so abruptly that both Herkimers were thrown forward.

Huge granite boulders lay in clusters between the base of the towering landmass and the front of Old Henderson's vehicle, which was now in total shadow. The mountain beyond these formations climbing upward into the still sunlit sky, appeared to be made up of a much different conglomeration of minerals than the solid looking boulders.

Trux was helping the Herkimers to their feet when Farley and the pig exited the right front of the vehicle's cab.

The former looked into the rear of the rig with a grin on his bearded face.

"Sure hope you boys like exercise," said Farley. "It's one hell of a hike up the side of this sucker!"

CHAPTER TWENTY TWO
REVELATION ON ALL FRONTS

The trek up the side of the mountain on foot after they left the truck was indeed 'One hell of a hike' as the bearded Maynard brother had predicted.

It was also treacherous, especially for the Herkimers. The dark red, and at times, bluish, earth was extremely unstable. Unless one knew exactly where to plant one's foot, there was a good chance a piece of the mountainside would immediately crumble and fall away.

Barney knew where the solid portions of the path were and led the way. Following close behind the pathfinder pig, was Farley. Then came Old Henderson, who was, of course, paying close attention to Thelma. The geriatric mining engineer wanted no harm to come to the lady's magnificent melons. They could get bruised in a fall.

Trux, helping the two frightened and stumbling Century City executives, who were both clearly out of their element, brought up the rear of the strange, uphill parade.

They were very nearly to the top of the mountain when the first uncomfortable buzz of a coiled rattlesnake reached their ears. Thelma screamed and Harold Herkimer would have fallen off the mountainside had it not been for Trux grabbing the city fellow as he jumped backward.

In the lead, Farley spoke quietly to the pig whose ears were already cocked and pointed in the direction of the obnoxious sound.

"Best take care of it, Barney."

Barney raced forward over toward a bed of red and blue rocks located just at this side of the mountain crest. He dove into the rocks and came up with the buzzing tailed reptile in his jaws. With a violent toss of his head, Barney flung the creature to the ground and methodically began to stomp it to death.

When at last, the snake was no longer moving, the proud pig trotted back to Farley and the rest of the group. He grunted importantly, indicating it was now safe for the humans to proceed onward to the top of the huge red and blue landmass.

"Told you the pig'd take care of us," Trux murmured to Horace Herkimer while Harold Herkimer tried to stop shaking.

"I'll be damned!" exclaimed Horace. "I wouldn't have believed it if I hadn't seen it with my own eyes."

"Anymore of those awful reptiles around?" asked Harold, whispering, when he was finally able to speak at all.

"I told ya before they're everywhere," said Trux. "But don't worry about it. That pig's worth his weight in gold around here."

He looked up to see Barney now leading Farley, Old Henderson and Thelma onward over the crest onto the apex.

"Come on, the others is hittin' the top. We'd better stick with em," said the broad shouldered co-owner of the mountain as he moved after the disappearing group.

Harold attempted another swallow. He still had no saliva.

"I think maybe we'll stay here," he said.

Horace reached out and took the other Herkimer's arm and began pushing him upward after the departing Trux.

"Don't be an idiot!" Horace whispered in his apprehensive brother's ear. "If that old fool up there finds out what we're after, we have to be there to discredit him. Lead on Trux!" he shouted after the man with the big chin. "We're right behind you!"

Finally, all reached their destination where they were forced to climb up over a ledge and then slide downward for about four feet, into a shallow gigantic crevice that made up the top of the mountain. The strange indentation instead of a peak, indicated that at one time, in aeons gone by, this was an active volcano.

Except for Old Henderson and Barney, who both immediately began looking around, the climbing party paused to catch their breath.

An extremely tall and narrow rock pinnacle, crudely reminiscent of the Seattle space needle which was obviously erected much later, towered above all else as it rose upward from the center of the top in the wide, round indentation. The tip of this strange formation of nature, accounted for the nipple of the breast as seen from below.

"What do you think, Mr. Henderson?" asked Thelma, "Any sign of gold or silver?"

The old man pulled a small hammer from his pocket and squatted down. He picked up one of the strange colored rocks and began chipping away at it as he answered.

"Of course not! I knew there wouldn't be. I've been climbin' and prospectin' this old volcano for years."

The aging engineer raised his head and studied the pinnacle formation in the middle of his surroundings. "Matter of fact, this is where I got picked up and taken away in the space ship by the Zorkanians."

"If there ever was a spaceship," added the old rock hound, turning his old gray head and giving Thelma a broad wink before returning to the task of chipping away at the chunks of solidified mineral matter in his hand.

Trux moved back to join the Herkimers who lingered near the incline of shale beneath the edge of the mountaintop.

"Don't pay no attention to that crazy old fart," Trux whispered to the two big city buyers.

"You can tell by the way he talks, least half his poop don't make it all the way down the chute. This property's well worth what you agreed to pay for it. You do still wanna' buy it don't ya?"

Horace saw the look of panic in the eyes of the big red neck and decided it was time to move this deal along. Harold looked like he might crack if he stayed up here on this mountaintop much longer and Horace wasn't that comfortable himself. He made an exaggerated face as he looked at the surroundings.

"To tell you the truth, Trux," said the man from Century City, "now that I've seen it first hand, I'm not sure."

The look of panic increased in the clear blue eyes of his pigeon and Horace knew his strategy was working. He had to be careful though. Pigeons could fly away, if frightened too badly.

"However," the lawyer continued, becoming smoother by the second, "a deal is a deal. Oh, why did I have that extra martini?"

Trux held up his hand, begging for patience, before turning and moving to Farley's side.

"Let's get our asses back down and sign those damn papers before they change their minds," the man with the big chin said in a low voice to his bearded brother. He then backed up a step and addressed the whole group in a loud voice he hoped sounded jovial.

"All right!" Trux announced, as he clapped his hands together, and deftly began herding Farley and Thelma back toward the Herkimers and the head of the trail leading back down the side of the mountain. "There's nothin' more to see here! Let's all go get a cold beer before we get snake bit!"

"Cinders!" said Old Henderson, who still squatted in the middle of the pile of rocks. He held one up for all to see.

Trux left the company of his brother and the beautiful lady wearing the shorts and halter, and hurried back to the old man. Beyond the gnarled old rock expert, Barney walked around in circles, keeping a vigilant eye out for snakes.

He leaned down and addressed the senior citizen in a harsh, urgent whisper.

"Henderson, you asshole," hissed the broad shouldered blond man. "Will you back off? You're about to kill a good deal for me n' Farley, here! We know all about them cinders. Ain't worth shit! We already busted our asses for five years tryin' to sell em' to a BBQ company! So knock it off and let's go!"

Over below the head of the trail, Horace decided the time had definitely arrived to move things along.

Old Henderson had just said the magic word that was the key to the property's worth. The attorney really didn't want the topic opened for discussion. He called over the heads of Farley and Thelma who stood between he and Harold to Trux.

"Well, let's go get that cold beer," said Horace. "Harold and I are buying. Right, Harold?"

The bones in Old Henderson's knees creaked slightly as he stood up and slipped the little hammer back into his pocket.

"I hope these city dudes is offerin' you boys a good price for this old mountain," he remarked, looking at the Herkimers who appeared to be quite anxious to make their descent to a lower elevation.

"Two thousand dollars!" replied Farley proudly.

"Four thousand dollars!" chimed in Trux at almost exactly the same time.

Farley turned toward Trux. He looked very confused.

"I was gonna' split it with you!" Trux assured his brother.

"So I been doin' a little wheelin' and dealin'," he continued when he saw the accusing look in Thelma's eyes. "I ain't exactly dumb you know!"

Old Henderson started to laugh.

"That's the truth, Trux! You sure ain't dumb," the gnarled mineral authority assured the Maynard brother with the pronounced jaw, when he could speak again.

"See?" Trux said smugly to Farley and Thelma, referring to what he assumed to be a compliment from the older man.

"But you sure are stupid!" cackled Old Henderson as he began dancing a little jig around the cluster of recently examined rocks beneath his feet.

"Gonna' sell out for a lousy four thousand dollars, when you could get at least a million, probably more."

Dust flew as he began dancing faster. His cackles became screams of hilarity. "Boy, you wrote the book on stupid!"

Trux stared at the dancing old man with an open mouth. Thelma pushed him aside as she walked from Farley's side to the delirious, experienced mining engineer and the small cloud of dust he was creating on the mountaintop.

"What are you getting at, Mr. Henderson?" she asked as the old man reached out for her hands and drew her into the dance.

Old Henderson continued to howl with glee, as he twirled the lady around.

Barney, standing nearby, wasn't sure what was going on, but it looked like fun. The pig began doing a little dance of his own.

"God! What great tits you have!" exclaimed the old man as he buried his gray head in the lady's ample cleavage.

He snorted, then looked up into her eyes, as he swung her around again, and began speaking in a high sing song voice. "There's gonna' be a new highway. Four laner! All the way from California to Washington! This mountain's full of the cinders they can to pave it with, and it's the closest place to get em'. Worth a fortune, but the state'll save a bigger fortune not havin' to process pavement! Call it an act of God, evolution, or as they say on Zorka, 'The will of Naba Naba.' Whatever! These volcanic cinders is already mixed with just the right ingredients! Spread em' out, press em' flat with their big machines, and, bingo! You not only got instant highway, you cut your maintenance bill way down below half. Cinders last damn near forever! Worth a fortune!"

Old Henderson screamed with laughter as he and Thelma joined hands and began dancing in circles around the pig who was having a wonderful time.

Perspiration glistened in the rays of the late afternoon sun on the old miner's weathered face. In spite of this, other than an occasional creaking of a few joints, his body, deserving of veneration due to the amount of time it had been around, displayed no signs of fatigue. The occasional, nearly silent, farts didn't count.

While there were no expulsions of gas or creaking sound coming from Thelma's magnificently proportioned frame, she was, nonetheless, showing just a hint of weariness.

Perspiration was indeed visible on her pretty brow also, but the beautiful woman hung in there. If Old Henderson could dance forever on a mountaintop so could she.

Near the edge of that same mountaintop, the Herkimers were sweating even more than the dancing couple. The overhead sun and the recent climb were only partially responsible for the open floodgates of sweat glands oozing from their pores onto the faces and other places of the Century City shysters.

"What are we going to do?" Harold muttered to Horace. "These Neanderthals out here get really mean when they're angry."

"We just have to hang in and hope nobody believes the insane old fool. I wouldn't," responded Horace. "Remember, Harold, faint heart never won a fat bank account," he continued, displaying far more courage than he really felt.

"You're not just stupid, Trux! You're a fool!" the old miner said.

Much to Thelma's relief and Barney's dismay, he had finally brought the dancing to a halt.

"Them city boys has slicked you and pricked you! You been hosed up the brown box canyon so deep, next time you let go with a fart, it ain't gonna make a sound!"

Both Maynard brothers spun almost in unison toward the Herkimer brothers and began advancing menacingly in their direction. The Century City lawyers weren't quite certain what the next move was to be.

Without warning, a thundering chopping noise in the sky directly above the group stopped all activity. Everyone's eyes turned upward.

A huge, sleek helicopter swooped down, seemingly out of nowhere, very close to the top of the mountain, kicking up huge clouds of dust, rocks and other debris.

"I don't believe it!" Horace said as he and Harold looked up at the overhead flying machine in total disbelief.

"Why would he be here?" whispered Harold, his sweat covered face was totally without color now. The younger of the two big city siblings actually looked like someone witnessing the appearance of a ghost.

"I have no idea, but it's time for us to leave!" responded Horace abruptly. His voice was filled with absolute panic as he and his brother wheeled around. They began slipping and sliding their way up the incline that would, in turn, lead them downward over the side of the mountain.

Barney suddenly forgot the overhead helicopter and cocked his ears toward something directly beyond the fleeing Herkimers. He let out with his famous squeal and charged this newest object of attention.

The pig's shrill squeal pierced through the thundering sound of the craft above. Harold, who had just reached the top of the incline with his brother, and was now standing on the very edge of the mountaintop turned back, reacting to the animals cry. All he could see was the angry looking Barney coming up through the shale right at him.

Harold Herkimer hadn't seen the damage done by the pig back in Darwin while he had been cowering inside that awful thing the called the jail, but he had heard the human cries of pain of the beast's victims. The Century City executive lashed out with his foot, kicking Barney in the stomach, just in front of the animals left rear leg.

Barney received the toe of the man's shoe in his groin just as his jaws clamped down on the head of the rattlesnake that was about to strike the owner of the footwear. The blow knocked the pig sideways onto an unstable piece of the mountaintop outer crest, which immediately gave way.

The dead snake sailed into the air as Farley Maynard's beloved four-legged companion went tumbling end over end, down the side of the landmass.

Barney did not experience the fright he had felt back in the cage at Dirty Socks Lake, as he fell down the mountainside. For some reason, fear seems to travel with hope. When there are no accommodations for the latter, the

295

former often declines the trip. He knew this life was over. He accepted the fact.

His catapulting body picked up momentum as it continued hurtling downward. There was nothing the falling stalwart swine could do except send out final mental missives to those he had loved since he could remember.

"I love you Daddy Farley. Good bye Uncle Trux. I hope they have Blue Ribbon beer and pigs have thumbs in Hog Heaven!"

There was no time for additional messages to either the beautiful lady or her sweet daughter, both of whom he also adored. His body crashed into one of the big boulders several feet away from the front of Old Henderson's parked truck, and then ceased to move.

The beer drinking, reptile repelling, fun loving Barney, as he was known in this world, was no more.

Farley's screams of anguish completely drowned all other sounds including those of the still hovering helicopter, as he raced down the unstable side of the mountain.

The horrified bearded man seemed to ignore the treacherous terrain as he rushed toward the remains of his beloved, four legged, cherished comrade. He fell, rose to his feet, ran forward, then fell again.

This process was repeated many times as he continued downward. His clothing was torn and blood oozed from his elbows, knees and fingers. Tears flowed freely from his eyes, soaking the strands of hair in his thick beard. He could no longer see, but Farley charged on blindly, still screaming.

On top of the mountain, it seemed inevitable that Harold Herkimer was destined for an immediate journey to his own Heaven or Hell. He struggled helplessly as Trux, his big hands gripping the floundering lawyer's armpits, pushed him up the shale incline toward the top of the precipice.

Horace balanced his pudgy body on the unstable silt footing, only a few feet away from the action. He look quite helpless. The father of the frog fixated Beverly Hills Princess seemed to be more concerned with the deafening sound of the helicopter still hovering overhead, than the fate of his sibling and business associate.

Just before Harold went over the edge, Thelma made her way up the slippery incline. She placed her hand on the angry Trux's broad shoulder.

"Farley needs you, Trux," was all the beautiful woman said. She spoke just loud enough to be heard over the noise from the aircraft above.

Trux paused in his efforts to push the other man to his death and looked down the mountainside past his intended victim. His brother could be seen far below, staggering toward the body of the pig.

The man with the square jaw set in an angry line, heaved a deep sigh and pulled Harold Herkimer back to safety. He tossed the whimpering man onto the shale and reached out for the Argus Queen.

Taking the beautiful lady's hand, and treating her with surprising gentleness, he helped her over the ledge. Together, they began making their way down the mountainside.

There was a lump in the big red neck's throat and tears stung his eyes.

He blamed it on the dust and grime being kicked up by that damned helicopter that had no business being up there in the first place. A macho stud like Trux Maynard would never cry over something so stupid as the death of a pig.

After making sure Trux and Thelma were well on their way, the Herkimers followed.

Finding himself to be the only one remaining on the mountain top, Old Henderson squinted up at the chopper that was now swooping away, out over the desert. His ancient eyes held a very strange look as he began unbuttoning his fly, taking advantage of the moment of privacy to relieve his bladder and think about things.

The sun was still above the far western horizon but no longer visible at the base of the mountain as Trux and Thelma finally completed their decent.

Farley was no longer weeping, but groaning and straining as he tried to lift the carcass of the deceased pig off the boulder. Trux and the lady moved forward to assist him.

The helicopter could be seen in the near distance. The large craft was creating new tumultuous upward outbursts of sand and other natural elements as it prepared to touch down in an area still exposed to the rays of the disappearing fiery planet.

At the base of the mountain, Horace and Harold Herkimer peeked out from behind one of the other boulders at the Maynard brothers and the lady, who were gently placing Barney's body on the ground. The remaining blood on the boulder where the unfortunate animal had originally landed shimmered with a subdued luster beneath the shadow of the old mountain.

Horace then looked at the helicopter. The sight of the landing machine obviously created more fear within the two city men than did even the Maynards.

"We've got to get out of here," Horace whispered to his trembling brother.

"How?" whimpered Harold. "This is all your fault, Horace. If we don't get killed, we're going to end up in prison, and it's all your fault!"

"Oh, shut up, Harold!" Horace whispered back as he looked around. The Century City attorney's eye landed on Old Henderson's truck still parked only a few feet away from where he and the other Herkimer were hiding. Horace jabbed his brother in the ribs and pointed to the vehicle. Using his hands, he pantomimed that they should make their way to the old transportation machine.

Harold, still shaking, nodded that he understood and followed the other man as he darted forth in the indicated direction.

None of the group gathered around the body of their departed friend with their heads bowed, even looked up as the Herkimers reached the old truck and climbed into it.

Inside the cab of the old rig, Horace who now sat behind the steering wheel, heaved a deep sigh of relief as he saw that the old mining engineer had left the keys in the ignition. He looked through the windshield first at the Maynards and the lady, then in the other direction at the helicopter that was now on the ground with its portal in the process of opening. He turned the key, hit the starter and the old engine sputtered to life.

Trux and Thelma both looked up as the truck backed up then turned around and sped away.

Farley, his attention totally on Barney's body, didn't seem to notice. If he had, it is doubtful he would have cared.

The truck was bouncing over the bumps in the desert road when its occupants suddenly realized that the noise of the whirling helicopter blades had diminished only to be replaced by the loud wail of a siren.

Horace gripped the steering wheel of the old rig and stared out through the windshield in disbelief at the sedan of the sheriff of Lone Pine coming directly at the truck he was driving.

The youthful face of Rodney Van Aukin could be seen through the windshield of the oncoming law enforcement vehicle. The sheriff himself had his rear end perched on the open window frame of the passenger door. Arty Dubs' legs and feet were still inside the car, but the rest of his torso was outside. He held the ever present Magnum in both hands as he aimed at the front tire of Old Henderson's truck.

"Okay punks! You just made my day!" whispered the lawman as he looked down the sights of the big pistol.

The fact that no one else could hear him didn't seem to bother Arty. He heard those reverent words, and somehow he felt Clint, wherever his hero might be at this moment, could hear him too.

The thunderous sound of the Magnum being discharged mingled with that of the screaming siren as the right front tire on the old truck exploded.

The vintage vehicle swerved and ran off the road. Its front bumper dug into a huge sand dune before it came to a complete stop.

Back on the road, Rodney brought the sheriff's sedan to a smooth halt and Arty nimbly leapt out of the remainder of the passenger window frame. Magnum still in hand, the sheriff of Lone Pine started sprinting toward the stalled old truck. Rodney quickly exited the driver's side of the official vehicle and followed.

At the base of the mountain, Trux and Thelma having left Farley's side, were standing a few feet away from the anguished man and his departed friend watching the activity. Old Henderson, now down from the top of the venerable volcano, was with them.

In the distance two other individuals were visible. One was a tall gray haired, extremely dignified looking gentleman. He wore dark glasses and held a white cane out in front of him. Beside him walked a handsome young black man as they advanced in the direction of the trio and the deceased animal.

Both newcomers, obviously previous passengers of the now stationary helicopter behind them, were impeccably dressed in very expensive looking suits. The black man seemed bothered by the setting sun in his eyes as the two walked toward the shade of the mountain. The gray haired man wearing the dark glasses and carrying the cane, appeared not to share in his companions discomfort as the pair, looking totally out of their element, continued onward toward the shade and the tragic scene beneath it.

At the recent crash site, several yards away, the Herkimer brothers were running away from the old truck, now minus one front tire, in different directions.

Rodney raced after Horace while Arty hobbled in his cowboy boots over the desert stones and other obstacles behind Harold.

The Magnum in the sheriff's hand went off accidentally and discharged harmlessly into the air. The report of the gunshot echoing out over the vast countryside didn't sound harmless to Harold. He skidded to an abrupt halt and lifted both hands high toward the brilliant panorama of the sunset lighting of the Owens Valley sky.

He only wished he knew the law better. He'd been so lazy throughout the years and left everything to Horace. There were so many archaic laws in the state statutes. Try as he might, Harold could not remember if killing somebody else's pig in California was a capital offense.

It had been an accident. Surely, if such a bizarre law did exist, he could plea the charge down to involuntary swine slaughter. A wet spot appeared and began to spread on the lower portion of the crotch of the apprehended fugitive's golfing trousers.

Horace Herkimer had never been plagued with an Honesty Monster. If he had, at that moment, he would be wishing he'd spent more time on the rowing machine, and less mixing martinis. The would be land grabber from Century City had never experienced a problem being dishonest with anyone, including himself.

There was only one person to blame for the situation he was in. Rodney Van Aukin! The very same young man whose breath he could now feel on the back of his neck was responsible. The wimp had done everything wrong.

Horace turned his head to look at his pursuer as he continued desperately trying to escape. Van Aukin was a fraud. Rodney had represented himself as a stupid little New Englander with no backbone and a skin condition. He may have come from New England, but the rest did not at all describe the healthy looking, tan faced, determined young man gaining on him.

The out of shape attorney decided, as he stumbled forward attempting to keep his legs and lungs pumping, that he must be the victim of some sort of supernatural, diabolic scheme. Some one or some evil thing had perpetrated a switch in Horace's perfect patsy.

These fleeting self indulgent thoughts came to a sudden end as Rodney leapt forward and brought his ex future father in law and superior to his knees with a spectacular tackle.

A variety of sand, minerals and tiny insects were scooped up into the open mouth of Horace Herkimer when his expensive dental work plowed into the desert floor. As he attempted to spit out the debris, at least fifty percent of the heretofore-mentioned dental work came with it.

Horace now practically toothless, was still spitting as Rodney drug his prisoner back to the road where Arty was waiting with Harold.

"Horace and Harold Herkimer," said the Sheriff, "You're both under arrest for attempt to commit felonious fraud and a bunch of other things we'll get into later when I get you back to Lone Pine behind bars."

Arty pulled a piece of paper from the pocket of his uniform shirt and proceeded to read the pair of unsightly captured fugitives their rights.

Horace who had developed a definite speech impediment from his header into the desert sands, interrupted him.

"You can't awest us! Dis iwent your jewesditun. You hab no atowaty in dis Cowntee."

Rodney retained a firm hold on the man whom at one time he had thought was to be his father in law as he and the sheriff exchanged knowing glances.

Arty reached into his pocket and withdrew yet another piece of paper. He smugly flashed it in front of the face of the protesting man with the desecrated oral cavity.

"Read it and weep Mr. Hot Shot Know It All," said the bucked toothed smiling lawman. "This here's a document signed by the sheriff of this County. Gives me total…"

Arty's eyes darted in Rodney's direction.

"Sanction," prompted the young man.

"Yeah! Sanction!" repeated the sheriff of Lone Pine. "Gives me sang-chunn to cross the line, arrest you two and haul you back to my own slammer. Sheriff Eggelthorp faxed it to me 'fore we ever left Lone Pine. You don't think I'd come all the way out here for you scum bags if I wasn't all legal do you?"

Arty not only had trouble with the word 'Sanction', he wasn't exactly sure what anything else in the paper really said. He did know he was on firm footing. Rodney had handled the whole thing. The sheriff was glad he'd let Arthell talk him into listening to the young man. The kid was about half smart.

"What does this mean, Horace?" the frightened Harold asked his brother.

Horace looked at the faxed document. He spit again as his pudgy shoulders began to droop as he brought a hand up to cover his injured mouth.

"It mean weaw scewed Hawod," he responded despondently.

The duly elected legal Lone Pine law enforcement officer completed his 'Reading of the rights' ritual and Horace and Harold were officially placed under arrest.

The gentlemen from the helicopter had already joined the others as Arty and Rodney proudly propelled their prisoners up to the base of the mountain.

The triumphant expressions on the faces of both the young man from Boston and the Lone Pine sheriff faded when they saw Farley in the background kneeling over the lifeless body of poor Barney.

Arty immediately removed his hat and placed it reverently over his heart. An awkward silence followed. The vacuous moment came to an end by the well-dressed newcomer with the dark glasses and the white cane. He spoke in an inquisitive cultured voice to his African American companion.

"Were they apprehended, Mr. Herkimer?"

Both Trux and Thelma did a double take when it was the black man, who answered, and not Harold or Horace.

"Absolutely, Mr. Herkimer!" the black man said to the older gentleman beside him before addressing Arty.

"Good shooting, sheriff!"

"Half the credit goes to Rodney here," responded the lawman. "He's one hell of a wheel man."

"Thanks Dad," said Rodney, whose attention was still riveted in disbelief on the grieving Farley and the remains of the bearded Maynard brother's friend.

Thelma gave both the young man and the sheriff a very strange look as she sidled up to Arty and murmured in the lawman's ear.

"You told?"

"I figured it was time," was Arty's response as he went about the task of handcuffing both his now extremely subdued prisoners.

"Does she know?" asked Thelma, still whispering.

"Like I said, it was time," answered Arty, before flashing his buckteeth at the miserable Horace, who now had next to none.

"You will let me know if them's too tight? I wanna' watch you suffer," said the sheriff as he completed shackling the man's hands behind his back. The lawman then moved to his other prisoner to repeat the procedure.

"Mr. Herkimer, we can explain," said Harold, sounding pathetic as he spoke to the new arrival wearing the dark glasses.

"Shut up, Hawod!" snapped Horace. It was also obvious that the very act of forming words was causing him pain. "The bwind old bassard won't wissen."

The dignified gray haired man turned to the black man beside him.

"Strange, that sounds somewhat like Horace, but…."

"It's Horace alright," the black man spoke up before his sightless companion could finish, as he looked at the suffering Horace. The latter's condition was obviously rendering him much delight.

"He's just had most of those phony teeth he's always flashing, knocked out. Looks good on him."

"Dear me," responded the blind man with a wistful smile, "I'd like to see that. Of course, I'd like to see almost anything. Who's responsible?"

"I'm afraid I am, Mr. Herkimer," confessed Rodney. "He was running away and I…"

"Who's that?" The gray haired man asked his African American traveling companion.

"Van Aukin, Mr. Herkimer," said the other.

The blind gentleman smiled again.

"Van Aukin, I'm sorry we've never met sir. You seem to be the hero of the day."

Before Rodney could respond, Harold spoke up again.

"Mr. Herkimer, it was all Horace's fault…"

"Horace was right about one thing, Harold," the gray haired man wearing the sunglasses interjected before the other could continue his whining. He obviously did recognize the voice of the man responsible for Barney's demise. "The bwind old bassard won't wissen. This 'bwind old bassard's heard enough. Are the Maynard bothers present?" He tapped the ground if front of him with the cane, while moving forward.

Trux looked at the man, realizing from the conversation the other could not look back.

"I'm Trux Maynard. What can I do for you?"

"Allow me to introduce myself," the blind man responded, turning in the direction of Trux's voice.

"I'm Christopher Herkimer. Head of the law firm, Herkimer, Herkimer, Herkimer, Herkimer. This is my nephew, W. P. Herkimer, better known as

Willis," he continued after indicating the handsome black young man at his side, who was now, in reality, slightly behind him

"Hopefully Willis and I arrived in time to keep you and your brother from being swindled."

"Their ain't a man alive smart enough to swindle a Maynard, buddy," Trux shot back, defensively.

"Shit!" Thelma muttered beneath her breath.

If the man who had just introduced himself as Christopher Herkimer heard Thelma's comment, he chose to ignore it.

"I'm relieved to hear that," he said in a very earnest tone. "I was concerned about the firm's reputation. While Willis and I were returning from the east coast, we received some very disturbing news from Mr. Van Aukin, here."

The head of the Century City law firm pointed the cane as he referred to Rodney in a direction the young man was not, then continued.

"It seems my other two partners whom I understand the sheriff and Mr. Van Aukin just prevented from escaping, and are now present, were up to no good. Would you explain it Willis? You're so much more articulate than I."

The other man in the expensive suit gave the two men now in handcuffs, a disgusted look. He did however, indulge himself in a gleeful grin as his eyes lingered momentarily on Horace's mouth. Quickly he recovered and began honoring his senior partner's request.

"Glad to Chris."

The black man then began addressing Trux and the others who had no idea what was going on. "Our firm was retained without the knowledge of either Chris or myself, by a well known contracting company who has been awarded the paving contract for a new highway that's going through this area. The assignment was to purchase your land for its valuable resources."

"Our partners here," Willis continued, using a very sarcastic voice as he uttered the three words, "were planning on buying it from you in their own names for next to nothing. Then they would resell it to the contracting company for the money they had been authorized to offer you in the first place. Of course, being the miserable miscreants they are, they were going to pocket the difference after making this transition, using our firms assets. Good old Horace and Harold, here were not only planning to swindle you Mr. Maynard, but us as well."

"And that really pisses us off," said the blind man.

"Well put, Chris," affirmed the black man giving Arty's prisoners a scathing glare.

Fortunately, Horace's head was now turned away and his lips were firmly pressed together hiding his ruined dental work so the attorney better known as Willis, didn't have to restrain a giggle to maintain his dignity.

Christopher Herkimer gave a nod of appreciation in no particular direction.

"Thank you Willis," he said, before jerking his well-quaffed head toward where he assumed Arty to be standing, but was not.

"Please take them to jail, Sheriff! They are both guilty of fraud and I will personally press charges."

Farley rose from where he had been kneeling beside Barney's body and moved to his brother's side.

"Trux, Can't you get these people outa' here?" he said in a low pleading tone. "I just wanna' be alone with Barney."

Trux nodded and addressed the others in a loud voice. "I don't really know what's goin' on here, but I'm gonna' have to ask everbody to leave."

The black Herkimer whispered to the blind Herkimer who spoke up immediately.

"I apologize. I didn't realize the circumstances," he said, showing genuine concern. "Perhaps we can talk business at a more convenient time."

Without another word the blind man and his companion turned and began walking back toward the waiting helicopter. The sun was down now and daylight was fading rapidly.

Arty spoke to Old Henderson who had been lurking in the shadows all through the previous conversation.

"Sorry about your tire, Old Henderson," said the lawman, "You don't mind ridin' in back with my prisoners for a spell, I'll give you a lift back to Darwin, 'fore I haul em' on into Lone Pine. You can fill out a reimbursement voucher for the tire on the way."

In spite of the awful mess he was in, Harold Herkimer heaved a sigh of relief. At least he wasn't going to be thrown into that awful Darwin monstrosity again.

"Preciate it Sheriff," Old Henderson said to Arty. "Gimme' just a minute here."

He turned to Trux as he dug into a pocket.

"Stupid of me to leave my keys in the truck. Getting' awful long in the tooth. Least I ain't so old I forgot this. You n' Farley probably need it more n' I do right now."

Trux accepted the full pint of whiskey the aging mining engineer handed him.

Rodney moved up behind Farley, who was once again kneeling beside Barney's body.

"I don't know what to say, Farley," said the young man, as tears matching those of the bearded man's, welled up in his eyes. Farley was too overcome with grief to respond.

"Then don't say nothin' punk!" Trux lashed out. The big red neck shoved the bottle into his own hip pocket as he moved in between the younger man and his brother.

"I don't know how you got your little ass outa' jail, but you'd best stay away from my daughter!"

Thelma walked to Rodney's side and looked Trux squarely in the eye.

"She's not your daughter, Trux!" said the Argus Queen in a tone of finality.

"So? She's Farley's then! Same thing!"

Rodney, sensing an upcoming altercation, maneuvered his way astern to join Arty who was now standing between his prisoners. The sheriff had a knowing smile on his face as he watched the exchange he felt was long overdue between the beautiful woman and the smartass with the big chin.

"Didn't you ever wonder about her name, Trux?" Thelma said forcefully. "Before you answer, think about it, Trux. Think about it hard!"

Trux just stood there. He had no idea what the woman both he and his brother were in love with, was talking about, but he felt certain she was about to tell him. He also had a sinking feeling he wasn't going to like it.

"What's my name, Trux?" she asked.

"Damnit, Thelma!" Trux retorted, indicating Farley with jerk of his head. "This ain't no time to play games."

"What's my name Trux?" asked Arty from his position between the two handcuffed Herkimer brothers who had no idea what was going on and were so preoccupied with their own troubles, they didn't care.

"You stay out of this Arty!" snapped Trux.

Suddenly a light could be seen in his blue eyes, in spite of the increasing darkness. 'Arty'…'Thelma'… 'Arthell'! He looked at Thelma in disbelief.

"You mean you and the asshole…?"

"In the future, you'd probably better come up with something less derogatory when describing my daughter's father," responded Thelma.

"It was just easier this way. Arty was just starting in politics. I was in love with you and Farley as I still am, and I didn't want to disappoint either one of you," she went on, attempting to be gentle as she furnished the facts.

"That's the way the old ball bounces," Arty called over his shoulder as Rodney helped him shove the Herkimers in the direction of the waiting patrol car. "She's my kid. Sorry about Barney, Farley. I mean that!"

Thelma gave both Maynard brothers one last look before turning to follow the others. Henderson stepped up to Farley and put his hand on the now sobbing, kneeling man's shoulder.

"Far as pigs go, he was my favorite," said the old man before he too headed off into the twilight and his ride back to Darwin.

Trux just stood there with a totally stunned look on his face. After a long moment, Farley rose and put his hand on his brother's broad shoulder.

"Ain't been one of our better days, has it Trux?"

The brothers embraced. Mercifully, the descending darkness and the fact that the moon had yet to rise hid the tears and the action of both from the rest of the world.

Everyone knows real men seldom cry, they don't hug, and they never need each other.

CHAPTER TWENTY THREE
NEGATIVE RITUAL WITH A POSITIVE TWIST

The sunrise was breathtaking.

Trux sat next to the remnants of the small fire he had built during the night to keep himself and his brother warm. The desert can get cold during the wee hours of the morning no matter how hot the preceding, or the following day.

The broad shouldered man with the pronounced jaw held the nearly empty pint bottle given to him by Old Henderson the previous evening. There was only little more than a healthy swallow remaining.

He decided to wait and give it to Farley when the bearded man finished decorating the grave with whatever wild desert flowers he had been able to scrounge in the vicinity. The mound of earth, under which the unforgettable pig was buried, lay against the foot of the mountain that only yesterday had been declared so valuable. Trux and Farley had dug and covered Barney's final resting-place with their bare hands. Now the latter was giving it final touches.

Farley's eyes were dry this morning, but his face was still quite somber. After he had placed the last piece of pathetic desert vegetation on the grave, he turned to Trux and accepted the bottle his brother now held out to him.

As the bearded man tipped the nearly empty glass container up to his lips, Trux saw something off in the distance and rose to his feet. A vehicle could be seen coming toward the mountain from the direction of Lone Pine. Trux studied it. Probably tourists, he thought to himself. Too early for any native to be out here in the middle of nowhere.

The car approached the intersection where the non-paved road split into several others including the beginning of Old Henderson's shortcut to Darwin. The ancient engineer's inoperative truck was still just beyond the forks, hood first in the sand dune.

Trux assumed the approaching vehicle would take one of the paths offered and be out of sight in a short time. The automobile, however, pulled to halt not far from the base of the landmass where Farley and he were standing in front of the grave.

"I'll get rid of em," Trux said, as he started forward. Suddenly, he stopped.

Beyond the parking car, long lines of other vehicles of various shapes, sizes and models were approaching on every road.

"Looks like the whole valley's comin," said Farley in wonder, after he drained the whiskey bottle.

"I'll be damned! There's the HOWDY HOSS!"

The cars kept on coming and people they'd known, some of whom that hadn't spoke to either of the brothers in years, began to disembark. The arms of most were loaded down with bouquets and various other types of pretty floral arrangements.

The motor home pulled up and parked off the side of the road nearest to where the Maynard brothers stood. Thelma, in the black dress she wore the day she and Rodney executed their plan, exited the old rig and walked forward. She carried a large, beautifully crafted, evergreen funeral wreath in her hands. The others followed her.

All were silent and respectful as they filed past the absolutely baffled Trux and Farley to pay their final respects to Barney and place the flowers on his grave.

On the road, Arty's patrol car could be seen pulling to a halt near the far end of what now looked like a huge shopping mall parking lot. Rodney, Arthell and the sheriff himself all dressed in their finest, climbed out of the official vehicle and headed for the grave at the base of the mountain to join the others. Arthell carried the pooper scooper from the Lone Pine jail.

Somebody had to remain behind to mind the store, so Jiggs had not been able to attend this final farewell. However, the red headed deputy had asked the beautiful girl he now understood to be Arty's daughter and not the Maynards', to say a prayer for him and bring along this token of remembrance.

More automobiles kept arriving, including an early model rattling station wagon from the Darwin direction. Its doors opened and Jake, Bobcat, Henry and the gaunt faced miner who had driven the tractor pulling the jail, all piled out.

Old Henderson climbed free of the rear seat of the same vehicle behind the rest, moving much slower. He wore a large, apparently stuffed, back pack. The senior citizen refused offered assistance from the other Darwinians. Instead, he sent them on their way to join the rest of those headed toward the base of the landmass and the grave. Once left to his own bidding, the old timer reached back into the station wagon and pulled out a tire already mounted on a wheel. He balanced the tire upright on the surface of the road, and wearing the heavy pack on his back, rolled the circular object off the road. He continued onward, pushing it across the sand to his truck.

After depositing the backpack in the cab of his old nonfunctional vehicle and the tire in the back, he returned to join the long procession heading toward the grave.

Old Henderson fell in behind the newly arrived Geraldine, Jeannie an Irene. All had flowers in their possession. With almost clinical interest, the aging man of the Owens Valley studied the very different types of feminine human derrieres in action as he plodded along. With the exception of the Argus Queen and a few others he'd seen during his long tenure on earth, the female posteriors over thirty sure as Hell held up better on Zorka.

In the near distance, a long limousine that must have been rented in Bishop could be seen coming to a stop. Christopher Herkimer and W. P. Herkimer, better known as Willis, were ushered out of the rear of the luxury machine by a uniformed chauffeur.

Both well-dressed executives moved on foot up the road between the multitude of parked vehicles. The other oncoming walking citizens of the Owens Valley parted with courtesy, as the handsome, sophisticated dark skinned executive and his blind companion with the white cane, moved toward the mountain.

Finally, after the cars stopped coming, all the people gathered in a deep semi circle around the place of the revered pig's burial. Mounds of flowers were piled high upon the final resting-place. The pooper scooper rested on the very apex of the colorful, floral display.

Thelma stood between her two red neck lovers, Trux and Farley. She clutched an arm of each, as everyone bowed his or her head in final, respectful farewell.

Arthell stood at graveside between Arty and Rodney. So much had happened to the sweet young girl in the last few days. She had not only discovered love; she had learned so many other things about herself. And now, when she should be happier than she had ever been, Barney, whom she had loved almost as much as Farley did, was gone. He had always brought sunshine whenever he showed up. It was so hard to believe she would never see the frolicking pig again.

Suddenly, through her tears, she saw the early morning sun falling over the heads of the mourners behind her onto the flowers; the sight was breathtakingly beautiful. The beloved Angel of the Owens Valley, realized, at that moment, Barney's sunshine would always be with those who knew and loved him forever. She started to sing in a clear, sweet, almost flawless voice, softly at first, then rising in volume.

"You were our sunshine. Our special sunshine.

You made us happy, when skies were gray.

I'm sure you know dear, how much we miss you.

Your special sunshine will never go away."

Farley began singing along with the girl whom he had always thought of as his daughter. He was definitely way off key, but the feeling in his voice was heartfelt and sincere. He sounded a little better when Thelma joined in, followed by Trux.

Soon everybody was musically vocalizing Arthell's paraphrased tribute to the departed pig, except Old Henderson. The white haired man, however, did mouth the words silently, as the singing filled the desert morning. It was indeed a special moment for a very special friend, none would soon forget.

As the singing came to and end, another replaced the voices. This one deep and booming. It came from the road behind the saddened group of people.

"Attention all ye who have gathered here today to pay tribute to the creature of the cloven hoof! You will all burn in the fires of everlasting Hell!"

All those around the grave, turned to see Brother Roy Ogles. The man of extra large cloth was standing up in the front of a small open topped Jeep parked in the middle of the road between the sizable assemblage of parked automobiles. The pastor of The Devotion To Divinity Church of Lone Pine, wore his large lavender robes. He ranted and raved, while shaking his huge fists indignantly at the group of mourners.

"The fires will be so hot, you will beg for one drop of water on your tongue, but no one will hear you! He will not listen to the pleading of sinners who have committed such an atrocity, and neither shall I, His special messenger! You are doomed! You must all hang your heads in shame!"

The look on the faces of those near the grave registered not shame, but building anger. Trux doubled up his fists and started forward. Thelma pulled him back as Brother Roy continued his sermon of condemnation from the front of the small jeep. The crowd, some of them parishioners of Brother Roy's church, began to mumble.

The vehicle had been the property of the late husband of the same misguided widow who had delivered the reverend his pants in jail after Barney had given the pastor his well-deserved ass chewing. Unfortunately, the poor lady was one of the many on this earth who fear God instead of loving Him. She knew not what she had done, by loaning Ogles the jeep.

"God will punish you for all for this idolatry! The Lord has said that the beast of the field…"

Brother Roy's speech was interrupted when a small stone struck the left temple of his fat face. He glared at the people to whom he was preaching and tried to continue.

"That man and God have dominion! He said that the building of altars for the cloven hoof will bring down fire and brimstone and that…"

A much bigger stone, undoubtedly large enough to qualify as a rock, hit him this time, right between the eyes.

"That creature should go on a BBQ, not desecrate God's green earth…."

The reverend began choking as a whole shower of rocks pelted his enormous robe clad body. One, extremely well aimed, entered his big, wide-open mouth.

The graveside mumbles became a mighty roar and the crowd an angry mob, as the majority of the people present thundered toward him.

Trux, Thelma, Farley and Old Henderson were not among those that stormed the jeep and pulled the obese intruder from his perch and began pounding on his rotund form. Neither were Rodney, Arty, Arthell, or the blind and black Herkimers, but they all seemed to enjoy the show.

Christopher especially seemed to be getting a big kick out of W. P. Herkimer's, blow by blow narrative of events.

On the road, Brother Roy somehow managed to cough up the stone from his throat and break away from those attacking him long enough to climb back into the Jeep. He started the engine and drove away amid a shower of more stones and rocks.

As Brother Roy sped away, the members of the funeral party whom he had escaped ran to their respective vehicles and scrambled into them. After a few moments of mass traffic jam, they all headed out after the fleeing fleshy robed figure in the undersized off road military inspired runabout.

In front of the grave, Farley suddenly cocked his ear toward the pile of flowers. After a second or two he nudged Trux who was standing next to him, yelling obscenities after the departed Ogles.

"Trux!" he said. "Listen up!"

"To what?" snapped Trux. He was more than a little put out that neither Thelma or his brother had let him join the mob.

"To that!" replied Farley displaying the closest thing to a smile that had appeared of his face since Barney's terrible accident. He pointed to beneath the ground below the mound of flora.

"Just listen!"

Trux heaved a deep, tolerant sigh and turned toward the grave. Slowly, as the rough and ready red neck listened, his wide grin began to spread.

"I'll be damned!" he said, as more and more teeth continued to be exposed to the sunlight. "Sounds like Barney's laughin'."

"Man, I'm sure as hell glad you hear it too!" Farley giggled.

"He is. He's laughin'! Barney's by God laughin'!"

"I hear im," said Old Henderson. The spot where years ago, the Senorita had knocked the tooth from his mouth was displayed as he also began to chortle.

"Can't blame im'! It was purty damned funny! I brung along some beer in my backpack. Even stole one of Darleen's fancy new fangled contraptions that keeps it cold," the old man added. "Should I fetch it?"

311

"Barney'd like that a whole lot, Old Henderson!" Farley answered, between huge guffaws. "Bring er' on!"

By this time, Thelma, Arthell and Rodney had joined in. Arty tried to keep a good Clint Eastwood stone face, but failed miserably as he too doubled over in mirth.

W. P. and Christopher Herkimer were standing a few feet away as Old Henderson crossed in front of them on the way to his truck. The dignified pair of civil rights defenders didn't exactly know what was going on, but they smiled.

"I'm glad everyone's in a better mood," the blind white man said to the black man. "I love the sound of laughter."

"So do I, Chris," the man better known as Willis responded.

"Excuse me, Willis," said the gray haired man, "I know this is quite rude, but doesn't one of them sound exactly like a pig laughing?"

Somewhere in the middle of the uninhabited desert, Brother Roy Ogles was not laughing.

The enormous evader of local wrath had finally taken advantage of the jeep's off road abilities to lose the long line of vehicles chasing him. Satisfied that those who seemed intent on dismembering his enormous body, were no longer behind him, he pulled the little topless machine to a halt next to a lonely Yuka tree. Still inside the front of the vehicle, the titanic Bible thumper struggled with his oversized girth until he stood upright.

His usually flowing robes were saturated, not only with perspiration, but blood. The moist red liquid had soaked through the reams of material covering his gargantuan gluteus maximus. The stitches had broken loose in that area of vast proportions, recently ravaged by the tusks of the creature of the cloven hoof. He looked up into the blue, sunlit sky and shouted to the Heavens.

"How could You let this happen?" the Pastor asked the Lord.

"You don't love me!" He was no longer questioning God. He was now accusing Him. Brother Roy's voice, still thundering, took on the tone of a suffering, self-indulgent petulant child.

"You've never loved me! You don't appreciate any of the many deeds I've accomplished in Your name! You don't believe in me!"

Suddenly, some sort of bird emitted a somewhat universally familiar, obnoxious sound as it flew directly overhead. The anguished huge man standing in the small Jeep looked up as a huge mass of something slimy splattered all over his fleshy facial features.

The airborne culprit who had just seen fit to use the man of the cloth's physiognomy for its toilet was probably a buzzard. However, to Brother Roy, as he attempted to watch its departure through the disgusting smelly gooey substance, the feathered creature fluttering away through the desert sky looked very much like a dove.

The fat boy from Bugtussle was, once again, all alone with bird shit smeared all over his face.

Several miles away, in the near vicinity of Maynard's mountain, Trux, Farley and their dear departed friend who had caused the defiled reverend so much distress, were not yet alone. The crowd of mourners, however, had definitely diminished. Among those no longer present were the honorable Herkimers, as opposed to their horrendous partners with the same surnames. They had since climbed into their limo and departed.

The desert crossroads were void of vehicles again except for the police sedan, the HOWDY HOSS and Old Henderson's truck. The latter, mounted on all four tires once more, was driving away. Strangely enough, instead of heading back toward Darwin, the aging mineral expert was traveling in the direction of Lone Pine.

Trux, Farley, the Argus Queen, her daughter, Rodney and Sheriff Arty Dubs stood at the forks of the unpaved wide paths watching the miner of many decades depart. They had all pitched in to help put the tire in place before sending him on his way.

Old Henderson had climbed the mountain alone one more time after the mass exodus of the others in pursuit of Brother Roy. The Maynards, especially Farley, might have objected, but the old man had been generous enough to share the portable ice chest of cold beer in his backpack. It would have been rude not to grant the senior citizen one last visit to the top of the landmass that now served as Barney's tombstone.

He had returned with the backpack filled with other things. He had made a gift of both the thermal container and what was left of the beer to the remaining mourners. Once the tire was attached to his truck, he had driven away.

Now all, except Arty, held a can of cold beer in their hands. Rodney had decided that a drink now and then was no longer quite so dangerous now that he had finally become acquainted with a young man named Rodney Van Aukin.

"Nice of him to show up. Wonder why he ain't headin' home?" pondered Farley, referring to the departing old man.

"You can ask that after knowin' that mean assed daughter of his all these years?" sneered Trux. "Beats me why the poor old peckerhead ever goes home at all."

"I wonder what he brought down from the mountain in that his back pack?" mused Thelma.

"Who gives a shit?" was Trux's intelligent response.

"Just be glad he didn't no have no more room for the beer. Nice of im' to bring it along in the first place though. Crazy old fucker, but he's got a good heart and he sure knows his shit," Trux further observed, as he dug into the still partially full cooler left behind by the senior citizen they were discussing, for another cold one.

"Fine line between crazy and crafty, Trux," commented Thelma, as she handed her empty beer can to the red neck with the big chin after declining another.

Rodney also refused a fresh beverage as he handed his depleted container to Trux. The young attorney then turned to Farley and held out his right hand.

"I really loved Barney, and I think you two guys are maybe the greatest and most real human beings I've ever met."

Farley accepted the young man's gesture of genuine friendship and shook the offered hand. Trux did the same as Rodney turned back to him. Now that he knew Arthell was not his or his brother's daughter, he understood the young man's interest in the pretty girl and accepted it with no reservations. Damned fine young man this Van Aukin. Arthell was lucky to land him. It was just a shame, such a nice guy was going to end up with Arty Dubs as a father in law.

The younger man continued, "Christopher Herkimer offered me a full partnership in the firm and the position of running the Century City office, but I turned him down. I'm staying in Lone Pine and hanging out my shingle. If you guy's ever need a lawyer...."

"Boy, even if you wasn't marryin' my daughter we'd still be see'n' a bunch of each other, now that you gone and said that!" said the Sheriff, snorting.

Trux shot the lawman a dirty look, but softened as Rodney moved away and the young lady everybody seemed to be either talking about or thinking of at that moment, walked up to face him and his bearded brother.

"You'll always be my Daddy Trux and Daddy Farley," Arthell embraced each one, then took Rodney's arm. The young couple headed off toward the parked patrol car with Arty.

It was Thelma's turn to take the Maynard brothers in her arms. The beautiful woman did so with gusto. When she was finally finished, she leaned back and spoke with words from the bottom of her giving heart to both of them, before handing the motor home keys to Trux.

"And I'll always love you crazy red necks. You're my guys and that's the way it is. Here's the keys to the HOWDY HOSS. Wedding's day after tomorrow. You both better be there. In the meantime, you know my door is always open. You know which door."

She turned away and hurried to join the others. Trux picked up the

314

remainder of the beer and the empty cans in the cooler. He and his brother stood there for a few minutes in silence watching the sheriff's vehicle and its passengers depart for Lone Pine. Finally they started meandering back toward the HOWDY HOSS.

The battered old rig was still parked near the base of the mountain and Barney's grave. Already some of the flowers were blowing away due to a newly arrived, soft desert breeze.

"Gona' miss ole Barney," said Trux as the two looked up at the floating flower petals. "Never be another like him."

"Funny you should say that, Trux." Farley spoke up. "I been thinkin'. You remember George Stubblefield over Ridgecrest way?"

"Hog farmer, with a little place just the other side of the naval base? Usta' have that daughter with a kind of mustache, named Bessie?"

"Daughter's name was Bessie. Mustache didn't have no name as I recall."

"Kiss my crack, smart ass! You know what I meant! Think she married some navy dude and moved away. You talkin' about that George Stubblefield?" asked Trux, finally coming back to the subject of his brother's original question. He already knew what Farley had in mind.

"That's him," responded Farley. "Think maybe we got enough gas for a ride over to Ridgecrest, Trux?"

CHAPTER TWENTY FOUR
DEARLY BELOVED

The baby's name was Barney Junior and he loved his Daddy Farley.

The tiny porker was snuggled up against the bearded man's fat belly inside the suit jacket of the person he was so fond of at this moment. He poked his cute little pink snout out through the opening of the coat, looking up at his Uncle Trux.

Barney Junior wasn't too sure about this Uncle Trux character. The human he already adored had told him the other human with the big chin would take some getting used to, but that he really was a great guy.

The eight-month-old piglet decided to take Daddy Farley's word for it, but he did wish the two would stop arguing.

"I'm takin' him in, and that's that!" said Farley, bringing the wish of the small animal beneath the front of his coat to immediate fruition.

Closing the jacket, yet still holding the little pig carefully, the bearded man with the adamant attitude walked away from Trux who was standing next to the parked motor home on the Lone Pine street.

The old battered utility rig sat about a half a block away from the front of the Lone Pine Devotion to Divinity Church. They had been lucky to find a spot at all.

The parking lot was overflowing and cars lined the streets belonging to folks who had come to attend the wedding of Thelma Houston's lovely daughter.

Trux let Farley proceed as the brothers headed toward the church. The big broad shouldered man didn't want his brother to see the grin that had taken control of his face.

The pig really was a cute little fart. The man with the pronounced jaw was secretly glad Farley had found him. It wouldn't do to let the curly tailed little son of a bitch know that too many people liked him, though.

Farley would spoil him enough. Pigs were like kids. Nothing worse than having one grow up thinking he's king shit!

However, what Trux was really smiling about at the moment, was that they were very close to the spot where Farley had shoved his tongue down Brother Roy's throat, when the reverend had been choking Trux's.

This time, instead of a pint, the Maynard brothers were in possession of a pig. One of the very critters the fat fuck had been yelling about, that had caused the whole fracas.

Trux and Farley were walking up the sidewalk, preparing to enter the church, when the limousine that had delivered the black and blind Herkimers to the funeral, pulled up beside them.

"The Maynards are here, Chris," said W. P. Herkimer, better known as Willis, as he and the gentleman with the dark glasses and the white cane exited the luxury vehicle.

"I have the papers right here," the handsome African American added, as he pulled some documents from beneath his impeccably tailored suit jacket.

"I see them, Willis," replied the dignified gray haired man proving that indeed he did not, by smiling in the wrong direction.

"Mr. Maynard, I presume?" he asked no one at all with a genuine smile.

Trux turned back toward the executives as their limousine drove away. Farley carried the pig beneath his coat on toward the door of the Church.

"Waddya' want?" asked the broad shouldered man brusquely. "We're late for a weddin!"

Christopher Herkimer, realizing his error, now turned in the proper direction.

"We didn't want to bother you before, due to your grief, but we really should get this settled," said the blind man.

"I really do apologize for the actions of my colleagues. I assure you, they are receiving proper punishment."

"Cruel and unusual, I'd say," remarked Willis. The handsome dark skinned man looked ready to burst into laughter.

"But that's just my opinion," he added, recovering quickly.

The man better known as Willis regained his professional face as he attempted to hand the documents to Trux.

"I think you'll find everything here on the up and up. If you and your brother will just sign these, you'll receive one million dollars a year over the next two. Two million, just like our client originally offered."

"Mountain ain't for sale at any price, Mister!" replied Trux, refusing the papers.

"We got a member of our family buried at the bottom of it. That mountain's his tombstone. Thanks anyway."

Trux started to turn away toward his brother who was now waiting at the front door of the church with the pig. Christopher Herkimer, having no idea the co-owner of the mountain was walking away, spoke up.

"I suppose if it's the method of payment that's bothering you, or the full amount...."

The head of the firm of Herkimer, Herkimer, Herkimer Herkimer, was not allowed to finish. Trux wheeled back to face the blind man.

"Mister, I know you can't see shit, and I'm sorry about that, but is somethin' wrong with your hearin' too?" asked the Maynard brother with the bright blue eyes.

"He heard you, Mr. Maynard," said Willis Herkimer, as a light of respect appeared in his own dark eyes. "Chris just isn't sure you're making the most intelligent decision."

Trux looked at both of the executives and spoke slowly, indicating he did not wish to repeat his words again.

"Well," he drawled. "I wouldn't know much about intelligence ' seein' as how I'm just a dumb red neck and all. I do know one thing though. There's always a way a fella' can scheme up money. Ain't no way, even in Hell, to scheme up love! Anybody thinks they can buy real love with money's even dumber'n I am."

Trux turned and swiftly joined Farley at the door of the church.

"You're really gonna' bring that damned pig in there?" he asked his brother.

"I don't wanna' discuss it!" said Farley, flatly as he and Trux disappeared inside the building.

"Strange breed, these red necks," said Christopher Herkimer, after W. P. told him the Maynards were no longer present.

"Let's go inside, Willis."

"Chris, I wouldn't miss this for the world," Willis responded with a wide grin filled with expectations.

Had the African American attorney more teeth, he would have greatly resembled a certain white red neck who had just walked into the church.

He took the blind man's arm, and the pair proceeded toward the door Trux, Farley and Barney Junior had just passed through.

The interior of the church was nearly overflowing but somehow the Maynard brothers had already managed to find seats in one of the far forward pews.

Thelma, looking more ravishing than ever, were that possible, was seated in the very front next to the aisle. She looked back and flashed a brilliant smile to both of the men she loved.

In the rear of the church, W. P. and Christopher Herkimer entered and stopped. As the organ up front continued to play, Willis looked around. He spotted two vacant spots in a pew near the entrance where they stood behind the other already seated people.

However, a tall, rather shabbily dressed man with long black hair flowing down over the back of his shirt stood in the aisle next to one of the pews. Beside him sat another man who looked very much like the first in hairstyle, dress, and skin color.

The two unoccupied places were beyond the second man.

Willis whispered to his sightless companion as he led him to the side of the man not seated.

"It's pretty crowded, but I see at least one seat, Chris. Maybe two. If there's only one, you can have it."

"Nonsense, Willis," replied Christopher Herkimer. "You take it. I don't mind standing up."

"You obviously don't know him," said the man with the long hair who was already standing in the aisle.

"I beg your pardon?" Willis responded to the complete stranger.

"Know who?" asked the blind man. "Or should I say whom?"

"Standing Up," replied the Native American named Sitting Down, who was the man standing.

"You wouldn't catch me sitting next to him. That's why I'm standing up."

"You're standing up?" queried the blind attorney, who of course, had a legitimate reason for asking the question.

"No, he's Sitting Down," the seated Native American spoke up.

"I'm Standing Up. And the reason Sitting Down's standing up, is because he's afraid if he sits down, he won't be able to stand up again. He drinks."

"Talk about the pot calling the kettle black," retorted Sitting Down from his standing position.

"I resemble that remark," said Willis, getting into the game.

"Damned if you don't," said the seated red man, seeming to notice for the first time, that the well dressed man in the aisle next to the standing Sitting Down and the well dressed white man was a black man.

"I'm confused," complained Christopher Herkimer. "Who is standing up and who is sitting down?"

"It's too complicated," replied Standing Up from his sitting down position. "Would you guys like a seat?"

"We'd love one. Two if the other's not taken," said Willis, trying not to ruin his image by giggling.

Standing Up stood and allowed them access to the spots beyond him. "Move it on in," he said. "Sitting Down ain't gonna' sit down."

The blind man started to speak again. Willis stopped him.

"Believe me Chris, just plant your ass. I've got a feeling it's better we don't know. Even if I'm wrong, I don't want to miss the show while we find out."

Up front, the organ playing finally came to an end. A clean-cut young man wearing clerical collar and robes entered from behind the chancel and approached the pulpit. He cleared his throat politely and began speaking to the crowd seated in front and below him.

"Before we begin this blessed event, I'd like to introduce myself. I am the

Reverend Roger Galloway; you're new pastor. I'd like you all to join me now in a short prayer for your former pastor, the Reverend Brother Roy Ogles, wishing him strength in his new position as assistant to the assistant pastor's assistant in his new church in Bear Wallow, Kentucky. I know God will watch over him."

The newly appointed shepherd of the Devotion to Divinity flock began to reverently bow his head. At the same time, all the citizens of the Owens Valley, including those who were members of this particular church, broke into wild applause, whistles and catcalls.

"Amen!" Reverend Galloway said quickly. He cleared his throat again and went straight to the business at hand when the hooting and hollering finally died down.

"Dearly beloved, we are gathered here together in the sight of God to join these six people in Holy matrimony."

"Six?" Muttered Trux to Farley from where they were seated in the audience. "What's this six shit?"

The organist resumed her playing and all eyes turned toward the rear of the spacious religious enclosure.

Rodney, wearing jeans, a pearl snap-buttoned shirt and a bolo tie beneath a western style jacket, had never looked more handsome or sure of himself. Jiggs walked by his side.

The redheaded deputy, the young man from Boston had chosen for his best man, also looked quite handsome in a much more conventional dark blue suit. He was able to attend this function because Arty had recruited two deputies from Big Pine to hold down the fort while his daughter got married.

In total contrast, Harold and Horace Herkimer, who entered behind the fine appearing young gentlemen, had never looked or felt more miserable. Horace pressed his lips tightly together attempting to hide the absence of teeth in his mouth.

Near the rear of the audience, next to the seated Standing Up and the standing Sitting down, Christopher Herkimer smiled pleasantly as he listened to the organ music.

The well-dressed African American sitting beside him, on the other hand, was biting the knuckle of his black right forefinger to keep from laughing out loud. The image he had been attempting to maintain was totally blown away by the appearance of the other two Herkimers.

The moment Willis had been waiting for was upon him. The cruel and unusual punishment he had referred to earlier outside the Church was about to begin. He was loving every second.

Life might get better, but right now W. P. Herkimer, better known as Willis, couldn't imagine how. What a wedding!

Had Horace and Harold, who followed Rodney and Jiggs up the aisle, been privy to their black cousin's thoughts, they would have been in total disagreement. The two men from Century City were pale.

Both not only looked like, but also felt as if they were active participators in the middle of the Baton death march.

The horrible memory of that night in the hospital when he had that unspeakable devise removed from his anal cavity had already paled in comparison to Horace's vision of the future.

On the chancel, ahead of the happy and unhappy men moving slowly toward it, the organ player paused in her task to sort through the sheet music in front of her to begin the wedding march.

Without warning, the atmosphere of solemnity was shattered by a searing fart.

The gastronomical rumble was, to be sure, not nearly the record breaker let by Old Henderson in his outhouse. Nonetheless it was loud enough to be heard by everyone present.

The baby pig in Farley's arms that was really the culprit, peeked out from his hiding place through the front of the bearded man's coat. His sweet little face was the picture of innocence.

The rest of the congregation, who were not aware of the tiny animal's presence, all turned with an accusing glare at both the Maynard brothers. The undignified disruption had definitely come from their direction; it had to be one of them.

Trux's face turned ashen, then crimson. The man with the big chin sunk as far down into the pew as possible.

Up front, the men from the recent trek down the aisle, all now stood in front of the new minister who was trying very hard to contain his mirth. To the pastor's right, the organ player somehow managed to compose herself and started the Wedding March.

Again, all heads turned back toward the rear of the church as the beautiful Arthell, in a wedding dress many girls only dream of wearing, came down the aisle on the arm of the beaming sheriff of Lone Pine.

As the music swelled, the baby pig let another fart.

"God damnit! I told you to leave him outside!" Trux snarled beneath his breath at Farley who was covering up the sweet little hog's head with his jacket so nobody would know who was responsible.

"You're the one fed im' the beans!" Farley hissed back.

As before, the congregation stared at Trux and Farley. This time Trux stared back.

Up front, Arty gave Arthell to Rodney and took his place beside the now standing Thelma.

He gave Horace and Harold his best 'Make my day' stare and actually mouthed the words when they looked like they might be contemplating sudden flight. For effect, the sheriff then opened his suit jacket.

While he may have been wearing civilian clothing, the Magnum was still with them all. Farley Maynard wasn't the only one with something beneath his coat on this blessed day. The lethal weapon was only inches from Arty Dubs' quick left hand.

Damn! What a team he and Clint would have made! The left and right hands of justice.

For at least a full minute it looked like the two that had come to Lone Pine to bilk the Maynards, might be tempted to challenge that appendage.

They weren't certain which fate might be worse, the Magnum, or what was coming up the aisle. However, they remained standing in front of the Pastor while again, the audience turned their attention in that direction.

Heffaroid resembled a gigantic helium balloon fashioned in the image of, and advertising the founder of Kentucky Fried Chicken. He lumbered up the space between the seated people in his white suit behind Catch Pen and Squeeze Chute as the organist continued to play the Wedding March.

It is doubtful, but to a select few of the older folks inside the Devotion to Divinity house of worship that day, the sight of the enormous owner of the rag tag Borax mine above Dirty Socks Lake in his wedding apparel, might have brought to mind another image. That of a rustic, fatter Orson Welles.

However, the memory of the Colonel seems to have lingered much longer than that of Orson's, even in the few minds familiar with him in the first place.

Half way up the aisle, Heffaroid's sisters let out a high pitched squeal in unison and thrust their leviathan older sibling aside.

They then thundered onward toward the chancel like two sexually excited buffaloes. Once the excited young ladies reached their destination, each grabbed a helpless Herkimer of her choice and began to simply engulf them.

Near the rear of the house of worship among the other seated wedding guests, Christopher Herkimer was explaining the situation regarding the newest aisle arrivals to Standing Up and Sitting down.

The two Native Americans, now that they'd been let in on the earlier details, were enjoying the sequence of events almost as much as Willis. The black Herkimer was laughing so hard, he was literally crying.

"I really believe it is definitely the right decision," said the blind attorney. He was speaking softly so as not to disturb the continuing ceremony, but his words were not unheard by those he was addressing.

Standing Up and Sitting Down were listening intently and not missing a syllable. As a matter of fact, Sitting Down was leaning over the lap of

Standing Up with his ear cocked as close as possible toward the blind speaker. He really wished now that he was sitting down. This was much better than the show up front.

"You see," Christopher Herkimer continued, "it wouldn't do to have any bad press that might well evolve should our ex partners go to prison. Never do at all. Willis and I deal mainly in civil rights cases and such a thing could bring about unfavorable repercussions. Much better to have them married to two beautiful country girls like those up there," said the senior partner of the Century City law firm, pointing in the wrong direction.

"This way you see, a benefit can be brought about from their wrongdoing," the blind man continued. "They cannot only help Mr. Hogg out with his labor problem, they may well develop some character as well."

Standing Up and Sitting Down had never heard a story quite so funny. They would definitely retell this one many times.

"You know Chris," Sitting Down said, between choking spasms of laughter, "for a white eyes with no eyes, you're alright!"

"Ain't he though?" chuckled Willis.

A moment in American history may possibly have been at that particular moment. Right there in the back of a church in a small town called Lone Pine California, a black man and two red men slapped hands in exclusive approval of an action initiated by a white man concerning the fate of others of his own race.

During Christopher Herkimer's dissertation, the vows up front had been taken and the 'I Do's' had all been declared.

While Catch Pen and Squeeze Chute, formerly 'Hogg' and now officially and legally 'Herkimer', practically raped Harold and Horace literally in front of God and everybody, Rodney and Arthell enjoyed the loving kiss of the century.

The insecure youth from Boston had become the man he'd never even hoped to dream of being.

"Hell of a wedding," said Farley, as he rose to his feet being very careful not to disturb Barney Junior who was sleeping.

"I just hope to Hell they got somethin' fit to drink at the reception," grumbled Trux.

CHAPTER TWENTY FIVE
OPTIMISTIC SOLUTIONS

Much to Trux's dismay, no booze was served at the reception, which was held behind the Devotion to Divinity house of worship.

However, Standing Up and Sitting Down had both brought presents for their beloved Daughter of the Wind. With the gifts, they had managed to smuggle in a gallon of wine.

The presents were now with the other wedding tokens of remembrances to be opened later, but the jug was hidden behind some garbage cans next to the fence. The Native Americans were willing to share. Therefore the gathering was at least tolerable for the Maynard brothers.

Neither were that fond of wine, but it went down better than the 'Pussy Punch' being served by the church ladies. Trux and Farley did accept the offered cups, however. They offered the contents of the containers to the newly awakened Barney Junior but he refused so they poured offensive non-alcoholic liquid out on the ground.

The small animal that had figuratively come out of the closet and literally out of Farley's coat, did however, approve of the taste of wine served him after the cups had been refilled. It also seemed to settle his tiny rumbling tummy.

The Maynard brothers congratulated themselves on making the right move, and poured themselves another immediately.

A really large folding table on which rested three medium sized wedding cakes, had been assembled not too far from the rear entrance of the Holy edifice. It stood in almost the same spot where Heffaroid had parked the Karmann Ghia on the evening prior to the big pignapping caper that now seemed to be forgotten. All feelings of ill will on the part of the oversized borax miner, now wearing the enormous white suit, toward anybody seemed to have been put to rest.

The big man smiled broadly as he posed for a picture along with Rodney, Arthell, Arty, Thelma and Heffaroid's two fat sisters as they all stood behind the table in front of the cakes. Of course, the spouses of Catch Pen and Squeeze Chute, who were the Hogg Enterprise's new labor force, were also in the picture. Each had the look of a zombie just awakened to the realization that life was only a distant recollection. At least Harold still had teeth.

"Hope he's got a wide angle lens on that thing," commented Sitting Down, referring to the camera in Jigg's hand who was recording the aftermath of the blessed events.

The Native American and his constant companion, Standing Up, were grouped together in a small semicircle with Christopher and W. P. Herkimer. They stood not far from where the Maynards sat with the pig.

The baby animal wasn't cause for concern, but Trux and Farley were a little too close to the wine stash for Standing Up and Sitting Down's comfort.

Both Standing Up and Willis got a big kick out of Sitting Down's remark. The blind man in the group simply smiled. Since he had no idea how really oversized the members of the Hogg family were, the gray haired man didn't find the joke as funny as the rest. Nonetheless, as he had stated before, Christopher Herkimer loved the sound of laughter.

While Jiggs moved in to take individual pictures of the newly married couples, Thelma wandered over to where Trux and Farley sat with Barney Junior. Now that her daughter was officially leaving the nest, the Argus Queen thought she'd better become acquainted with the newest member of the family.

In front of the church's back door, Rodney took a big bite of the piece of cake his wonderful bride was feeding him while Jiggs immortalized the moment. He had no idea how it tasted.

The confection could have been made from vinegar or even those awful umbrella steaks Arty served in his jail. This was the most perfect day of his life.

The young groom didn't even regret his parents' decision not to attend the wedding due to such short notice. It was undoubtedly all for the best. The sex life of their son's new mother in law alone, was going to take some time for the terribly politically correct Van Aukins from stoic New England to understand.

He was afraid he would never get his father to comprehend honesty as a blessing rather than a curse, but one thing was certain. They would both adore this new Mrs. Van Aukin. Nobody could resist Arthell's open and honest charm. Perhaps, through her, even the senior Van Aukin would learn the value of truth.

Louise Herkimer had also declined her invitation to the wedding. That too, was probably a good thing.

"Come on, Rodney! They've brought out the presents!" his bride said.

Arthell's gorgeous eyes were sparkling with happiness as she took his hand and led him back to the table that was now covered with pretty packages and gleaming small kitchen appliances. At least seven blenders, sixteen toasters and a dozen can openers of various shapes and sizes now rested on the tabletop.

Over by the fence near the garbage cans, Thelma held the sweet little piglet in her arms. It snuggled close to her fantastic breasts, rubbing its tiny pink snout against the generously exposed portion of her cleavage.

Barney Junior's position was the envy of every man in the crowd who happened to be looking in the Argus Queen's direction.

"Is it a boy pig or a girl pig?" asked Christopher Herkimer, who had just been informed what Thelma was holding.

He and Willis, who was now sporting Standing Up's broad brimmed hat with the feathers, had moved over to this spot with the owner of the headwear and his companion. Both of whom were behind the garbage cans at the moment.

"Barney Junior's a boy pig!" Farley answered proudly.

"Hell yes, he's a boy pig! Ain't that hard to figure out. He's doin' okay!" Chimed in Trux as he headed behind the garbage cans to join Standing Up and Sitting Down. The man with the big chin was afraid the Native Americans would deplete the contents of their own jug without informing him. Indians have a habit of doing things like that to white people.

"Bless whoever's in charge," Trux called back over his shoulder. "He's already hung better'n Farley!"

"Ain't the size wins the prize!" Farley shot back.

"I'll bear witness to that," smiled Thelma, as the little pig continued to nuzzle her bosom.

"Dear me," said the blind, gray haired attorney, referring to Farley's statement and not Thelma's, as he spoke in the direction he assumed Trux to now be.

For a change, he was correct. Farley's brother was returning from behind the garbage cans with his paper cup now filled with wine. Standing Up and Sitting down, each carrying two of the containers, originally intended for the church ladies' innocent punch, walked behind him.

"It would seem your brother, in addition to being an animal lover, is also a poet."

"That may be Chris, but ain't nobody gonna call Farley Maynard, Longfellow," remarked Sitting Down as he handed one of the cups to Willis Herkimer. Standing Up carefully placed his extra paper container in the hands in of the older gentleman bearing the same surname as the black man.

Everyone thought this was terribly funny except the Maynard brothers. Trux laughed anyway. He had no idea what the connection between poetry and the length of a man's member might be, but he knew the joke was on Farley.

Fortunately for Farley, another subject totally unrelated, replaced his least favorite topic of discussion.

Arthell swept forward through the peripheral wedding party group. She wrapped both of her arms around Standing Up's neck, pulling the Native American into an embrace and knocking off his hat.

She was now wearing a sparkling silver choker around her own pretty neck that wasn't there before.

"It's the most beautiful painting I've ever seen, Standing Up. I just love it!"

The beautiful bride was referring to a nine by eleven inch water color, that a smiling Rodney who stood behind her, held up for all to see. The piece of art was indeed exquisite.

While it was a indeed done in water color, to even the most critical connoisseur, the masterfully executed craftsmanship had to be carefully scrutinized to discover it had not been created in oil.

The wonderful painting depicted an image of Arthell herself, seeming to flow upward out of a horn of plenty made up of surrealistic human faces of all races and creeds. The replica of the gorgeous young woman was throwing hearts of love out over a vast brown desert, turning it in to rolling green meadows. The blend of colors was magnificent.

"Best I could come up with on such short notice, little one. Next time you get married let me know a little more in advance," said Standing Up, modestly.

"This is the one and only, Standing Up!" she said, laughing. "Start working on my anniversaries. I warn you, you're going to need a lot of paint."

"He didn't use paint," stated Sitting Down. "That was all done with spilled booze and marijuana. He just smeared it around on the canvas along with some dog poop and made a picture out of it. He's so cheap he don't want to waste nothin'."

The new bride turned to Siting Down and gave him a hug while Rodney stood by awkwardly in the background still holding the painting.

Behind him, Catch Pen and Squeeze Chute could be seen beyond the other guests squealing with delight as they piled blenders and toasters into the arms of the helpless and unhappy Horace and Harold.

"And I adore my necklace, Sitting Down!" Arthell said, referring to the silver choker around her throat as she gave the Native American a kiss on his hairless cheek.

"You guys are just too much!"

"Don't tell Arty," Standing Up muttered out of the side of his mouth as he picked up his hat from the ground, "but Sitting Down robbed all the parking meters on Main Street to get enough silver to make that stupid trinket. I tried to talk him into spendin' it on wine, but he wouldn't listen."

All conversation among everyone present at the church backyard wedding reception halted abruptly as Old Henderson's truck came to a screeching stop in the driveway leading beside the building from the direction of the street. The old vehicle backfired just once before the aging miner turned off the engine and climbed out of the rig. He was absolutely filthy.

"Trux Maynard!" yelled the old timer as he waved his backpack in the air while all the wedding guests and participants looked on, many with distaste. "I wanna' talk to you!"

Arty moved up to face the old man. "You've got one hell of a nerve, bustin' in here like this, Old Henderson!" snapped the lawman as he started to draw the Magnum from beneath his civilian suit jacket. "I oughta' run your wrinkled old ass in!"

Thelma swept up in front of the sheriff with Trux on her arm. Farley was behind them, once again in possession of the baby pig.

"Oh, for Heavens sake, Arty!" she said. "Stop that! This happens to be a friend of mine."

"Damn! You've got great tits!" exclaimed Old Henderson by way of greeting and gratitude.

Arty backed away with a disgusted look on his face. The sheriff looked at the old mining engineer and then at the Maynards. This beautiful woman made great babies, but with the exception of himself, she had lousy taste in men.

"And smart too!" the old party crasher continued. "Can't believe God had sense enough to put such great bazooms and brains all in the same package!"

"All women have brains, Old Henderson," replied Thelma. "You see, God created man in his own image. Then He created woman to make up for His mistake."

"Never know it by lookin' at that daughter of mine."

"Your daughter's not stupid, Mr. Henderson. She's been smart enough to keep the two of you eating out in that ghost town. She's just bitter. Woman's function is to worry about life. Men worry about women. Unfortunately, Darleen screwed up by taking on both."

"Ain't much in the tit department, but I'll take your word on it. I'll believe anything you tell me," said the old man nodding his head up and down as he looked at her breasts. "That other shit you said sure has got me thinkin'."

"What the Hell you want, Henderson?" asked Trux. He hated it when people started discussing religion.

"You gonna sell that mountain to them city dudes over there?" queried the aging desert rat as he waved the back pack in the direction of Christopher and W. P. Herkimer who still stood near the garbage cans with Standing Up and Sitting Down.

"Not that it's any of your business, But no," answered Trux.

"You sure about that?" asked the old man. "Don't bullshit me now, or you're gonna regret it!"

"I told you no, damnit!" said Trux who was really getting tired of repeating himself. "That mountains the tombstone for Farley's pig! We ain't sellin' no matter what the price! Now stop askin'! You're startin' to piss me off!"

Farley covered Barney Junior's ears and quickly retreated with the small animal to the table where Heffaroid and his sisters were supervising the unhappy Harold and Horace as the unhappy pair stuffed wedding loot into large burlap bags. This was not a conversation for the ears of the very young.

"Figgered' you to say that and I respect you for it," the old man responded. "But I hadda' make sure. Now get outa' my way."

With out another word Old Henderson pushed his way through the crowd to face Christopher and Willis.

"Understand the Maynards ain't sellin' you their mountain. What your people gonna do 'bout pavin' that new highway?" the old man asked the pair of city attorneys point blank.

"Quite honestly we don't know, Mr. Henderson," replied the blind man.

"How'd you get so dirty, Old Henderson?" Standing Up wanted to know.

"Been climbin' around on that ole mountain on the back part of the Reservation," Old Henderson told the Native American silversmith.

He turned back to say something else to the white and black attorney, but was interrupted this time by Sitting Down. "You go climbin' around out there old man, that white hair of yours is gonna end up hangin' from the top of the chief's lodge pole. He don't cotton to white eyes fuckin' around on our land."

"That ever happens, his balls' n' pecker'll be hangin' next to it!" the Owens Valley senior citizen snapped back in cantankerous fashion.

He pulled some chunks of what appeared to be formed of the same substance as the rocks on Maynard's mountain from the backpack, which he now had slung over his shoulder. The aging miner then held the chunks up in front of Christopher Herkimer.

"You see these?" Old Henderson asked the blind man.

Willis, still wearing Standing Up's hat, moved in beside the more mature man whom he called Chris. He looked down at the filthy items in Henderson's even filthier hands.

"What is it?" asked the African American.

"Jeezus! Are ya' blind?"

"Yes I am," admitted Christopher Herkimer.

"No, I'm not!" denied Willis Herkimer at almost the same time.

"Volcanically formed cinders!" explained the old man, obviously frustrated with the ignorance of those he was talking to.

"The same shit as these here I picked up on Maynards mountain! Whoever your people sent through here in the first place didn't find it 'cause ain't nobody allowed on the Indian Reservation! But this is what they're lookin' for."

"You know what kind of trouble you've caused?" asked Standing Up of the aging mining engineer. "The whole Tribal Council'll end up corrupt because of you!"

"Ain't no reason you people shouldn't be like everone else in the Owens Valley!" the old man retorted. He turned back to the attorneys.

"Anyway, that's where you can find what yer after, be ya' interested. Me, I gotta go. Ain't been home for two days. Darleen's gonna' be howlin' like a hyena in heat with a hernia!"

The ancient expert on minerals shoved the backpack and its contents into Willis's hands, then turned on his heel. He charged back through the crowd to his truck.

He gave one last wave in Thelma's direction, climbed in his vehicle and started the engine. After a loud grinding of gears, the old truck lurched. Then miner and machine backed out of sight.

"Wonder what's in it for him?" pondered Trux as he watched the old miner's truck disappear.

"Probably doesn't want the new highway closed for repairs every six months. Less maintenance if they use the cinders. That's why they're so valuable," Thelma informed him as she gathered what few gifts the hefty Herkimer brides hadn't stuffed into the gunny sacks still held by their helpless and hapless looking new spouses.

"How come you to know so much?" the square jawed man asked. The look on his face that immediately followed showed he was sorry he had. He held up both hands, palms forward.

"Don't go into that creation shit again! We're too close to the church to talk about God!"

The Argus Queen laughed.

"Actually, I was going to ask if one of you could pull the HOWDY HOSS around front. I've been so busy, I may not have mentioned, I told Rodney and Arthell it would be okay with you guys if they drove it to go on their honeymoon to Reno this afternoon when this is all over."

"What?" boomed Trux.

Then he added in a quieter, if not less irritated tone, "I didn't even know they was goin' to Reno."

"Why would you go and say somethin' like that, Thelma?" Farley wanted to know, as he kneeled in front of little Barney Junior. The infant swine was now beneath the table nibbling on a piece of wedding cake that had slipped through somebody's fingers.

Thelma gave each of the men she loved a look of adoring exasperation.

"Are you boys ever going to learn to trust me? Can they drive it or not?" she asked each question with arched eyebrows.

Farley sighed as he pulled the pig out from beneath the table and scooped the tiny animal up into his arms.

"Let's go get the HOWDY HOSS, Trux," he said.

Over by the garbage cans, Standing up was wearing his own broad brimmed headgear again and the now hatless Willis Herkimer was just finishing making a call on Rodney's cellular telephone.

The black attorney handed the portable communications instrument back to its owner as he spoke to Christopher Herkimer.

"Limo's on its way Chris. Thanks Rodney."

The new groom proudly held the beautiful painting in one hand while he slipped the phone beneath his jacket with the other and acknowledged the expression of gratitude.

"Anytime Willis. You really should carry one of these with you at all times. I know I'd be lost without mine. I've read that they'll give you a brain tumor, but I say it's the people that write that crap that give you brain tumors."

He didn't even feel guilty about stealing Thelma's material. He did feel that way now and besides, he was well on his way to becoming a genuine red neck. Red necks are allowed to screw around with the truth a little when there's a point to be made.

The young man from Boston then turned to the two Native Americans. "You've got my number. Like I said, feel free to give it to your Tribal Council members. I'd be happy to help out on the land deal anyway I can, if they need legal representation."

"We'd better be careful, Chris. We're up against the big time now," the black lawyer said to the white blind lawyer after both had shaken the hand of the young man who would rather be a red neck in the Owens Valley than a big executive in Century City.

"Do me a favor, Rodney. Keep me posted on the progress of Horace and Harold. The welfare of my dear cousins mean a lot to me," Willis continued, now speaking to the groom.

The black man, feeling the effects of the red men's wine, made certain his words were loud enough to reach the ears of the poor miserable souls to whom he was referring.

"I will," Rodney promised. He obviously didn't find the other two Herkimers' situation as funny as Willis did. He was, however happy that, in a way, justice was being served. Just the fact that both men the handsome

African American was talking about, had resigned from the California Bar, and neither would ever again be able to practice law, made him feel a lot better about his chosen profession.

"I hope you're able to find honest replacements for them," he said, addressing his words this time also to Christopher Herkimer, although it wasn't quite clear if the latter knew he was one of the recipients right away. "I know 'Honest' and 'Lawyer' are words that aren't supposed to go together, but after meeting you two, I know it doesn't have to be that way. I sure plan on doing my part to prove it doesn't."

"I do believe the loss of our firm, is indeed Lone Pine's gain," said Christopher Herkimer, really meaning every word. He then looked in the direction where he had first heard his black companion's voice. "Well, Willis, we really should go and notify our clients of the new developments."

"It was awfully nice seeing all of you," said the blind man as he prepared to leave.

"And awfully nice hearing you, sir," Standing Up responded.

The Native American artist's remark evoked a genuine laugh from the gray haired man with the white cane and dark glasses.

"I'm told you both do excellent art work, but you could also fare very well at stand up comedy," Christopher Herkimer told them.

"Me maybe," Standing Up retorted as he gestured to Sitting Down. "But this dude's humor all comes straight out of the toilet. Even in there, when he's standing up, he's Sitting Down."

This remark brought laughter to all of the remaining garbage can area stragglers.

Willis and Christopher said goodbye once more and headed for the driveway leading to the front of the church and the street beyond it.

"I'm happy for Young Van Aukin. He's his own man of course and entitled to make his own decisions, but I really am sorry we're losing him. With Horace and Harold otherwise disposed, Van Aukin would have been the perfect man to commandeer our Century City office while you and I are on the road," commented Christopher Herkimer as he allowed Willis to steer him forward.

"I've been thinking about that Chris," replied Willis. "Why don't you start running home base? Let me keep the civil rights thing cool. If you feel I can handle it."

"Of course you can," the gray haired man with the dark glasses and cane responded. "I will think about it. I hope I can get along with Miss Wayling. I really never have gotten to know the woman."

"Chris, I've got a feeling that after a few months with Miss Wayling, You'll both be seeing everything in a brand new light."

332

The black man's eyes were twinkling merrily. He was enjoying the moment, yet he was still quite serious. Willis really thought this man and the lady who never made it to cheerleader could learn a lot from each other.

"I'm looking forward to it," said the blind man as the pair disappeared from sight.

The other guests were also starting to disperse. Thelma, standing by the table gave her daughter a beckoning wave.

Near the beautiful lady, Arty, Jiggs and Heffaroid kept a watchful eye on Horace and Harold Herkimer who were once again being strangled by hugs and smothered by kisses from Catch Pen and Squeeze Chute.

"Thanks again, Sitting Down and Standing Up, for the wonderful gifts," said Arthell as she hugged each one again. "Either my mom's trying to fly or she's giving Rodney and I the high sign that it's time to go."

"Just remember, Husband of Daughter of the wind," Standing up called after Rodney, as the lovely young happy bride wearing the stunning silver necklace, dragged her new husband and the fabulous painting toward her mother, "Follow the tumbleweed of life to learn the secret of the raven!"

"I'll remember!" Rodney called back. He had no idea what the statement meant, but neither did the man who had made it.

The Native American silversmith turned to the Native American painter. The latter was digging the nearly empty wine jug out from behind the garbage cans. He unscrewed the lid from the glass container and tipped it up to his mouth.

"You know that painting really is damned good," said Sitting Down to Standing Up.

"Thank you. You did some excellent work on that necklace," replied Standing Up to Sitting Down before draining the jug.

"You just drank all the wine!"

"Wasn't enough for both of us."

"Second thought, the painting really sucks!"

"Necklace ain't worth a shit either."

"Want to go get another jug of wine?"

"Don't know. If them rocks Old Henderson found out there on the Reservation really are gonna make my people rich, I better think about it. Might hurt my standing in Lone Pine society if I was to be seen walkin' down the street with a white man."

"I ain't a white man."

"You're Grandpa came from Italy."

"So?"

"So, Eyetalians are white."

"You think Eyetalians are white, you shoulda' traded your hat for Chris's cane."

"I like ole Chris. Sees life in a better light than most."

"You wanna' go get that jug of wine or not?"

"Might as well. Nothin' goin' on here."

"God! You're negative! You know what they'd say about someone like you in Kiowasua?"

"I know what they'd have to say about a screwball like you in Rom!"

As they headed out in search of additional libation, the two strange men with the strange names, began cursing each other in the two different tongues.

Neither understood the other. Neither cared.

Such is the way of the world.

EPILOGUE
DISCARDED YESTERDAYS

Standing Up and Sitting Down had hence departed in search of libation. However a few of the wedding guests remained in front of the Devotion to Divinity house of worship, including the new pastor, to see the newly married couples off.

The HOWDY HOSS with Rodney behind the steering wheel and Arthell sitting beside him, was now parked at the curb directly in front of the church.

The sad looking little Karmann Ghia sat behind the big battered rig. It had, in turn, an even more pathetic looking horse trailer attached to its rear.

Heffaroid was, once again stuffed into to the front of the little topless German made automobile. The huge man in white looked back from his cramped quarters. Arty and Jiggs stood by while Catch Pen and Squeeze Chute dragged Horace and Harold Herkimer into the horse trailer with their burlap bags of gifts. Once the girls had their men inside, the sheriff moved in and closed the gate.

Arty then gave a wave to Rodney in the front vehicle, signaling that it was time for all those recently joined in Holy Matrimony to 'Move on out' as John Wayne, or perhaps Clint himself, used to say.

All those still standing in front of the front of the church waved as both vehicles and the trailer pulled away.

Inside the front of the motor home, Rodney looked in the rearview mirror at the image of the Karmann Ghia and its passengers. Arthell leaned out though the open passenger window across from him, returning the waves of those left behind.

The young man, originally from Boston, now from Lone Pine, couldn't help but think of Louise again for one fleeting second, as he continued to look in the mirror. It was definitely a good move on her part not to have attended this ceremony. The Beverly Hills Princess could have handled watching her ex fiancée that she had never really cared for drive off into the sunset with this beauty beside him. She might also have been somehow able to stomach the marriage of her father and uncle to the two mammoth mamas. She would never have recovered however, from the sight of what her beloved 'Slum Mobile' now had become.

"The Ghia was my present to the Hogg family," said Rodney as he pulled his eyes away from the back of the HOWDY HOSS to concentrate on where he was driving.

Arthell turned from the window and maneuvered the jump seat up close to her new husband as he continued to operate the big rig's controls.

"God! I'm glad I married you!" she exclaimed as she threw her arms around him.

Rodney couldn't do a thing to stop her as she began fondling his body. He was the designated driver.

In the rear of the same old motor home's interior, behind the curtain, Thelma, Trux and Farley lay on top of the bed. All were naked and drinking champagne as they snuggled together beneath the covers.

The baby pig, on the same bed, nestled happily against Farley's exposed bare feet.

"Thelma, think you'll ever get married?" asked Trux as they all clinked glasses.

Thelma waited until they had all drained their drinks before she answered.

"You know I'm too much woman for just one man," she said as she collected their dainty goblets and put them aside along with her own. The Argus Queen then opened her arms and pulled both totally naked men down on top of her own fabulous nude body.

"Come to Mama boys. It's along way to Reno, and when we get there, we've got an even longer night ahead of us."

*** *** *** *** *** ***

It had been a long night, but several hours still remained before daybreak.

Old Henderson wasn't sure just how long he had been sitting on top of Maynards mountain in the moonlight, beneath the shadow of the tall rock pinnacle. He did know his case of beer was nearly depleted.

He looked up into the sky. One star seemed to be getting bigger and brighter. He couldn't be sure. Old Henderson wasn't even certain why he was here. The aging mining engineer just knew that somehow his presence in this particular spot on this particular night was mandatory.

The white haired master of yesterday's unearthed ductile metallic chemical elements had arrived at the base of the landmass shortly after darkness had set in, the prior evening. He hadn't climbed to the top of the formation right away. The old man had spent at least two hours beside the grave of the pig. The components of this naturalized structure towering above Barney's final resting spot had induced a chain reaction of rapacity among certain humans.

This emotion of greed had not only caused great turmoil for many, but was directly responsible for the demise of an innocent animal. Somehow the entire situation seemed totally inequitable and somehow off balance.

Nothing seemed fair in the old man's world any longer. After disclosing his discovery regarding the volcanic cinders on the Indian Reservation to those big city lawyers the day before, he had returned to Darwin to another. One so disastrous, he thought at first, he must be experiencing an egregious optical illusion or having a horrible dream.

Unfortunately, he found himself to be undergoing neither. What faced him, upon returning to the place he had called home for well beyond four decades, was blatant reality. Darleen had finally carried out her previous threat. The outhouse behind the saloon had been destroyed.

The hole beneath it was filled with earth, and its pieces carted away. Old Henderson's last symbol of solace was no longer an entity. Darleen had even burned all issues of the catalogue, including the ladies underwear sections.

He knew his daughter was angry that he had become involved with the affairs of outsiders, but he really never thought her ire would lead to an act of such devastation. She was also mad because he'd taken her ice chest and never returned it. Nor was she overjoyed with her father for raiding her precious ice supply that day. He hadn't realized just how irate she could become.

Now Old Henderson knew his daughter's wrath would soar way beyond all limits. When eventually informed her father to be responsible for bringing wealth to the Indian Reservation near Lone Pine. Darleen hated all people who weren't pure Caucasian, and most who were, if they didn't hail from Darwin. He didn't wish to be around when that news reached her.

Then, from somewhere deep inside him had come a missive. Thankfully, there was no other soul to whom he needed to explain this strange phenomenon.

It wasn't even clear to him, but the old miner knew he wasn't supposed to stay in Darwin any longer. It was time for this old prospector to push off. To where, he wasn't exactly sure. He did know the first stop was to be Maynard's mountain.

He had taken the first opportunity when his bitch of an offspring wasn't watching, to steal one last case of beer. The old man without an outhouse had then lighted out in his old truck for that designated destination.

Now, here he was. The case of beer was the only thing he'd brought with him and that was nearly empty. He wasn't even in possession of his trusty old revolver. There was no need for a weapon. Old Henderson had nothing left to defend. He knew the premises were thick with rattlesnakes but they never seemed to bother him. Perhaps it was his smell. Or possibly, in Old Henderson they found a kindred spirit. Snakes didn't seem to have much of a reason for hanging around either.

Prior to climbing the mountain, the old miner had urinated on Barney's grave at least three times after consuming twice that many beers. He felt it was the least he could have done. He really had been fond of the animal and he truly believed, were the situations reversed, Barney would have done the same for him.

Now, as he looked around the shallow crevice that made up the mountaintop he realized how everything in life seemed to be one big contradiction.

The only things that Barney had ever really disliked were snakes. Now, the very place that served as the marker of his memory, was infested with the very reptiles he hated..

Everything seemed upside down. Until yesterday the old man had always assumed men to be smarter than women. Tonight he knew that to be false. He was fully aware now, after talking to the one they called the Argus Queen, that he had certainly shown no intelligence escaping from the Zorkanins because the big titted women on that planet had no pussies.

What was it the lady seemed to know everything had asked him? 'What was the alternative?'

He had no answer for the beautiful woman. He was Henderson, the man renowned for daring to explore other places where others said there was no silver and proving them wrong by finding the precious metallic mineral.

He was also the man too stupid and too nearsighted to search the unknown for sex because he'd come up against something different.

He had been telling the beautiful woman the truth when he'd quipped that he could only manage a 'Sideways' erection in his old age.

What if the female plumbing on Zorca was fashioned to accommodate just that? What if 'Sideways' was the way it was supposed to be on that planet? While he was there, these simple thoughts had never entered his mind. He had been horrified to find that the women weren't 'Normal' as he knew the word.

He had become a classic example of Moronic Xenophobia, even though Henderson didn't really know the definition of that word.

There was probably another word in the English language that the old rock hound didn't know, one that meant beyond stupid. He was now fully aware, however, if such a word did exist in the dictionary, his picture deserved to be above it.

The soul searching old man was down to the final beer. He wasn't sure what he would do when the last can he now held in his gnarled hand was empty. Then again, he wasn't even sure what he was doing here in the first place.

Suddenly, the whole top of the mountain was bathed in a blue, almost blinding light that seemed to be pale, yet bright all at the same time. A high pitched barely audible sound accompanied the surrealistic illumination and he knew.

The man on the mountain looked up to see the saucer bathed in the bright, yet pale blue light settling down in front of him. He well remembered this particular light. It's unique hue prevented all earth radar systems from detecting unidentified objects on their screens.

The Zorkanians had returned. He was being afforded a second chance. He drained the beer down his throat. Henderson was ready.

The old man rose to his feet. Suddenly he didn't feel old anymore. He carefully inserted the empty can in the case before picking it up and placing the whole carton of aluminum containers against the pinnacle.

The master of minerals on earth, and newly self discovered neophyte on sex everywhere, then stood very straight. Slowly he turned to face the craft from another world.

The high pitched, almost indistinguishable hum continued to permeate the moonlit night as slowly and silently, the doors of the heavenly vehicle began sliding open.

"Dro- gjavax dalcoa?" asked a melodious female voice from somewhere deep within the craft.

"Broner- azalog -ejutas- zov!" he replied with great emotion and conviction as he walked forward beneath the pale, yet piercing light.

Old Henderson let an ear shattering fart.

This one may have been a record breaker even for him. Quite possibly it was even louder than the gastronomical explosion escaping his aging body not that long ago before the demise of his beloved outhouse.

The old red neck could have cared less. He was off to look for love in strange places. As far as Old Henderson was concerned, it was the last sound on earth.

THE END

Printed in the United States
1425500001B/232-249